# A
# Moorland Hanging

# MICHAEL JECKS

# A Moorland Hanging

**SIMON &
SCHUSTER**

London · New York · Sydney · Toronto · New Delhi

A CBS COMPANY

First published in 1996 by Headline Book Publishing

This edition published in Great Britain in 2013 by Simon & Schuster UK Ltd
A CBS COMPANY

1 3 5 7 9 10 8 6 4 2

Simon & Schuster UK Ltd
1st Floor
222 Gray's Inn Road
London
WC1X 8HB

www.simonandschuster.co.uk

Simon & Schuster Australia, Sydney
Simon & Schuster India, New Delhi

A CIP catalogue copy for this book is available
from the British Library.

ISBN: 978-1-47112-647-5
eBook ISBN: 978-1-47112-648-2

Typeset by Hewer Text UK Ltd, Edinburgh
Printed and bound in Great Britain by CPI Group (UK) Ltd, Croydon, CR0 4YY

For Nicky, Martin, George,
and especially Keith and Lynn,
who first suggested I should be a writer.

# AUTHOR'S NOTE

For those readers unfamiliar with my two earlier novels featuring Sir Baldwin Furnshill and Simon Puttock, a quick guide to early fourteenth-century history may be useful.

The late 1200s and early 1300s were years of massive change for Europe's population. Conflict over the papacy in Rome had led to the Pope moving his court to Avignon in France; thus the French King, Philip IV, became the most powerful man in Christendom, directly influencing God's vicar on earth.

As proof of the French King's new authority one need look no further than the 'Poor Fellow-Soldiers of Christ and the Temple of Solomon' – the Templar Knights. They had been the leading institution in Europe for almost two hundred years, reporting only to the Pope himself. Considering themselves warriors for God, the monks fought for the defence of the Kingdom of Jerusalem, often recklessly throwing their lives away in battle, so strong was their faith in the Order's mission to protect Christ's country from invasion by pagans. These men were knights in their own right, but gave up secular pleasures and personal wealth in order to take the oaths of their monastic order: poverty, chastity and obedience.

The Templars flourished with the Crusades, earning vast sums from their ventures in banking and commerce; indeed they could be described as being the first retail bankers, issuing notes to confirm deposits which could then be redeemed in other countries. Massive estates were given to them by supporters, providing rich sources of income to help maintain their army. By the end of the 1200s the Templars were a force to be reckoned with.

However, Philip IV was in dire need of funds. In 1306 he moved against a rich but disliked and unprotected group. In one day, every Jew in France was arrested. All their records and assets were seized and auctioned to the benefit of the Crown. Meanwhile, Jewish citizens were thrown out of the kingdom with nothing. Conveniently, all notes confirming royal debts to the Jews were destroyed, though monies owed by subjects were now payable to the King – and he required prompt payment. All in all, this proved a thoroughly successful venture, and soon Philip began to cast around for other similarly wealthy groups to fleece.

The Templars were hardly an easy target, but they were certainly rich – although as a religious Order, they were protected by the Pope. How could the King gain access to their money while the Pope was nominally responsible for them?

Fortunately, Pope Clement V was a man with a thoroughly modern attitude. He was absolutely committed to his own wealth. Usefully, he was also close to hand, now that he lived in France. Still, even he would have balked at the idea of robbing the Templars, so the King moved without telling him.

The Templars' fate was really sealed earlier, in 1291, when the last significant holding in Palestine was captured, because their whole reason for existence disappeared with it. Acre was the sole remaining possession of the old Crusader Kingdom of Jerusalem. It was attacked in April 1291, and on 28 May it fell under the massive Muslim onslaught. With it died the hopes of the whole of Christendom for the old Kingdom. Much of the respect for the Templars died at this time, too. Other Orders were similarly held in some disdain after the fall of Acre, but only the Templars had their head-quarters in France, and this was their downfall.

On Friday, 13 October 1307 – a date which has given us the popular superstition – every member of the Order in France was arrested. Many wild conspiracy theories have been proposed about their destruction, but only one fact is absolute and inescapable: beforehand the Templars were wealthy; afterwards their wealth disappeared. Philip was the prime mover in accusing them of various crimes, at a time when he sorely needed money. The Pope soon came round to agreeing to the charges pressed by the King. It seems likely that Clement V enjoyed some financial benefit from the Order's destruction, and this helped him to believe the allegations.

The Order was disbanded. Some of the knights were already dead. Others, especially the more prominent, were burned publicly. Of the rest, many were allowed to disappear into monasteries, a few faded away and joined the Teutonic Knights or the Knights Hospitaller, or one of the other Orders fighting pagans at the fringes of Christianity.

In England and Scotland there was never much faith in the accusations against the Templars. The English King, Edward II, trusted them, for they had helped his father in battles against the Scots and their Master had died in the war against William Wallace. When Edward received a papal communication ordering him to arrest his old friends, he dithered for some weeks. He was a weak man (who was later to be ousted by his wife and her lover), and he already had too many enemies to want to lose the Templars and their support. By the time he made a move the majority of the Templars had disappeared – as had their treasure.

Most of the Templars were never found; some almost certainly made their way to Scotland. In that miserable event for Edward II, the Battle of Bannockburn, it was said that the Templars' standard was seen. The Scottish King, Robert I ('the Bruce'), had no fear of upsetting the Pope – he was already excommunicated and his country under Papal Anathema: no holy rites could be performed by the priesthood.

In 1315 and 1316, the whole of Europe suffered from a devastating famine. Fragile economies were disrupted, especially those of England and France, and hundreds of thousands died. Floods destroyed crops and entire flocks of sheep. Bands of outlaws took to the roads, robbing and killing to try to survive, and there were rumours of cannibalism.

This was a bleak and brutal time, when warlords bickered and fought. King Edward was ineffectual and considered a fool. Arguments between him and the French were soon to flare, which led a few years later to the Hundred Years War. Theologians battled among themselves, disputing such fine points of Christianity as whether humour was blasphemous. Yet at the same time, men like Bacon were inventing spectacles and gunpowder, classical learning was being taught in the new universities, and trade was booming. Only some seventy years later, Chaucer would write his *Canterbury Tales* and Froissart his *Chronicles*. Gradually, English Common Law was developing, and litigation made lawyers wealthy – and objects of disgust!

In the midst of the hardship, some areas were still relatively calm and ordered. While the coastal towns were raided by pirates, and English possessions on the Continent were taken over by the French King, and while the border regions were overrun by Scottish reivers, and Ireland was invaded, the West Country stayed peaceful.

This was the time of Sir Baldwin Furnshill, who had been a Knight Templar, and his friend, the Bailiff of Lydford Castle, Simon Puttock.

*Michael Jecks*

# CHAPTER ONE

Clambering up the long, shallow gradient to the mass of rock at the summit, the last thing on Thomas Smyth's mind was the man who was shortly to die. Smyth was concentrating solely on the dull pain of his strained muscles, and wondering how much further he must go.

Just before the last slope he had to pause to rest, his hands on his hips as he panted. It was becoming cooler as evening approached, a relief after the day's searing heat. Glowering at the tor above, he gave a brittle smile. After this expedition he knew he must accept he was no longer a young man. Though his mind was the same as when he had first come here, a lad of not yet twenty, that was more than thirty-two years ago now. Thomas was well past middle age.

Gazing around him, he saw thin feathers of smoke rising eastwards in the still evening air: the straggle of crofts on the Chagford road were settling for the night. He could hear a dog barking, a man shouting, shutters being slammed over windows, and an occasional low grumble from oxen in the byres. After the misery of 1315 and 1316, when the whole kingdom had been struck with famine, it sounded as if the country had returned to normal. This little vill in the middle of Dartmoor stood as proof of the improvement in the weather, which now, in 1318, promised healthy harvests at last.

But Smyth's anger, never far from him now, would not let him survey the view in peace. He felt his gaze being pulled back. South and east, he knew the grey mists were caused by his new blowing-house, whose charcoal furnace melted the tin which was the primary cause of his wealth. It was the other fires northwards which made him set his jaw and glare, the fires from the other men, the miners who had arrived recently and stolen his land.

He himself had not been born here. It was many years ago, while serving as a soldier in the Welsh wars, that he had first heard tell of the huge wealth to be amassed from working the ore that lay so abundantly on the moors. Thus, when the battles were done, he had meandered southwards, intending to take his share.

Back then, in 1286, he had been a gangling nineteen year old – a poor man with no future. In those days, a large part of this area around the West Dart River had been uninhabited, and only a few tinners struggled to work the land for profit. Taxes were crippling, raised whenever money was needed for wars – and it was rare for the old King *not* to be at war. Many had already left the land by the time Thomas arrived, allowing him to increase his works for little cost, and though it had taken some years he had steadily built up his interests until now he was the wealthiest tinner for many miles, employing others to keep the furnaces lighted and the moulds filled with tin. If he did not own the land, that was merely a technicality – and a financial saving. By all the measures he valued, the land was his: he could farm tin and take the profits; he could bound tracts of land wherever he wanted; he had a seat at the stannary parliament. These were the ancient rights of the stanners of Devon, and he made full use of them.

But others had come, stealing parcels of land he considered his own, working it to their own advantage, ruining his efforts and making him look foolish in front of his neighbours. It was intolerable.

With a last baleful glare, he set his face to the hill once more and continued climbing.

Behind him, George Harang smiled in satisfaction. He had caught a glimpse of Thomas' expression, and knew what it signalled. At last the old tinner had made up his mind; he was going to defend his land and investments. From George's perspective, the retaliation was long overdue – not that he would ever have said so openly. He respected his master too much.

They were ascending the southern side of Longaford Tor, and soon George could see the yellow glow of a fire up near the conical mound of stone at the top. Nodding towards it, he walked a little ahead, his hand on his knife, but there was no need for caution. The three men were waiting for them in the shelter of the small natural bowl in the grass as agreed. Barely acknowledging them, Thomas Smyth's servant strode past the little band, to stand with arms folded as the discussion began.

Watching his employer, George could see that the inner strength he had admired as a lad had not diminished. Though

MICHAEL JECKS

he was only some five feet six inches tall, Smyth had the
build of a wrestler, with massive arms and thighs, and a chest
as round and solid as a wine barrel. He had a natural way
with the men who worked for him, a commander's ability to
put all at ease in his company. As always he squatted with
them by their fire, his square chin jutting in aggressive
friendliness as he spoke, dark eyes alight, thick eyebrows
almost meeting under the thatch of greying hair. In the kindly
light of the flames, George felt sure his master could have
been mistaken for a man of ten, maybe even twenty, years
younger. The fierce glitter in his eyes, the sudden stabbing
movements of his hands as he spoke, the quick enthusiasm in
his words, all seemed to indicate a man in his prime, not one
who was already one of the oldest for miles around.

When Thomas had finished speaking, his eyes held those
of the other men for a moment as if to confirm that he had
selected the right group. Then, satisfied, he clapped the two
nearest on their backs, rose and started off back down the
hill, moving more quickly now, George following behind
him.

'They'll do it,' Thomas said meditatively, gazing eastwards with his hands hooked into his thick leather belt as
they walked south to their horses.

'Yes, sir,' George agreed, and was surprised when his
master spun round to stare at him, frowning in
concentration.

'You think they're right for this, don't you?'

George nodded with conviction. 'Harold Magge, he'd do
anything you'd ask,' he said firmly while the almost black
eyes held his. 'And Stephen the Crocker and Thomas
Horsho'll do what Harold tells them.'

Thomas turned back to the view. 'Good,' he said softly. 'I've had enough. I want my land back.'

South and east of them as the two men descended, Adam Coyt was putting the last of his cattle in through the gate, and setting off with his dogs to stroll round the old moorstone enclosure while he checked for weaknesses in the wall.

He had spent all his life on the moors. As a boy he had played out on the open lands, the huge rolling plains between Lydford and Chagford, watching the creatures through the seasons. Rabbits, deer and hart, wolves and foxes, he knew them all as well as he knew the animals on his own farmstead. A moorman, he had known no other life. His father had lived here and his father before him, all the generations working in the cruel climate which so often broke those who did not respect it.

Like a tinner, Adam felt a close affinity for the land, but in his case it was bred of experience and fear. Though he had prospered, Dartmoor had exacted its toll, taking his wife and son. He could not blame the moors; it was the way of the forest, that was all. She should not have gone out when it had begun to snow, and was mad to try to return later. Crockern, Dartmoor's spirit, deserved respect from people. There was no use in praying to God for help, not when Crockern had sent the bitter winds to scour the land. When Adam had found her body, slumped and curled into a small ball of agony, the flesh frozen blue-white, he had wept, but not for long. There was no sense in tears – he had work to do. A year later his son too had succumbed, unable to survive the bitter winter of 1316 when the food spoiled under the sheeting rains. Then Adam had not even been able

MICHAEL JECKS

to cry. It had been hard, he had tried to give the lad enough, taking from his own meagre portion to feed him, but it was insufficient and the crying had increased in volume daily until Adam was almost relieved when it faded and at last was stilled. A month later when the thaw had come he had made the cruel journey to Widecombe Church – the small pathetic body could no longer be kept in its barrel, protected in salt like a haunch of pork, and he wanted the boy to be buried with his mother.

For all that, the moors had given him a good life. His cattle thrived, his life was unaffected by the miseries of warfare or disease which all spoke of in the towns when he went to buy goods, and he lived in peace, far from others. Only the miners occasionally disrupted his life, digging holes on the land he needed for pasture, and stirring up the streams where he watered his animals.

To a moorman like Adam Coyt, the world was formed of two groups of men: those, like him, who were of Dartmoor, and others – foreigners – who came from other parts of Devon or the world. Now, as night fell, their fires could be seen as glittering points of light, some far off, others closer. These were the places where the tin miners lived. He sighed at the sight, but patted his dog's head and continued up to his house. There was nothing he could do about the invading metal hunters.

Henry Smalhobbe yawned and sat back in front of his fire, keen to see what the dark ore would yield up to him. Last week he had dug a new leat from the River Dart to his little plot so that he could have running water to help him sort the valuable tinstone from the lighter soil around it; this was his first fire since finishing the leat, and his first attempt at tinning in this area.

It was hard work compared to what he was used to, and his hands still blistered too easily. Many days of labour were needed to generate enough ore to make a fire worthwhile, but at least this parcel of scrubby ground appeared to have more potential than the last area he had tried. For the best part of a year he had covered a few hundred yards of the little river bed, separating the good ore from the useless spoil, and piling up the waste at the edge until he noticed tinstone in a hole dug for a fire. Interested, he had begun to investigate the ground nearby. At first there had been little, but then he located a rich-looking deposit. Parallel to the old river bed there seemed to be a thick layer of tinstone only a foot or so under the ground, and now he had given up the search in the stream and was concentrating on the store lying just under the ancient banks.

Stretching, he relaxed and leaned back on his elbows, a slight man in his late twenties with roughly-cut, mousy hair. He looked over-tired, with strained features and bright brown eyes which held a feverish glitter. No matter how many hours he spent in the sun and rain, his skin never tanned, just went an unhealthy red.

On hearing a noise he glanced over his shoulder. Sarah, his wife, was approaching carrying a bowl of beans and soup on a platter with bread and a pot of ale. A dark, plump woman in her early twenties, she watched while he ate. Seeing him look up, she smiled, her cheeks dimpling. It made her look fifteen again, the same as when they had first met. She chatted, and he was pleased that she did not mention her fears. They had talked about the threats and dangers often enough.

It was pointless going over the same sterile ground day after day. She nodded towards the fire as he gulped his ale. 'Is there much tin in that lot, do you think?'

Placing the pot carefully on the ground, he glanced at the smoking charcoal. This was the easiest way to obtain the metal from the ore. You dug a hole and started a fire with layers of charcoal and ore over it. Once the fire had died, the tin could be pulled free from the ashes in jagged, black chunks. He broke off a crust of bread and chewed. 'I don't know. It was dark, and felt heavy, but it's hard to tell. Sometimes the best metal comes from the worst-looking scraps, and the best-looking tinstone sometimes yields little . . .'

He could see her thoughts were not on his words. Her gaze had risen to the flickering glow to the north, where their neighbour had his hut. 'There's no point in worrying, Sarah,' he said gently.

'No,' she agreed, but went on staring. 'Still, I wish he would come here and stay with us at night. It would be safer, for us as well as him. While we stay apart . . .'

'Sarah, he won't come. Anyway,' he shot a quick glance at the distant fire, 'he'll be all right.'

'Smyth's men have threatened us too often. If he wants us gone, he can attack us easily, and Peter's too far from everyone else, out there on the moors. There's no one to help him.'

Her husband stood and shrugged. 'I know. But he's convinced he's safe. Anyway, I see no reason for us to fear. We're tinners no less than Smyth, and we have the same rights as him. He can't make us leave.'

Sarah nodded, but her eyes avoided his. She knew he was right under the law, but that did not dispel her fear. Three times now the men had come – twice when Henry was away at his works. The first time they had only made lewd comments, surrounding her and barring her escape while they amused themselves by insulting her, speculating why she had no children yet: was it her or her husband? Was he not good enough? Maybe another man, a real miner, would be better? And all she could do was stand silently, her face reddening in shy embarrassment at their talk. That time they had soon gone.

The second time Henry had been with her. One moment they had been alone, the next they were encircled by four men who stood with cudgels ready and told them to go, to leave this land. She recalled her husband's courage with a flush of pride. He had shoved her to safety behind him, facing the men and cursing them, stubbornly stating his right to the tin within his bounds, ignoring their threats and hissed warnings. The men had left as suddenly as they had appeared, but their menacing words seemed to hang on the still evening air for hours afterwards.

But it was the third visit which had scared her the most. While she was inside their hut, a man had entered without knocking. She recognised him immediately: it was Thomas Smyth. Uninvited, he crossed to a stool and seated himself, and in a calm, soft voice he had begun to talk, resting his elbows on his knees and staring at her with his unsettling dark eyes. At first she had thought he was rambling: he had spoken of his life, of his marriage, then of his love for his daughter – and it was only then that she realised he was trying to intimidate her. 'I wouldn't like to think of my daughter being so far from anyone. I wouldn't want to think she could be widowed so easily, could be left to fend for herself, as you could be if your husband was to die out here on the moors.'

This time her fury had been sparked. That this man should dare to enter her house and threaten her, in defiance of all laws of hospitality, was obscene. It was so shocking that she had forgotten her fear, and, raising her wooden spoon, she had shrieked at him to go. He did, with a cynical, half-amused glance at her weapon, as though measuring it against the swords, knives and arrows of his men. But at the door he had paused, looking back at her and saying slowly and deliberately, 'Think about what I have said, Mrs Smalhobbe. After all, even now your husband might be dead. You might already be a widow. Think on that!'

The terror of that visit was still heavy on her soul. That strange, dark little man with the gentle voice, comparing her to his own daughter, had given her an impression of cruelty which had not faded with time. She knew that her husband had been anxious for her when he returned home that night. Her terror was all too plain, and as soon as he arrived she had launched herself into the protection of his arms. It was some time before he could persuade her that he was perfectly safe – indeed, he had seen no one all day.

'Do you want to leave the moors?'

His words, unexpected, and so soft she was not at first sure she had heard him correctly, made her spin, eyes wide in astonishment. 'What?'

Her obvious amazement made his mouth curl into a dry grin. 'I said, "Do you want to leave here?" I don't, but if you're not going to be able to find peace here, maybe we should move on to another place.'

'But . . .' She stopped and considered. This land was all they had in the world. They had come here – was it only a year ago? – to try to make a new life after losing their old home, and had, by the grace of God, been able to earn a meagre living. Were they to leave now, would they ever be able to settle elsewhere? For the first time since the first visit from Smyth's men, she contemplated the options left to them: stay and run the risk of violence from their rich and powerful neighbour, or leave and try to find a new living somewhere else. They had tried that for a year before coming here to the moors, and the very thought of it made her shudder. She could not face it again.

Turning to her husband, she held his gaze for a minute. 'We will stay,' she said at last.

He gave her a tender smile. 'At least we have each other,' he said.

'Yes,' she whispered, but glanced fearfully one last time at Peter Bruther's small fire, so tiny and sad in its distant solitude.

The decision to remain had left a hollow pit of fear in Sarah's belly. The haven they had thought so safe only a few weeks before had proved as insecure as any of the other places in which they had attempted to hide. At least she had her husband with her, she thought. Poor Peter Bruther had no one. How could he defend himself, all alone out there, if Thomas Smyth's tinners chose to attack him?

Leaping from his horse and tossing the reins to the waiting ostler, Sir Robert Beauscyr strode quickly to the steps leading to the old hall, his narrow face pale, lips compressed into a thin line. He took the steps two at a time, threw open the great door and passed through the curtain into the hall itself.

'Father!' he began imperiously. 'That damned cretin, your man who—'

'Be quiet!' The angry bellow from his normally calm and composed father made Robert pause, and it was only then that he noticed the other two men in the room. His fury dissipated as he studied them warily. One – young, broad-shouldered and with the powerful right arm that spoke of a life spent in training for war – he recognised immediately.

Sir Robert could see that his younger brother had grown to maturity. The slim, lithe boy of fourteen who had left home six years before had developed into a swarthy warrior. Blue eyes held his calmly, but the face had changed: the nose had been broken, and a thick scar marred the flat of his right cheek which would, Robert was sure, attract all the women in Exeter.

For his part, John Beauscyr was unimpressed by the sight of his brother and had to conceal a grimace of disgust. Always more interested in study than in fighting, Robert had the ascetic thinness of a priest; his skin was waxy from spending too many hours indoors. Even his handshake felt limp and pathetic. John was sure that his older brother would have made a better merchant than knight, and it was a constant source of aggravation that in the lottery of life he should have come second: it would be Robert, not he, who would inherit the old Manor of Beauscyr in Dartmoor.

The second visitor was a tall man, standing a little away from the fire as though keeping back until sure that Sir Robert was no danger. Having seen the welcome given by John, he stepped forward, and Sir Robert was struck by the sense of power emanating from him, not strength of muscle alone, but of purpose and of will. John introduced them.

'Robert, this is my master, Sir Ralph of Warton. I have been his squire for over two years now. Sir Ralph, this is my brother.'

Sir Robert glanced quickly at his father, then gestured to the waiting servant. 'Sir Ralph, I am pleased that you have come to visit our house, you are most welcome. Are you to be here for some time?'

Sir Ralph graciously inclined his head. 'Not for long, I fear, sir. This is simply the last stage of our journey to the coast. I confess I find the current state of the kingdom depressing, and will be glad to leave when I may.'

'Who would not?' said Sir William shortly, instructing the servant to fetch more wine and some cold meats. 'Since the famine there are hardly enough villeins to work the fields.'

'But it is peaceful here.'

'I suppose so. At least down here we are safe from the raids of those murderers from Scotland.'

'They are the devil's own brood,' Sir Ralph agreed.

'Of course, sir. Mad! They must be mad. One victory and they seem to think they can raid with impunity as far into the kingdom as they choose. Don't they realise that they will suffer the Pope's extreme displeasure? Their leader is already excommunicated, I believe – do they want their whole country to suffer anathema?'

'They already do.' It was John who spoke, and Robert was interested to see that he reddened and looked down as his knight shot a keen glance at him. It was as if he suddenly realised he had said something wrong. Sir Ralph spoke then as he took a mug of wine from the servant.

'Yes, the Scottish are all under an interdict. The Pope decided to punish them for refusing to seal their dispute with King Edward, who is, after all, their liege lord.'

'Good,' said Sir William, rubbing his hands together with a smile of satisfaction. 'Let us hope they will realise the error of their ways, then. Perhaps this will make them see that they cannot live by simply stealing what they want all the time. Those Scottish are no more than a tribe of outlaws.'

'More to the point, it also stops any chance of a new crusade to the Holy Land, and that is what the Pope wishes for,' Sir Ralph continued, staring into his mug. 'While the Scottish continue raiding in the north, and with the French King threatening the south, King Edward can hardly be expected to agree to travel to Palestine. The Pope's desire for a new attempt on the Holy Land must stay just that: a desire, with no chance of being satisfied.'

'At least the Pope's trying to cow the Scots into submission.'

'Yes, sir. And the news from Ireland sounds better. The King's justiciar over there has apparently forced the Scottish invaders back. Thanks to God for a wise man who can command his troops!'

'If, er . . . if there was to be a new crusade, Sir Ralph – would you join it?' asked Sir Robert, and was fixed with an intense stare from the knight's grey eyes.

'Yes, sir. I am like your brother here. I have no property; my brother inherited it all from our father. What I crave – what I *need* – is an oppportunity to win glory and favours. Where else should a knight be, but in battle? If there was a new crusade I could win fame and wealth. But be that as it may, there will be no crusade. Not while the French and English kings bicker among themselves at every opportunity. No, I will not be going to Palestine. But I want to cross the sea, to see new lands and fight. There are wars in Italy where a knight can earn good sums. I may go there.'

Motioning for more wine, Sir William burped and agreed. 'Yes, the Italian cities offer good opportunities.'

Sir Ralph nodded, but his eyes remained on Sir Robert. After a moment John cleared his throat.

'So how is the demesne? The Manor looks as though it's hardly suffered, compared with the rest of the kingdom.'

'We've been lucky,' Sir William agreed. 'The estates have not been so badly affected as others. And not many villeins have died.'

'But some have run away.'

Sir Robert's sharp tone made his brother and the knight look up. His father opened his mouth to speak but Sir Robert carried on, his anger rising again swiftly as he remembered the incident. 'Oh, yes, some have run. Like Peter Bruther . . .'

John frowned. 'Who, old Martha's son?'

'Yes. She died, and he ran away some nine months ago. We thought he must have gone east, to try to win his freedom, but I saw him today on the road to Exeter. The cretin did not run far, apparently, he just went to the moors. He saw me, too, and went to the trouble of stopping me to show he does not fear us any more, the cur!'

'Did you beat him?' his brother asked, curious.

'He was surrounded by miners, like guards round a king. I could do nothing. If I had, they would have attacked me.' Sir Robert glared at the fire, while John could not hide his sneer at this weakness.

21

Shrugging, Sir Ralph said, 'Well, if you want him, go after him. If a villein runs away he must remain free for a year and a day to gain his freedom. If he has not been gone for a year yet, you have every right to bring him back.'

'Not here, Sir Ralph. The moors are different. And others will see him get away with it, without punishment! He will see to that: the rogue promised it, and laughed at me. Him – a villein – laughing at *me*!'

Sir William wore a worried frown. 'This could be bad for the demesne. What can we do? If we do nothing, the other villeins will see that they can go when they want, and the Manor will fail for lack of workers, but if we try to pull him back, the miners could fight us.'

John was unconcerned. 'Demand that the warden at Lydford comes and sorts it out. He has responsibility for the tinners in Devon under the law. Peter Bruther must come back, and the warden can make him.'

'Maybe you're right,' muttered Robert. Looking up suddenly, John was surprised by the fury on his brother's face as he ground out: 'One thing I do know: if I catch that bastard alone, out on the moors, he'll regret his laughter at my expense.'

'You mustn't harm a miner,' his father remonstrated mildly.

'Me? I mustn't let villeins run away, Father, and neither should *you*!'

# CHAPTER TWO

'For the love of God, Simon!'

'What?' Simon Puttock turned in his saddle, and peered at his friend.

His companion sighed dramatically, but when he caught Simon's expression he could not help breaking into loud, but not unkind, laughter. 'Your misery, that's what! You've been like a bear with a leg in a trap all the way, complaining about this visit. Are you going to keep it up until we get there? What are you so troubled about? The journey is not long, there's a meal at the end of it, and at least the weather is good for a ride over these moors you've told me so much about.'

Simon, bailiff of Lydford Castle, gave a surly shrug of his shoulders, but was forced to confess the validity of at least the last part of the statement. From here, up at the far eastern fringe of Lydford, the moors did look inviting in the sunshine – a deceptive series of softly moulded green hillocks in the distance, rolling and merging one into the other, touched with bright yellow and gold where the sunlight caught the gorse, with occasional licks of purple and mauve where the heather lay. The scene looked as rich in colour as the robes of an emperor, the flanks of the hills spattered here and there with white where sheep grazed. Overhead a hawk soared in a cloudless sky, while ahead of them water sparkled in brooks and pools.

But the view gave him no comfort, and the worst of it was, the bailiff wasn't sure he could fully explain his problems. It had been two years now since he had first met Sir Baldwin Furnshill, the Master of Furnshill Manor near Cadbury, and in that time the two had become firm friends. As Simon knew, after investigating murders with him, Baldwin was shrewd and learned, and had a good grasp of law – especially now that he was a Keeper of the King's Peace – but the troubles Simon was forced to contend with almost daily would be incomprehensible even to a man trained in legal matters. Though Baldwin had travelled much in his youth, in those days he had been a member of a wealthy and powerful organisation. Local issues were a very different kettle of fish.

The bailiff threw him a doubtful glance. In the sunlight, Baldwin was tanned and fit-looking, the thin knife-scar on his cheek shining red in the sun. His brown eyes moved confidently over the country ahead, and with his strong, square face he looked the picture of a modern knight. But the neatly trimmed beard which followed the line of his jaw jarred, as did his clothing. The old tunic was stained and worn, his hose faded and dusty, making him look as if he had fallen on hard times. It was not so, Simon knew, for the knight's estates were prosperous, but Baldwin had simply no

interest in his appearance. He was content to appear poor if
others wished to believe him so.

'Come along, Simon. How can you be so miserable on a
day like this?' Baldwin asked again. It was unlike his friend
to be so introspective and oblivious to the world. If anything,
it was usually Baldwin himself who was prey to dark
thoughts, and Simon who had to pull him back to the present.
But not this time. Baldwin was relaxed and refreshed after
staying with the bailiff for three days, and he found it hard to
understand why the message from an obscure Manor towards
Widecombe should have so unsettled his friend.

Simon rode along in silence for a while, jogging in time
with his horse's slow gait. 'It's these damned miners,
Baldwin,' he said at last. 'Wherever they go, there's trouble.'

'But this man Beauscyr only has a simple complaint,
surely?'

'It's not as easy as it seems,' Simon grunted. 'This is not
like your Manor, where you have the right to treat your peasants as you wish. This is a forest.'

'A forest?' Baldwin repeated dubiously.

'Yes. It used to be a hunting ground for the King until he
made Piers Gaveston Earl of Cornwall and gave it to him.
Since Gaveston's killing, it has reverted to the King – and the
miners fall under the King's demesne.'

'How so?'

The bailiff explained. 'There has always been a lot of tin
on the moors, and the farming of it has become a profitable
occupation for many – not least for the King. Edward taxes
all the metal mined here, so he has given rights to the miners
to protect them and their interests. More or less anything that
helps them find tin, they are allowed to do.'

'But the man is a runaway, surely? All of this is irrelevant.'

'I wish it was. The trouble is, as soon as he bounded land, he became a miner. It follows that he's a member of the King's demesne. Beauscyr may not like it, but his man is now *de facto* a tin miner working for the King. There's little Beauscyr can do about it.'

'Well, then, Beauscyr must accept that he has lost his man, whether he likes the fact or no. He can petition the King if he feels he has a claim.'

Simon studied his friend with an embittered eye. The knight stared back with open, cheerful incomprehension, and Simon sighed again. 'Sir William Beauscyr won't see it like that, *Sir* Baldwin,' he said drily. The knight chuckled at the sarcastic use of his title as the bailiff scowled at the track ahead. 'As far as he's concerned, he's got rights too – the same as you or anyone else. This man was his villein; he has run away, therefore he should be returned.'

'Except that now the man falls under the King's protection,' Baldwin said lightly.

'Except that now the man is the King's,' Simon agreed. 'The trouble is, many villeins run away and *call* themselves miners, just to escape their lords. Some men on the moors have claimed stannary rights and privileges – that is, they've declared they're miners and behave as such – until they have a new tax imposed, when they suddenly change their minds and say they're merchants, or farmers, or foresters . . . anything! That's what Beauscyr alleges: that this man – who was it? Peter? – this man is claiming to be a tinner out of convenience, and has no intention of mining.'

'That I cannot understand,' said Baldwin. 'What would be the point of it? All it means is, he has gone from one master to another. It's not as if he is free . . .'

'Yes, it is!' said Simon emphatically. 'As a tin miner, he has most of the rights of a freeman – that's the whole point. He can farm tin as he wants, for as long as he wants. The miners have ancient rights, since time out of mind, so the King can be sure they'll bring in the greatest quantity possible. He certainly earns a fortune each year from their efforts. The King imposes few rules on the stanners, and they make their own laws. That's why they can go anywhere on the moors. They have the right, given to them by the King, to wander anywhere, on to anyone's land, to dig for tin, to cut turves for their peat fires, to redirect water for their workings – almost anything. This Peter "Whomsoever" knew what he was doing when he ran away. To all effects he's free now. And this bloody fool Beauscyr wants me – *me*! – to sort out problems which have been brewing for centuries . . .'

Baldwin grinned to himself as his friend muttered on. At thirty-two Simon was some thirteen years younger than he, and still occasionally prone to the kind of angry outbursts which Baldwin more commonly associated with the wild red-haired men of the north. However, the knight knew that these fits of temper never lasted long. Tall, with swarthy skin and brown, nearly-black hair, Simon was normally phlegmatic, accepting what life threw at him, and as he grew older his grey eyes studied the world with a reserved calmness that hid a sharp mind. Having been educated, he was more keen to listen to arguments and strive to find a fair and reasonable line through any dispute, a trait Baldwin found reassuring in a man responsible for the well-being and fortunes of others.

The bailiff's logical mind was able to accommodate most petitioners, and it was only rarely that he lost his temper, when matters appeared to be unfair, or when people were intransigent.

This time it was frustration at being sent to mediate between two parties whose views and wishes were so utterly at odds with each other. From the little Baldwin had heard, there was no likelihood of Simon being able to please both groups. The needs of the miners and the landowners in the moors were too intertwined and yet mutually exclusive to permit of an easy resolution – the King himself would have to rule an agreement. He studied his friend sympathetically for a moment.

'Still, Simon, I was pleased to see that your own Peter has thrived.'

The bailiff threw him a quizzical grin at the mention of his son. 'Thanks for changing the subject,' he said. 'Yes, Peter is fine, thanks to God! And Hugh is devoted to him.' The boy was a long-awaited blessing. Simon and Margaret, his wife, doted on their daughter Edith, but both had longed for a brother for her. Their wishes had finally been fulfilled the previous year, and Simon's servant Hugh had taken to the baby immediately, a fact which occasionally led to arguments between him and Simon's daughter as they bickered over who should look after him.

Some way further on, Baldwin shifted in his saddle. 'Have you heard about affairs on the Scottish marches?' The bailiff threw him a baffled glance as he continued: 'It seems that the Pope has been so infuriated by the wars between the Scottish and English that he sent two cardinals to try and negotiate a peace.'

'A peace between the Bruce and Edward? Never!' Simon snorted. 'None of the King's men in England want to see the Bruce keep what he's stolen, and he's unlikely to agree to give it all up.'

'It may become easier. Now that the Irish have begun to force his men back, he may accept that over there, his conquests have stretched at far as they are going to. Perhaps he will think about agreeing to peace at last.'

'I'm not so sure. A man like that's got no honour. He swore fealty to the King's father when he was Earl of Carrick – how could he be trusted again?'

'Easily, old friend. That was a political promise,' said Baldwin cynically. 'Since then he has been crowned King. After all, our own blessed monarch Edward is a vassal of France for Gascony, and yet he has not given homage to King Philip, has he?'

'Ah, but that's different. King Edward's an honourable man, and he's gone to France to pay homage over the last few years – but how often should he be expected to go? Each time he returns, the French King dies, and he must turn around and go back to swear to the successor. No, it's different with the madman of Scotland. He refuses to come and pay homage to his English King.'

'I am not so sure it is quite that straightforward, Simon. Still, we can but hope for peace. The last thing the country needs is more war.'

'Were the cardinals successful?'

'No. Not quite,' Baldwin said slowly, and then he chortled quietly. When he continued, it was in the unhurried manner which showed he was choosing every word with care. 'In fact, they were somewhat incommoded on their way. They landed on our shores in July of last year, but did not, it would appear, arrive in Scotland until much later. Seemingly they were met by a group of brigands between York and Durham, and were robbed.'

'What happened to them?'

'Oh, they were unharmed. Their pride was more hurt than their persons! Of course, their horses and money were stolen, but they were not hampered apart from that. The additional exercise will probably have done the honourable cardinals some good.'

'I suppose that'll put paid to any hint of peace. If those damned Scotch rebels dare to attack and rob the Pope's cardinals on the way to meet their lord—'

'Ah, Simon!' The knight roared with laughter, making his friend stare at him uncomprehendingly. 'You mustn't jump to conclusions! It wasn't the Scots who attacked the cardinals, it was a band led by an Englishman.'

'No Englishman would dare!'

'Sir Gilbert Middleton did. He had resorted to outlawry. I hear he thought that if the King was unable to protect people up on the northern marches, he might as well take advantage of the fact. He was caught at the end of last year, and I expect his head is on a lance in London even now, for the embarrassment he has given the King.'

'How do you find out these things?' Simon muttered, torn between resentment at the laughter and an urge to join in.

'Simple,' the older man told him. 'I speak to travellers. Most people are happy to tell their news to an interested man. And I still sometimes have . . . friends come and visit me.'

His words made them both quiet for a minute. It was more than ten years since the arrest in 1307 of the 'Poor

Fellow-Soldiers of Christ and the Temple of Solomon', the Knights Templar, and here in England they were all but forgotten, their lands divided and sold off or in the hands of their rivals, the Knights Hospitaller. But neither Baldwin nor Simon could forget the Order, for Baldwin had been a member of the outlawed and disgraced group.

There was a view, commonly held in England and Scotland, that the Knights Templar were innocent of the crimes attributed to them, and were merely the victims of an elaborate plot hatched by the French King to seize their wealth. After the Order had been destroyed, many men who had been members were used by the English King as diplomats, and other warrior monks were welcomed in Scotland, where King Robert I wanted as many trained soldiers as he could find. There were reports that the 'Beauséant', the black and white banner of the Templars, had been seen at Bannockburn, where the English forces were routed so disastrously. Thus there were a great number of men all over the country who had been comrades of Sir Baldwin of Furnshill in the past, before he had become Keeper of the King's Peace in Crediton, and he often entertained guests at his small Manor. Though Simon knew this, he preferred not to enquire too deeply.

'So,' Simon mused after a time, 'the Pope wants to see peace as well, does he? That could be helpful. Maybe he can persuade the Bruce to stop his raiding.'

'Do not place too much store on his ability to bring an end to the wars, my friend.' Baldwin smiled wrily. 'The Pope has already excommunicated the Bruce, after all. And if you had been crowned King of the Scots, I doubt you would be pleased to receive a letter from the Pope addressed to "You, who *call* yourself King of Scotland"! If Pope John wants peace, he will need to try harder than that!'

They were still chuckling at this as they rode down a shallow slope from which the sweep of the moors could be seen. For Baldwin, unused to the area, it was an awesome sight. Bright grass gleamed in the sun, some thin and cropped by cattle, some long and spindly like reeds, both sliced apart in places by silvery trails of glistening water trickling to blue pools. Their path was a dark slash meandering between softly moulded hillocks surmounted with moorstones, a landscape which would have been bleak in winter, Baldwin felt, but which now seemed full of promise with the high singing of larks in the clear sky and the constant tinkling music of the water.

For several miles the knight and his friend saw no other person. The route was well-trodden, the grass flattened and in places worn away, but there was no sign of habitation. The ground became, if possible, even more profusely covered with the grey boulders. Their path took them into a low valley, and soon they were trailing around the fringes of a little wood on the steep hillside, where the trees grew among the litter of stones and boulders.

'God above! Simon, what's happened here?'

The trees were unlike any the knight had seen before; it was as if each of the plants had been shrivelled. All were stunted, misshapen caricatures of the great boughs he knew from his own lands. None was more than twenty feet tall, and most were much shorter.

'I'm glad it's a surprise to you,' Simon smirked. 'You're always so pleased to amaze me with your tales of foreign countries, it's pleasant to repay the debt, if only in part.'

'But what has happened to these trees? Why are they so . . . deformed is the only word I can think of. These *are* oaks, aren't they?'

'I think so, yes,' said Simon, his voice thoughtful as he glanced at the trees near the track. 'But they only grow so high out here, in Wistman's Wood.'

'What about other parts of the moors?'

'I've heard there are some other place where the trees are similar, but I haven't been to them yet. All the other trees I've seen are normal.'

'They are certainly very curious. All the branches point in the same direction – had you noticed that?'

'It's as if they're pointing to something, isn't it? There are rumours I've heard . . .'

'Yes?'

'Well, you remember the stories, don't you? About the Devil and his pack of wish-hounds baying after lost souls? This is where those stories come from, Baldwin, out here on the moors. They say that the wish-hounds are heard here when the winds blow hard.'

Baldwin gave him a sour stare. 'I suppose you think the hounds come here to piss on the trees? Diabolical hounds peeing on the branches kills them off, and that makes the oaks die on one side? Really, Simon, I—'

'No, of course not,' said Simon, hastily holding up a hand to stem the knight's ironic flow. 'But I know *I* wouldn't want to stay here after dark.'

'No, I can see why,' said Baldwin reflectively, gazing at the trees. The atmosphere was oppressive, he thought, and it was easy to understand how people could imagine the worst of such a place, especially if the wind howled among the boughs as night fell. Baldwin did not believe in old wives' tales himself, but it was natural for anyone to be affected by the menacing power of a place like this.

'The people here think there's some kind of strangeness about it,' Simon continued. 'Maybe that's where the name comes from. Round here, "wisht" means uncanny, or weird. Certainly these trees look it.'

'Yes, they do. But I think these trees grow this way for some mundane reason. Wish-hounds!' His voice betrayed his amusement, and the bailiff shot him a suspicious glance.

Another mile southwards, after they had breasted another hill, Baldwin at last understood why Simon had brought him this way. He reined in his horse and stared.

'This is what I wanted you to see, Baldwin. Welcome to the tin mines of Dartmoor!' Simon announced as they came to a halt.

Baldwin found himself staring at a wide encampment on a plain surrounded by low hills, the whole unmarked by wall or fence. Dotted here and there stood small, grey turf and stone cottages. One, larger than the others and set in their midst, gave off a thick plume of smoke which straggled in the slight breeze. The broad area was pitted and scarred with holes and trenches. Through the middle trailed a narrow but fast-flowing stream, from which sprang several man-made rivulets, and there was a large dam over to their right. Other leats were fed by this, tailing off into the distance, and Baldwin guessed that they led to other workings.

'With all these houses there must be many men here,' said Baldwin, eyeing the area speculatively.

'An army. Over a hundred in this camp alone,' Simon agreed, and kicked his horse on.

They had only travelled a short way when they saw a pair of men at the outskirts of the vill, and Simon smiled with sardonic amusement at their reaction – it was all too typical of the attitude of miners out here that they should be suspicious of strangers. One pointed in their direction before running off, while the other man grasped what looked like a pick and faced them resolutely. By the time the bailiff and his friend had come closer there was a group waiting for them, looking like trained soldiers to Baldwin's military eye. The man who had run for help had returned, joined by a thickset character who looked as if he was in charge.

Simon rode up to him, smiling in a friendly manner until the tinner snapped: 'Who're you? What d'you want here?'

The bailiff sighed. It was infuriating that these miners should feel free to be so arrogantly discourteous – even more that they had the right and strength to behave so. He heard Baldwin's intake of breath and could almost feel the waves of disapproval from the knight.

'Good day,' he replied pleasantly. 'We're on our way to visit a friend, to the east. My companion here hasn't seen how tin is farmed, and—'

'He won't find out today, either,' said the man firmly, and Baldwin moved his horse a little closer to Simon. The miner was short and sandy-haired, with skin tanned by the sun and wind to the colour of old saddle leather. Though he looked quite old, Baldwin could not be sure whether that was a sign of the harshness of life on the moors or an indication of his age. If fitness was anything to go by, the man was not ancient. His belly was taut, the breadth of his shoulders was almost the same as his height, and the knight quickly came to the opinion that he would not want to fight such a man without a superiority in weapons. As it was, the man merely carried a long dagger at his waist, but Baldwin could see that he was wary in the way his hands rested close to its haft, his thumbs hooked into his thick leather belt.

'At least tell us how far it is to Sir William Beauscyr's Manor,' Baldwin said sharply, and was pleased to see a quick flicker of doubt in the miner's brown eyes.

'You're friends of Sir William?'

'Not quite,' Baldwin said, then glanced at Simon. 'But the bailiff of Lydford and I are on our way to see him.'

'The bailiff?' His gaze moved suspiciously back to Simon.

'Yes, I'm the bailiff,' said Simon, exasperation beginning to take him over. 'And yes, I'm on my way to see Sir William. Now answer my friend's question and tell us how much further it is to the Manor.'

Directions were grudgingly given while the other men watched, hands fiddling with mattocks and spades, and Baldwin was glad when they could finally set off once more and leave the tense little knot of miners behind. Once they had passed by the village and were making their way up the slope at the far side of the camp, he glanced back and was disturbed to see the sandy-haired man standing motionless in the same place, his eyes still fixed on them.

At a time when so many lords were finding difficulty in financing their country estates, Beauscyr Manor came as a surprise to Baldwin. The family was known to him, of course – they had rendered so many years of loyal service to the kings of England that it would have been hard *not* to be aware of them . . . yet he had not expected quite such a grand Manor. But then, as he reminded himself, Sir William

Beauscyr had fought in Scotland and Wales, and spent time with the old King Edward in France. He must often have been in a position to profit, and after the manner of wealthy men who have made their own way in life, Sir William evidently enjoyed flaunting his riches.

The imposing fort lay some miles beyond the miners' camp, out at the eastern edge of the moors towards Widecombe, on a small hillock formed in a loop of the East Dart such that the river swept around the rear of the buildings to form a narrow moat. Nearby were cottages for the servants of the household and a few of the villeins who laboured in the fields, but these were dwarfed by the Manor itself. As they rode down a slight hill some way off, Baldwin could see the layout. Rectangular and built of local stone, the Manor held inside its walls all the essential buildings. One imposing section at the front, facing west, contained the main gate, behind which was a walled passage, barred with a second door to secure the compound behind. The hall was at the opposite side of the cobbled courtyard, standing high over its undercrofts, a massive structure with a solar block attached at one end where the family could retreat from their retainers. North stood the kitchen area, with what looked like rooms for the garrison, while the stables were at the south. Any attacker attempting to storm the place would have to run the gauntlet of missiles rained on them from the top of all the buildings. Even if both gates were breached, allowing access to the courtyard, the hall itself would withstand a sustained assault.

At the first gate the two men had to wait for a few minutes, but were soon admitted and gladly dropped from their saddles. The Manor was only some twelve miles from

Lydford, but after all the hills on the way and the streams they had needed to ford, it felt much further. Simon stood rubbing the small of his back, and Baldwin gave a pained grimace.

'I think I must be out of condition for journeys like that,' Baldwin admitted. 'Ah, is that our host?'

At the top of the staircase to the hall a man had appeared. Seeing the two visitors, he made his way down the steps and marched over to them. Simon could see he was not the man who had sent the peremptory message demanding help in recovering his villein. Sir William was well into his fifties, while this man was only some twenty years old.

'My father asked me to greet you,' he announced. 'I'm his son, Sir Robert Beauscyr. You're the bailiff? Come with me, and—'

'No,' Baldwin interrupted quickly as the man motioned. '*This* is the bailiff. I am merely a friend.'

Robert Beauscyr flushed angrily as he looked at Simon, as if the bailiff had deliberately misled him. Simon's heart fell at his haughty and dismissive glance, and the thin, tightly-pursed lips. They showed how unlikely it was that there would be any calm and logical discussion. He sighed as, with a curt wave of his hand, Sir Robert Beauscyr motioned the two men to follow him and led the way to the hall. Here, Simon knew, he would be asked to explain himself, and it was bound to be an unpleasant experience.

# CHAPTER THREE

At the top of the steps, they found themselves in the narrow screens passage. On the left was an open door, leading into a buttery filled with casks and boxes, where a man was filling a jug with ale – a welcome sight after their ride. Baldwin followed the others into the hall. Here a fire smouldered in a hearth in the middle of the floor, and benches and tables stood haphazardly on the dry rushes. Tapestries darkened by age and woodsmoke covered the walls, illuminated by shafts of light from the high windows. Before him was a dais on which, round a large table, sat three men and a woman. Simon was almost at the dais, Robert Beauscyr introducing him, and as the people were named for him, Baldwin studied them with interest.

'My father. Sir William Beauscyr.' A large man, and ungainly, was the knight's first impression. The body was misproportioned for his short legs, and the arms swung, long and heavily-muscled as an ape's, under the short-sleeved blue tunic. A large star-like scar marked both cheeks, as if from a lance-thrust. His brows were heavy and intimidating, while his thick mouth was a vivid pink, fleshy and sensuous in the pale-coloured face. Although he had once been a fighter, it must have been many years ago. Sir William was no longer a man to instil fear, Baldwin decided, noting the heavy paunch spilling over the leather belt.

'My mother, Lady Matillida.'

Watching the elegant woman nod regally, Baldwin was impressed. She looked little older than her son, but must have been in her late thirties to have had a lad of his age. Tall, certainly not less than five feet six, and dark-eyed, she was slim and graceful, with movements as quick and assured as an eagle. She gave Baldwin the definite feeling that she had the bulk of the intelligence in her marriage.

'My brother, John.' This youth was clearly training to be a soldier. Well-formed, with lighter hair than the others in his family, he had surprisingly clear blue eyes for such a dark coloured skin, which flitted over Simon and then passed on to Baldwin with an intensity the knight found curiously unsettling. Then there was one more.

'My brother's master, Sir Ralph of Warton.' Slim and elegant in his flowing green tunic, he struck Baldwin as being a well-travelled man. It showed in his calm eyes, dark, hooded eyes under thin eyebrows. He had no visible scars, but Baldwin knew all too well that many men of war carried their battle honours under their clothes, at the points where their armour was weakest. As he studied the knight, Simon introduced them, and as his name and title were given, Baldwin was suddenly aware of his interest being reciprocated. Sir Ralph of Warton was plainly disconcerted by his presence, as if for some reason he had cause to fear Baldwin – or his position.

Food was brought, bread fresh from the ovens and cold meats, and Simon and Baldwin, as guests, were invited to join the family at their board. Gratefully they accepted, sitting together at the end of the table opposite Sir Ralph. By common consent all avoided mention of the reason for Simon's visit until the meal was finished, then Matillida, her son John and Sir Ralph all rose and looked enquiringly at Sir Robert, expecting him to join them. He steadfastly refused to meet their eyes, staring instead at his father, who gave a petulant shrug of his shoulders in assent.

As soon as the other three had left them alone, it was the son who began to set out the case for the return of the wayward villein, his father toying with his empty pewter goblet.

'So what d'you intend to do, bailiff? We asked the chief warden of Lydford to come and investigate; instead he's sent you, so what're you going to do? This leaching away of our villeins must be halted or we'll be ruined.'

It's difficult, of course,' said Simon soothingly. 'The chief warden asked me to come and talk it through with you. But you understand the difficulties. Your villein's now a miner, a stanner, and—'

'We know all that! The question is, what're you going to do to get him back? If the Manor can't produce food, we'll have no money: we'll be unable to pay our taxes. Mark my words, if this miserable cur gets away with his disloyalty, others will soon follow his example.'

'Yes, but the stanners have ancient rights—' Simon sighed as he was interrupted again.

'You don't need to tell me of them! I was born here, I know about the stannary privileges. This isn't the same. Peter Bruther's no tinner. He's not digging for peat or tinning. He's just sitting in his new cottage and enjoying doing nothing. Don't take my word for it, go and see for yourself!'

Speaking patiently, Simon said, 'Even if I did, what good would it do? It makes no difference whether I see him lazing around or not. As far as the law's concerned, he's no longer your responsibility now, so . . .'

'None of our responsibility?' The boy's voice rose to a shout. 'He's our villein, and the law's allowing him to run away! Just to satisfy a few thugs on the moors . . .'

'And the King,' Baldwin interjected mildly.

Sir Robert shot him a glance of loathing. His voice shook with contempt as he sneered: 'The King? That runt! What—'

'Be silent, Robert!' His father leaned forward at last, resting his elbows on the table. Like others Baldwin had known with wounded cheeks, the old knight had a slight lisp as if his tongue was damaged. He looked tired, and Baldwin was sure that it was not his idea to send to the chief warden for help. 'Now, bailiff, you know my son is right. Something has to be done; I cannot allow my villeins to fade from my lands. What will the position of the chief warden be if I go and fetch this man Bruther back?'

'You mustn't,' Simon said bluntly. 'If you do, the miners will be within their rights to prevent you, and the chief warden doesn't want a fight.'

'You will do nothing to help us, then?'

Simon held up his hands in a gesture of despondency. 'What do you want me to say, sir? Do you want me to lie? To promise something you know I can't offer? I've got no massive force to call on, I'm merely the King's man here – and I can't sanction any breaking of the law. Bruther has the law on his side. If you try to get him back, I must tell you I'll have to support the miners if they want to stop you. But you already know that. Look – if you wish, I can try to lend some support to your plight by writing . . .'

'So, after many years of looking after the King's interests, I must now accept the loss of my principal wealth, is that it?'

'This man has gone. Forget him. He's effectively a free man now, owning his own land for mining.'

'Bailiff.' Sir Robert Beauscyr leaned forward, and his voice hissed as he spoke. 'As far as I'm concerned, that man's still our villein, and *our* villeins own nothing! They've use of some of our property while we let them, and that's all. If they own anything, it's their bellies and their hunger. Nothing else.'

'Sir William.' Simon ignored his son's outburst. 'There's nothing I can say will change the facts.'

'No, there isn't, is there?' said Sir Robert, and rising suddenly so that his chair slammed over, he glared at Simon. 'But I'm not prepared to see my inheritance fail because of the stupidity of the law – and its officials! If you'll not help us, we must sort out the issue ourselves!' And he swept from the room before Simon could answer.

For a moment, all three were silent. Baldwin's eyes were on the curtain, still fluttering after Sir Robert's angry passage, when he heard Sir William speak quietly, his tone thoughtful.

'He's very worried, as we all are. Out here in the moors, it's hard enough to keep the peasants working without losing the young ones who hope to gain their freedom and make a good quantity of money in the process.'

'Yes, I understand the problem, but what can I do? As bailiff, I must uphold the law.'

'And you think *this* is the way to do it? In God's name!' He turned to Simon in despair. 'I stopped my son from saying anything villainous about him, but – Christ Jesus! – the King cannot control the people. Look at affairs in Bristol – only two years ago, the city had to be assaulted with artillery because they refused to pay taxes due to the Crown. In the countryside, trailbaston is a growing problem, and outlaws are springing up everywhere. Villeins dare open rebellion. Nowhere do people want to obey the law; they all hold the King in contempt since Bannockburn. What'll happen to us if this man is allowed to get away? We could have an uprising here, in my Manor. The villeins could decide to revolt – and what would you do then, bailiff? Would you come and apologise to my corpse? And to the bodies of my wife and sons?'

There was nothing Simon could say, and after a moment the old knight's gaze dropped to his hands. He had hoped for some help, something constructive, but it was obvious that he would get nothing from the warden or his bailiff. As the miners well knew, they had power and the strength of the law behind them. There was nothing more he could do – all was now in God's own hands. Slowly he stood and walked from the room, suddenly feeling his age. He must at the least stop his eldest son from behaving foolishly and provoking the miners.

When the curtain had fallen behind Sir William, Baldwin heard a heavy sigh. Glancing at the bailiff, the knight gave him a wry smile. 'I think I begin to comprehend your trepidation about our visit here.'

Simon grunted. Then, looking quickly at the curtained doorway, he stood. 'Let's go and have a look round the Manor. This room makes me nervous. I feel like a prisoner waiting for the gaoler to return.'

Once more in the courtyard, Simon took a deep breath of the warm, peat-tainted fresh air. He had expected the Beauscyrs to be angry, but that did not make it any easier. After all, he was in agreement with them, and he had no wish to be responsible for any harm to them should they be attacked by their villeins in an uprising. His friend's sympathetic voice broke into his thoughts.

'Come now, Simon. There is nothing else you can do for them. As you said, Peter Bruther is legally entitled to stay there if he wants.'

'I know, I know, but that hardly helps. After all, like Sir William said, a Manor is only as good as its workforce, and if the villeins here find they can ignore their lord's will, they'll lose respect for him – and that can only lead to rebellion.'

Baldwin waved a hand at the buildings ringing the yard. 'You need not fear for Beauscyr overmuch,' he said drily. 'Look at this place! It would take the posse of the county to break in here.'

Simon could see what his friend meant. From inside, the defences could be better appreciated, and appeared even more impressive. Apart from the tall walls, the storehouses beneath the main hall looked full. Judging from the number of men bustling around, there was a fair complement of guards as well as the servants. Simon pointed with his chin at a couple standing idly near the gates. 'Looks like the Beauscyrs can afford their own army.'

Following his gaze, Baldwin nodded slowly. 'Yes, well, it's no surprise. Sir William was a soldier with the King for a number of years. He was known to have captured several of Edward's enemies, so he must have made a lot of money from ransoming them. And no doubt he won plenty of loot.'

There was a cynical note to his voice. 'What is it?' Simon asked. 'You used to fight – you must have taken captives and won your own loot. It's the spoils of war which make it worthwhile, after all. No one would bother to join an army unless there was a reward.'

Baldwin smiled but said nothing. Because they rarely discussed his time as a Knight Templar it would be difficult for the bailiff, so strongly rooted in the secular world as he was, to understand that the Templars had fought not for profit but for God. When they gained wealth, it was not for an individual, but used to enrich the Order so that it could continue to perform its vital function of protecting pilgrims in the Holy Land. All else was unimportant compared with that holy task. But then, the Knights of the Order were not worldly soldiers fighting for their own profit; they were the vanguard of Christ, the warrior monks. Their chivalric code made the concept of mercenary soldiering distasteful to Baldwin.

'Come, my friend. Let's go back inside,' he said quietly. 'At least we will be returning to Lydford tomorrow.'

'Yes, but I'll not be allowed to forget this issue, I'm sure. With a young man like Sir Robert Beauscyr involved, who feels his inheritance is threatened, this matter will be bound to come up again before long.'

Standing on the casde walls above the gate the following morning, watching the two men ride away, Sir Robert Beauscyr was filled with righteous indignation. He had always had faith in the rule of the law, had believed it gave protection to those who needed it, and was convinced his family had right on their side. It was not just unfair that Peter Bruther should be allowed to escape justice, it was *wrong*. Worse was the fact that any attempt to put things right would mean breaking the law.

'So, brother. No satisfaction there.'

John had stepped quietly to his side and was also staring at Baldwin and Simon as they cantered up the gentle slope. Sir Robert could not resist a scornful jibe. 'All alone for once, John? Where's your master, Sir Ralph?'

'Oh, he wanted to go for a ride to see the moors.' He gave his brother a faintly amused, questioning look, but then half-shrugged as though Robert's mood was to be expected, and was, in any case, of little consequence. 'So, the bailiff will not help. That seems certain.'

His brother nodded angrily. 'What's the point of the law if it'll not uphold what's right and good?'

'Ah, but this time the law has to try to find a way between the interests of a small family in the moors and the King.'

His dry sarcasm made Sir Robert stare. 'What do you mean? Our father, and his before him, have aided the kings of England in all the wars over the last fifty years. We've the same interests as the King. He must know that.'

'Are you certain about that?' Now John's voice was scornful. 'From what I hear, this King of ours is too weak to choose what tunic to wear of a morning. All he wants is money so he can show largesse to his friends – and the miners give him that money. What are we worth? And how much can he value our loyalty when he has the choice of great lords – the pick of men such as Aymer de Valence and Thomas of Lancaster? Does he need the Beauscyr family to protect him as well?'

Irritably gesturing with his hand as if slapping at the suggestion, Sir Robert snapped, 'Rubbish! The King knows who his real friends are. It's the knights in the shires like us who are his real guards, the men he needs to call on in time of war, not—'

'Brother, brother, please! Can you really believe that? The King cannot be stupid enough to think it. The knights who, as you say, he calls on when there are battles to be fought, are either abroad and earning money fighting with the Pisans or the Venetians or any others who will pay, or they are loyal to their lord before their King. After all, who do most knights give their word of allegiance to? The King or their local magnate? Anyway, Edward does not even need to worry about that here. Here his choice is very clear: does he support the miners, who provide him with many tons of tin and the taxes they produce, or does he side with a few knights whose lands border the moors, and whose wealth can only be measured in a few pounds?'

'In fairness he must—'

'Oh, no! Life is not fair. The King, God bless him, is forced to look to his own and the kingdom's good. I fear that our father – and you – weigh rather low in his estimation compared with the tin miners.'

'What's the matter with you?' asked Sir Robert, stung by the sarcasm. 'You know the King needs men like us, we're the backbone of the kingdom. Where would he be without the knights and—'

'Who's that?'

The sudden concentration on his brother's face made Sir Robert wheel round to the view. A pair of riders approached down the slope from the west. He frowned as he tried to make out the figures. 'Good God! It's that miner, Thomas Smyth, and his henchman. What do they want here?'

'I have no idea,' said John imperturbably, his eyes fixed on the horsemen. 'But as the heir to the Manor, I'm sure you'll know soon enough.'

Muttering an oath, Sir Robert spun on his heel and strode to the staircase in the small tower at the corner of the stables. This was just one more cause for concern. The miners were a constant irritation, and any visit from them was unlikely to be for social purposes, as Sir Robert knew.

Curious to see how the meeting went, John remained up on the wall where he could see down into the courtyard. From his vantage point he had a clear view of the reception. The old tinner dropped from his horse, tossing the reins to his servant with a haughty flick of his wrist, plainly feeling there was no danger to him even here in the stronghold of his enemy, John saw with some surprise. Sauntering across the yard, the visitor left his servant and made his way to the hall's steps, at the top of which stood Sir William, his face grim. They met and said a few words at the door, then passed inside. A few moments later Sir Robert emerged from the stable block, rushed to the hall and stormed inside.

It was possible to hear what was being said inside the hall from the top of the steps, and for an instant John toyed with the idea of eavesdropping. Here was an opportunity for harmless fun, the chance of overhearing something with which he could prick his brother's pride . . . but the embarrassment if he was caught outweighed the potential for any advantage. He shrugged and put the meeting from his mind. It was hot on the wall, and he was about to leave and fetch himself a pint of ale when he heard the raised voices.

It was obvious that there was a heated debate going on. He could make out his father's voice, apparently raised in an attempt to calm someone, then the hoarse bellow of his brother: 'You can't – I won't allow it! This is madness, complete madness! You want to take this foreigner's word – it goes against all reason! I won't have it!'

There was more in a similar vein, and John could see that the miner's servant found it as intriguing as he did. At the first shout, he wavered visibly, undecided whether to go to the hall or not. With one hand on his dagger, the other pulling at his bottom lip, the man soon reached a decision and began to move towards the hall, but before he could cross the yard, the door was thrown open and Sir Robert hurtled out, rushing down the steps and across the cobbles to the stables. There he shoved a slow-moving groom to his horse. Under his bellowed orders it was saddled and bridled, and then he mounted and galloped through the gate, off up the slope before the Manor.

John watched dumbfounded until his brother had disappeared among the trees at the brow of the hill, then he turned back to the courtyard. At the top of the steps stood his father, the tinner in the doorway behind him. He could see the quick motion of the miner's hand, the slow loosening of the servant's grip on his dagger's hilt, but most of all what John saw, and what made him smirk secretly to himself, was the expression of despair on his father's face as he stared after his eldest son.

# CHAPTER FOUR

With the troubles caused by outlaws, Sir Ralph had decided to take the advice of his host and bring a man-at-arms with him on this ride. He was also aware, after talking to his young squire, that there was another good reason for bringing someone along with him who knew the area – for Dartmoor could be a dangerous place even in the middle of summer. Bogs proliferated, and often trapped unwary travellers as well as the sheep and cattle of the moormen. Even so, in the warm sunshine it was hard to be too fearful, and he soon threw off his feelings of caution and began to canter, enjoying the sensation of the wind pulling urgently at his cloak and the feeling of precise, elegant power in his horse's stride. He was not dressed for war, clad only in his riding clothes of hose and a simple tunic of green wool, thin and cool. There had been no need to bring his great horse. Today he rode his palfrey, a light-framed roan mare who ate up the miles with eager joy.

His guard, a cheerful young man called Ronald Taverner, was happy enough with the ride. It was good to be out from the Manor for once. He had no knowledge of this knight, but he was an optimistic soul, eager to please Sir William and keen to impress any friend of the Beauscyr family. Right now the wish uppermost in his mind was that they might be able to stop off for a while and buy some drink, and for that he was taking the knight out north and west, towards the alehouse where the Dart River crossed the east-west road over the moors. The farmer there always made too much ale for himself, and was happy to sell it on to any passerby.

They had gone some four or five miles when they found themselves at the edge of a low cliff; they reined in and peered into the valley formed by a tight loop of an old river bed. Below them were the remains of what must have been a powerful watercourse, now reduced to a little stream, trickling down in a narrow rivulet between rocks, curving sharply away to their left and right. All around was a mess of grey moorstone and mixed gravels, with here and there a small bush or stunted tree. There was also a man, who stood as the two figures appeared over the brow above him and shielded his eyes against the sun behind them as he peered up.

Sir Ralph ignored him. Clearly the man was merely one of the tin workers, and thus of little importance. But then he heard the sudden hiss as the man-at-arms drew in his breath. 'What is it?'

'That man there. It's Peter Bruther, the runaway from my master's Manor.'

'Is it?' Ralph looked back. He saw a man in his late twenties, thin and worn, dressed in a faded brown tunic and what looked like a shabby fustian cloak. Dark eyes held his, but not with suspicion or fear, merely with a kind of vague curiosity. After a minute, he shrugged and began scraping muck from the stream and tipping it into a leather bucket. Somehow Ralph felt let down. From what he had heard, this villein was the embodiment of evil, and yet the reality was rather pathetic. Making a quick decision, the knight smiled to himself. Spurring his horse on, he rode down the slope to where the man stood.

Hearing their approach, Bruther straightened again and watched as they splashed through the stream, glancing behind him once as if expecting a sudden attack, then waiting patiently. Ralph smiled at the look. Even if he wanted to, there was nowhere for him to run to – and little point in trying to escape from men on horseback, the knight reasoned.

'Are you Peter Bruther?'

On hearing his words, Bruther straightened and stared up at him. 'I am a miner.'

Ralph felt his mouth twitch. It was pleasing that the man had a defiant spirit. 'I assume that means you are, then. You are the runaway from Sir William Beauscyr's estates.'

'I used to be one of his men,' Bruther confessed with an air of calm; if he had been admitting to owning a sack of corn for sale he could not have been more casual.

Studying him, Ralph was suddenly aware of a certain dry humour in his intelligent eyes. It was unsettling. As a knight, he was used to a range of expressions on the faces of peasants: usually anxiety and trepidation, often outright fear. Never before had he seen the open contempt which was now evident in the curl of the man's lip and the raised eyebrow.

Fury welled up in him. In a merchant or another freeman it would have been disrespectful. In a runaway, it was blatantly impudent. Ralph spurred his horse closer.

'If there is something which amuses you, share it with me.'

'Oh, no. Not until you have explained why you want to speak to me. You are the trespasser here, after all, not me.'

*'Trespasser!'* The knight spat the word, astonished by the daring of this insignificant little man. Beside him, he heard the intake of breath from the man-at-arms.

'Sir Ralph, I think we should return—'

'No,' he interrupted, his eyes fixed on the slight figure before him. 'I think we should take this man back with us. If for no other reason, his insolence deserves punishment. And it would be a good turn to Sir William for the hospitality he has shown me. After all, the Beauscyr family cannot be held responsible for me bringing the man back in error, can they? And I will soon be gone. Once he is back on the Manor's land, he can be punished as a runaway. Tie him and give me the end of the rope – he can come back with us to the Manor and explain his amusement there. If he will not walk, we can drag him.'

'Sir Ralph . . .'

This time it was Peter Bruther who stopped the man-at-arms. 'It's Sir Ralph, is it? You know that I am a tinner – you see my tools here? You must know that I am responsible to the King now and am bound by stannary law, and yet you want to take me hostage?'

Ralph smiled bleakly. 'I know you are a runaway villein from Beauscyr and that is all that matters to me.' He turned. 'I told you to tie him . . .'

55

His voice faded at the sight which met his astonished gaze. Where before there had been an empty sweep of river bed, now there was a group of eight men. From the mattocks and shovels gripped in their grimy fists, they must be miners, and he realised too late that they must have been working further upstream, round the bend. There was no doubt in his mind, as he looked them over, that they were prepared to fight. Unconsciously, his hand fell to his sword, but at the movement he saw the point of a pick rise threateningly. He took his hand away, but kept it close. 'Leave us alone,' he hissed.

'But, you see, these men are my friends – other miners like me. I think you should leave, though. This land is stannary land. *Our* land. You have no rights here.' Bruther was almost at his horse's head now, peering up at him. His voice took on a harsh, jeering tone. 'Go on, sir knight. Leave us. Or do you prefer to try to take me back, like you threatened?'

'You'll regret this!' Ralph leaned low in his saddle and glared at Bruther, eyes wide in impotent fury. But there was nothing he could do. Viciously yanking the reins round, so that the metal bit cut into his mare's mouth, he whipped and spurred her up the slope. Before Taverner could chase after him, Bruther snatched his pony's bridle, and stood smiling up at the nervous man-at-arms. While his men laughed, the miner slipped the thong on his small coil of rope, then weighed it in his hands.

'You tell your Sir Ralph that I'll keep this,' he said mockingly, and chuckled. 'Tell him he can come and get me whenever he wants. I shall always keep it handy. If he wants me, he can come and tie me up and take me back with him.'

He slapped the pony's rump and Ronald clattered off after the disappearing knight.

But the man-at-arms had to travel a long way before the jeers and laughter of the men behind him had at last died away.

Straightening up, Henry Smalhobbe groaned and rubbed at his back. The sun was low in the western sky, and as he winced at it, face screwed into a walnut of wrinkles, he could see it was late. He should return to his hut; it would be dark in another thirty minutes or so. In Bristol the hills and trees all round quickly blotted out the sun and its light, but here twilight crept slowly towards true night, the stars gradually flaring above like tiny diamonds.

Shouldering his small leather sack of rocks, he hefted his shovel and pick and began to make his way homewards. The ground rose shallowly from the old river bed, and he had to climb the slope to the flat plain above, cutting straight across country to get to the hut and Sarah. It was a path he had trodden every day for some weeks now, and he knew it well. There were no dangerous marshlands, providing he walked carefully and kept the grey mass of Higher White Tor before him and Longaford Tor to his left, and the way was easy, being fairly level and grass-covered. There were few rocks.

The stream chuckled merrily behind him as he clambered upwards, and he soon missed the sound as he walked on. Apart from the birds, his only company during the day had been the trickling water. At this time most of the birds were nesting, and the moors were quiet. Only the soft whispering of the wind could be heard. It made him shoulder his pack and frown ahead. There were too many stories here of Crockern for any man to feel entirely comfortable as night thickened and the light fled to leave the moors to the spirits.

But Henry Smalhobbe was not unduly superstitious, and he thrust all thoughts of the spirits of the moors to the back of his mind. He had learned to do that while still a small boy, leaving unproductive fears behind like so much unwanted baggage. There had been little which could upset the peaceful, even pace of his boyhood. Once he'd reached adulthood, most of his time had been spent in loyal service to his master, and the work had kept him too busy to have any terrors of ghosts or spirits. But that was before . . .

Stopping, he rubbed at an eye with the heel of his hand. His eyelid kept twitching – a strange but irritating quirk which had developed over the last few months, and which occasionally preyed on his mind in case it was the precursor of blindness. That thought terrified him. To be blind was to be the target of abuse, or worse. There was no protection for a blind man unless he was wealthy, and Henry Smalhobbe was not rich. If he were to lose his sight, he knew what would happen. Other miners would take over his land; he and his wife would be driven from the moors. How could a blind man find work? Their only hope would be for Sarah to earn them a living, and there was only one way she could do that.

He set his jaw and carried on. It was foolish to waste time worrying about such things. After all, there were many other dangers here on the moors. He could be bitten by a rabid animal or snake, fall into one of the bogs or catch leprosy. There were many ways to die horribly without exercising the imagination.

As if on cue, a low howl shivered on the soft breeze and he glanced at the horizon. Wolves – but a long way off, from the sound. He strode a little faster.

It was almost dark, and he was relieved to see the flickering light of the fire in his hut's doorway. He and Sarah had built their small cottage with regular-sized stones from what appeared to be an old wall a few yards away, jamming pebbles and mud into the gaps to stop draughts, but they had only an old, thick fustian blanket to act as a door. It was little good in winter-time, but it served well enough now, in the warmth of summer. Sarah always left it open at night until he got home, to help him find his way.

The ground was flat here, with a light scattering of moorstone. One or two bushes broke the soft undulations of the grassy plain before his door, but in the main the area was empty as far as the eye could see. While some way off, Henry stopped, frowning. Up ahead, between him and his hut, a bush appeared to have changed. When he had left that morning, it had been a thin straggling plant, but now it seemed larger, and more substantial.

For a moment he felt as if his heart had stopped. All the terror of the moors struck him anew: he suddenly recalled the stories of the moorland spirits. The tales he had heard when sitting before the hearth of the inn with a quart of ale in his hand had seemed laughable then, but now, miles from anybody else, he felt defenceless. A gust of wind flicked the hair from his forehead, and in its light caress he felt the icy trickle of sweat. When the shadow-like figure slowly moved, the hairs at the back of Henry's head rose like a dog's hackles in a chilly spasm of fear.

Whatever it was blocked his path. He could not get to his door without passing it; could not see how Sarah was. She must surely be inside, but he dared not call to her – not for his own sake, but from fear of what the thing might do to her.

Then the fear disappeared as if blown away with the wind. The figure had coughed! Any creature which made such a mundane sound was only flesh and blood like himself. Gripping his mattock, he quietly placed his pack on the ground and crouched. Whoever it was seemed to want to remain hidden. The small explosion of sound had been stifled, as if smothered by a covering hand. It had only been the breeze, carrying the sound to him like a friendly spy, which had betrayed the man. Who he was and why he was here was a mystery, but one which Henry was keen to have answered. Carefully placing one foot in front of the other, he stalked his prey, circling widely to come upon the man from behind.

The figure slowly resolved itself into that of a squatting man, resting easily with elbows on his knees. Clad in a dark cloak, he surveyed the land ahead, occasionally glancing behind him at the hut with a cautious deliberation. Henry felt the blood hammer at his ears. This was no casual moorman, this was clearly an ambush, and the miner felt a rising anger. This man was waiting for *him*. There was only one reason, as Henry knew, why anyone would want to attack him, and if he could surprise the stranger, he might be able to capture him and gain the upper hand.

With infinite care, he crept toward the dark shape. Each time he saw the head begin to move he froze, holding his breath. Then, as it turned back to the path, Henry continued, his feet rising high and slow in a parody of normal motion before being carefully placed down, testing each step to make sure that it would make no sound. There were no twigs or dry leaves to betray his presence here. In a state of exquisite tension, his scalp tingling with his excitement, his hands locked like cast iron round the stave of his mattock, his mouth open to silence even his breathing, he painstakingly moved forward.

But then it all went wrong.

'Henry? Henry?'

His wife's call, betraying a slight anxiety, came clear on the night air from the doorway. She stood peering out into the gloom. It was only because he was late. Sarah had been waiting with his food ready since dusk, for he normally returned before full dark. Now it was quite black outside as she walked to the curtain and twitched it aside. Henry was never this late, she thought to herself, and she wondered whether he could have hurt himself, maybe falling into one of the bogs which proliferated in certain areas, or perhaps having an accident while digging. But that was ridiculous. He knew all the land around here, had walked over the whole area with her to make sure that it was safe. Her husband was a careful man, she knew, and unlikely to harm himself. But though not yet worried, she nonetheless felt a vague trepidation. It was unlike him to be so late, he loathed walking across the moors in the dark.

Head thrust forward, she frowned out, staring. Up ahead there was a shadowy figure. She called, saw his face turn to her, yellow-white in the gloom, and scared, and then she saw the other form spin and rise, and the two men springing from beside the path. That was when she screamed.

\*     \*     \*

Setting off from the hall, Samuel Hankyn burped gently to himself, smiling under the relaxing influence of the strong ale in his belly. He was mildly interested in what had made his master send him home so early, for it was unlike Sir William to go on without a man-at-arms, especially since he was going to meet the man who, as all in the Manor knew, he considered to be his enemy.

Samuel noted that Ronald Taverner, his companion, still wore his vague and faintly stupid expression; he gave a quick frown of exasperation. He should not have listened when Ronald suggested they should go for a drink before making their way home. After all, he had seen often enough before how little the lad could drink.

Strange, though, he reflected again, that his master should have decided to dismiss his men at the miner's door and enter alone. After the row that afternoon he would have expected Sir William to take a strong force with him, rather than just Sir Ralph, his son John and two men-at-arms – himself and young Ronald. A show of strength would have been more in keeping with a man of his standing, and since all the men in the fort knew of the argument which had led to Sir Robert rushing out in a rage, there was even more reason to make a strong showing before the miners. If they even suspected that they had sown dissension in the ranks of the Beauscyr family, the miners might decide to ask for more, or even to take the knight hostage against a large ransom. It had happened before.

For now, though, Samuel just felt grateful at having escaped. If it came to a fight, he wanted to be far away. Knights were well-enough protected, for they had mail and armour to cover them, and if that failed and they were captured, few would kill them. Keeping them prisoner against a goodly charge for release was vastly more profitable. Not so for the poor man-at-arms. He was never wealthy, so could not afford much more than the legal minimum of arms – Samuel's sword and helmet were paid for by Sir William – and was therefore not worth the keeping. If caught, a man-at-arms was lucky if his only punishment was a knife across the throat.

Facing the road ahead, he frowned. That was the thing that niggled at him. Sir William must know that he was riding into danger in going to the miners' camp, so why go there unprotected? It was madness. Surely Sir William was not going to give in – that was almost incredible.

The facts spoke for themselves nonetheless. They had ridden out from Beauscyr to Thomas Smyth's hall at the vill in the middle of the moors, and there Sir William had ordered the men-at-arms to leave him. When Samuel looked back, he saw John and Sir Ralph leaving the knight at the door and riding off on the Chagford road. They would not have left the old knight unless he knew himself to be safe, and that meant he must have been going to accept the miner's terms – paying money to stop damage to the estate.

Samuel and Ronald could have gone straight back to the Manor, but the whole place still felt as if there was a storm brewing after the afternoon's argument, and so Ronald quickly persuaded Samuel to find an inn. Both men had seen John and Sir Ralph heading north-east on the Chagford road, and guessed they were going to the Fighting Cock. It was no secret that the two often went to that tavern for their drinking and other entertainments, and Samuel and Ronald wanted to go somewhere else where they would not be under the amused and patronising eyes of the squire, so they went off the other way, to the farmer's hall where the Dart and the Cowsic Rivers met the road. Here, in the little valley, they were soon happily clutching pots of ale and forgetting their master and his troubles.

Now, some hours later, it was getting dark and Samuel was in a hurry to return to the Manor. He had no wish to be out when night fell, he was too well aware of the tales, and he was fearful of the response of Lady Matillida if they should arrive late. In a small fort like Beauscyr she would be certain to hear about it. Others had endured her fury: he had no wish to.

After leaving the stableyard they turned east. It wasn't long before Samuel saw a pair of riders before them. He felt sure that they were miners, and cursed. Even a single quart of ale made Ronald useless in a fight, and today he had consumed three. Nervously, Samuel glanced south. He remembered this area, it was close to the River Dart, and the ground was often little better than a mire. On the other side of the road there was a path north. They could follow that for a mile, and then turn east on to the Lych way. It was hardly a direct route, but better than getting involved in an unequal fight. Cursing quietly, he spurred his mount to the trail.

Ronald seemed unaware of any change in their direction. He jogged along happily after Samuel, his face beaming. Samuel muttered bitterly. With this detour, they would be travelling a good two miles out of their way. But there was no alternative – the two riders were at the end of the lane, staring after him suspiciously. Praying that they would not follow, Samuel led on.

This track wound along near the river at first; gradually the hills began to rise upon either side. It would have been easy to turn off to the right and make their way down to the road again, but that would have taken them close to Crockern Tor, the seat of the miners' parliament. Anything associated with tinners was unattractive tonight, and Samuel determined to stay on the track until it met the Lych way.

The rocks on both sides grew more plentiful, and the horses began to climb. A hillock stood before them, and when they reached its summit, another lay beyond. Soon Samuel could see the grey-green mass of a wood ahead, and he pursed his lips at the sight. It was only a short way after this, he knew, that the main track lay, and he kicked his horse again. The rest of the journey would be faster, and the sooner they were on their way the happier he would be. The sun was low in the west. Its glow was a rim of gold and purple above the hill to his left, and it gilded the top of the bank on his right with impossible, fiery colours. Down here in the valley he felt the cold rising from the river, and there was an eerie quality to the deadened sounds of their horses' progress as they circled the little wood.

'Is it much further?' he heard Ronald call. The lad's brain was still sodden: his face had not yet lost its expression of bemused happiness.

'Shut up, you daft bugger,' he snarled. 'If it wasn't for you we'd be most of the way back. Can't you see where we are?' Ronald gazed at him in blank incomprehension. 'Look around. We're miles out of the way, hadn't you realised?'

They were at the top of the wood now, and Samuel was about to turn in disgust and make off along the Lych way, when he saw something new in Ronald's expression, 'What is it now?' he asked irritably.

In answer, the young man-at-arms pointed a shaking finger. There, just to their left, stood a large tree, with a rock at its base. And from one branch, spinning slowly, head drooping, hanged a man.

# CHAPTER FIVE

It had been dark for almost an hour when Matillida Beauscyr heard the cry from the gate, then the heavy snort of a horse and a stamping of hooves in the courtyard. Peering through the open door, she saw the grooms holding her older son's horse while he dismounted and curtly instructed them to feed and groom the great creature. Then he made his way over to her.

She stood quite still as he came near, one hand resting on the doorframe, and though she made no sign he knew immediately how angry she was.

'Mother. My apologies for being out so late. I—'

'Be quiet and come inside.'

The words were forced out between teeth clenched so tightly together she looked as if she had lockjaw. Following her, he could feel his face reddening just as it had in his youth in anticipation of the sharp cutting edge of her tongue. With an effort he kept his head up, determined not to show his feelings.

It was the same whenever he knew he had upset her. Robert feared no man greatly, not even his father, but his mother was different. The daughter of a wealthy burgess in Exeter, Matillida had been reared to behave imperiously, confident in the knowledge that her wishes carried authority. She still had the deportment of a princess – but now, in the Manor she had taken for her home, she wielded more power than any queen.

In the hall, she led the way to the fireplace, swearing at the bottler and curtly ordering him out, and sat, staring at her son. 'Well?' she demanded. Her voice was deceptively cold. She would not let herself fly into a passion, that would be too demeaning, but she could not hide her contempt as she stared at her eldest son. He had good reason to squirm, she thought.

To move to the middle of the moors after the busy social life of Exeter had not been easy, but she had understood her duty. Her father had been glad to have won for her the hand of a man such as Beauscyr. To Matillida's mind, Sir William was maybe not so comely as other knights, but he was a man of wealth and power then, in 1289, and she was pleased with the way that she had fitted into his household. In the nineteen years since, never had she forgotten her twin responsibilities: to look after the Manor and give her husband the sons he needed. And she had, although two other sons and a daughter had died young, too weak to survive in the harsh moorland climate. Only two had lived, and now the eldest had left the family open to attack. The fool!

'I'm sorry if you were worried for me, but—' Robert began stiffly.

'Don't be stupid! If you were mad enough to get yourself into trouble on the moors, you know well enough how to look after yourself. And if you were to get yourself killed, at least then you would save us from any other problems caused by your lack of thought.'

'What's that supposed to mean? I was angry – I *had* to leave, otherwise I might have said something which could have made problems for us.'

'No, not angry. You were sulking like a child whose plaything has been taken away. You rode off from an important meeting where your father needed you,' her voice began to rise, 'and you did it in a manner which guaranteed that all the men in the yard would see and hear. "Oh, the poor young master," they will all have thought. And where does it leave you in the future? How do you expect them to respect you now? What happens when your father dies? He's over fifty-five now, he can't last much longer – and how can you take over his responsibilities if the men think you will run away each time there is a hard decision or negotiation to undertake?'

'That's hardly fair,' he said, his face flushing. 'That cretinous miner Smyth was threatening us, the bastard! He rode in here as if he owned the place, and—'

'You dare to call *him* cretin?' Her voice was low, but her hands gripped the carved arms of the chair tightly. It was galling that her son was so dense. After the privileged education he had received, he should have realised the implications to the Manor and himself. '*He* at least knows his power here – you seem to forget it. Do you not recall that under the King's law, if a miner says there is tin on our land, he can come and seek it out? If he says there is ore beneath our fields, he can ruin our crops if he has a mind to, and don't–' she held up a hand to stop his attempt at interruption,

'– don't tell me he wouldn't dare. He has the men to do it. And when he came here to talk, you ran from the room like a maid scared of losing her virginity!'

'I suppose it would have been better for me to stay and challenge him. You'd have liked that,' he said bitterly.

'Don't be even more of a fool!' Abruptly she stood and stared at him with her hands clasped. 'When your father dies, you will be responsible for the Manor, and for me. This man Smyth must not perceive any weakness in you, because he will use it against you. If he thinks that each time he comes here to negotiate with you, all he need do is enrage you, he will know he can control you.'

'But he wants us to pay him not to come on to our lands!'

'I know that. For now, as you say, he wants us to pay him to protect our Manor. If we refuse, he will claim there is tin here, or he will demand that he be allowed to divert the waters from our stream for his workings, or he will cut down our trees to make charcoal for his furnaces – anything. And we know there is nothing we can do to stop him. But soon there might be something we can use against him. For now we must calm him, remain on friendly terms with him, try not to insult or demean him, and persuade him to stay away from the Manor. That is what your father and brother are doing now, trying to keep him happy. After your outburst, it was necessary. Now we will pay. We will mollify the man, befriend him, make sure he is content. Later, maybe, we will gain the advantage and make him regret his presumption!'

'How can we? He's only a common peasant, no better than Peter Bruther, a runaway villein. Would you negotiate with *him*?'

'I would negotiate with the Devil himself if it would keep this Manor together!'

The words sank in slowly. For his own mother to spit out such a blasphemy stunned him, but there was no mistake. There could be no misunderstanding her words or her commitment, and suddenly he was not sure that he had ever understood her. Mumbling another apology, he took himself out of the room.

Alone again, Matillida let her breath escape slowly; her rage had dissipated. Surely the boy must understand. He had responsibilities, not merely to the land and the Manor, but to the family. Today, his behaviour had endangered all that – and it was unforgivable. She was filled with a sense of approaching danger, suddenly fearful for the safety of this place and her family.

In the yard Sir Robert dragged his feet on the cobbles. He was confused, unsure of himself and even more of his mother. At least soon she would have to treat him better – like a man, not a brainless child. He paused by the stables and watched a groom assiduously rubbing sweat from his horse's flanks with a handful of straw. Today, with luck, a new life had begun for him. Sir Robert climbed the staircase in the corner which led up to the walkway on the wall.

He was still there, out by the main gate, when two riders came into view. With dull uninterested eyes he watched them canter down the hill. They were men-at-arms, he noticed, from the Manor.

'Open the gates!' one yelled as they came closer. 'Is Sir William here yet?'

As the bolts were hauled back and the gate unbarred, Sir Robert could hear the surly response from the doorkeeper.

'You should know – you were out with him. Of course he's not back!'

'God!'

Sir Robert watched the man jump down from his horse and lead it through the second gate to the courtyard, the second trailing after, both exhausted after their ride, their mounts tired and flecked with sweat. Soon they were surrounded by a milling crowd of guards and grooms. Something in the hushed anxiety of the scene made him hurry to the inner wall and shout down: 'You! What is it? What's the matter?'

His voice sailed the hubbub below, and he found himself peering down at a group of pale faces. One stood out. It was one of the men, who now stared back with a mixture of nervousness and suspicion. 'Sir, it's the runaway, Peter Bruther. He's dead!'

The following afternoon, Sir Ralph of Warton was looking out at the view from a low tower, mulling over the news about Bruther, as four figures rode towards Beauscyr Manor. The bailiff of Lydford and his friend were easily distinguishable out in front, and the other two must be servants, he thought. One was close by the knight, moving at the same pace like a well-trained squire, and he caught Sir Ralph's attention almost immediately. The man was clearly a warrior, and from the way he rode, never more than a few feet from his master's horse, the two were used to working together. Like his master, he was clad in a light woollen surcoat, but both wore mail beneath, as the occasional glints at wrist and ankle revealed.

The last man in the group lolloped along behind the others like a grain-filled sack, radiating discomfort and misery. He was small of stature and wore a simple short-sleeved shirt with a padded jacket. Clearly this was not a man-of-war in any sense of the word – he looked like a labourer.

Hearing a step, Ralph turned to find John peering over his shoulder.

'So the bailiff and his friend are back, then. And they've brought guards, too. Very sensible. You can never tell where your enemies are, can you?'

Ralph gave him a frosty smile. 'We need not fear each other, anyway.'

'You think so?' John faced him. 'But after your humiliation by that man . . .'

'Don't be ridiculous! He was a peasant, that's all. He was not worth my anger. And certainly not the risk of being hanged for murder. Why? You don't think that I—'

'Perhaps. It was an embarrassment, wasn't it? I hope that the man-at-arms who was with you does not feel it necessary to tell our friend the bailiff. That could mislead him unnecessarily.'

'The man-at-arms?' Ralph surveyed him warily. 'What can he tell?'

'Only what happened, of course. But maybe I should have a word with him and see to it that his memory is . . . modified. The last thing you and I need is to have any suspicions raised about either of us, after all.'

He bowed and made his way down the stairs just as the first gate was opened to welcome the visitors, and Ralph found his attention drawn to the four men entering the barbican. 'Yes,' he murmured, 'that's the last thing *I* need – I am a stranger here. But what about *you*, my friend? What do *you* want?'

In the courtyard, the four men slowly swung from their saddles. Hugh, Simon's servant, was the last to get down. He had always hated riding. Born and raised at the north-eastern edge of Dartmoor, the second son of a farmer, he had never needed to mount a horse while a boy. Nor was there an opportunity. In the small hamlet where they had lived, they had been more or less self-sufficient, bartering with travelling merchants for any goods they could not produce themselves. It was hardly ever necessary to travel anywhere.

But since he had gone into service with Simon, Hugh had been forced to get used to regularly covering long distances. And that meant learning to ride. He hated it! Horses were far too large for a man to control, he felt, and every time he clambered up and squatted uncomfortably in the saddle he found his thoughts turning to the hardness of the ground so far below. In Simon's service he must go up to Tiverton, east to Exeter, sometimes cross the moors to visit the stannary towns of Ashburton, Tavistock and Chagford, or make the long journey down to the coast. All were, for him, excursions of despair. During the journey, all he could think of was the pain and anguish of the trip, and even when he finally reached their destination, he could not enjoy the triumph of safe arrival: his thoughts were already bent on the agonies to come while returning home.

Today, though, he did not feel so bad. The weather had been good, so his fear of getting lost in a moorland fog was unfounded, and the warmth of the sun, and regular gulps from his wineskin, had made him almost mellow. Still, he had no wish for his master to think that he was becoming used to riding, so he maintained his glower of disgust as he released his feet from the stirrups and dropped heavily from the saddle, standing rubbing his backside with both hands.

While a lad, Hugh had been sent out with the sheep, protecting the flock from thieves on either two or four legs. Much of his suspicion of people came from those days, and now, as he turned and stared at the walls of the Manor, his face set hard. All around them men bustled, some coming to take the horses, others pulling their bags from the saddles. The pair standing and talking to his master and Sir Baldwin were, he learned, Sir William Beauscyr and his son Sir Robert. Beyond more men stood watching idly, common soldiers who could have been outlaws the week before, leaning against posts or lounging with thumbs hooked into sword-belts. To Hugh they looked like executioners gauging their prisoners, and he gave a quick shudder at the thought.

The ageing knight and his son greeted Simon and Baldwin, then led the way to the hall, Hugh trailing along behind. Edgar, Baldwin's man, kept as close to his master as a shadow.

'Sir William,' Simon said as they entered the hall, 'as I understand it, Peter Bruther's death was no accident.'

The man gave a wry smile. 'No, bailiff. It was no accident.'

'Why are you so sure?' asked Baldwin.

'Because he was hanged – that's why! Two of my men found him swinging from a tree,' he said curtly.

Simon and Baldwin exchanged a look. Both were troubled by the news, the bailiff most of all. With all the existing problems between the tinners and landowners, it only needed one small spark to start a conflagration which could engulf all the lands under his authority. This death could easily be that spark.

Sir William plainly did not hold the same fear. He was reserved but not fearful as he strode to the fireplace where his wife sat quietly stitching at a tapestry. She smiled up at him as he touched her shoulder. When she returned to her work he said, 'Certainly, it's a nuisance. But it's a problem solved as well.'

Baldwin was not surprised at his words. It would have been strange for the old knight to feel otherwise. After all, he reasoned, the death of Bruther must have been a relief to Sir William, and the man was no hypocrite.

Seating himself at a bench near the fire, Simon gazed at the old knight thoughtfully. Robert wandered to the dais and leaned back on the table, listening carefully. Simon glanced at him, then back at the knight. 'Solved?' he prompted.

'Yes.' Sir William dropped heavily into a chair. 'Solved. Bruther is dead. He was a sore problem to me and my family while he lived, but now he's dead, the example he set to my peasants has been killed with him. If any other villeins had ideas about running away, they'll think again now.'

Baldwin had seated himself beside Simon, and now leaned forward. 'Do you have any idea who might have killed him?' he said. He was surprised when Matillida Beauscyr answered, her eyes on her stitching at first, but then rising to meet Baldwin's gaze.

'Yes. *He* did.' Her voice carried certainty. 'He killed himself as surely as if he had put the rope round his own neck.'

'I'm sorry?' said Baldwin, frowning. 'How did he do that?'

'The miners hereabouts are a tough group, Sir Baldwin, and they have their own kind of justice. They rely on all tinners holding to certain principles. If a man makes a claim to some piece of land, it is his. This fool Bruther went on to a plot and began tinning there. I have no doubt you will find that he was on someone else's land. To the tinners, that would be as good as theft. I rather expect you will find that he was trespassing and the real miners decided to punish him.'

Sir Robert frowned, unsure of her point, but then it came to him and he almost gasped. In a few short words, Matillida had put the blame firmly on to Thomas Smyth.

'You mean that he was hanged as a punishment for working on another man's claim?' Baldwin probed.

Sir William spoke again. 'Yes. We've no doubt about it. He was lynched by a mob.'

Simon stirred. 'You've got his body here?'

'Yes, in an undercroft – it's cool down there.'

'May we see him now?'

Shrugging, the knight led them back into the courtyard and up towards the kitchen area, leaving his son and wife behind. At the back of the building, near the wall closest to the river, he took them down a short stair and into a shallow, pit-like cellar. Here wine and ale barrels lined the walls, and when Hugh tapped one experimentally, it thudded dully, sounding comfortingly full. Up at the far end of the chamber was a large box; within it rested the corpse of the man who had caused so many problems to the landlord.

Walking towards it, Sir William beckoned the others forward with a proprietorial gesture. Peering inside the box, Baldwin and Simon found themselves staring into the face of

77

a man in his late twenties, slimly built and dressed in a rough sleeveless tunic of thick reddish cloth which left his arms bare.

'Poor devil,' Simon heard Baldwin mutter, and he could easily understand why. Lank dark hair fell over one eye, almost covering it, but not hiding the unfocused stare. Bruther had plainly died from strangling. His eyes were wide and staring in the suffused face, his mouth open, tongue a blackened, bloated mass with a line of toothmarks where his jaws had closed in his death throes. Around his neck were the remains of a hemp rope. It was a light cable, of the kind used for lashing, not the type normally associated with a hanging, and was tied loosely. While the bailiff watched, Baldwin studied the body, his hands resting on the edge of the box while his eyes ranged over the figure. Copying his stance, Simon forced himself to stare down as well.

Bruther's was not like the other corpses he had seen. He was becoming familiar with death, having viewed men dead from burning and stabbing in the last two years, and all too often he had felt the need to vomit afterwards. He had witnessed enough hangings, too, as a legal representative, and seen the results. To his mind, the bodies of those who had been hanged were less distressing than those of murdered people, probably, he knew, because he was content to see the guilty punished, but also because there was less overt violence visible. This one felt different from them because it was that of a man who had been killed for no good reason, without trial, in a violent crime. And Bruther's end must have been horrific. It was as if the final terror of the victim managed to transmit itself to him, and in his mind's eye he could imagine the group of men grabbing him, tying his hands, throwing the rope around his neck, hauling the kicking, choking victim aloft, and leaving him there while his face blackened and his eyes rolled. The thought made Simon shiver. He swallowed heavily and turned away.

As usual, Baldwin appeared unaffected by the sight of death. Having finished his quiet survey of the body, he called his servant forward. Edgar had armed himself with a candle, and he held it near the dead man to the knight's instruction, first next to the feet then slowly moving upwards, halting at the hands and wrists, then on up to the face. Last of all Baldwin took the head in his hands and studied it, muttering to himself, not just the face but the scalp as well.

Sir William shot a look of astonishment at Simon, who gave him a weak smile. 'Do not worry, Sir William. My friend's always like this.'

'And lucky I am too!' snorted the crouching knight. 'Right, Edgar. Now, near his neck while I look at the rope.'

'But why?' The older knight tapped his foot impatiently, arms crossed over his chest. 'Haven't you seen enough? The man is dead, and there's an end to it.'

At this Baldwin glanced up, his face thrown into deep lines and shadows where the orange candlelight caught it. 'I don't know about that yet, sir.' He motioned to Edgar. 'Cut the rope from him. Sir William, how can you say there's an end to it when we don't know who did it?'

'But as my wife said, it must have been—'

'The miners. Quite. However, I have little doubt that the miners will say it must have been someone else. Who knows – they might even say it was *you*, Sir William. Now, where did you say this man was found?'

The older man stared from Simon to Baldwin, aghast. '*Me?* They wouldn't dare!'

'Or one of your sons,' Baldwin continued cheerfully. 'That is why we must study this body, to see whether there is any evidence about who really *did* kill him. So, where was he found?'

'In . . . in Wistman's Wood – a little wood some distance from here.'

'And he was hanging from a tree?'

'Yes. My men saw something swinging as they passed by. When they looked, they found his body.' Sir William was still wide-eyed with shock.

'Thank you. I think it might be interesting to see where this was, if you don't mind. Could you ask one of the men to take us there?'

'Yes. Yes, I suppose so, if that's what you want. I'll arrange it.'

'Good. Now . . . ah, thank you, Edgar.'

Taking the heavy cord from his servant, Baldwin studied it carefully. It was strong hemp. Edgar had cut it from the neck, preserving the knot so that the interwoven threads could be studied in one piece. While Simon watched, Baldwin tested the noose, pulling at the knot so that it ran up and down the rope easily. Then the knight threw a glance at the body. Simon held out his hand, and Baldwin wordlessly passed him the rope. He was concentrating on the figure again, oblivious to the others in the room.

Simon had always had a squeamish side to him which the knight found either endearing or infuriating, depending on his mood at the time. For Baldwin, who had experienced warfare and seen death in many forms, there was a certain fascination in a new corpse. He was driven by a pure curiosity, not to prove a principle, but merely to find truth. Each

time he saw a new body, he wanted to study it, and discover
the reasons behind the death, as if the corpse could explain
to him if he would but listen and observe. And he was determined to give each the time it needed to tell him.

Long ago he had realised that when a man or woman died
in a specific way, the signals were roughly the same for
others dying from a similar cause. From experience, then, it
was clear enough that this man had died from hanging. That
was plain from the marks on the face. Baldwin had seen
them often before in hanged men, and he nodded to himself
as he noted them dispassionately. The skin of the head and
upper neck was a dusky colour; the eyes had small red haemorrhages in their whites; the cheeks and scalp, when he
pulled some hair aside, showed even more. No, he had no
doubt that this man had died of being throttled.

He stood back and surveyed the body. One thing was
niggling him. When he studied the neck wound itself in more
detail, he could see something that looked odd. The rope had
lain across the neck, and a thick mark was visible where the
skin had been pulled away in places. It was, he decided, a
little like a long blister, as if a thin scraping had been peeled
away to leave the weeping, exposed flesh. Logically, he
considered, it must be a kind of rope burn. But what confused
him was the *second* mark. Underneath the heavy scar was a
narrower line, stretching from one side of the throat to the
other. He took the candle from Edgar and held it closer.

'Is that all? Or do you want to stay here all afternoon?'
said Sir William, fidgeting irritably. 'It seems clear enough to
me. Bruther is dead from the rope – what more do you want?'

Baldwin frowned, then picked up one of Bruther's hands
and stared at it, examining the wrist. Letting it drop, he

slowly straightened and smiled at the master of the house. 'Yes, of course. Now, if you could take us to the men who found the body, sir, we shall leave you in peace.'

Sir William stomped up the stairs which led to the kitchen, waiting for his guests before marching out into the yard. He gave orders to a guard, who eyed the strangers suspiciously before strolling off to fetch their man. In a few minutes, Samuel Hankyn appeared, looking to Simon like a starving ferret, he was so thin and sharp-faced. He was dressed in russet-coloured wool with a leather jacket. Looking enquiringly at his master, he managed to glance at Simon and Baldwin from the corner of his eye as Sir William explained what they wanted.

Before long they were on their way. Judging from the position of the sun, they had a good three hours before dark, and as none of them wanted to be stuck out on the moors when night came, they struck a brisk pace which made conversation difficult. Samuel was out in front, while Simon, riding behind him, felt stiff, his muscles protesting at so much time spent in the saddle. After a half-hour, they turned off northwards in a broad valley between two low hills.

'This wood,' Baldwin said when they caught sight of greenery up ahead. 'Isn't it the one we passed the other day?'

Simon peered ahead. 'Yes, it's Wistman's,' he said, and something in his voice made the knight look at him.

'I suppose now you will tell me the man was killed because he upset the wish-hounds!' he said lightly.

'There are some things you can't laugh at, especially out here on the moors, Baldwin. Strange things can happen, it's not like other places. Take this wood: all the trees are shorter than they should be. Crockern looks after *his* land the way *he* wants.'

Baldwin was about to say something when Samuel pointed. 'That's where he was,' he said simply.

Up ahead was a wall of moss-covered trunks. A small breeze made dry leaves rustle, chilling the men as it cooled the sweat on their backs. They paused and stared. Beneath one, which stood a little taller than the others, was a large rock, and beside this lay an untidy coil of the same hemp they had recovered from Peter Bruther's body.

'He was hanging off that branch there,' Samuel continued, a finger indicating a heavy bough directly above the stone.

The knight nodded, then dropped from his horse and walked over to the tree. The hemp had been sliced through, he saw. He stared hard up at the oak, then below at the stone. 'You cut him down?'

'Yes, sir. When I came back with the other men.'

Baldwin clambered up on top of the rock. It stood some two feet above the ground, and when he was on it he could just reach the branch overhead with his arms stretched upwards. He gripped the branch and stared at it for some time, then let it go and sprang down, studying the ground all round while Simon observed him. He had seen his friend like this before, searching for any hints like a dog seeking a spoor.

Samuel grunted to himself and kicked his horse, moving out of the wind into the shelter of a rock. Hugh went over to join him and offered him a sip of his wineskin. The guide nodded to him gratefully and took a long pull of the cool drink, passing the skin back and wiping his mouth with the back of his hand.

Jerking a thumb at the knight, who was now squatting and moving twigs and leaves aside as he examined the ground,

Samuel asked: 'Is he always like this? He looks like he's searching for roots.'

Hugh burped quietly and stoppered the flask. 'Often enough. But he seems to see things sometimes which you'd never have expected,' he explained, with a certain grudging respect. 'What he's looking for now, though, I can't imagine.'

'There's nothing to look for. Men came here and hanged him, that's all.'

'He lived out here, did he?'

Shrugging, the man inclined his head slightly northwards. 'A little way off north of here. Most of the miners live out in the open, but this one was nearer the middle of the moors than the rest. Must've been mad. Anyone who's been out on the moors for any time at all learns to stay away from the middle.'

'Why?' Edgar had ridden closer, and now sat easily and clearly comfortable a short way from them.

'Because no one who knows the moors wants to tempt *him*,' Hugh muttered, and the guard nodded sagely.

'Tempt who? What are you on about?'

'Look,' Hugh said, 'this area, it's Crockern's, all of it. The spirit of the moors. He doesn't like people trying to take from him. Even the miners know that, that's why they all stick together, more or less. They keep to their villages, and leave most of the moors to the old man. Otherwise . . .' His voice trailed off as he caught sight of the cynical, raised eyebrow.

'Come on, Hugh. Otherwise what?'

'There was a farmer, not far from here. He had a good living, earned enough to feed himself and his family, but he got greedy. He wanted more. So he started increasing his land, taking more and more from the moors. Well, Crockern doesn't mind people living here as long as they don't hurt his country, but as for taking over bits they don't really need, he doesn't like that. So he stopped anything from growing on the new fields – thought that would stop the farmer. But it didn't. The fool kept trying to increase his lands, draining and hedging and ditching, planting more and more all the time, until Crockern had had enough and decided to put a stop to it. The farmer found his animals died, all his plants withered, not just the ones on the new land, but on his old fields too, and then his house burned down—'

Samuel interrupted. 'House? No, it was his barn.'

'House or barn,' Hugh amended diplomatically. 'Anyway, he lost everything, and he was ruined. And that is Crockern. If you upset Crockern here on his own territory, you see, you'll be destroyed by him.'

'And that's what happened to this miner, you think?' Edgar was amused. Having spent most of his life in great cities he felt able to treat the superstitions of country folk with scorn. 'He tried to take too much from the land, so the old man of the moors killed him?'

Offended by the bantering tone, Hugh was silent, but the man-at-arms stared at Edgar, his dark eyes pensive. 'I wouldn't laugh if I's you. Crockern may not like it, not here on his land. Who's to say why Bruther died? For all I know he might have killed himself, but I'll tell you this: as far as I'm concerned, that boy's as likely to be Crockern's corpse as the victim of the miners hereabouts.'

'If that was the case, why were no other miners hurt? Surely Crockern wouldn't want to differentiate between them, would he?'

The man-at-arms studied his face carefully, then motioned southwards. 'You know what that hill's called?'

Edgar glanced round, back the way they had come. There was a hill, but from where they sat it was impossible to see more than the flanks. He shook his head.

'That's Crockern Tor down there, where the miners all meet for their parliament,' Samuel said slowly. 'And Bruther, well, he lived close. Too close, maybe. Crockern doesn't like his bones being disturbed.'

'You can't believe that!' Edgar scoffed, but the man ignored him and, kicking his horse, meandered a short distance away. When Edgar turned to Hugh, he noticed a speculative expression on the servant's face. Hugh looked almost as if he was wondering whether a bolt of lightning might strike Edgar down at any moment.

# CHAPTER SIX

The knight had finished his study of the ground and remounted his horse, frowning thoughtfully. 'Simon,' he said softly, 'I think this will be an interesting matter before we're done.' He swung his leg and settled, grasping his reins, staring back at the tree. 'There's something strange about this death.'

'What's that?'

'First, the land hereabouts. What was Bruther doing over here – fetching wood or something? There's no axe. Then there's his body . . .' He lapsed, glowering at the tree as if expecting it to answer his thoughts.

'His body?' Simon prompted after a few moments.

'Yes. If you were going to lynch someone, what would you do to him first?'

'I don't know – gag him, I suppose.'

'And?'

'Well, it would depend on how many men were with me, how powerful the man was, lots of things.'

Baldwin shot him a look. 'One of the first things you'd do would be to tie him up, surely?'

'Yes, of course.'

'So why wasn't Bruther tied?'

'I suppose the men who cut him down must have unbound him . . .'

'No, Simon. He was *not* bound. If he had been, his wrists would have been bruised. They weren't. I checked.'

'Could he have been unconscious? Maybe he was knocked out before they strung him up?'

'Possibly.' His voice was noncommittal.

'There you are then. He was attacked and knocked cold, then someone threw the rope over that branch, tied one end to his throat, hauled him up, and fastened the other end to the tree to hold him there.'

'I suppose so,' Baldwin said dubiously. He still wondered about the thin mark on the dead man's neck, but did not want to discuss it in front of the man-at-arms. He wheeled his horse to face the others.

'Hey, you!' Simon called out, and their guide came forward. 'You found this body with another man from the Manor, is that right?'

He nodded, 'Yes, I was with Ronald Taverner.'

'Why were you all the way up here? It's miles from Thomas Smyth's place, and I understand you went there with Sir William.'

Samuel explained about their decision to go for a drink, and about their circuitous route homewards after seeing the two miners on the road. Baldwin listened carefully as the man spoke. His story rang true, but he seemed reticent on one point.

'I don't understand why you came all the way out here,' Baldwin probed. 'Isn't there a nearer tavern or inn? Surely there's one on the way to Chagford?'

'John and his knight went there. I didn't want to be with them.'

'Why not?' asked Simon.

'Because . . .' He stopped and stared at the ground.

'Come on, Samuel. It will go no further,' said Simon reassuringly.

'John can be a hard man,' he muttered.

Baldwin nodded. From what he had observed he felt sure that the young squire could be a cruel master. After all, he was being tutored by Sir Ralph of Warton. Mercenary knights like Sir Ralph were all too common, and none were noted for kindness or generosity of spirit.

'So you went all the way out to the alehouse near the Dart and drank there,' Simon stated. 'And on the way back you left the road because of some miners. What were they like?'

'One was tall, both were young. They were cloaked and hooded.' His face took on a pensive frown.

Simon had the same thought. 'It's rare for miners to own horses; they usually ride ponies if anything, don't they? And you say they were cloaked . . . Wasn't it a warm night? Why would they have been cloaked?'

'I don't know. At the time I just assumed they must be miners. Who else would be out on the moors at that time of day? Farmers would all be bedding down their animals, and there's no merchant would want to travel at that hour. I just thought . . .'

'Could it have been a knight, a man riding with his squire?'

Again Samuel frowned. There had been something odd about the two, now he came to think of it. 'I don't know . . . One could have been well-born, but the other . . .' He stumbled into silence.

After some moments, Simon cleared his throat. 'All right, Samuel,' he said kindly, 'tell us if anything comes to you. For now, do you know where this man Bruther used to live?'

'Yes, over beyond the Smalhobbes' place.' He jerked a thumb over his shoulder.

'Good, so it's not too far out of our way, then. Take us there.'

Simon and Baldwin followed as he led them past the rock where the two servants waited. Simon saw Edgar give Hugh a patronising sneer and overheard him mutter, 'Crockern's corpse!' The bailiff made a mental note to ask his man what the comment meant.

They toiled up the bank of the hill. Within a short distance they found they had left the boulders behind; rocks only seemed to lie in the valley around the wood. Towards the top of the hill the land was firm, undulating grassland for as far as the eye could see, with small yellow and white flowers lying among the grasses. The ubiquitous grey tors towered over the skyline in all directions. At the sight of the emptiness, Simon gave an inward groan. By now he was longing to get down from his saddle, but that pleasure was obviously some way off.

It was a good mile and a half to the little hut where Peter Bruther had lived. After some minutes, they could see it – a small, stone-built place, with turves carelessly tossed over for a roof. A fast-flowing stream wandered before it, cutting deeply into the black soil. Behind lay a patch of cultivated soil, where some crops struggled against the bitter winds which scoured the land.

At the sight of the building, the five men slowed to a trot. All were struck with the urge to approach quietly as a mark of respect to the dead man who had lived there. Their passage was almost silent until they splashed through the stream and headed to the door. And only then did they hear a shrill scream and see the woman dart from the entrance, ducking under the head of Baldwin's horse, and pelting away to the east.

The men were so surprised that at first no one could move. Baldwin's horse seemed as astonished as his rider, shying only when the woman had passed well beyond, but even as he snorted and jerked his head, his rider was beginning to get over his shock. While Simon exchanged a dumbfounded glance with Hugh, the knight set spurs to his horse, and with Edgar close behind, made off after her.

He had no desire to harm or scare her, but he was intrigued to know who she was and what she had been doing in the dead man's house. Approaching obliquely so as not to alarm her unduly, he overtook her and slowed to a trot. She was sobbing. He smiled, trying to look reassuring, and held up his hands to show they were empty of weapons. It appeared to work, for as he reined in, she stopped a short distance from him, wiping at her eyes and panting.

It was impossible for the knight to miss the signs of her poverty, the threadbare dress and dirty wimple, the holes at the elbows and knees, but he was impressed by her carriage.

She stood tall and straight, looking almost like a lady, and was not scared to meet his gaze. This was no fearful rabbit of a serf, he could see.

'Please stop, madam. You are in no danger, I assure you.'

'Who are you? Are you with Thomas?'

His expression of frank incomprehension must have been convincing, for her eyes left his at last, and moved to take in the straggle of men at the hut behind her, then Edgar, who had pulled up to her side and now sat resting his elbows on his horse's withers. Baldwin shrugged to emphasise his ignorance of the name. He had no knowledge of this Thomas.

'You aren't miners, then,' she said doubtfully, and her mystification increased as the dark-faced knight laughed aloud.

'No, no, we're not miners. I am Sir Baldwin Furnshill, and the gentleman back there is Simon Puttock, the bailiff of Lydford. We are here to find out who killed Peter Bruther.'

'He *is* dead, then?' she cried, and covered her face with her hands.

Edgar led Baldwin's horse back to the hut while the knight walked with the weeping woman. By the time they had returned to the other men, he had managed to learn that she was Sarah Smalhobbe.

'Why were you here, Sarah?' Simon asked when Baldwin had introduced her.

'I wanted help after they attacked us. They came to my house yesterday, three of them, and they set on my husband. He's there now, in his cot. Three against one! Where's the victory in that, eh? The cowards hit him and kicked him while he was on the ground, beating him with cudgels just because he refused to leave the moors. But where else can we go, sir? We have no family to protect us, we're just poor people, and we cannot leave and find somewhere else to live.'

'You do not come from around here, then?' Baldwin asked gently, and her gaze immediately moved to him. She hesitated, nervous of saying too much. 'No, sir. We come from the north.'

'Where from? Why did you come all the way down here, to this miserable place?'

Unaccountably she began to snivel again. 'Sir, it's hard, but there has been nowhere to earn a crust – the famine affected richer people than us. We had to go somewhere when we could no longer get food, and when we heard about the mining down here, it seemed a chance to build our lives again.'

Simon glanced at Baldwin, then back at the woman. 'We can protect you on the way to your house, and perhaps help your man. But you must tell us who did this to him.'

The fear returned to her eyes. 'If I tell you they'll come back.'

'If you tell us, we can see that they never come back,' he said reassuringly.

'How can I depend on that? What if you're wrong? They may burn us out, or kill us both!'

'Sarah, calm yourself. I am the bailiff. They will not dare to attack you if they hear you're under my protection.'

'I don't know . . . I must speak to my husband.'

'Very well, I won't force you. But think on it. We may be able to help you – after all, the last thing we need down here is mob-rule.'

'You already have that, bailiff,' she said sadly, and turned away.

While she waited outside Bruther's hut with Hugh and Edgar, Simon and Baldwin entered the little dwelling. A baulk of timber in the centre supported the roof, while a burned patch and twigs nearby showed where the miner had kept his fire. A simple stool formed the only furniture. The man's sad collection of belongings lay on a large moorstone block which jutted from the wall in place of a table: a cloak, a hood, a small knife, a half-loaf of bread, a paunched rabbit. A thin and worn sleeping mat lay rolled up on the floor beside it.

Baldwin picked up the dead rabbit and weighed it in his hand. 'This can only be a day old. In this heat it would hardly last much longer. If he caught this, surely he would not have committed suicide shortly after?'

'Why – do you think he might have killed himself?' Simon asked sharply.

The knight sighed. 'No, but suicide would explain why his hands had not been bound. Then there's the second mark . . .'

'What second mark?'

Baldwin explained while Simon listened intently. 'It more or less proves it must have been murder,' the knight said, tossing the rabbit aside.

'It's not very honourable, is it?' Simon mused. 'Stepping up behind a man and throttling him. Not the kind of behaviour you'd expect out here. Usually if there's a fight it's with daggers or fists. This . . . it's sickening.'

'Yes. As you say, it is hardly chivalrous. But then, there are many miners on the moors, and I doubt whether any of them have noble blood. In any case, there is not much reason here to kill a man, if they killed him to rob.'

'Could they have taken something from him?'

'From a villein? Maybe he had a purse on him, but he hadn't been living here for a year yet. He can't have earned that much. No, I doubt whether the purpose was robbery. Besides, since when have robbers hanged their victims?'

There was nothing more for them to learn here. They went outside and mounted their horses. Baldwin offered Mrs Smalhobbe a ride with Edgar, but she refused. It wasn't far to her house and she would be happier to walk. 'So would I,' Hugh muttered fiercely when he saw that Simon was within hearing, but his master chose to ignore the comment.

At the Smalhobbe holding they found a small and neat square stone cottage. Sarah immediately ran to the door and entered while the men dismounted. Inside it was tiny. By the light of a guttering candle, which made the air rank with the foul smell of burning animal fat, Simon could see the slim figure lying on a palliasse at the far end of the room, his wife kneeling beside him. On their appearance, the miner lurched up to sit, his brown eyes showing anxiety – but not fear, Baldwin noted approvingly. The man looked unwell, his gaunt features bruised, but though he was slight of build, Smalhobbe looked wiry and fit.

'My wife says you are trying to find out what happened last night,' he said, his voice weary and strained.

Baldwin glanced round the room, then sighed as he realised there were no chairs or benches. He squatted. 'Yes. Peter Bruther was killed, as your wife has presumably told you. We understand you were attacked as well.'

Henry Smalhobbe watched as Simon crouched down beside the knight. The miner's expression was reserved and suspicious, but Simon thought he could detect a degree of hope there, as if the man had been praying for some relief and now felt he could see the approach of rescue. Simon cleared his throat. 'Could you tell us what happened last night? Maybe we can help you at the same time as clearing up the matter of who killed Peter Bruther.'

'Maybe,' said Henry Smalhobbe quietly, and sank back on to an elbow. His face was now in darkness, below the level of the candle in the wall, so that his expression was difficult to read; Simon wondered whether the move was intentional. He chewed his lip in concentration as the miner continued: 'There's not much to tell. I was out all day, same as normal, working the stream a little to the south of here. When I came back it was just before dark. Well, I was almost home when I saw a man hiding outside. He must have been waiting for me.' He spoke dispassionately, as though recounting another man's misfortune. 'After I heard Sarah call out, I had to look at her and make sure she was all right. Well, before I could turn round, something caught me across the back of my head.' He broke off and gingerly touched his scalp. 'I fell down, and someone whispered in my ear, said that if I didn't go and leave this land to the one it belonged to, I could die. And my wife . . .'

'I understand. Please, what happened then?' said Simon softly.

"They beat me. Someone was kicking me, another had a cudgel, I think, and hit me all over – my legs, back, head, everywhere. I passed out when they got to my head.' He spoke simply, not trying to embellish his tale, and Simon felt sure he could be believed.

It was Baldwin who leaned forward and asked: 'Did you see any of these men?'

'I didn't need to, sir. I know them all. There's three of them: Thomas Horsho, Harold Magge and Stephen the Crocker.' He explained briefly about their previous visits, how they'd threatened him and his wife. 'Usually George Harang is there too, when these men go out to scare people, but last night it was Harold who spoke. If George had been there, it would have been him.'

'Did you hear them say anything about Peter Bruther? Any comments at all?'

'No, sir, not that I recall. I'd tell you if I did.' His voice carried conviction.

'Have you heard of anybody else being attacked recently? Do you know if anybody else was hurt last night?'

'No, sir,' said Smalhobbe, glancing at his wife for confirmation. She shook her head too, her eyes huge in her concern.

Baldwin subsided, and Simon stiffly rose to his feet, his knees cracking. 'Thank you for all that. We'll see what we can do. If you're prepared to accuse these men, perhaps we can get them punished.'

'Oh no, sir!' Sarah Smalhobbe's face was twisted with fear. 'We can't! What will happen to us if we do that? You can see what the men are prepared to do when we make only a little trouble for them . . .'

Simon cocked his head. 'What do you mean by "a little trouble"? What have you done to deserve this beating?' he asked.

She stared at him for a moment, then her eyes dropped, flitting nervously, or so Simon thought, to her husband.

'Henry?' he prompted, and was sure that the man started nervously.

'When we came here, we did all legally, bounding our plot, marking it out and registering it. All we wanted was to be left alone to make some kind of living, and so far we have. But some tinners, all they want is to keep people off the land.'

'Tinners? Surely you mean the landowners? It is they who wish the miners to leave,' said Baldwin.

'No, sir. The landowners want us to leave them alone, it is true. Some miners damage their lands and pasture, but no, I did mean miners want us off this part.'

'Is it very wealthy, then? There is a lot of tin here and others want you to leave so that they can take it?'

To the knight's surprise, the wounded man gave a harsh laugh. 'Hardly! There might be enough for me and Sarah to live off, but not enough to become wealthy. No, it's because another man has paid miners *not* to work this land so that he can keep it for his own pasture, and they are enforcing the agreement.'

'So these men, they beat you because they were paid to keep the land empty?'

'Yes, sir. They work for a powerful man, for Thomas Smyth, and he is paid not to mine this far into the moors. So he has told them to get rid of the likes of us.'

'Did you know of this, Simon?' asked Baldwin, glancing at his friend in astonishment.

'I've heard of it,' he admitted. 'It's hard to stop. When the Devon miners separated from the Cornishmen thirteen years ago and formed their own stannary parliament here in Dartmoor, they became more powerful locally, and this type of thing has happened a few times. But,' he stood and nodded to the Smalhobbes, 'I'll do what I can to stop it, now I know who's responsible.'

Simon was quiet during their return to the Manor, and Baldwin too was content to hold his peace. Although the bailiff had warned him about the troubles caused by the tinners, he had not realised how the bands of men affected the people in the moors, terrorising some in return for money from others. He was still frowning thoughtfully when they arrived at Beauscyr Manor. Dusk was approaching, and they were all relieved to drop from their saddles. Samuel Hankyn went off to the kitchen, while the two men and their servants made their way to the hall. Here Baldwin was pleased to see that food was laid out for them on a table before the fire, and he had filled a trencher and was eating before the others had seated themselves. But for them, the hall was empty.

After some minutes, Sir Robert Beauscyr twitched the curtains aside and strode in. He marched across the rush-covered floor to a bench opposite Simon and sat, staring at the bailiff. 'Well? Have you discovered anything?' he demanded.

Simon regarded him silently while he chewed on some tough, dry beef. He had disliked the older of the two brothers since their first meeting. His arrogance was insulting, and Simon was unused to such treatment. Swallowing, he leaned back on his bench and picked up his pewter mug. Ignoring the question, he said, 'How long has the Manor been paying money to Thomas Smyth to keep off the Manor's lands?' and drank.

Robert Beauscyr was dumbfounded. The whole affair had only blown up over the last few days. Before that, even he had not known of the arrangement. He regained his composure with an effort and tried to pass the matter off with a shrug, aware that his shock had been visible. 'What has that to do with this murder?' he snapped. 'It is irrelevant.'

'No, not irrelevant. If, for example, you had paid a man to protect lands which were yours, and he tried to do that by killing a man, it would be the same as you paying for the murder.' The bailiff nonchalantly popped a crust of bread into his mouth, delighted by the young knight's discomfort. 'Wouldn't it?'

'No . . . I mean, maybe. But that's not important here.'

'Why? Do you consider yourself above the law?' asked Baldwin mildly.

Sir Robert glared at him. 'No, of course not. But Wistman's Wood is not part of the Manor. It falls outside our demesne. If it's anyone's, it's Adam Coyt's, a moorman. He has rights of pasturage there. Anyway, we wouldn't pay to have a villein killed!'

'Even one who had run away and was proving a continuing embarrassment to the family?' said Simon with raised eyebrows.

Before Robert could answer, the outer door slammed and his father entered. Sir William was irritated to see that his son was already there. Noting how tense the men round the table looked, he hesitated and offered up a quick prayer. 'What's the fool said now?' he wondered under his breath. Nodding curtly to the visitors, he dropped down beside his son, feeling exhausted. He knew that his fatigue was visible. Baldwin's suggestion that the miners could accuse him of

Bruther's murder had come as an appalling shock, and he found it hard to meet the knight's gaze now. The past week had been hard enough, and he knew it would not get any easier until the bailiff had gone.

Sighing, he said: 'So I suppose you found the spot where he was killed, then, bailiff?'

Immediately his son burst out, 'You didn't say – did you find anything?'

There was a hint, Simon thought, of nervousness in his voice; he subjected the youth to a pensive stare. 'It seems unlikely he killed himself,' he told the Beauscyrs. 'We think he was probably killed by a gang.' He did not want to mention their visit to the Smalhobbes' plot yet, not until he was sure that the latter would be safe from any retaliation. 'As you said, the miners are a hard group of men. No doubt some of them were annoyed at Bruther's mining activities.'

'I see. What will you do about it?'

Simon stared at his pot, then glanced at Baldwin. The knight had no doubts. He lazily stretched his legs and sighed happily. 'We will go and speak to these miners tomorrow, and see what they have to say.'

'Good,' said Sir Robert, and stood. 'I want this affair sorted out quickly so that we can get back to normal.' He marched swiftly to the door and left them.

'Forgive him his rudeness, bailiff. It is only the impetuousness of youth. He's had an anxious day today; he's convinced the miners are going to create more problems. And he's argued with my other son.' Sir William sighed heavily. 'And one of the men-at-arms was hurt at practice today . . . Why does everything always go wrong at the same time?'

Giving him a frosty smile, Simon nodded curtly, while Baldwin had to hide his grin by drinking from his pot. If the boy continued being so 'impetuous', he thought to himself, he might soon find himself being taught manners at the point of a bailiff's sword.

# CHAPTER SEVEN

After receiving directions, they left early the next morning to meet the miner they had heard so much about: Thomas Smyth. On the way they spoke about the corpse. Simon was not convinced by Baldwin's preoccupation with the thin mark on Bruther's neck. 'Are you sure it wasn't anything to do with the rope he was hanging by?'

'It could not be the rope,' said Baldwin with certainty. 'If a man is hanged, the rope makes a bruise; if a man is throttled, fingers and thumbs will show as marks. But you can hit a dead body as hard as you like – it does not bruise.'

Simon shrugged. 'Perhaps so, but what's that got to do with it?'

'On this body, the rope did not bruise. It burned, it's true, but did not bruise. What does that mean? It means that Bruther was already dead when he was hanged. The thin cord killed him because that one *did* mark his neck.'

'Fine! So someone hanged him after killing him to show how he had died. Very kind of them,' said Simon sarcastically.

Baldwin smiled. 'Someone strangled him before he was hanged,' he agreed. 'But then someone – presumably the same "someone" – went through the charade of hanging him for some purpose.'

'And you're sure he was strangled?'

'Oh, yes. There can be no doubt about that. He had all the signs of being throttled. Didn't you see the red splotches all over his face? The little haemorrhages in his eyes?'

'I felt no need to study the corpse as closely as you,' said Simon drily, and the knight chuckled. 'What else did you notice?'

'Is it that obvious?'

'Yes, Baldwin. You look as smug as an innkeeper who has just sold a barrel of six-month-old ale to a sot. Come on, then. What is it?'

The knight scratched reflectively at his neck. 'As I said, Bruther's hands were not tied. There was no bruising to his wrists. The line on his neck was well defined at the front of his throat and the sides, not at the back. I saw some scrapes on his head, but I cannot tell whether they would have happened when he was alive or not. It seems to me that he was attacked from behind.'

'I can see that. Sneaked up on and garotted.'

'Yes, but it points to something else too, of course.'

'What?'

Baldwin gave him a long-suffering glance and sighed. 'Think about it, old friend. If he was caught by a group of men, there would have been signs of a fight. There were none though – just the single mark. As I see it, Bruther was either knocked on the head, producing those scrapes, and then throttled, or he was caught unawares by a single attacker who threw a thong round his neck and strangled him in that way. I think it was the second rather than the first.'

'Why?'

'In God's name, Simon!' Now his tone was openly exasperated. "Think, man! If he had been knocked out, why would the killer bother to fetch a thong, when all he need do was slip his hands round the fellow's throat? It wouldn't take above a minute, and it would be as quick as killing a rabbit or a chicken. The murderer might have happened to have a cord about him, I suppose, but isn't it more likely that he was prepared for his victim? He already had the thong tightly wrapped round each fist as he saw Bruther approach, then all he had to do was slip it over his unsuspecting victim's neck and—' He gave a vicious gesture with both hands. 'And that was that. One less miner on the moors.'

Simon frowned. 'It makes sense – but we're still no wiser about who killed him.'

'No. All we can do is try to find out who might have had some reason to want him dead, and then question them. The trouble is, there appear to be quite a few people who wanted him gone from his mine.'

'Well, maybe we'll find out something here,' the bailiff said. They had topped a small hill and were looking down a shallow slope to a village.

It stood out incongruously among the great rolling plains of the moors, or so Baldwin felt. The dingy-looking longhouses and cottages were built in the same style as those in the little hamlets like Blackway or Wefford on his own estate, though the colour was wrong. At his home the earth was red, and the mud used to build walls coloured the houses, staining the lime wash. These dwellings were insipid and grimy-looking. Then, as they drew closer, he saw that he was wrong. These were not the normal cob and timber places he was used to. Back on his Manor, mud and animals were always to hand and the woods bordering almost every vill promised logs. Here in the moors there were no such easily available building materials; only one substance proliferated, moorstone, and the people made use of it everywhere.

The houses straddled the road, which ran oddly straight from one horizon to the other before them. Behind the houses were the plots which provided food for the people and their animals, with back lanes forming the outer boundary of the village. A stream slashed a scar through the countryside, bisecting the village and feeding a fishpond behind, and where it met the road a wide ford offered a safe point to cross. The men made for this. They had been told that the miner owned the property nearest on the western bank.

Coming closer, Baldwin pursed his lips in a soundless whistle. Though it had no battlements, no moat or great gate, this place was obviously the possession of a wealthy man. Baldwin had known many rich houses, but there was none which could boast a finer appearance. The hall at the centre was wide, with broad and tall windows under a slated roof. Opposite was a storage area, and a separate square building like a kitchen block stood nearby. All gave a feeling of comfort and calmness. When he glanced at Simon he could see that the bailiff was similarly impressed.

'Makes Lydford look a bit pathetic,' he heard Simon mutter, and the knight laughed. As he knew, Lydford had gained notoriety in the bailiff's family from the many draughts. The bitter wind whistled up the Lydford Gorge, battering the square keep and making life inside miserable, and Margaret, Simon's wife, was relieved that as bailiff, he could choose to live in a house nearby rather than in the castle itself.

This house was separated from the road by a wide field in which a group of oxen stood, munching contentedly as the men rode past. A straight path led to the stables, and the four made for it. As they dismounted, a tallow-haired man shuffled into sight, rubbing the sleep from his eyes. He took their horses, staring at them with evident surprise that anyone should visit so early.

They had started towards the house when another man appeared through the door. 'Ah!' said Baldwin. 'I think our meeting is about to get interesting.'

Looking up, Simon saw that it was the same man who had warned them to leave the miners' camp alone on their first visit. Recognition was mutual. The sandy-haired man hesitated, staring at the group advancing towards him; he glanced around at the doorway, then faced them once more, his face fixed into a distrustful scowl. Somehow this made Simon more cheerful.

'Hello – I think we've met before,' he said heartily.

'Aye. Maybe.'

'Of course. You were the man who helped us find our way to Sir William's Manor, weren't you?' The man glowered at him without speaking. 'We're here to see Thomas Smyth. Is this his house?'

The man sneered as he looked Simon up and down. 'I don't reckon he'll want to see *you*.'

'I think he can judge that better than his servant,' said Simon shortly, moving to walk past him. To the bailiff's surprise, he found his path blocked. The miner stood before him, hands stuck into his belt.

'What do you want to see him about?'

Baldwin watched with interest as different emotions chased each other across the expressive features of his friend. Stunned outrage was closely followed by dry amusement, but both were chased away by a sudden attack of anger. Simon's face reddened and his jaw clenched, and Baldwin quickly moved to his side.

'I think *we* should tell your master what we want to discuss with him,' he said hurriedly, and smiled. As he did so, Edgar stepped beside him, his hand already grasping his sword hilt. 'So, your master,' Baldwin continued. 'Where is he?'

George Harang stared at him. He was unused to having his will thwarted. No miner would dare to defy him like this, but with the bailiff and his friend, he was unsure how to respond. Steeling himself, he was about to bellow for help, when a voice came from behind him.

'What's all the noise about?' Looking up, Simon saw a newcomer leaning on the doorframe. He was scruffy-looking but cheerful, and wore a genial smile.

To Simon he looked like Baldwin's mastiff – though less ugly. A short man with grizzled hair to his shoulders and eyes like chips of coal, glittering with amusement, he could have been a poor serf; there was nothing about his clothing to denote wealth. His leather jerkin was scarred and worn, his shirt a simple woollen shift, torn and darned in many places, and the only personal adornment the bailiff could see was the gold ring on his forefinger. Ostentatious display was unnecessary, for from his demeanour he could only be the master of the house.

Straightening, he motioned to his dumbfounded servant. 'Out of the way, George. Of course I'll see these guests. I can't turn the bailiff of Lydford away, can I?' And he waved them inside, Hugh scuttling after the knight and Simon while Edgar stood staring at George; only when the guard's gaze wavered did Edgar stride inside after the others.

As Baldwin had expected, the house was magnificent. The door gave on to a panelled screens passage, above which was a minstrels' gallery, while beyond was a long hall with high windows throwing immense pools of light on to the rush-strewn floor. The fireplace was a huge circle of packed earth in the middle of the floor and an enormous log lying smouldering on the bed of glowing ashes hissed and crackled softly. Tapestries sheathed the walls and kept in the warmth, while all the visible woodwork was richly carved. Two wolfhounds lay by the fire, rising at the noise of the visitors' entrance and watching their master.

Thomas Smyth walked to his dogs and rested his hands on their two heads briefly. Immediately, as if at a signal, the animals dropped down again and rested. Nearby was a bench at a table, and Smyth sat, waving a hand for the others to do likewise.

Simon found himself assailed by sudden doubts. This man did not have the look of a brutal extortioner – far less a killer. He looked calm and reasonable, with the self-assured aura of wealth. He watched as Baldwin stepped over to the hearth and crouched before the dogs, stroking their heads. When Hugh walked too close, one stared at him and there was a perceptible rumble, making the servant scurry to a bench and sit, but the animals submitted to Baldwin's patting with apparent pleasure. The bailiff shook his head. Somehow Baldwin always had that effect on dogs.

'So, bailiff. What can I do for you?' Thomas Smyth sat easily, his hands on his knees, the very picture of amiable friendliness.

'How did you know I was the bailiff?'

'Ah well, when someone as important as you and your friend pass through the moors, you're bound to be noticed. And my men cover a wide area here. After all, I have over a hundred men working for me.'

'Of course,' said Simon, but he was aware of the implied threat in those innocuous words. Only a rich man assured of his power could afford to have so many men in his pay, and this miner was pointing out the numbers he could count on. As if to emphasise the fact, Smyth glanced casually at the other three men before his eyes rested on Simon again. But then, seeing the understanding in Simon's face, he grinned, as if this was all a game, and since both knew it, why not get on with it and to hell with verbal fencing. And with a feeling of faint disgust, Simon found himself liking the brash confidence of the man. He decided to approach the true aim of their visit obliquely.

'There was an attack yesterday,' he began. 'Why did your men beat Henry Smalhobbe and tell him to leave his works?'

'Who?'

'Henry Smalhobbe. He named your men.'

110

'That's a serious allegation, bailiff,' Thomas Smyth said, his eyes hardening into black ice. There was an intake of breath behind him, and Simon turned to see that the doorman had followed them into the hall and now stood near at hand. He glared angrily at the bailiff.

'Very serious,' Simon agreed mildly, turning back to the miner.

'Did this man say exactly *who* beat him?' This time the miner affected a display of surprise.

'Harold Magge, Thomas Horsho and Stephen the Crocker. All your men.'

'George?' Smyth looked at his servant.

'Sir,' he said, 'they've all left the mines. They must've gone the day before yesterday.'

'Ah. So, you see, bailiff, they've all left my camp. They must be doing something on their own if they attacked this – who did you say it was?'

Simon ignored the question. 'Why would they have left your camp?'

'Ah, well now, bailiff,' said Smyth, shrugging expansively and smiling. 'There're as many reasons for a man to leave as I have men working for me. I'm a master tinner, I've got a controlling interest in many works over the moors, and it's hard to keep track of all the men who labour in my mines. There're all sorts: journeymen paid by the day, labourers contracted to me yearly, and many others. Do you really expect me to know all of them personally? It's impossible! And then, of course, there are foreigners, men who aren't local and grow to dislike the moors – or get scared by them. They often get depressed by living out there, and just leave.'

111

'Others have suggested that you keep very close control of your men – *and* your mines.'

'Oh, yes. Well, of course I do.' His affable smile widened as if in sympathy that this was the best that Simon could do. 'I have to control them with vigour. The men are a tough bunch, bailiff. They need considerable . . . let's say "supervision", shall we? Out here, there are many who might not wish their past to come under too close a scrutiny. Quite a large proportion, I'm sure, only came to Dartmoor because they knew that they would then fall under stannary law, and be safe from any embarrassments they wished to leave behind. That doesn't mean I know them all by name.'

'You mean you've outlaws working for you?' Simon asked bluntly.

'Bailiff, please! Do you expect me to ask all the sheriffs and reeves in the land about the past life of every man who comes to me asking for a job? Anyway, most of them will never return where they came from, so you could almost say that I am *helping* the law by stopping them from being outlaws! While they are here, working for me, they aren't living in the woods and robbing merchants – if they ever did, that is.'

Baldwin stood, grunting. 'These three men – were they outlaws?'

'I've no idea. I didn't ask them,' said Smyth.

'Is it true that you have been trying to force Smalhobbe and others from the moors?'

'*Force?*' He paused, head on one side as he stared at the knight as if astonished.

'Yes, force them from the moors. By threatening them, suggesting that their wives could be raped or widowed . . .'

'Oh, really! I already have widely spread works, I don't need more.'

'And yet a man is wounded and holds you responsible – and another is dead.'

'Dead?' The look he threw at George Harang was not faked, Baldwin was sure. There was genuine surprise there.

'Yes, a man called Bruther,' Simon said shortly.

'Who did you say? Peter Bruther's dead?' The tinner was transfixed, staring in disbelief.

'Murdered,' said Simon. 'Someone hanged him. Do you have any idea who could have wanted Bruther dead?'

Smyth's expression was wooden. The bailiff could not know the truth, he thought. If he did, that question would never have been asked. Before he could collect his wits and respond, there was an interruption.

The door banged open, and Baldwin came face to face with a pair of women. One was a cheerful, contented-looking lady of forty at most, a matter of ten years or so younger than Smyth, and the knight guessed from her smile that she must be his wife. She was short and plump, with the clear, fresh complexion he associated with moorland dwellers, but with none of the dour stolidity he had seen elsewhere. Her dark hair was braided and curled under her wimple, the stiff severity of the headgear out of place beside her laughing brown eyes.

With her was a younger woman, obviously her daughter. She had the same dark hair and sunny, warming smile which betrayed her vivacious spirit. Seeing the guests, she paused at the door, but then her eyes went to her father, and she crossed to him. Baldwin could see that she was only some fifteen years or so old, still a little coltish in her movements,

113

and slim as a foal, but with none of the gawkiness which was sometimes so evident in girls of her age. The maid was very self-assured, and clearly knew she was being watched by four men from the way she elegantly and decorously floated across the floor to her father. Baldwin noticed that her mother had observed this too. As if in mild despair at this forward behaviour, she sighed, and then grinned when he caught her eye. He had to smile broadly in return.

'Father, you promised to come and ride with me this morning.' The girl's voice was deep, at odds with her slender figure. Though her attention was apparently fixed on Smyth, she walked to his side and turned with her hand on his shoulder so that she could study the visitors.

'Yes, but we're busy for now, my sparrow,' he said, putting an arm round her waist. Otherwise he ignored her, frowning intently at the bailiff . Simon felt that Smyth was controlling himself with difficulty, but that was no great surprise. Nobody likes being accused of extortion and murder in the same day, he thought.

'Will you be long?' Her eyes were on Baldwin now, challenging, and the knight was not sure whether the question was aimed at him or not. Meanwhile the tinner grunted and addressed Simon.

'Who wanted Bruther dead, you asked? You need to ask the bastards he ran from, the Beauscyrs. They wanted him back to stop other villeins from leaving the Manor, and they made no secret of it.'

'But why would they kill him?'

'A warning – to show what any other runaway could expect. He was hanged, you say? The Beauscyrs must have wanted his punishment to be as obvious as possible! A short rope and a long drop. How else can they keep their Manor together? They can't afford to let anyone leave their work and run when they want to; the Manor needs men.'

'They suggested it might have been you had him killed.'

For a moment there was no sound, and then the miner's servant leaned on the table behind Simon, his face taut and harsh. 'They said that? They dare accuse my master of—'

'Be silent, George!' The command was immediate and uncompromising, and Simon saw that Smyth's eyes had gone black with a quick fury, but his rage died as quickly as it had flared, leaving him looking tired and oddly vulnerable, and the bailiff was reminded that this man was already old compared with most. When he spoke again, Smyth's voice was slower, but the emotion was still there in the precision of his speech.

'Bailiff, I have lived here for many years and, as I said, I have a rough group of men to keep under control. Sometimes there have been troubles, but not very often, and each time I have kept the peace here, not like other places where even the knights have resorted to robbery. These last few years have been hard, but here on the moors I have made sure that the rule of law has survived. If I thought any of my men had killed Peter Bruther, I would see them pay. Compare that with the Beauscyr family. Look at that old fool Sir William, and his two young whelps. If you want to find the murderer, you need search no further than this family. Sir Robert Beauscyr in particular is a—'

'Father, that's unfair!' His daughter's outburst caught him by surprise. She spun away from his encircling arm. 'Robert would never consider murder!'

'Alicia, be quiet!' His voice was not raised, but it was cold and angry. 'Your views are not important; this is nothing to do with you. This is serious. Someone has done murder, and I think it may have been Robert.' He turned to Simon again, his daughter throwing him a tragic glance and walking over to George's side as he continued: 'Robert Beauscyr has always had a cruel thread running through him, and he can call on many men to assist him from his father's men-at-arms. It would have been easy for him to have gone to the moors and killed Bruther.'

Baldwin's eyes were on his daughter. She sat beside George, her eyes fixed on her father, while the old servant patted her on the back, his face filled with sympathy. She looked as though she was about to burst into tears, and the knight could see how close she and the heir to Beauscyr Manor had grown. They were of good ages: the boy a little over twenty, the girl ready to wed at fifteen or so, and they had presumably known each other almost all their lives, dwelling so close together here, while other settlements were far distant. There could be few others of their age nearby.

Simon was saying, 'But what about you, sir? Where were you on the night Bruther was killed?'

'Me?' Disbelief faded, to be replaced by cold rage. 'Here, bailiff – I was here! And if you want to check with an independent witness, ask Sir William Beauscyr. He was here with me. Now, if you'll excuse me, I have other matters to attend to.'

He made his way to the door, but before he could leave, Baldwin said, 'One thing, before you go, please. If you have no objection, could we go to your camp and ask there if any man knows what has happened to the three miners? If we can, it would be best to speak to them as quickly as possible, either to confirm their innocence in this affair, or . . .'

Thomas Smyth stared at him with a slight sneer. 'Of course,' he said. 'George will take you there and make sure your questions are answered, won't you, George?' And then he was gone, the door slamming behind him.

# CHAPTER EIGHT

'How long have you known your master, George?' Simon's voice was conciliatory as they jogged their way down the incline from the house, heading south-west to the miners' encampment. They had already left the stream far to the left, and were now passing through empty lands where the only sound came from their jingling harnesses.

Harang glanced at him suspiciously, his eyebrows almost meeting in a sandy line. Reassured by the frank openness he saw, he gave a shrug. 'Some seventeen years, I reckon.'

'That was when you first came down here?'

'Yes.'

'And you began to work for him then?'

'Yes.'

'You've stayed with him since?'

'Yes.'

His taciturn unresponsiveness made Simon falter. He glanced at Baldwin, who said mildly, 'So I suppose Alicia was born some time after you started working for Thomas Smyth?'

'Yes.'

'She must be . . . what – fifteen? Sixteen?'

'Fifteen. Born back in 1303. In the May time.' For the first time his voice grew softer, and his face showed the strength of his feelings for the girl.

'She looks a bright girl.'

'Very bright,' he told the knight, who now rode beside him. 'Quick and alert, she is. I remember when she was young, I only ever had to tell her once what bird was singing and she always remembered afterwards.'

'It's a pleasure to be with someone who learns fast, isn't it?'

'Oh yes, sir. And she's nearly as strong as a lad, too. Growing up round here, she knows the moors as well as most folk know their own garden. She's often out for hours at a time on her pony.'

'She obviously likes Sir Robert Beauscyr.'

'Why do you say that?' Suspicion darkened George's face.

'She hardly made a secret of it, the way she leapt to his defence, did she?'

'Well . . . yes, they know each other,' George admitted unwillingly.

'Isn't it . . .' Baldwin hesitated. 'I mean, you must agree, this Robert Beauscyr, he may be wealthy, but he's hardly a perfect example of a knight, is he? I'd have thought he'd be too dull for her.'

'That's what I've said to her, but once she's . . .' His face reddened as he went silent.

119

'A little wilful, perhaps? She looked like she had her own mind.' George threw him a quick glance, then grinned suddenly and gave a definite nod. 'Ah!'

'Look, sir.' George settled in his saddle. 'It's not that, see. If she'd set her cap at someone else, a farmer or someone, I doubt whether I'd have any complaint about it, but I don't trust the Beauscyrs. I've known some lords in my time, and they're never as strong as their sires, if you follow me. The sons always seem to be weaker, whether in the head or the arms, just as if the strength is reduced in the children. And that's what I reckon has happened with the Beauscyrs. Sir William is strong enough, I can't argue with that, he's proved it in fighting for the King – but what of his son, Sir Robert? He's got some brains, but he uses them all in books and reading, and that's not natural. No, I don't think he's right.'

'Right for Alicia, you mean? Or do you mean he could kill?' Baldwin laughed at the man's expression. 'Come, George. Like your master said, Robert Beauscyr had good reason to want the man back. Do you think he could murder?'

'Sir Robert Beauscyr kill Peter Bruther?' He considered, riding in silence as he thought through the implications. As he knew, the Beauscyr family had little enough reason to like Peter Bruther, but killing a man was different from disliking him. 'I wouldn't have thought he could kill, but if he had a group of men with him and they would do his bidding, he might order them to.'

'What do you know about his brother?'

'Him?' He spat. 'If Robert's got the brains, then John's got the muscle. He's one man I'd always want in front of me, never behind. But he's no interest in the lands, he's always riding out with his knight looking for more loot or spoil. Their sort are never satisfied, they always want more.'

'Their sort?' Baldwin shot him a glance, but George felt he had said enough and refused to explain himself, maintaining a reserved silence for the remainder of their journey. Luckily it was not much further, and soon they were at the broad plateau where the miners held their camp. George led them to the blowing-house, where there was a small stable area near a slow-turning waterwheel. Leaving their horses there, he took them to the house itself. 'You wanted to see this last time you passed near,' he said, and motioned the knight inside.

Baldwin found it was as hot as a smithy, with two men working bare-chested at the furnace. Its flames filled the square room with an unearthly glow of angry red light. He puffed out his cheeks at the heat and winced. The air was so dry and pungent with the fumes of charcoal that it was difficult to breathe after the coolness of their ride, and with each squeeze of the bellows the atmosphere bludgeoned at him.

The building was a simple two-roomed affair, built of sturdy rock and turf to keep out wind and rain. A doorway to his right led into a storeroom, and the fire was opposite, set into the wall. It looked like a series of rocks set vertically, four feet wide at most. To the left was a massive bellows, which appeared to be driven from outside by the waterwheel in the stream, and which fed air into the bottom of the hearth. Behind the rocks, George told them, was a tall clay pot, shaped like a cone standing on its point.

'We fill the clay pot with layers of charcoal and ore,' George explained when asked. 'The bellows are needed to get the furnace hot enough so that the tin melts. When it does

121

it runs into that trough at the bottom.' He indicated a deeply grooved stone under the furnace. 'Then all we have to do is ladle it into an ingot, ready for coining at the stannary town.'

The temperature was too extreme. Though Baldwin would have liked to stay longer and see what else went on, he was eager to leave. 'Fascinating,' he murmured to Simon outside as he wiped sweat from his forehead, 'but distinctly uncomfortable!'

'Aye, but good when the snow lies on the ground,' said George cheerfully. Since seeing the room he appeared to have recovered his good humour, Baldwin thought, like a devil after receiving a brief but warming blast of hellfire.

'Can you show us where these three men used to live?' Simon asked. He was bored with seeing blowing-houses and the other machines and paraphernalia of the miners. To him it was all as exciting as watching cob dry – if a great deal more profitable.

George Harang shrugged unconcernedly and led them to a series of cottages at the southern edge of the hamlet. Stopping at one he waved a hand for them to enter, leaning against the wall with every sign of relaxation. Exchanging a glance, Simon and Baldwin ducked under the lintel and entered.

It was a miserable hovel, only ten feet by eight, and it stank of urine and smoke. A tiny hearth held a few burned twigs and pieces of wood, while a bundle of faggots stood to one side. There was a sad palliasse, bleeding straw, and a canvas sack beside it with a wooden platter and pot atop, all covered with soot. Apart from that the room was empty.

Outside, a stranger had joined Hugh, Edgar and George. Short and slight, he had the sallow skin and bright eyes of overwork. George cocked a thumb at him. 'This is a friend of theirs. He used to share the cottage with them.'

Simon saw that the youth was nervous, perhaps from shyness. He said, 'We would like to ask you some questions about Harold Magge, Thomas Horsho and Stephen the Crocker. Do you know where they are?'

'No, sir,' said the boy, shaking his head emphatically. 'I never saw them go. They just weren't here the day before yesterday when I went to sleep, and I haven't seen them since.'

'Did they always sleep here?'

'Yes, sir.' The nod was as pronounced as the shake, and Simon began to wonder whether his head was firmly set on his shoulders. If not, it was likely to fly off at any moment.

'When did you last see them?'

'I don't know, sir.'

'Roughly, lad. You don't have to be precise.'

'Some days ago, sir.'

'*Where* did you last see them?'

'I can't remember, sir.'

'Surely you can tell us whether they were here at the hut or out somewhere else when you last saw them!'

'I don't know, sir.'

Staring at him, Simon felt the exasperation mounting until he caught a glimpse of George Harang's face. He was resting against the wall of the cottage, exuding relaxed nonchalance as he smiled at the miner. And then Simon caught on.

'Thanks, anyway. You've been very helpful,' he said, and the man hurried away like a startled hart. Turning, Simon smiled at his friend. 'I think we have taken up enough of George's time, don't you?' Seeing the disbelief on Baldwin's face, he took him by the arm and began to walk with him back to their horses. 'Come, we need to speak to the Beauscyrs, don't we?'

Their guide accompanied them to their horses. 'I'm sorry you found out so little,' he lied cheerfully.

'Yes,' said Simon reflectively. 'Just one last thing, though. Where were you on the night Peter Bruther died?'

'Me?' George smiled. 'I was at the house with my master, of course. Where else would I be?'

'That was a complete waste of time!' Baldwin muttered angrily as they rode at a steady pace up the incline from the camp. Simon glanced at him, smiling.

'Not entirely, Baldwin. We have learned something from our visit. It's clear that George Harang and Thomas Smyth do not want to help us track down any of these three men. They know exactly what their men were doing that night and don't want us to find out – which raises some interesting points to consider. For example, if Thomas Smyth is hiding the men or preventing us from finding them, did he know that the three men were going that way? Did he tell them to go? Did he actually *instruct* them to go and beat up Henry Smalhobbe? And if he did, did he also tell them to go on to Peter Bruther's place and attack him too?'

'He could have, from the look of him,' said Baldwin, his dark eyes brooding as he frowned at the horizon ahead. Simon followed his stare to where a man herded cattle. The knight continued, 'I think Smyth would stop at little to get what he wants. He's a man who has carved out his own empire here, and no one can tell him what to do. There are any number of men to do his bidding, and if that poor, terrified rabbit of a man was anything to go by, many of them are fearful of upsetting him. I'm sure that's what he was scared of, aren't you?'

'Yes, I have no doubt about it. That was why I thought we might as well leave, as we were obviously not going to get anywhere – at least, not while George Harang was hanging around in earshot. No, if we want answers from any of Thomas Smyth's men, we'll need to get them away from their master and his servant.'

Sir William watched the small party riding off to hunt with a sense of relief. Three retainers had joined his sons and Sir Ralph. The two boys had been niggling at each other almost from the moment John had returned, and though he was very proud of his sons, both of them, Sir William was beginning to look forward to the time when Sir Ralph and his youngest decided to leave and continue their travels abroad. Sighing, he turned back to the hall, where his wife would be waiting. Matillida too was feeling the strain of the constant sniping; she was becoming waspish.

Something was wrong with Robert, he reflected. His oldest son usually responded pragmatically to problems, but now he appeared to be incapable of seeing how to avoid conflict – indeed, he sought it out. In the past he would always have avoided an argument, preferring to get on with work, but since the affair of Peter Bruther, and especially now that his brother had come home again, he seemed to relish quarrelling. Sir William frowned. It was almost as if he had suddenly discovered a new strength of character.

And John too was a different person. Of course, a lot of that was due to his training as a warrior. Before that he had been a mere boy, but he had now returned as a man, and that was hard for Robert to understand. John had his own opinions on a number of matters where before he would have bowed to his brother's view. No longer. He had left home a shy, quiet boy; now he was used to work and hardship after six years of steady training in service to his master. Confident and self-assured after living for years on the Scottish marches, a warrior now after fighting the border raiders, he had seen too much to be able to go back to a state of happy obedience, constantly deferring to his older brother's wishes. Perhaps that was it. Maybe it was just that Robert could not understand that John had grown to maturity, Sir William decided.

Climbing the steps, he found his eyes being dragged back to the main gate, as if trying to look through it to the men riding off. He was still unsure of Sir Ralph. The knight had certainly trained his son well in the arts of war and chivalry, he had seen that in numerous little signs, in the way that he shared money unstintingly with the guards, in the way he offered to give alms to beggars at the door, but most of all in the way he could handle a sword. It had been impressive, Sir William admitted to himself – but troubling, as well.

The day before, John had been fretful, apparently bored, and had asked one of the guards to practise with him. One of the men-at-arms Ronald Taverner, had been persuaded, and they had used training swords built of heavy iron, with edges and points blunted. For protection they wore bucklers – small, circular shields. The idea had been to keep John in training, or so he had said, but when Sir William had gone to the stables to watch, he had been surprised by something Sir Ralph had said.

The knight had joined him, resting his forearms on the rail, a small dry smile on his face, and Sir William had said, 'It's good to see the young working to achieve the best they can, isn't it?'

Sir Ralph had glanced at him, then back at the circling fighters. 'To learn, surely the young should pick fighters as good as themselves, or better?'

Surprised, Sir William had watched the two men. It was plain what the knight had meant, and he had seen it for himself. Whereas John had demonstrated his skill, battering with his sword at any point of weakness like a good soldier, the guard had been clearly uneasy and far below John's standard. He had held his sword well enough, but seemed not to have enough strength to use it effectively. His buckler was never quite fast enough to parry the crushing blows of his opponent's weapon, his own blade was always just too slow to take advantage of an opening. Though John had managed to make it look as if he was having to work hard, the real effort had all been on the other side.

'They do look unmatched,' he had said, and had been surprised by his guest's chuckle.

'More than a little. Any moment now John will lose interest. Ah, there it is!'

John had faltered, a foot dragged and made him stumble, and immediately the guard was on him. But as soon as he moved forward, the squire feinted to the right, then swung his buckler, knocking the man to his knees. Before he could move, the heavy sword had chopped downwards, and he had collapsed, rolling in the dirt of the yard in his pain and clutching at his neck while John sauntered over to the bar and thrust his sword into the ground, casually tugging his gauntlets free.

'So, Father. I fear your guard missed my little trick.' His eyes were partly lidded, and Sir William had not been sure what expression they held. 'Still, he has learned not to trust a swordsman who trips.'

'Did you have to hit him so hard? There was no need . . .' Three men had rushed to the rolling figure, and helped him to his feet as Sir William watched, stunned. Even when propped upright, his head dangled loose as though his neck was broken.

'Of course there was,' John said imperturbably. 'If he was not hurt, how could he learn? It is only by thrashing dogs – and servants, too! – that they get the point of their lesson. He'll be all right. Just have a headache for a couple of days.' And then he had stared at Sir Ralph, who met his gaze evenly. 'Anyway, the main thing is, I won. Winning is all that matters when you hold a weapon, isn't it? Winning and surviving.'

'John, that's not the way of a knight. It's not only victory that matters, it's the honour of the match,' his father had protested.

'Perhaps, Father. But sometimes the honour doesn't matter,' John had said, and Sir William had been shocked into silence by his cynicism. Half-shrugging, John had walked away, leaving the two men standing and watching him go. As he was half-carried away to recover, the wounded man also watched John go, and cast a baleful glare at him.

But more than the distaste which he felt for his son's words was his shock at hearing the knight beside him murmur, 'Your man should be grateful. If his sword had been real and edged, John would still have struck him.'

Now, a day later, Sir William could still recall the strange sadness in the northern knight's voice. It was as if Sir Ralph had, with those words, confessed to himself how poorly he had trained his squire. Though a warrior should be resolute and determined in battle, he should still be loyal, honourable and courteous – to those beneath his station as well as his superiors. John's behaviour showed no chivalrous qualities whatsoever. That, Sir William felt sure, was why Sir Ralph looked so unhappy, so distressed, as if for the first time he d understood the nature of the squire he had created.

A noise at the gate made him look up, drawn once more to the present. It was the bailiff and his friend, back from their visit to Thomas Smyth. Anxiety surged through him as he watched them enter and dismount, but there was nothing he could do. If Thomas had told them, he would soon know about it. Then he drew himself up sharply. Sir Ralph could have had another reason for his black mood the day before, he thought. There was no indication of when Peter Bruther had died: Sir Ralph might think John had played a part in the villein's death.

Simon saw the figure of the old knight slowly making his way up the stairs and nodded toward him. 'This has hit him hard. Sir William looks older than when we first came here.'

'Yes. He feels his responsibilities. It is strange how death can remind a man about his own weaknesses – or those of his family.' Baldwin's face was pensive, his eyes fixed on the now closed door.

'Should we leave him alone for a while, do you think?'

'We must question him at some point. It might as well be now,' said Baldwin, setting off for the hall.

Inside, the old knight and his wife were resting in front of the fire. Simon could see how exhausted Sir William was when he raised his eyes to the four men. 'Bailiff, Sir Baldwin – please come in and have some wine.'

'Thank you,' Simon said, reaching forward to take the proffered goblet, then settling on his bench. Baldwin sat beside him, while Edgar and Hugh took their seats unobtrusively some feet behind.

'Have you had a useful morning?' asked Matillida Beauscyr graciously, and Baldwin smiled at her as he sipped some wine.

'Very, thank you,' he said. 'Yes, we have been to see Thomas Smyth, and the miners' camp. And, tell me: we saw a man on the moors near your mining camp with cattle. Are there many who use the moors for pasture?'

Sir William nodded. 'There are some. It's not the same as it used to be before the famine – then we had five thousand head or more, but there's less than half that number now . . . But there are still some farmers who use their rights of pasturage. The man you saw was probably Adam Coyt. He lives over west of here. I think he's been on the moors all his life, which has been a hard one. His wife and son are both dead, and he's kept his little farm going alone ever since.'

Baldwin said, 'It must be hard for a man like him. Working all alone, and with no one to leave it to.'

'It happens all too often, I fear,' Sir William sighed. 'The moors are cruel to all those who choose to live here. To be a moorman you must be as hard as the moorstone itself.'

'But your Manor is not like that!' Simon protested. 'It is successful, with good crops and growing herds.' As bailiff, he knew; he saw the records of production each year. Sir

William shot him a glance as if expecting an immediate tax increase.

'We have been lucky so far, bailiff. Luckier than some,' he admitted heavily.

'You must be glad you have two strong sons to leave all this to,' Baldwin continued.

'Of course. It would be difficult if I had no heirs,' and Sir William shrugged.

Baldwin did not meet his look. 'Thomas Smyth has no son, does he? Could you tell us anything about him?'

Sir William stared at the fire for a moment. 'I should have thought,' he said drily, 'you could have found out all you needed to know from the man himself while you were with him. Anyhow, he is not a local man, as you probably guessed. I think he came from the north somewhere, and moved here back in '86 or '87. He was only a lad then, of course, but enthusiastic. Well, he began mining and was lucky. Many men go for ages without finding anything, but he was one of the fortunate ones. He happened on a piece of land which bore a good quantity of metal, and he was shrewd with it, getting other men to look after it for wages while he searched for more. Soon he was not satisfied with just finding tin. He had to aim for better, more efficient ways of refining it. Most men are pleased to find tin and smelt it once, but not he.'

'Smelt it once?' asked Baldwin. It was Simon who answered, resting his elbows on his knees.

'There is a first and a second smelting, Baldwin. When miners find ore, they break it into small chunks and melt out the tin over their fires. That's called "first smelting". There are lots of impurities in it from the charcoal and other

131

rubbish, so it has to be smelted again to produce "white tin", which is clean enough to be coined at the stannary towns.'

'I see. And Smyth was not satisfied with that?'

Sir William gave a sour grin, 'Oh no, not old Thomas. He's too sharp. He had to build his own blowing-house, The furnace is so clean he can smelt tin faster and recover even more, and it's all white tin. There's hardly any dirt mixed with it. He can produce as much as he wants, and smelt other men's metal too, so he charges them to use his fires, and that makes him even more powerful here.'

Simon stated the obvious inference. 'You do not like him. Sir William.'

'I do not. It is wrong for a man like him to be able to live like a lord. He is only a commoner – I don't even know if he's a free man. He could well be another runaway peasant like Bruther, someone who managed to escape to the moors. Just because he has accumulated money does not make him any better.'

'He told us you were with him on the night that Peter Bruther died. What were you doing there if you dislike him so much?'

Sir William stared at him, anger flaring briefly, only to be washed away by a kind of tired acceptance. 'For a guest you are very inquisitive, bailiff,' he sighed. 'No matter. I was negotiating: I was there to agree terms with him so that he would not damage my lands.'

'So you went to pay him not to come here?'

'Yes. If I didn't, he promised a small army of miners taking my water, digging on my pastures and cutting down my trees for charcoal. They have the right, after all. We settled on a sum.'

'I see. The men who found the body, they were riding with you, were they not?'

'Yes. But I sent them off before I went in to speak to Smyth.'

'Why?'

'I wanted to talk to him without two inquisitive men-at-arms listening.'

'Were you alone with Smyth for the discussion?'

'Apart from his man, George Harang.'

'You had no men with you?' Simon's voice was openly amazed.

Sir William looked up, frowning. 'And who should I have had with me, bailiff? A son like Robert, who loathed the fact that I must negotiate with a blackmailer? Or perhaps John and his master, who travelled with me, but . . . Ha! Each would prefer to slice his own throat than deal with a commoner. They left me when we arrived at the miner's house. I sent the men-at-arms back so they would not hear what I was there to discuss with Smyth. How could I let one of my guards hear that kind of talk? It would take no time at all for news to travel all round this fort that I, the master of the Manor, was being threatened by a common tinner and forced to pay up. How could the men here respect me if they heard that?'

His wife put her hand on his shoulder and William gradually subsided, sinking back into his chair exhausted. Surely, he thought, the bailiff must understand. A fortress like this was only as strong as the men inside it. If the guards all felt unsure of their master, they might run off and desert him or, worse, decide that he was too old for his responsibilities. Weak lords did not live long – there was always someone prepared to organise a mutiny among the common guards. It was not like the old times when honourable men worked for their master for life; now castles like Beauscyr had to rely on hirelings, on paid mercenaries. That was why this castle, like so many other new ones, had dormitories for the men-at-arms separated from the solar where the family lived. In the past all would have slept in the same hall, but mercenaries were not to be so well-trusted as guards, and it was not unknown for a lord to find himself having to fight his own men, defending his solar from the very soldiers he had trained for war. Surely, the bailiff could understand that, too?

His wife looked at Simon coldly. 'Is it not enough that we must demean ourselves in front of this miner? Do you have to rake this up and embarrass us with it?'

'I am sorry, my lady, but though Peter Bruther was only a villein, it does seem he was murdered, and we must ask everyone who could have been involved.'

'Who *could have been involved*? Are you saying that you suspect my husband of involvement?' Her brows rose in angry disgust. 'I do not wish to hear more, sir. You are our guests, but there is no need for us to accept insults. I would like to be left alone, now. Please leave us.'

It was not a request. Feeling ashamed, and not a little saddened at upsetting the lady of the Manor, Simon led the way from the room.

'This is how I used to feel when I was a small boy and my nurse sent me from the room for misbehaving,' Baldwin murmured to raise his spirits, and Simon smiled gratefully.

Once they had left, Matillida knelt at her husband's feet, her hands in his lap. 'You see how their minds are working? That whoreson Smyth has them on his side already. You have heard about the corruption of officials – well, obviously the bailiff thinks about his purse more than he does about justice! You must do something to make Puttock realise what a danger the miners are out there.'

Sir William looked old and tired, and for the first time she could see how the years had exacted their toll on his spirit. Resting one hand on hers, the other in her hair, he smiled weakly. 'Poor Matillida! All you want is the family strong and secure, and all you find are threats on every side. What do you want me to do? Have Thomas Smyth murdered? Or maybe just have him tortured until he admits to killing young Bruther?'

'Don't be foolish. No, we need to keep him with us, that's certain. We cannot allow this affair to get out of proportion, to turn Smyth against us. You know that Robert is set on Alicia?'

'What! My son wants her? But he hates Thomas . . .'

'Of course he does, but that means nothing, not when it comes to the girl. And she would be good for him. She is intelligent and should bring a good dowry.'

He gave a harsh bark of a laugh. 'A good dowry? Yes, very good! It will be our own money which is returned to us.'

'Yes, husband, but better that it should come back as a dowry than be lost to the family for ever. And the girl would make him a good wife, as I say. Especially with me helping and training her. So we must ensure that her father is not at odds with us, mustn't we?'

'But you said we need to make the bailiff realise how dangerous the miners are. How can we—'

'We must help the bailiff understand how unsettling it is to have outlaws and thieves masquerading as miners, of

course. We do not object to freemen coming here and working, only the brigands and cut-throats. And if they are
allowed to remain, is it surprising that people sometimes get
killed by them? Of course not! That is the point you must
make to the bailiff and his friend, that it is hard enough
surviving here without having murderers and outlaws living
nearby in a miners' camp.'

He stood and sighed, looking down at her. 'I will see what
I can do.'

'You must! We have to try to keep Thomas Smyth happy
so that he will smile on his daughter's marriage to our son. It
will make sense for him, to marry into a good family, and it
will be good for us to have the use of his power and wealth.
But he needs to be curbed a little. He must be made to realise
that his power ends at the border of our lands, and he must
not try to extort money from us again.' Nodding, Sir William
made his way to the door, but before he could leave, her
voice stopped him. 'And if the bailiff listens to you, we might
be able to break the power of other miners like him for ever,
and regain control of the land for ourselves.'

# CHAPTER NINE

Sir Ralph of Warton rode back slowly, his mind on the argument between Robert and John. He was fully aware how easily brothers could come close to blows. Not many years before, he had drawn sword against his own older brother, and that was over a bet on the price of a falcon. It was hardly a shock to see Robert and John so much at loggerheads – they were merely acting like brothers the world over – but he did find the degree of mutual animosity surprising in its virulence. There were undercurrents whenever either of them opened his mouth. Robert, slim, pale, weak-looking, and as a result, obnoxious – to the knight's way of thinking, was still at least loyal and honourable, whereas John was openly flippant and insulting, with no regard for any man.

Today it had been Sir Ralph's idea to go out hunting. He felt it would be good to get away from the claustrophobic atmosphere of the Manor, away from the grey eyes of the bailiff and the astute questions of his friend from Furnshill.

Sir Ralph had anticipated a pleasant ride out to a quiet part of the Beauscyrs' private park where they could set the hounds at a deer. It was some time since he had been able to enjoy hunting as a pastime rather than a necessary chore, and the prospect was attractive.

The reality had been very different. They had ridden eastwards, away from the moors themselves, and out into some thick woods, and almost immediately the two brothers had started at each other. One – and he was not sure now who it was – had passed comment on the other's choice of area for the hunt, and suddenly he was in the middle of a battle. It was a matter of pure self-defence to drop back as the insults and curses flowed, and all peace was gone. They had found a small buck and chased him for a mile or more, but then lost the scent, and of course each brother said it was the fault of the other. After biting back his rising anger for a further mile, Sir Ralph had lost any desire to be with the two and had announced his intention of returning. Hastily refusing any company, he turned his horse to the west and left, ignoring the pleading look from a man-at-arms who clearly wished to avoid any more bickering and also wanted to get back to the castle and a pint of ale.

There was some tension between the two young men that he did not understand. It seemed to go beyond the normal rivalry. Maybe it was simply the jealousy of the younger. In most families John would have been sent to a convent instead of into training as a knight. All too often, the second son was diverted to the religious life while the older carried on his education and training as heir. In this case, though, it should have been the other way around. Robert, for all his posturing and prideful behaviour, was more suited to a cloistered life, while John was the resolute, strong and wilful one. He would, the knight thought, have made a very good master of the Manor.

At the gate he called to the doorkeeper, dropping from his horse and walking into the courtyard. There he saw the other knight, the bailiff's friend, and he stiffened. Squaring his shoulders he led his horse through to the stables.

'A good mount,' he heard Baldwin say, and nodded, avoiding the man's gaze. He would have turned and made off, but the dark-haired knight was too close for him to pass, and so he stood dumbly, tugging off his gauntlets.

His indecision was painful to watch, Baldwin decided, and he smiled, trying to appear as friendly as possible. It only served to heighten the man's anxiety. Baldwin patted the black horse's rump, and then his eyes caught sight of the mark, visible on the left outer thigh although partly concealed – a large capital M. When he glanced back at the knight, he could see the sudden stillness in his face, the tautness in the way he held himself.

'Sir Ralph, don't worry,' he said, so softly that the groom could not hear. 'Matters up at the Warbeck are not important down here.' And he turned and left. But he could feel the knight's eyes on his back all the way across the yard.

Simon was at the entrance to the kitchen, Hugh and Edgar beside him. The bailiff and his man were drinking from large pots of ale, served by the old bottler.

'Drinking again, Simon? The beer will addle your brains.'

'Too late,' Simon said, and took another long draught. 'My brain feels addled enough already. Miners, knights, squires, villeins . . . pah! We're wasting our time here! I have no idea who might have killed Bruther, I don't even have any idea what the man was like. How can we find out who did it when all we have to go on is a series of vague dislikes about him?'

'You are right,' said Baldwin, taking a pot from the servant and holding it out to be filled, then placing his hand over the top when it was only half-full. 'Thank you. Yes, Simon, you could be right. We know that he was a sore embarrassment to his master, to old Sir William, and to Robert Beauscyr. He was disliked by Thomas Smyth for being a foreigner, and not bowing to the miner's will, so it is possible he was killed by Smyth . . .'

'Or by the gang who beat up Smalhobbe,' Simon interjected. 'And then there's that knight too,' he said, pointing with his chin at the tall figure by the stables. 'I don't trust him. He's too aloof.'

'I know what you mean, but I think I might be able to clear up a few points about him soon. Leave him to me.'

'What about the other brother?'

'Who, John? He's hardly been here in three years or more. What possible reason could he have for murder?'

'There are many reasons for murder, Baldwin. Maybe he wanted to remove a problem from his father and brother.'

Sir Ralph had just emerged from the stables. He stood staring across at the small group of men, as if undecided, but then strode off to the hall. Baldwin cocked an eyebrow at the bailiff. 'Did you see that? I think if I had been alone here, he would have come over to speak to me.'

'Why on earth do you say that?'

'I was looking at his horse just now, and there was a brand-mark on its rump.'

140

'Really? Well, now so many lords need to hire additional warriors, they often do that, don't they? Brand the horses, so if they're stolen they can be found. And it's not uncommon for a man to *say* his mount was stolen when he bartered it for money, if he feels his master doesn't pay enough – and if he knows his lord will replace it for him. And if mercenaries decide to run away before their contract is up, it's an easy way to find them again. It's not very pleasant, I know, but many do it. It's another foreign habit we've been lumbered with, and—'

'Simon, please! You must never travel, old friend, you would surely be lynched within a few yards of the coast in any foreign country. What is important is, do you know of any place which brands horses with a capital M?'

'Moretonhampstead?' Simon's face screwed up as he tried to think of places far away.

Laughing, Baldwin clapped him on the back, spilling much of his beer and making the bailiff give a low growl of disgust. 'Simon, you're priceless as a guide to these parts, but you're hopeless as a man of the world. Who in that little town would care about hirelings? I'll give you a hint: try far, far to the north. Near Scotland, where John and Sir Ralph were living.'

Just then, a cry came from the gates. Immediately there was a bustle of men in the yard. The haughty figure of Robert Beauscyr rode in; his brother, grinning broadly, followed with three hounds trailing along behind him.

'While you're congratulating yourself on how much more knowledgeable than me you are, Baldwin, why don't you go and speak to Robert?' Simon murmured. 'And I'll have a word with the other brother. We should try to discover whether they know anything.'

When the knight nodded, the bailiff wandered idly toward the squire, who was rubbing down his horse, while Baldwin followed Robert to the far side of the stables.

Hugh glanced at Edgar. 'Are we supposed to go too, do you think?'

The man-at-arms was watching his master. 'I don't think we can help them – we'd probably only get in the way.'

'That's what I thought.' Hugh belched happily and held out his pot once more to the bottler.

Robert Beauscyr was critically observing a groom remove the saddle and bridle from his horse and making dry comments about the man's abilities when Baldwin approached. He looked up quickly on hearing the knight's step, and seemed relieved to see who it was – or who it was not.

'A good ride?' Baldwin asked pleasantly.

'The ride was fine, but the conversation was dull. Very dull.'

Leaning on a trestle, Baldwin crossed his arms comfortably. 'It's very difficult with brothers. You feel you should like them – but sometimes they can be impossible.'

'He's so superior sometimes – he was never like this before he went off to the north. Then we used to be able to talk about things and enjoy each other's company, but now it's "Oh, you still do that here . . ." or "Well, of course, in the north we didn't have all these luxuries . . ." and "I suppose living out in the middle of nowhere you have to do this sort of thing, but in decent company . . ." It makes me want to knock some sense into him.'

The knight smiled. 'You can choose friends, but you're stuck with your family,' he agreed.

'Not for long, thank God! He leaves soon with Sir Ralph, and I'll be glad when they've gone.'

'Don't be too hard on him, Robert. He is very young, and he will grow out of it in time. The trouble is, he has been fighting with other men he respects. Once he has won his spurs, he will begin to understand that life is not so straightforward. Right now, all he knows is that he has been tested in battle and has won – or at least hasn't been killed, but as a knight, he'll discover that it's not so easy to be in command. He will have to send men to their deaths, and that is a sobering responsibility.'

Robert glanced at him, and saw the faraway look in his eyes. 'You have fought, and led men?' he asked.

Stirring himself, Baldwin gave a wry smile. 'Oh yes, my friend. And seen them die. And I was very much like your brother, full of hellfire and gallantry and a constant source of embarrassment and pain to my older brother. He had the responsibility to protect the family and the Manor, while I could go and enjoy my freedom, and I do not think I ever realised how hard his task was. It took the death of a city to show me what real duty meant, and by then it was too late to say anything. I was too far away. Don't worry, John will calm down. He will improve, and you will be proud and happy to call him your brother again, once he has got the lust for power and money out of his system.'

'If he ever does,' Robert said, throwing a surly glance over his shoulder at his brother. 'It's not as if a knight going to the Continent nowadays returns wealthy, not like the old times when there were estates to be won.'

'There are still some who succeed,' Baldwin said mildly. 'I think while he is in the service of Sir Ralph he will be well looked after; that man is very astute.'

'Possibly.'

'Robert.' Baldwin's tone was reflective. 'I know this is annoying to you, but I must ask it: what were you doing on the night Peter Bruther died?'

The man whirled to face him. 'Me? I . . . Do you mean to accuse *me*?'

Baldwin's eyes held his in silence, and Sir Robert had to drop his gaze. He frowned and shrugged. 'I suppose you're right. After all, I did have cause to hate him after he ran away and made the family look foolish.' He stared down at his boots. 'You already know about that devil's bastard, Thomas Smyth, and how he demanded that we should pay him money to keep off our lands. That was the afternoon he came to see us. We had the rest of the day to think about it. He made it sound reasonable, said he had a need for more water, and it would cost a lot of money to bring it from the moors. His alternative, he said, was to divert our streams – it would be much cheaper for him that way. But then he said that if we agreed to pay him the *difference*, he could tell the miners to leave our water alone and get it from further off. It was sheer blackmail, nothing else.'

'How did your father react?'

'My father's an old man. Old and tired. In his life he's fought hard and long in many battles and yet he still has to contend with the likes of Smyth. He thought we had no choice. I . . . I'm afraid I lost my temper. Bargaining with Smyth was like haggling with a thief for the return of your own purse! That was what made me mad, the way that the thief was going to get what he wanted. I left them to it, I wanted no part of a discussion of that sort, and rode to Chagford, to the tavern.'

'Did you go near Bruther's place?'

He did not hesitate. 'Yes. In the afternoon I went past Bruther's holding. But I didn't see him, nor anyone else nearby.'

'When did you get back?'

'A little after dark. I was furious. It took me that long to calm myself. The thought that my father was giving away my birthright, first in letting that villein get away, and then in paying off the miners – well, it was better that I was away for a while, that was all.'

'How did John react to the miner's offer?'

'How should he react? When he heard about it he was amused. It's my estate, not his, when my father dies. To him, anything that reduces the Manor makes me look foolish, and that appeals to him.' His voice was bitter.

'You say you saw no one near Bruther's place. What about elsewhere?'

Frowning, Robert thought for a minute. 'I saw Adam Coyt, a moorman, north of Crockern Tor in the afternoon. He was cutting peat, I think. Apart from him I saw no one except miners.'

'Where? And at what time of the day?'

'They were heading north, a little after I saw Coyt, walking up to the road.'

'How many were there?' asked Baldwin, trying to keep his voice casual to hide his sudden tension.

'Three. They were making their way up from their camp to the moors. They weren't far from Coyt at the time.'

'I see.' Baldwin nodded, considering. There was something shifty about Sir Robert's manner, he thought. He asked casually, 'And you were alone all this time?'

MICHAEL JECKS

'Oh, yes. All the time.'
And Baldwin knew he was lying.

Seeing Simon walk towards him, John's smile broadened.
He stood with his hands in his belt, waiting for him. 'So,
bailiff, have you found the men who killed poor Peter yet?'
he said cheerily.

Simon regarded him sourly. The youth's hectoring manner
was as annoying as his older brother's. 'Not yet, but we will,'
he said sourly.

'Yes?' His eyes drifted off to where Baldwin was talking to Robert. 'And you will do it by talking to us individu-
ally, I suppose. Is that so we cannot concoct a story
between us? If so, you're too late; we've just been
completely alone for some time – since Sir Ralph became
bored, I think, with our conversation. Ah well, what can I
do for you, anyway?'

'Peter Bruther was surely killed for a reason. Who could
have hated him enough to want to hang him?'

'A good question. I suppose you already know the obvious ones: Thomas Smyth and his merry men, my father, and,
of course, my brother. It's for you to take your choice
between them.'

'What about you?'

'Me?' For a split second Simon could see his surprise.
'But . . . ah, bailiff, I think you're playing games. What
reason could *I* have? It's not as if I stand to gain anything
from Bruther's death. He was an annoyance to the family,
but that's none of my concern now. The whole estate will go
to Robert, and I have no wish to help him by removing obsta-
cles to his happiness. Why should I?'

146

'You really are angry about Robert inheriting the Manor, aren't you?'

'You are most observant, bailiff,' John said drily. Then his lip curled, and when he continued his voice was scornful. 'My beloved brother is a clerk. He is good with books and accounts, which is, I suppose, what the place needs for most of the time, but for the rest it needs a strong grip. He's not capable of providing that: I am.'

'To keep the peasants under control?'

'There is that,' he nodded. 'With trailbaston becoming a serious problem, with outlaws attacking outlying places, it's time we got hard on the people who foment discord. They are prepared to upset the balance of the kingdom, and they must be destroyed.'

Simon watched him. He was smiling as he pronounced his cures for the nation as if there was a joke the bailiff could not understand. 'So you think all outlaws should be hunted down and killed,' he said.

'Oh yes, bailiff. Anyone who wishes to create disharmony: common peasants who become outlaws, thieves, cut-purses, draw-latches, brewers who water down their ale, tinners who mix impurities with their metal . . . and men who cannot keep their estates in order. All need the rope, don't you think?'

'Including knights?'

'Oh, no.' Now his expression became serious. 'You can't lump a well-born knight into the same category as the rest. A knight is the holder of all the prime virtues, no matter what. He is the highest order of the land, fighting for what is good. After all, of the three levels in society, the knights, the clergy and the people, it is the knights who are the most important; for they are the men who must keep order.'

'Many would say that the clergy should be the highest order.'

'They can give direction, but little more. The crusades proved that; the bishops and their men showed that we should take back the Holy Land, but could they have taken it without the knights? Of course not.'

'But,' Simon's Christian soul was aghast, 'it was the knights who *lost* the Holy Land, by consorting with the heathens there! If they'd—'

'If they had not been misled by others, you mean. The Pope and his bishops began to fall into bad habits, didn't they? The Popes have been too interested in their own wealth for too long. Look at Boniface, and all the rumours about him being a Devil-worshipper and a sodomist. It is no wonder that God decided the Holy Land should be taken from us after all that.'

'That has nothing to do with it! Boniface was not Pope until years after the Fall of Acre!'

'And you think he was the first to be so debauched and heretical? No, it has been going on for years. And the knights have always been pure, because a knight's only duty is to look for honour and glory in battle. Courtesy, honour, largesse . . . these are the main principles by which a knight must live. All a bishop need do is profess a love of God to increase his wealth a hundredfold; as soon as he's considered a holy man people will flock like sheep to give him their money.'

'You have a very cynical view of the world, John.'

'Perhaps. But at least I will not be disappointed by it. I've seen too much already to trust anyone or anything more than I trust myself and my sword.'

'If you feel this way, do you think a runaway villein is of no importance compared to a knight, and should be punished for bringing shame to a knight's family?'

'Very good, bailiff!' he said delightedly. 'So you bring us back to the point at the same time as suggesting I have a motive to murder him. But no, I fear you must look elsewhere. I would not trouble myself over someone who was a cause of pain to my brother. Why should I? Bruther was merely a thorn in Robert's flesh, and as such he gave me pleasure.'

'Even so, where were you on the day Bruther was murdered?'

'Ha! I wondered how long it would take you to get back to that. Well, now. I was here almost all day, with Sir Ralph and my mother or father, I saw, for example, the row between Robert and Thomas Smyth – so embarrassing to see one's elder brother running out of a meeting like a whipped brat. After the evening meal I joined my father to ride over to Smyth's place. Sir Ralph came too. My father paid the tinner the money he demanded, by the way, Shocking, I know, but there it is.'

'And you stayed with your father?'

John stifled a yawn, 'No. Sir Ralph and I did not want to get involved in such a sordid matter. We left my father there and went to the inn – the Fighting Cock. It was some time later that we returned home.'

'And which way did you come back?'

'We didn't come past Bruther's place, if that's what you mean, bailiff. We came straight home again.' He smiled, waiting for the next question.

Out of the corner of his eye Simon saw Baldwin leaving Robert. There was no point, he decided, in carrying on trying to interrogate the squire. John was clearly unworried by his questions. If he was concerned, he had learned how to hide it, the bailiff thought, staring at his openly amused expression.

'Don't worry, bailiff, I'm sure you'll find the murderer,' John said, a mocking tone in his voice.

Simon nodded impassively, then walked away and joined Baldwin.

'How was John?' the knight asked, peering over his shoulder at the squire.

'Insufferable, in short. If he'd made it any more obvious he thought I was a fool, I'd have had the right to strike him. As it was, I got the impression he was mocking our attempt to find out who was responsible for Bruther's death. How about the older Beauscyr?'

'Oh, calm and reasonable for once. He didn't even lose his temper with me,' Baldwin said, amused by the bitterness in Simon's voice. 'But he has no alibi for that evening. He was out on his own for most of the day.' He explained what Robert had told him, and then Simon summarised his conversation with John.

Finishing, the bailiff said, 'So at least John has some sort of witness to the facts. Sir Ralph was with him, so he says. That means that if he can confirm what John told me, I suppose the most suspicious character must be Robert, eh, Baldwin?'

The knight was staring after the brothers. 'I suppose so,' he said meditatively. 'But I think I would like to confirm John's words too. Perhaps it would be worthwhile for us to ride to this inn and try their ale.'

\* \* \*

'Brother?'

In the blackness of night the soft, low call made Sir Robert spin, his hand gripping his sword. There was a dry chuckle, then a shadow detached itself from the wall near the stables. In the faint light from a sconce he saw that it was his brother. 'What do you want?' he hissed.

John's face was anxious. 'Did the bailiff or that damned knight question you as well today?'

'Yes. So what?'

'I think you should be careful, that's all. The bailiff seems to think you or I could be the murderer.'

Robert felt the strength drain from him. 'And?' he said, experiencing a quick stab of fear.

'We may disagree about many things, brother, but this is important. Those miners killed Bruther, there's no doubt about that in my mind, but it looks as though they've either bribed the bailiff – he is responsible for the tinners, after all – or have succeeded in making it look as if it was someone here, at the Manor. We can't allow that.'

'What do you suggest?'

'This murder – it must have been the same three men who attacked Smalhobbe. What can we do to find them? Thomas Smyth is a devious old devil. I've no doubt he'll have hidden them well enough. Of course, if only we could get hold of one of them, and make him admit what they did to Smalhobbe and Bruther, it would go a long way to showing the bailiff that we're all innocent.'

'Where could he hide three men, though?' Robert said thoughtfully. 'There aren't that many places on the moors. Unless he hid them in the miners' camp itself . . .'

\*         \*         \*

Sir Ralph was keen to leave. The Manor held nothing but danger, and he felt that whatever he did was open to scrutiny. His only option was to get away and carry on with his journey. The enforced delay was making him fretful.

It was just after dark, and up here on the battlements near the gate the countryside seemed to have disappeared, hidden by the relative brightness of the sconces and braziers which lighted the wall and walkway. He wrapped himself up in his cloak and stared glumly to the south. Though his heart was still in the north where he had been born, he knew he had to go, and that as quickly as possible.

Hearing a noise, he peered down. In the courtyard, he could see John, his squire, and Robert, huddled together by the stables. When the door to the hall opened, he saw the brothers quickly retreat into the darkness of the stables, and raised an eyebrow in surprise. Why should they be so surreptitious, he wondered.

In the open doorway he saw the tall knight standing alone, and began to understand the pair's desire for obscurity. The very sight of the bailiff or his friend was becoming tedious – and worrying. To be so near the coast and escape, and yet cut off here on the moors, was as frustrating as being caught in a siege, and he was nervous of speaking to the knight after his quiet hints earlier that day. Baldwin of Furnshill, he was sure, guessed more than he had let on.

There was a guard in the courtyard, and Baldwin walked down the steps and over to him. Their voices rose to Sir Ralph as a soft murmur in the still night air, and then the guard pointed up to him. Sir Ralph stared down as Baldwin glanced in his direction, and he felt the blood stop in his veins as the knight made his way to the stairs and climbed up to join him.

'Sir Ralph, I'm glad to find you.'

'I was about to go indoors. It is cold up here,' he said, pulling his cloak tighter round his shoulders.

'This will not take long. Come, let's walk along here a little further.'

It was impossible to refuse the calm, grave voice, and Sir Ralph soon found himself unwillingly pacing with the knight by his side. All he wanted was peace and solitude so that he could plan his future, not a continuation of the oblique conversation of earlier in the day. To his surprise, Baldwin did not want him to talk.

'I used to serve with an honourable army, you know,' he began. Smiling, he stared out over the hill before the Manor. 'I fought in the last battle for Acre, back in 1291. A long time ago now, of course. All I wanted then was a chance to win renown, which is right for a young knight, isn't it? But afterwards I found myself in a position where my allegiances were called into question. It is hard, when you have taken an oath from the most honourable motives, to discover that you have been betrayed. That happened to me.'

Pausing above the main gate, Baldwin sighed. Thinking back and recalling his past had seemed a good idea earlier, but now he could sense Sir Ralph's nervousness and distrust. When he continued, he spoke wistfully. 'It still happens a lot, of course. Men swear loyalty, and then find out that their master is not honourable. And what should a man do then? Go away and find another master? Or wait until he is released from his oath? It is very difficult.'

153

Listening, Sir Ralph felt trapped. He would like to be able to trust this stranger. There was integrity and understanding in his dark brown eyes, a kindness he usually associated with priests which conspired with his own feelings of loneliness and danger to make him want to blurt out the truth, to share his secret. But he did not dare.

He looked lifeless, pale and sickly in the flickering light. Baldwin stood with his hands resting calmly on the wall as he peered out remembering, as though he was lost in his own thoughts and unaware of Sir Ralph's presence.

'In any case,' Baldwin continued, 'whatever may happen in the north is none of our concern down here. The marches are always in turmoil, and if the Scottish attack, men must defend themselves.' He turned, facing Sir Ralph with an eyebrow raised as he subjected the knight to a dubious stare. 'But if a man was to murder, I could not condone that. If I found that a man had murdered, I would have to make sure he was held. And if I thought I knew who had killed this villein Bruther, it would not matter whether he was the son of a serf or a lord, I would hold him in gaol until his trial.'

'Do you accuse me of killing the boy? What reason could I have?'

'A good question. I too wonder what reason you could have,' Baldwin said, seeing the tautness of the man's stance. 'But no, I do not accuse you, Sir Ralph. I think you know something of the affair, though, and I would like you to trust me. Perhaps you will, in time.'

Sir Ralph glanced away. He wanted to believe the knight's words, but he could not speak. It was too dangerous. He was not from this area, and he had no family or friends on whom he could count for protection. Suddenly he felt very alone.

After a moment Baldwin sighed. There was nothing more he could say, and the determined glower on Sir Ralph's face spoke of his resolution to maintain his silence. Baldwin turned to leave, pausing when he faced the inner courtyard. Now what were they talking about? he wondered. Sir Ralph followed the direction of his glance and saw John and Robert standing near a wall sconce.

Alone once more, Sir Ralph gazed out to the south. Whether it was guesswork or not was irrelevant to him – all that mattered was that Sir Baldwin evidently knew about his past. How he had found out was unimportant. The fact was, he *did* know. And that could mean the bailiff knew as well . . .

That thought made him shudder.

# CHAPTER TEN

Simon groaned as he hauled himself upwards from the bench which had been his bed for the night. In the past, when he was younger and had not qualified for the privilege of sleeping in a hall, he had often spent nights in barns while travelling. It was preferable to this, he thought. In a barn or stable there was hay and straw to make a comfortable bed, but now he was a bailiff, his hosts always seemed to think he deserved a chance to sleep on one of the family's best wooden benches in the main hall. Probably, he winced, because of a general dislike for bailiffs.

It would not be surprising if it was some kind of punishment. Though he himself tried to behave honourably, there were many bailiffs in the land who were known to be corrupt and dishonest. Even among the bailiffs responsible for the moors, there were some whose actions were, at best, dubious. The chief warden regularly received complaints from people claiming that bailiffs captured men of the county and held them in gaol until ransoms were paid, or that juries were coerced into giving bad decisions in court in return for money. Few trusted the moor's bailiffs.

Stretching, he glanced around. True to form, Hugh was still snoring gently in the corner by the wall. It always took the equivalent of a charge of warhorses to wake him in the mornings, no matter where he rested. There was no sign of Edgar or Baldwin. Their benches were empty.

He stood, yawned, and wandered to the fire. The large blocks of wood which had fed it the night before were almost burned through, and he had to push some glowing embers together and blow at them to restart the flames. It took some time, and he was still crouching there when he heard the door crash open. Startled, he looked round to see Baldwin stamping in, Edgar hurrying along in his wake.

'Quick, Simon, get ready to leave. I've ordered your horse to be saddled, and food to be prepared. There's no telling how long this will take,' He kicked Hugh's bench. 'Damn them!'

'What in the good Lord's name is the matter with you?' Simon asked reasonably, grinning maliciously at the sight of Hugh who, shocked into wakefulness in an instant, tried to leap up, forgetting where he was. Arms flailing, he slipped backwards and disappeared.

'What's the matter? War, bailiff. That's what's the matter! Those mad fools have gone to the mining camp with some men-at-arms!'

'What? Who?'

'Wake up, Simon. Hell's teeth, you'd try the patience of a saint when you're half-asleep! Robert and John, of course. They've got it into their heads that Peter Bruther's murderers

157

are in Thomas Smyth's camp, and they've ridden there to catch them.'

Hugh's face reappeared over his bench, his eyes massive in his alarm, though whether at falling or at the thought of a fight, Simon was in no mood to guess. 'Hugh! Stop staring and get ready.'

They were on their way in a matter of minutes. Their horses were ready and waiting and it took only a moment to clamber up, snatch the reins from the grooms, and whip their mounts through the gates, passing rapidly over the moors to the miners' camp.

The sun was well into the sky when they approached, and Simon was reflecting with longing on the breakfast he should have been eating, had it not been for the stupid actions of the two brothers. At the Manor, he thought dreamily, there would have been cold cuts of the calf they had eaten the night before, and his belly rumbled at the memory. When Baldwin came alongside, he contemplated him sourly.

The knight ignored the bailiff's look; he was frowning seriously. 'What's that – can you hear it?' He cocked his head, and Simon followed suit. Dimly, over the thudding of hooves and squeaking of harnesses they could make out a crashing and clanging, like an army of blacksmiths. Baldwin cursed through gritted teeth. 'God! We're too late!'

Kicking his horse to greater urgency, Baldwin fumbled for his sword hilt. Now that they were almost there, he was beginning to wonder whether it was such a good idea to have chased after the two brothers and their men. There were only the four of them, and if it came to a battle their force would be inadequate to keep the two sides apart. His sword was loose in its sheath, and he had just taken fresh hold of the reins when they came over the brow of the hill and could see down into the valley of the miners.

'Thank God!' he heard Simon say, and nodded to himself. There were no bodies on the ground, and the sides were not closed yet. They charged forward.

The crowd was thickest at the blowing-house, and it was here that Baldwin aimed his mount, thundering down the shallow incline, through the stream, the water leaping up on both sides, and then on to the yelling and swearing men.

Bellowing '*Stop!*' at the top of his voice, Baldwin drew his sword and pounded towards the miners. Now he could see what had created the harsh metallic ringing. It was not sword on armour, it was rocks raining down on the brothers' shields. They were standing before the doorway to the blowing-house with three men-at-arms at their sides, while the tin workers hurled rocks, going to the stream's banks to use its plentiful supply of moorstone. At the front Baldwin could see the sandy hair of George Harang. He appeared to be directing the attack, yelling to urge the tinners on.

A man hurled a stone which bounced from John's shield, making him curse and stagger, but that was the last one. Even as it struck, Baldwin arrived between the two groups. He screamed at the miner who had thrown it, pointing with his sword: 'I said *stop*! If I see another missile I'll have your head – *do you understand*?' The man nodded dumbly, aghast to find a knight suddenly appear in front of him. When Baldwin was sure he would obey, he whirled his horse round to face the Beauscyrs, and found Simon was already with him, Edgar and Hugh to either side. The bailiff's horse was pawing at the ground, as he stared at the men, his rage clear for all to see.

MICHAEL JECKS

'Well? What excuse do you have for this trespass?' Simon said, his voice as cold as a moorland stream. 'You are guilty of invading the King's forest, of armed attack and threatening men of the King's demesne – what excuse can you give? Robert? Speak!'

'We wanted to come and catch the gang who killed Peter Bruther.'

'Oh? You know who it was now, do you?'

John came forward, a bemused frown on his face. 'Bailiff, it had to be the miners. They were threatening us, as you know. It's only a small step from extortion to murder.'

'Rubbish!'

'It's true. And this same gang has been beating up outlying miners. What about Henry Smalhobbe? Doesn't he deserve protection from these moor-based thugs? Or don't you care about them, bailiff?'

Simon, white with fury, was about to kick his horse forward when Baldwin's hand gripped his arm. The knight's voice was calm. 'John Beauscyr, you are a fool. Be silent. The bailiff is right to protect all miners, not one or another but *all*. You are at fault in being here, let alone in drawing weapons against those who have a legal right to be here. We will deal with you later. For now, you will come with us.'

'And what of our prisoners?' the youth sneered.

'What prisoners?' asked Simon.

John disappeared into the blowing-house, and they heard a shout, then a curse. In a moment, three men came out, all with their hands bound, blinking in the sunlight and stopping uncertainly at the sight of the four large horses blocking their path. Following, John nonchalantly waved his sword in their direction. 'Just for you, bailiff, I am pleased to present some

men you wanted to meet: Stephen the Crocker, Harold
Magge and Thomas Horsho. Aren't you going to thank us
for finding them for you?'

'You, *bailiff*, are supposed to be the protector of the rights of
the miners here,' Thomas Smyth roared. 'You're not here to
disrupt our work and support foreigners who decide to
molest my men!'

Baldwin and Simon had ridden to his house after Hugh
and Edgar had escorted the Beauscyrs and their man back
to the Manor, leaving the three gang members behind. It
was going to be impossible for them to be made prisoner
and taken away, that was plain from the angry mutterings
of the crowd of miners, but Simon had spoken to George
Harang, and he had agreed, after some show of reluctance,
to keep the three under guard until they had all spoken to
Thomas Smyth. The bailiff had persuaded him that he
would be held personally responsible to the chief warden
of Lydford for them. If they escaped, he would answer for
them.

The bailiff and his friend sat quietly while the master of
the house thundered, stamping like a bear waiting for the
baiting. Simon's eyes followed the miner, but inwardly he
was seething. It was one thing to take advantage of the
Beauscyrs, but quite another to lie to the chief warden's bailiff, and he was wary of speaking until he could control his
anger. Unaffected by any legal implications, Baldwin was in
a position to enjoy the encounter, and he did so, watching
Thomas Smyth's ranting with open amusement. Seeing his
evident pleasure did nothing for Smyth's temper. His face
was as black as the sky in a storm, glaring at the two men.

161

George Harang stood before them, his eyes reflecting his open contempt.

'How can we work the King's tin if we're to be obstructed? And if this isn't an obstruction, God Himself only knows what is! It was madness to let them come to the mining vill. If I'd been there, the bastards wouldn't have left alive, I promise you that. And you let them go! They should've been arrested immediately – by *you*, bailiff. It's why you're here, it's your job, and if you won't do it, someone else'll have to. The impudence of them! They force their way into my blow-ing-house, beat two of my workers like a gang of outlaws, and then you let them *get away*! They should've been held – yes! Sent to Lydford Gaol and held for the next stannary court, that would've cooled their ambitions! Two of them with men-at-arms! God in Heaven!'

Baldwin thought he was running out of invective. Smyth stopped beside George Harang, surveying the seated men, but then caught sight of the expression on his servant's face. If anything, it only served to heighten his fury. 'And you . . . you can stop looking like a lawyer with a new client, you bastard! If you'd done your job properly that camp would have been better defended. How did the Beauscyr whelps manage to get into the compound? Hey? They should've been seen from miles off and stopped. How can we protect our tin if the miners don't look after the blowing-house and storerooms?'

George quailed. He had suffered the rough edge of his master's tongue before now, but this time it was worse. He had never seen Thomas look so angry, not even at those times when a lot of it was for show and he was browbeating one of the men for an infringement of his rules. This was no acting, though, this was the raw, fierce rage of a man who was close to the end of his tether. 'Sir, I did what I—'

'Shut up!' Thomas turned back to Simon. 'So, then, bailiff. What are you going to do about it? I want them arrested.'

'No.'

'What do you mean, "*No*"? Have you no idea what your—'

Simon cut across the fresh tirade. 'I will not arrest the Beauscyrs, or *your* three men. I'll question them all, but until I know what's really been going on down here, I'll not take any more action. There's been too much latitude taken by your people, as well as the Beauscyrs, and it'll stop now. You will immediately halt your attempts to bully people away from the moors.'

'You dare to tell me – *me* – what I must do?' His voice was lower now, and his face was quite pale, as if the blood was draining from it. 'You dare tell me you'll question *my* men? I shall say this to you, bailiff: no one has ever had the arrogance to threaten me in my own home, and if you think—'

'Thomas Smyth, I am the bailiff of Lydford, as you have pointed out. I am here on the orders of the chief warden. If you presume once more to interrupt me, I will arrest you and have *you* thrown into the gaol. Do I make myself clear?'

Although Simon's tone was deceptively soft, Thomas was aware of the iron beneath it. He bit his lip and glowered, but then stamped to a chair and stood by it tensely, ordering his man to fetch wine and staring at Simon.

Staring back at him unblinkingly, the bailiff continued. 'Good. I have had evidence of your men beating up legitimate miners on the moors, of your charging money from

MICHAEL JECKS

landowners to stay off their lands, and now I find that you
have lied to me. When I asked you about these men, you
told me that they were not here any more, that they had
disappeared from the mining camp. Now I find that the
Beauscyrs were quite correct to assume that you had lied,
and that you were, in fact, hiding them in the storeroom of
your blowing-house. Under the King's forest laws *or* the
stannary laws, you're guilty. However, before I sort out the
mess you have created, I intend to discover what happened
to Peter Bruther, and I expect your complete cooperation. If
I do not feel I am receiving it, I will have you arrested. I
trust that is clear?'

'You're in the pay of the Beauscyrs,' the miner jeered.
'That's why you won't do your duty.'

Angered by the accusation, Baldwin made a move as if to
stand, but Simon's hand caught his arm and he subsided,
saying, 'This is getting intolerable! My friend here is trying
to unravel a murder, and all you and the others who live here
want to do is argue about ancient privileges.'

'Ancient enough, sir knight, but important,' Thomas spat,
but then he collapsed in his chair. He had seen the knight's
anger, and it made him hold his tongue. George had returned
with the bottler, a thin grey-faced man, who carried a goblet
and jug. Sighing, Smyth took the proffered wine, then realised that there was none for his visitors. 'What of them, you
fool! Do you expect them to drink from the jug?' he snapped,
glaring after the bottler, who quickly ran from the room.
Sighing, he could not help a faint, disgusted smile. 'It seems
my world is falling apart,' he muttered. 'Very well, bailiff, I
believe you. You have my apologies. You'll do your duty.
What d'you want from me?'

Simon surveyed him woodenly. He had been close to losing his own temper when Baldwin had leapt to his defence, and was glad now that he had managed to keep it on a close rein. More could be achieved with the miner on his side than against him. But he was sure that something was wrong.

'First, I want your permission to speak to whomsoever I wish in your camp, whenever I want, and without interference from your men.' He glanced up as he said this. George Harang and the bottler had returned with two more goblets and a jug.

'Very well. If it will help to find Peter Bruther's killer, I agree.'

'And I may want to speak to others. Your daughter . . .'

'Alicia? But why? She was—'

'She knows Robert Beauscyr, that's all.'

'Very well, but I'm sure she'll be of little help. Anyway, I'll not let her see the whelp in future.'

'And last, I want to know at what time you saw Sir William on the night Bruther died.'

'He was here when we arrived back,' Smyth said, glancing at the bottler. 'You! When did he get here?'

The bottler's head snapped round. He was an old man, too thin to be healthy, his sandy hair going pale as it greyed. 'He arrived here in daylight, sir. I brought him in here to wait and he stood in the middle of the room, shouting every few minutes for more wine. I had to keep coming back with fresh jugs for him.'

Smyth nodded contemptuously. 'He looked drunk when we returned.'

'Where were you earlier?' Simon asked.

'We had spent most of the day with our men, checking on their work and how well the blowing-house was working. It's very new still, and I've been worried that it might not be functioning properly, so we were there for much of the time. We got back after Sir William and sat to eat immediately – though he was not hungry. I think the thought of sharing our food would have hurt his pride too much.'

'I know what he was doing here.'

'He told you?' Smyth was surprised.

'He didn't like it, but yes. I assume he agreed to your terms?'

'Yes,' Thomas said tightly, 'although he wanted to pay less than I asked and I was forced to point out how much trouble it would save him. In the end he accepted.'

'And when he left, what sort of mood was he in?'

'I won't pretend that he was happy, bailiff. But he seemed to realise that he had little choice.'

'I see.' Sipping his wine, Simon said, 'What do you think of Robert Beauscyr?'

'A hothead. He's so keen on his studies, he never thinks about his actions,' said Thomas dismissively. 'Today shows that. Any other man would have thought through the attack better and been gone before the men there were awake, but oh no, he had to ride in noisily and make such a row that they all awoke. And then it had to go to a fight if he wanted to get away. Sheer stupidity.'

'Would you have said that of him before today?'

'How do you mean? Oh, I suppose . . .' The miner reflected a moment. 'No, probably not. I'd have thought he would be one of the more sensible of the landowners in the area because of his learning. No, you're right. He acted out of character today. Usually he's happy enough to accommodate the miners.'

'What about John?'

'Ah, bailiff. Now you are asking me about someone I cannot understand. Young John is a hard man, I'm sure of that. I don't like or trust him, he always looks like something else is going on in his head when he speaks. He resents his brother as the heir to the estate. Not just from jealousy – I think he honestly believes he would be the better master. He might have been, too. When he has a mind, he can charm the larks from the skies, and he certainly has the diplomatist's skill of lying while seeming to be honest.'

'Robert Beauscyr could have wanted to capture Bruther and take him back to the estate; if the man refused, he could have killed him. He had a motive to murder, to remove an embarrassment to his Manor and punish someone he saw as merely a runaway, but I know of no motive for John to kill. Do you?'

'John?' Frowning with concentration, Thomas looked deep into the fire. 'No, there's none I can see. He's been away too long to have been insulted by Bruther, and he doesn't strike me as the sort of lad to want to help his brother overmuch.'

'Who else could have wanted to see Peter Bruther dead, do you think?'

The old man gave him a helpless glance. 'I don't know, bailiff. There's nobody could have wanted to hurt him, as far as I know.'

'What do you know of Bruther?' Simon was beginning to feel desperate. 'Where did he come from?'

'He was son to Martha Bruther, a widow in Shallow Barton, a small vill out on the outskirts of Widecombe. Her husband was old Arthur Bruther, who died before Peter was born, and she brought the lad up on her own.' He hesitated. 'I can't imagine anyone wanting to kill him.'

There was a quietness about him which Simon found curious. For a powerful man, who must surely have been a hard taskmaster to so many of his miners, to feel so sympathetic to the dead man was unusual, especially when Bruther was living out on a parcel of land in which Smyth had an interest. The bailiff found himself wondering whether this was a show put on for his benefit. Thomas Smyth was more than capable of acting sadness, he was sure. The miner silently refilled his goblet and drank deeply, staring into the distance.

Baldwin leaned forward. 'Do you think he was involved in something illegal? Stealing cattle, for example? Could he have been killed for a theft?'

'No!' The emphatic denial made the knight's eyebrows rise in surprise. 'I would have heard about it if he was, I'm sure. I look after a lot of men out here, and I try to make sure they all keep to the law. Otherwise I'd have the bailiff visiting me every other week.'

The knight nodded, but his eyes remained fixed on the miner as Simon said, 'I don't think there's anything else we need to know from you. If you do think of anything, I want to hear it as soon as possible. Now, I need to see your daughter. I must ask her about that night as well.'

'But she won't have seen or heard anything – she was here all the time.'

'Maybe, but anything is possible. And I want to know more about Robert Beauscyr. She can help me there too.'

With a bad grace, Thomas Smyth motioned tersely to George Harang, who left the room and came back very quickly with the girl. Baldwin smiled. The speed of her entry and her red face made it clear that she had been listening at the door.

Studying Alicia, Baldwin found it easy to understand why Robert Beauscyr could be interested in her. She had breeding – from her mother, no doubt. It showed in the way she walked. Her face, without the heaviness which showed in Christine's features, was high-browed and smooth-skinned, while her eyes were large and wide-spaced. Alicia moved slowly to her father's side once more and stood defiantly with her chin up as if expecting judgement.

Simon began to question her. He had no wish to cause her upset. His own daughter would someday be like this girl, teetering on the edge of adulthood – and hoping to fall over the brink very soon. 'On the night that Peter Bruther died, my dear, we know your father had Sir William Beauscyr come to visit. Where were you that afternoon and evening?'

Glancing quickly at her father, Alicia said, 'I went out with Mother to Chagford in the morning, but we were back here by mid-afternoon. When my father sat down in the hall with Sir William, we left the men and went to the solar.'

'And you stayed there all night? You saw no one?'

'No.'

'I see. In that case, we can move on. Robert Beauscyr: he's a friend of yours?'

She stood a little straighter now, like a haughty queen. 'He and I have known each other since we were born.'

'Tell me, then: how would you describe his temper?'

'Robert's temper? Oh, mild. He is always calm and polite. It's rare for him to raise his voice, and when he does it's only after a lot of provocation. Of course, he's very brave as well.

MICHAEL JECKS

He may not have spent his strength in wars far away that mean little to us down here, but he would always defend anyone who needed help.'

Baldwin rubbed at his brow as he listened, sighing inwardly. That was the trouble with asking young people about their peers, he thought. Either they were the embodiment of all evil or perfect heroes. There hardly ever seemed to be a middle ground. If one thing could be gleaned from her answers to Simon's careful questions, it was that she was fond of the youth. He exchanged a swift glance with the bailiff, who gave a nod.

'That's very good, Alicia. Thank you for that, it's been very useful. Now,' he stood, 'I think we should go. We have many other people to see and speak to.'

Thanking Thomas Smyth and his daughter, the bailiff and his friend went out to their horses. 'And now, Baldwin,' said Simon with a wolfish smile, 'I think we ought to have a brief look at the Fighting Cock, don't you?'

# CHAPTER ELEVEN

The inn was a pleasant surprise when it came into view. A large central block stood a little apart from store-rooms, stables and kitchens, all made from stone. But while other buildings seemed depressing and grey, this place sparkled in the sunlight. It was trading well, too, judging from the number of horses which waited outside.

They left their horses tied to rings in the inn's walls and entered. It was a large hall, the ceiling supported by huge pillars which rose up like the masts of great ships. In the middle was a fireplace, and the rushes on the floor smelled fresh and fragrant, almost overcoming the sour stench of spilled ale. The windows were tall and narrow but lighted the room well.

As they had expected, the place was full. Baldwin saw craggy-featured miners in one corner, a foppishly dressed merchant with four servants holding court near the fire, a knight with two men-at-arms standing and leaning against a wall and watching the others with a mocking smile, a laughing group of farmers at a table, two older men with rosy cheeks sitting primly as if with distaste at such noisy displays, and in and among them moved three serving girls, daintily circling round the men with pots and jugs in their hands.

Striding to a table which was for the present deserted, Baldwin beckoned to a pretty, pale young girl, whose auburn hair was loose and flowing. She smiled at him and nodded, soon making her way to them between the tables.

'So, Simon. We need to find out whether Sir Ralph was here like young John said, don't we?' the knight said as he sat.

'Sirs?'

Baldwin glanced up to find the girl at his side. He returned her smile, ordered for them, and she disappeared into the throng once more. Before long she was back, carrying full earthenware pots of ale. When she had set them down, Baldwin asked if she could wait for a minute.

'Oh no, sir. Not while there are so many to be served. I have to keep working, or I might lose my job here . . .'

'This won't take long,' Baldwin promised. 'It's just that my friend and I know the Beauscyrs, and John told us that his knight and he were here the other day.'

'Yes, sir. They came in an hour or so before dark. We know John here.' Dimples deepened and the light beamed like flakes of gold in her hazel eyes. Happily she said, 'But I can't stop now. Anyway, that was Molly, if he recommended one of us, not me. I'm Alison. But I can get her to come to you later, if you want.'

The knight stared at her. 'Oh! I . . .'

Seeing his friend's embarrassment, Simon began to shake with laughter. Baldwin himself was incapable of speech. While the girl stared from one to the other, Simon struggled to bring his humour under control. At last he managed to say, 'Alison, there's just one thing, if you could: if John was with Molly, where was his friend?'

'His friend? Oh, no! You misunderstand me – Molly was *with* his friend. John wasn't in the mood at the time.'

'I see. And his friend was here for how long?' Simon asked while Baldwin coughed and leaned forward attentively.

'Most of the night, sir.' Her eyes went to the knight with a faint nervousness. She knew the Beauscyr family was wealthy and powerful, and she did not like being questioned about them.

'So John and his friend were here until late, then?' Simon asked.

'No.'

'What?'

'John wasn't here for long. After Molly took his friend away, he went out – for a ride, I daresay!' she giggled. 'He didn't come back till later.' Seeing a man wave urgently, she left them, steering a course back through the people.

'Bugger!' Simon swore, and up-ended his pot.

'Yes, that does change matters a little, doesn't it? If she's right, both brothers were out and about that night.'

'Yes, and it would have been easy for either to have got Bruther and killed him.'

'I wonder . . . Although the two brothers show every sign of hating each other, perhaps *both* were out there trying to kill Bruther . . .'

'You mean they might have formed an alliance?'

'Well, it is possible. Obviously Sir Robert wished to see the villein returned or be punished, and it is not impossible that he could have persuaded his brother to help him – by pointing out that their mother depended on the stability of the Manor, for example.'

'I suppose so, but having seen how the two of them react to each other I would have thought it was unlikely. Maybe John himself had his own reasons to want Bruther dead?'

'Yes . . .' Baldwin's expression betrayed his doubt. 'But it seems a little far-fetched to think that both wanted the man dead and coincidentally happened to be out looking for their victim on the same night. I find that too unlikely. There must be a more simple explanation; we just do not have all the facts yet. Come, let's be off. I want to hear what these three miners have to say for themselves.'

At the miners' camp they found a short but well-muscled guard standing before the blowing-house with his sword drawn. He watched the two men suspiciously as they approached, and seemed unwilling to stand aside until Baldwin rested his hand on his own sword and stared at him unblinkingly. After a moment the guard shrugged ungraciously and let them pass.

The three miners were back in the store-room where they had been hidden, sitting sullen and uncommunicative. Though they glanced up as Simon and Baldwin walked in, none made any move to show that they recognised their questioners.

It made little difference, for there was no point in trying to talk. The waterwheel rumbled and clattered, and men added to the din, pounding chunks of ore with iron-shod clubs on moorstone mortars, reducing the stones for the furnace, and there was a continual hiss and suck as the great bellows worked. The room was stuffy, and acrid with a stench that Simon was coming to recognise: the metallic tang of tin, the smell of money. Motioning to Baldwin, he invited the three to follow them outside, where the air was cleaner and they could speak free of the clamour of the machines and hammers.

Blinking and wincing after the darkness, the three men followed Simon and Baldwin to the stream's bank, the guard trailing along in their wake, unsure whether he should allow his prisoners to move from their gaol but unwilling to force the issue with a knight.

When they were all seated some distance from the slowly revolving wheel, Simon surveyed the men. 'Which of you is Magge?' he asked. There was no point in scaring these men further, he saw. Their fear was all too evident. They knew their lives were at risk. From their shuffling and limping, they must have suffered a beating; Simon would raise this with the Beauscyr brothers when he next saw them. In his opinion there was no excuse for torturing a prisoner.

Harold Magge lifted his head as though it weighed as heavily as a rock on his shoulders. Bloodshot blue eyes gazed back at the bailiff with immense weariness from a face tanned brown as the dark soil all round. In a happier time, Simon thought, and with a tankard of cider in his fist, this man could have looked as cheerful as a free-born farmer with his roughly cut hair and the thick grey bristle on his square jaw. Now a dark bruise showed on one cheek, the edges an unhealthy yellow, and there were scratches on his face where the skin had been scraped. He gave the impression of great sadness and near despair.

'You know that you're all suspected of murder?'

Nodding slowly, Magge said caustically, 'Yes. Our master has betrayed us.'

'You are not from these parts?' asked Simon.

'No, I come from the east, from Kent. I have been here for fifteen years, working the mines. I have been loyal to my master all that time.'

'We don't doubt you, but we must know all that happened on the night Peter Bruther died. We already know that you attacked another miner. Why?'

Sighing, Magge picked up a pebble, then tossed it up and caught it, tossed it up and caught it. He carried on flicking and catching it as he spoke, his eyes on the stone and never meeting the bailiff's. 'It was some days ago now. Thomas Smyth came out and spoke to me, asking me to meet him with these men at Longaford Tor.'

'Was he there alone?'

'George Harang was with him.'

'Does he always go abroad with George?' Simon asked.

The eyes remained on the rising and falling stone. 'Yes. George has worked for him for more than seventeen years, or so they say – a little before my time, anyway. Well, he asked us to help him get rid of the miners up on the moors – all the ones who didn't work for him.'

'Like Henry Smalhobbe and Peter Bruther?'

'Like them,' he agreed, but then caught the stone and stared at Simon. 'But he didn't ask us to do anything to Bruther. He told us to leave him alone.'

'He told you to leave Bruther alone?' repeated Simon sarcastically. 'I suppose he wanted to make himself feel good, leaving one man free on the moors while he got rid of all the others.'

The irony of the comment seemed to elude the miner. Still gripping the pebble in his fist he said, 'All I know is what I say. He told us to leave Bruther alone. He wanted all the others to be scared off, but not Bruther.'

'Very well. What then?'

'We'd spent some time trying to scare them already, but they're a strange lot, these squatters and foreigners.' He voice was disdainful. 'None of them would go. That was the problem. Thomas wanted them gone, so he told us to beat them. So we did.'

'Henry Smalhobbe. You were there.' It was not a question, and Magge gave a short nod before tossing the stone once more, apparently calmed by the monotonous rhythm of throwing and catching. Simon found it irritating, and longed to snatch the pebble from the man, but intuition made him sit still and silent, waiting for the man to continue. It was not long before his patience was rewarded.

'We were there. I was out on the path, waiting for him, when his wife called from the hut.' He spoke without expression as he described the short ambush, how Smalhobbe had almost caught his attackers but had been betrayed by his wife's anxious call, how they had wrestled him to the ground and then begun to beat him. 'He was game, I'll say that,' he said at last, his tone meditative. 'If we hadn't been three, if we'd only been two, he might have been able to keep us off. As it was he had little chance; we came at him from all sides.'

Nodding, Simon was half-amused at the grudging respect the miner held for the man he had beaten so viciously. Catching sight of his friend, he was surprised to see an intense concentration, and then realised what had caught Baldwin's interest. It was strange that Henry Smalhobbe could have displayed such a skill for hunting his attacker. 'He fought that well?' he said thoughtfully.

'Yes.' There was no doubt in his mind. 'Like a trained man-at-arms.'

'And then you went on to Peter Bruther's place?'

The bloodshot eyes looked at him with a flare of anger. 'No! I told you, we never went there. Thomas told us to leave him alone and we did.'

Beside him, one of the other prisoners, a thin, ill-favoured man with sparse grey hair and pale almond eyes, looked up and spoke peevishly. 'Why don't you believe us? Why would we go and kill him? We had no reason to.'

'Shut up, Stephen.' Magge's terse command, made the other silent, and Baldwin studied him with a frown. That Crocker was a weak and ineffectual man who would obey orders Baldwin did not doubt, but there was a sense of whining injustice about him that indicated he felt genuinely hard done by.

'Very well,' Simon said at last. 'So you absolutely deny having anything to do with the murder of Peter Bruther. Did you see anybody else on the moors that day – either before or after your attack on Smalhobbe?'

The stone was caught once more, and remained in his hand while Magge drew his brows down in concentration. 'There were a couple of men, I've seen them before at the Beauscyrs' Manor. They went off up to Wistman's Wood.'

'You saw no others?'

His bloodshot eyes wavered. 'No,' he muttered, and Baldwin and Simon could both see he was lying.

'Why would *we* hurt Bruther, anyway?' Stephen the Crocker's voice was a miserable wheedle. 'Ask Smalhobbe – he could kill! He probably wanted Bruther's land, and he used to be an outlaw, so—'

'What's that?' Simon's head snapped round to stare at the man and he gestured curtly to Harold Magge to be silent. Magge glared at his companion, but held his tongue. 'How do you know?'

'I saw him.' There was an underlying satisfaction in Crocker's voice at the reaction to his words. 'He was in a band that robbed a merchant up north, over a year ago. I saw him. That's where he learned to fight, with a gang of killers.'

When they finally got back to the Manor, they did not have to seek out Sir Ralph. Hardly had they reached the hall and seated themselves before the knight came in.

'Where is everyone?' asked Simon, vaguely waving a hand at the empty room.

'Lady Beauscyr has gone to the solar to rest, and Sir William is out hunting. He was not best pleased with his sons, as you may well imagine. Robert has gone out, and John was down at the stables when last I saw him,' Sir Ralph said with his eyes on Baldwin. It appeared that the northern knight wanted to speak to him alone, but Baldwin was not prepared to permit that. He motioned to a bench, resting his chin in a hand.

'It was only a few days ago, Sir Ralph, that I was telling my friend here about some news I had received from a traveller. He had just come from the north, from the armies protecting Tynemouth, and had some interesting stories to tell about the events up there.'

To Simon it was as if the man suddenly lost all energy. He fell on to the bench and stared at Baldwin with the eyes of a hare frozen to immobility as it watched a hunter creep close.

'He told me of groups of men up there, knights and soldiers who were taking advantage of the Scottish troubles to make their own mischief, robbing and pillaging over a wide area while the King is absorbed with other matters. A disgraceful state.'

'Yes,' Sir Ralph whispered distractedly, but then sat up, as if finding a new source of strength and courage, meeting Baldwin's serious gaze with resolution.

'I understand that they are called "shavaldores", and they ride out over the land like soldiers,' Baldwin said, and seeing the tight nod carried on. 'And two men led them, Sir Gilbert of Middleton and Sir Walter of Selby. They attacked two cardinals, Luke of Fieschi and John of Offa, who had been sent to negotiate with the Scottish King. They didn't harm them, did they? But they did take their horses and money and everything else, so it was a grave insult to the Pope. And a slight to the King, of course.'

Now Sir Ralph's face was as grey as the ashes in the hearth. Simon felt no sympathy. There were too many supposedly honourable men up and down the country who had resorted to violence in the last few years for him to have any feelings other than disgust.

'That was last year, of course – 1317. Since then, all of Sir Gilbert's neighbours have been persuaded by his actions that he must be stopped. I understand that they were to attack his castle at Mitford. I merely wondered whether you knew of this affair, Sir Ralph? No? There was a knight with Sir Gilbert, too, I recall.' The vagueness of Baldwin's voice was deceptive; there was no loss of concentration in his eyes as he stared at the man before him. 'His name was Sir Ralph, I think. Sir Ralph of Oxham. Have you heard of him, I wonder?' Without giving the other man time to respond, he immediately moved on. 'Of course, it doesn't matter to us down here. It's irrelevant. If a knight swears fealty to a more powerful knight, he should be honoured for keeping to his vows. It is hard to condemn a man for holding to his oath if his master then decides to become, for example, a shaval-dore. In any case, we have enough trouble keeping the peace in this county without worrying about the affairs of others many hundreds of miles away. After all, there's this murder to think about, even if it was only the killing of a villein.'

Sir Ralph breathed out slowly, the exhalation whistling through his pursed lips. 'Yes,' he said raggedly. 'Murder is a more serious crime, isn't it?'

'Tell me, Sir Ralph. On the night that Peter Bruther died, you went to an inn with John, didn't you? We have been to that same inn today, and a girl there told us that you spent the evening with one of them, but that John was out riding.'

'Out riding? No, he told me he was there all night. He was certainly there when I returned to the room.'

'Asleep?'

'No, he was already awake, sitting by the fire.'

'Was this in daylight?'

'It was still dark. The cocks hadn't crowed yet.' There was little doubt in Simon or Baldwin's mind of Sir Ralph's sincerity. 'He was there all night, I thought,' he continued.

'Or at least, that was what he told me. I mean, where else could he have been?' His face went white as he suddenly realised what he had said.

'Sir Ralph, we would be very grateful if you did not mention anything about this conversation to John or his family,' said Baldwin quietly. 'You are not a fool, so I won't explain why.' The knight nodded again, slowly, his mind dwelling on the surprise revelation about his squire. 'And now, could you tell us what he was like while he was with you in the north?'

'Very good,' said Sir Ralph shortly. 'He always appeared brave, prepared to put himself at the front of any raiding party, whatever the risk. And he was bright, too – not a mindless thug like some: he could think an attack through. When it came to a defensive action, he was very quick to see the lie of the land and use it to best advantage, siting archers and men-at-arms effectively. I have to say, there was no better squire while I was in . . . the north.'

'Was he honest? Would you call him honourable?'

'Honourable, yes. He would make sure that a captive was well looked after until a ransom could be sought, and what more can a soldier do? I'm not aware that he ever mishandled a prisoner; he always looked after them.'

'You didn't answer the first question: was he honest?'

Sir Ralph thought back to the raids, the times when his leader, Gilbert, had led them out to the villages, to the churches and the priory. The clashing of the arms, the arguments over the spoils, the looting, women weeping at the sight of their dead men, and the inevitable, cynical smile on his squire's face as he looked to their portion of the profits, playing at dice with other soldiers and always winning their loot, secretly finding food while those same men starved, and his ability to lie to them, saying he was as hungry as they.

'No,' Sir Ralph said sadly. 'No, I do not think he was very honest. Not now I think back.'

Baldwin nodded slowly. From the expression on Sir Ralph's face, it was clear that the knight was seeing his squire in a new light. 'I think,' he said, 'we should see this other man-at-arms who was with Samuel Hankyn when he found the body, so that we can check his story.'

'Yes,' said Simon, his eyes still on the knight. 'What was his name?'

'Ronald Taverner.'

The start was unmistakable. Sir Ralph had been reaching for a pot of wine when Baldwin spoke, and on hearing the name, his hand almost knocked the drink from the table. He remained there, fixed, contemplating the pot in his hand as if to avoid meeting the gaze of the bailiff, then carefully set it back down.

'What is it, Sir Ralph?' asked Simon, his voice betraying his frank surprise.

The knight's face turned to him. He looked tragic, but without speaking he rose and strode quickly from the room, and Simon and Baldwin could only stare at each other in amazement.

George Harang walked carefully into the hall. He had managed to avoid his master for some hours by riding to the camp on the pretext of checking on the blowing-house, but the messenger had not left any room for doubt. 'Master Thomas wants you, George, and he wants you now. I don't think he's of a mind to wait,' the boy had said, and his eyes told of the urgency of his mission.

Questioning him on the way back, George found that Smyth had hardly moved from his seat at the fire since the bailiff and his friend had left. When the bottler had gone in to speak to him, he had been bellowed at, and since then all had left him alone. Then, after some hours, he had suddenly come back to life, roaring for wine and demanding George.

As he crossed the floor to where Smyth sat contemplating the small fire, chin cupped in one hand, the other resting idly on a hound's flank, George felt his anger mounting. This shrivelled old man was not his master. Thomas Smyth was a strong and courageous man known throughout the moors. The figure before him was that of a huddled old man, tired and weak after a lifetime of struggling.

'Master? I heard you wanted me,' George said tentatively, and the black eyes fixed on him.

'Wanted you?' Smyth sounded pensive, as if his mind was elsewhere, but then he stood, and George saw that he was not humbled, but consumed with rage. 'Of course I want you. Who else? That bailiff and his friend – what do you think of them?'

'I don't like the knight. The bailiff seems straightforward enough.'

'Oh, yes. Straightforward, certainly. But can we trust him? I don't think so. For a start, how well does he know this area? Not as well as us, George. And all the time he's here, he's staying with the Beauscyrs, listening to their poison about the miners and *me*! I don't like him and I don't trust him, and I think the Beauscyrs can wind him round their fingers like a ring. All that family wants is to see us off the moors, and while they've got the King's own man living with them, they can get him to think their way. In any case, I doubt he'd cost much to buy – most bailiffs are cheap enough.'

'Do you think he'll take their side, then?'

'I think we have to make sure he isn't going to. You'll need to keep an eye on them, George. Keep an eye on where they go and who they meet, and then we'll see, won't we?' His gaze turned away, and he stared once more at the fire. 'I think that bailiff could be a great danger to us, a real threat. And I want to make sure we're safe . . .'

# CHAPTER TWELVE

Ronald Taverner was lying on a palliasse below the hall, in a quiet room where he could rest. Samuel Hankyn knelt by his side, feeding him sips of hot sweetened ale. He watched his friend with concern. Gone was the cheerful lad he had known for so long. Now Ronald was pale and nervous, starting at the slightest noise. Chewing his lip, Samuel was angry to see how his friend had changed. As Simon and Baldwin entered, Samuel stepped back to the wall, throwing them a suspicious glare.

Simon felt claustrophobic in the small room. Only a little light crept through the narrow slit window in the wall and the open doorway. Apart from a bench, well chewed by wood-worm and rats, there was nowhere else to sit. The bailiff tried it tentatively. It appeared able to support him, but after giving it a cursory glance, Baldwin preferred to stand. Testing it with two bodies, he reasoned, could prove to be too dangerous.

Though he was used to seeing wounded men, the sight of this latest victim made the bailiff scowl with compassion. Taverner was little more than a boy from the look of him, a slight man in his late teens with an unruly shock of mousy hair above a narrow face with a high brow. Dark eyes met his with a look of trepidation and slender fingers plucked at the frayed edge of the worn blanket. Ronald Taverner was unused to meeting officials.

'What has happened to you?' asked Baldwin, and Simon could hear from his voice that the knight was as struck by the lad's condition as he.

'I got hurt in practice, sir.'

'How?' Baldwin could see no visible sign of a wound, but the stillness of the form under the blanket showed the degree of his suffering.

'Sir, it was while I was with John, sir. We were practising with blunted swords, and he caught my neck.'

'An accident, then.'

The quick glance shot at Samuel was seen by the bailiff and his friend. Simon leaned forward. 'Was it an accident?'

'Oh, yes, sir!' The boy's voice was emphatic, but his friend snorted in disgust.

'Samuel?' Simon said, looking up.

He needed no further prompting. The injustice of the attack had at first shocked him, but then his anger had been ignited, and through all the hours of looking after his companion he had found it growing. 'No, sir, it wasn't an accident. It was a warning,' he said bitterly.

'A warning?' His tone made Simon raise his brows. 'What do you mean? A warning about what?'

'Go on, Ronald, tell them. Tell them how that mad bastard nearly killed you. You might as well, you owe him nothing.'

Faltering, with many a glance at his friend, Ronald told of the match between himself and the younger of the two brothers, how he had tried to get his strike, how John had stumbled, then whipped his sword round hard. It was easy to recall. The memory of the sparkling agony in his head, the intolerable pain, was too vivid. He shuddered. 'It was just to teach me, he said, sir,' he finished miserably.

'Let me see,' demanded Baldwin, walking to the rough bed and kneeling. He examined the swollen and bruised neck for a moment before gently helping the white-faced boy to lie back again. Glancing at Simon, his eyes glittered with cold fury. 'This is ridiculous! His wound is far too heavy for a training session – that damned fool John must have tried to inflict as much pain as possible. This lad could have been killed.'

'What was he trying to teach you, Ronald?' said Simon, leaning forward.

'I . . .'

'Tell them, Ronald. There's no point keeping it back now. If they throw us out, at least we'll still be alive. If he does this to you again, like Sir Baldwin says, he might kill you. You don't want to end up like poor Peter, do you?' Samuel's voice betrayed his frustration.

'Well, sirs. It was to stop me telling anyone about me and Sir Ralph meeting Peter Bruther on the moors a little while before he was killed.'

Listening to the story, Simon felt his face creasing into a perplexed frown. When the boy finished, sinking back on his pillow with a slight gasp then wincing as he tried to wriggle into a more comfortable position, Baldwin and the bailiff exchanged a baffled glance.

'Tell me, Ronald,' said Simon after a minute or two of reflection, 'do you have any idea why what you have just told us should have led to your beating?'

'No, sir. I mean, unless—'

'Because John and his friend killed Bruther,' said Samuel flatly.

Simon considered him. 'John and Sir Ralph?'

'We saw them riding off together and they came back here together. It must have been them who killed Bruther, and John hurt Ronald here to stop him talking – maybe even meant to kill him.'

'Oh, come on, that's—'

'Why else? They wanted him to keep his mouth shut.'

'It would seem that Sir Ralph was with a woman all night at the tavern,' Baldwin said mildly. 'He could not have killed Bruther.'

'A slut from the tavern? If she was paid enough she'd probably say she was with him all year,' sneered Samuel. 'Those tavern tarts only want money. Are you saying you think she's honest?'

'But if you're right,' said Simon patiently, 'I don't understand why you think they would kill Bruther.'

With a quick movement Samuel pushed himself away from the wall. He found it hard to believe that the bailiff could be so naive. 'It's obvious! This Sir Ralph couldn't take the insult from a runaway villein, and he went back there with his squire to murder Bruther because of Bruther's rudeness. They didn't want anyone to hear about the affair. They tried to avoid having anything to connect Bruther to them.

That's why they had to have any rumour about the meeting on the moors quashed, because it shows why Sir Ralph wanted Bruther dead! A noble knight turning tail like a cur! What more reason do you need?'

'But that can't be it!' Ronald protested, gesturing weakly with a flapping hand. 'He's always been good to me, and generous, not like others. And after all . . .'

'I know all that,' said Samuel quickly, and Baldwin glanced keenly at him. The interruption was too hasty, he felt, but the man-at-arms met his questioning gaze unflinchingly. 'There was no one else out there, so who else could it have been? If you're right and this woman is telling the truth, maybe the knight *did* stay in the tavern that night – but was John there? He'd think an insult to his master was an insult to him too.'

Simon and Baldwin left the room shortly afterwards. There was nothing more to learn – or, as Baldwin ruefully admitted to himself, there was nothing more that the two men were prepared to divulge. When he spoke, his voice low and guarded against the servants running to and fro around them, the bailiff was deep in thought, and had to ask him to repeat his question.

'I said, "What do you think, Simon?"'

'It would make sense, wouldn't it?' Simon mused. 'If we didn't know Sir Ralph was at the tavern that night, the two of them would be perfect suspects – *if* what Ronald said was true. There's little I *wouldn't* think the Beauscyr sons capable of,' he added darkly.

'Simon, Simon, Simon!' Baldwin laughed. 'You mean John killed Bruther for the insult offered to his master? Do you not think that it would show a little too much loyalty?

From what I have seen of John, I would hardly expect him to be *that* devoted to anyone.'

'No. You're right. He's too self-confident to care what might be said about his master. And he cares nothing for the estate or his brother.'

'Did you notice how Samuel silenced his friend? Just when Ronald was saying how Sir Ralph was better than others, Samuel shut him up.'

'Yes. But I've no idea what the lad was going to say. Maybe we can question Taverner alone.'

Baldwin shook his head. 'Too late. From the way those two behaved in there, I would say that Samuel was the stronger – and he wanted whatever it was kept quiet. I expect Ronald will already have been persuaded to hold his tongue. He will do Samuel's bidding – who else will he feel he can trust here at the Manor after his injury?'

'Could it be that they saw John, do you think? Is that what Samuel was hiding?'

Shrugging, the knight's mouth drew into a doubtful crescent. 'I have no idea. At present we seem to have no lack of people who disliked Bruther, but nobody at whom we can point a finger. Unless Samuel decides we deserve to be let into his confidence, I begin to wonder whether we will ever learn more.' He frowned. 'Let us look at it the other way: who *was* on the moors that night and had reason to want Bruther dead?'

'We know from the serving girl that John left the inn. He could have joined his brother on the moors and committed the murder then.'

'It would have been possible. But the two of them hardly speak to each other without having a row.'

'That could be to hide their act! And it would fit in with John's attempt to conceal the meeting between Bruther and his knight, too!' He slapped his thigh in a brief display of delighted incisiveness.

'Wait!' said Baldwin, and put a hand to his friend's shoulder. 'Why would John have attacked Taverner?'

'To put suspicion on to Sir Ralph. He didn't try very hard to silence Taverner, did he? Just enough to anger the boy and his friend. If he was serious about it he'd have paid them money, not threatened and beaten him up. It almost guaranteed that the story would come out, treating the lad like that.'

Baldwin frowned and sighed. 'I'm not certain. From what I've seen, John may well feel that the only way to keep a man quiet is by fear. No, I think he probably did try to keep the story secret in the only way he knew how, and had no idea that it would all come out like this. He is a soldier, Simon, don't forget that. He was a shavaldore with Sir Ralph. They lived by robbing and extortion in all likelihood. It probably would not occur to him that he could get what he wanted by more subtle means. No, I think we must try to find out a lot more before we accuse anyone of this murder.'

Simon stared, but gradually his enthusiasm faded to be replaced by a sombre reflection. 'Very well, Baldwin. But I think I may be right.'

'You may well be. But for now we are living in the Manor of the boys' father, and you should be careful how you proceed. We have no proof of anything, only guesses. All we really know is that there were two strange characters on the moors that night and no one seems to know who they were. Apart from that it is all conjecture.'

'In that case we must get some proof.' Simon began to walk to die hall, but then suddenly stopped dead.

'What is it, Simon?'

'Baldwin! Bruther: he had a group of miners with him, according to Ronald Taverner! Why . . . come!'

He led the way to the stairs and climbed them swiftly. At the top, Baldwin followed him along the line of the wall to where Sir Ralph stood peering out, his hands on the battlements. Hearing their approach, he turned slowly, then sighed.

'Sir Ralph, we have heard about your meeting with Peter Bruther out on the moors,' Simon said as they drew near.

'I guessed you would.' His lip curled bitterly. 'It's the sort of thing a man-at-arms would not forget, a knight running from a rabble.'

'We must know exactly what happened. It could have a bearing on the murder.'

'You mean, you think I might have killed the fellow.' His eyes searched their faces for a moment. Their doubts were all too obvious, and he knew he would be suspicious if he was in their position. 'It is true that I was humiliated,' he admitted, 'but that's no reason to kill!'

'You should've told us before, Sir Ralph,' said Simon shortly. 'It would've saved us time, and stopped us having to wonder about you. As it is, you can make up for your mistake now. We understand you met Bruther and tried to bring him back?'

'Yes. He was digging among the rocks when we saw him and I wanted to get a closer look. Then he insulted me, and I was going to punish him for it. And it would have helped my host, of course, to have his runaway brought back. I thought Sir William would be grateful. But it was impossible.'

'Of course. You were thwarted by the men with him?'

'Yes.' The knight's face twisted into a grimace of self-reproach. 'I should have ignored them, but . . .'

'How many men were there?'

'Oh, I don't know. Seven, maybe eight.'

'And how were *they* with *him*? Simon asked, frowning.

'What do you mean?'

Baldwin interrupted. 'What were they like with him? Was he scared of them, do you think? Could they have been his friends? Were they guards holding him – or were they protecting him?'

Blank amazement stole over the features of the knight. 'I have no idea. I . . . They seemed well-enough disposed towards him, that much I know. They didn't strike me as being his enemies.'

'So you would not say that he was being held by them against his will?' Baldwin persisted.

'If he were, he would hardly have been so rude to me, would he? He would have tried to come away with me. Anyway, why on earth should he have been held by his own kind?'

'You felt that? That they were his own kind?'

'God in Heaven!' Sir Ralph's patience was running dry. 'Of course they were! They were miners, weren't they? So was he!'

'Think, Sir Ralph,' Baldwin said calmly. 'Are you quite sure about it? You are sure they were his friends! Not just holding a man who happened to be a miner? How did they behave?'

Sir Ralph stared. 'They . . .' He broke off. 'Now I come to think about it, they *were* almost like a guard. They stood around, but none of them spoke, as if he was their leader. If they had all been equals, I suppose I would have expected more of them to speak, but only he did.'

'While you were with your woman, you said you did not know that John had left the inn,' Simon stated.

'That's right. I had no idea he had left.'

'So you don't know how long he might have been gone for? Or whether he could have made it to Bruther's place?'

Throwing his hands in the air, Sir Ralph felt he was being tested beyond endurance. He stared at the bailiff in exasperation. 'In God's name! How could I know? Until you told me, I had no idea he had gone!'

Baldwin leaned against the battlement and folded his arms. 'We don't know what to think. But it does seem as though John had an opportunity to kill Bruther. It was light when you got to the inn, wasn't it?' He nodded. 'And was it still light when you were with the woman?'

'I suppose so. The shutters were over the windows. I couldn't say.'

'So it comes to this. John knew that Bruther had insulted you, his master. He knew Bruther had caused problems for his father and the Manor. And we know he had the chance to kill Bruther because he disappeared for some time.'

'But surely others had more reason to kill than he?'

'Possibly, but we can't ignore the fact that John seems to have had the chance as well as reasons aplenty. Did he kill while he was in the north with you?'

Sir Ralph wetted his lips nervously. 'It's possible,' he managed after a moment.

'So he could have killed again.' Baldwin's tone was definite, and Sir Ralph slowly nodded. They had no more questions and a few minutes later he left them, walking meditatively over to the stairs. They watched him slowly crossing the courtyard to the hall.

'Now I think Sir Ralph feels sure it is his squire,' said Baldwin.

'Yes, but he could be wrong. Don't forget, the three men working for Thomas Smyth could have been telling the truth when they said they were told not to attack Bruther,' Simon reminded him. 'From Sir Ralph's words, it would appear that Bruther was *protected* by miners, so it must be less likely that it was Smyth's men who killed him. But why would that be? Why was Thomas *not* after this one man to go away and leave the area? If he was so determined to have Henry Smalhobbe and others thrown off the moors, what would've made him let Bruther stay?'

'From all we have heard, this Peter Bruther was no coward. He seems to have been prepared to stand up for himself against his master, Sir Ralph – *anyone*. Perhaps he fought against Thomas Smyth as well. After all, we do not know who these other miners were who defended him against the worthy knight. Maybe there were others like him and Smalhobbe – a little group of the weak protecting themselves against the strong.'

'Possibly. We must speak to Henry Smalhobbe and ask him about that.'

'We could go and ask the miners, too, of course, but I doubt whether we'd find out much more than we have already learned,' mused Baldwin.

'No. It's Smalhobbe I wish to see. I want to know more about that man's past.'

\*       \*       \*

At his hut Henry Smalhobbe paused at the door and dropped his sack of tools with a sigh of satisfaction. Hearing the clatter, Sarah rushed to the doorway and twitched the curtain aside, gasping with relief as she saw her husband. She had been on edge and anxious ever since the attack, and especially after hearing about poor Peter's death. From that appalling day onwards she had not been able to relax.

The air was still and humid, and she had felt on the brink of fainting all day in the smothering heat. Even the birds had seemed to find it too exhausting to sing, apart from an occasional lark. There had been a haze which had hidden the further hills when she stared out to the south and east, and the land nearer shimmered under the smothering blanket of intense dry heat.

As she performed her chores, sweeping the hard-packed earth of the floor, washing a tunic and mixing dough, Sarah Smalhobbe could sense a brooding danger all round as if the moors themselves hated her and wanted both her and her husband to die. These moors were not soft and gentle like the northern ones nearer their old home, they were brutal and unfeeling, and she could feel them watching her.

She was not fanciful, but the tales of the old man of the moors, Crockern, kept crowding back into her mind. How the spirit hated men, hated the way that the tinners dug deep into his body to bring up his riches, disturbing the grey rocks which were his bones. This might be the fourteenth century, but she could feel the weight of his disapproval, and though she was Christian, she knew better than to tempt him here in his own land.

At least her husband was back safe again. She hugged him, feeling the tears close once more, and even when she heard his short gasp of pain as she gripped him, squeezing his bruised chest, she could not let go. It was too good to be able to hold him after the loneliness of the day.

Henry caressed her fondly and kissed her head. The pain was receding, though one arm was still almost useless. He had only gone to his workings to make sure that no one else was stealing his ore, but nobody had been there all day, and he had spent much of his time merely sitting and wondering about their future here. The miners working for Smyth were becoming more violent, and he was not going to be able to protect himself and his wife from their attacks if they continued. Perhaps they should leave now, while they still could, before any fresh assault? But to do that would be to admit defeat.

As his wife's grip tightened, he smiled through his pain. He could not bear to see her suffer, and if he was to run away with her, how could they earn a living? They had no profit yet from his workings, and they had lost all their belongings before they arrived. He gently stroked her back and led her inside the hut, where they sat and ate their bread in silence. There was no need to speak. Both knew the nature of their peril and the risks of taking to the road again. If nothing else, it was possible that one of their old enemies might discover them. At least here on the moors they were protected by the stannaries. Out in open country they could be challenged, and it was not so very far to their old home. Henry knew that they might be able to get to Cornwall, to the mining areas there, but who was to say it would be any better?

After eating, and drinking a little of the ale Sarah had brewed, he stood, stretching. Groaning with a mixture of pain and pleasure as tired and knotted muscles ground under the bruises, he smiled at her, then walked outside.

The moors glistened under a full moon, the rolling hills and plains coloured silver-grey, as if illuminated by an inner light. They looked as if they were covered in a thin frost which lay as light as down over the stark landscape. Now, in the early evening, he felt aware of how ancient this land was, and how different from the pleasant woods and farmland around their old home in Bristol. He sat, his wife beside him, and they stared out together, lost in their thoughts and heedless of the world. They did not speak. There was no need, they simply sat and pondered, enjoying each other's companionship and the coolness of the evening.

They were so engrossed they did not notice the riders making their way towards them until a hoof clattered on a stone, and then Sarah clutched her husband's arm as Thomas Smyth bellowed and cantered towards them.

# CHAPTER THIRTEEN

Supper that evening was a dismal affair, though John
Beauscyr found it amusing. Simon, Baldwin and their men
sat at the table on the dais with the family, and servants filled
the hall beneath them, but there was a stilted quality to the
atmosphere. Sir Ralph, John saw, was sullen, and moodily
chewed his food scarcely aware of the others near him, as if
he was already marked out as a coward or murderer. On the
few occasions when he caught John's glance, he looked
away hurriedly, almost guiltily. Matillida was snappy, and
short with the servants, at one point flinging a pot at a man's
head and screeching at him when he spilled wine on her
dress, while Sir William ate quietly with a determined
concentration, trying to avoid the gaze of his guests and
family alike.

For his part, John was carefree and enjoying himself. His
only cause for concern was Robert, his brother. He sat quietly
but with a degree of nonchalance as he fastidiously pulled

shreds of meat apart and ate them, which John found disturbing. If I were the bailiff, he thought, I'd want to know why he seems so free of all worries now. Out of the corner of his eye he kept a surreptitious watch on his older brother, looking for any signs which might explain his evident easiness, but as the meal finished and his father and mother made their way into their solar, the servants leaving for their rooms and the guards going to their duties or barracks, he was still no wiser.

Baldwin could see the boy's interest in his brother, and wrily acknowledged his own fascination with Robert's demeanour. The latter was apparently finding it hard to contain his amusement or joy. Something must have happened this afternoon, he thought. As the room emptied, Baldwin rose. Seeing Robert making for the door, he strolled after him, only dimly aware of Edgar, who immediately stood and followed. After so many years, Edgar's presence was only remarkable when it was absent.

Seeing his prey in the stables patting a horse, Baldwin motioned to Edgar to wait, then walked over to join him.

'So, Sir Baldwin. Are you following me?' Robert Beauscyr raised an eyebrow as if to suggest sardonic amusement.

'No. But I thought I might as well come outside and enjoy the evening air when I saw you leave.'

There was good reason for his words. The sun was slowly dropping, and the sky had taken on a pink and mauve tint, making the fort and surrounding hills look like a varnished picture, smooth and gleaming. It reminded Baldwin of the fine silks he had seen traded in Cyprus. He felt as if he could reach out and touch the warm, vibrant colours. The sun had washed Robert in glowing hues. His face looked almost golden, transforming his normally dull features.

But it was not only the colour. There was an urgency to the youth's movements as he strolled round his horse. He was different now, more alive. Even when he spoke there was a new vitality to his voice. 'More questions? Or are you just a bored guest seeking entertainment?'

Baldwin's smile faded. He had known others who had been listless and vapid, only to become energised after violence. After the death of Peter Bruther, he wondered whether Robert's new-found excitement had the same cause – whether Robert could have been the killer. 'You had a pleasant afternoon?' he asked, and was rewarded by a quick glance.

'Yes, thank you, Sir Baldwin,' he said mockingly. 'I had a very pleasant ride, uninterrupted either by my brother's needling or your questioning. I trust you had an enjoyable time too?'

Ignoring the jibe, Baldwin stepped forward and stroked the horse's rump. 'I am sure you would have found it very boring. We asked questions of a lot of people, that is all. It is interesting, though, is it not, to speak to people you would not usually meet?'

'You've questioned the three we caught?' Robert peered at the knight with sudden concentration.

'Yes. Harold Magge and the others.' Baldwin was a little surprised to see that the young man had become reflective. 'Who beat them?'

'Beat them? What do you mean?'

'Just that. They have been beaten severely. Did you and your brother torture them?'

202

Sir Robert stared in astonishment. 'Why on earth would I have done that? We thought they were there so we hunted for them, but we had no time to harm them – as soon as we found them we were attacked by the others.'

Baldwin raised a doubtful eyebrow, and the young knight sighed and turned away. He looked sad now, deflated, and Baldwin was sorry to see how his happiness had fled. In a more conciliatory tone, he said, 'The three were very helpful.'

'What did they have to say?' As he spoke he moved further round the horse, so that now his face was hidden in the gloom of the stable and Baldwin could not see his features.

Sucking at his teeth to extract a fragment of meat, Baldwin said, 'They confirmed it was they who attacked Smalhobbe, though they deny absolutely having anything to do with the death of Bruther.'

'Did . . . did they see the two riders noticed by Samuel?'

A revealing question, Baldwin considered. 'Why such interest in the riders? Do you think it was they who committed the murder now? This morning you were convinced that it must be the miners.'

'I . . . well, they would hardly admit it themselves, would they? They will surely have tried to put the blame on to someone else. I just wondered if they had tried to accuse the two riders they saw. Did they say?'

Baldwin smiled and nodded. Now he was sure that at least one of the riders was known to him.

The next morning was dry but overcast as the four men set off from Beauscyr Manor, and Baldwin found the difference in the weather daunting. In the gloomy light the rolling plains and hills appeared more threatening on either side, their flanks invaded by dark-coloured heather, the higher points malevolent with their variously-shaped moorstone tors. Some looked like fantastic creatures waiting to spring, others like giants towering over the land seeking smaller creatures to crush. Although he was not usually given to unwarranted fears or superstitions, the sight of the massive shapes looming on all sides made him aware of how remote this place was from any town.

To his vague irritation, Simon was unaffected by the malign feel of the area. He rode on steadily, whistling tunelessly, and apparently unaware of the menace which the knight felt. In a strange way, his very lack of interest in the views was reassuring to Baldwin. His very unconcern seemed to keep the monsters Baldwin could sense at bay, as though they needed belief to make them whole. But it piqued his pride to find that for once it was he who was being superstitious.

They made their way west, then north by west until they came to a small group of trees – not like Wistman's Wood, Baldwin noticed, but ordinary, straight and tall oaks and chestnuts. Here they had to encircle a wide area of marsh-land, and to make a broad sweep before they could continue riding along well-trodden tracks of packed earth up and down the gentle slopes of the moorland hills until they came to a brook. Trailing along its banks, they continued northwards, Simon leading the way. A scattering of trees rose around them. At last the sun broke free of the silvery clouds above, and they were enclosed in a verdant glow as it glimmered through the leaves.

Coming to a clapper bridge, where a massive block of stone had been laid over the stream, Simon turned right. Here there was a track leading east, and they were soon out of the trees, climbing a slight hill. At the top Simon slowed, and here Baldwin caught his first sight of Adam Coyt's farm.

It was a well-cared-for barton, lying a scant half-mile from the road in the lee of a wooded hill which protected it from the worst of the winter storms. The long house was sturdy and strong, built of moorstone which was hidden under the white lime render. A few yards away was a byre, with three outbuildings leaning close by as if for warmth. From the roof of the house came a thin ribbon of smoke which was immediately wafted away by the gusting wind.

From the barn where he was axing branches from a series of tree trunks, preparing them for cutting into manageable planks, Adam Coyt watched them approach with slitted, suspicious eyes. Strangers out here were a rarity, and letting the axe drop from his hand, he walked out to meet them.

Hugh was relieved to fall from his horse. He knew full well that today his master wished to travel widely and see several people, and was determined to take his rest when he could. Seeing Adam walk up, he nodded. From his youth in Drewsteignton he recognised the sort of man he was. Hard as the elements, as much formed of the land around him as any of the trees in his little wood, this was one of the old Dartmoor men.

Simon dropped from his mount and smiled reassuringly. 'Good morning. I—' As he spoke, two sheepdogs suddenly bolted from the barn and stood snarling before him.

Giving a whistle, Adam commanded them to be silent without even glancing in their direction, and Simon was

205

relieved to see them obey. Both immediately sat, and one began to scratch, changing in an instant from wild animals with slavering jaws into friendly companions with wide smiling mouths. At home with dogs, Baldwin ambled over to them, let them smell his hands briefly, and began to stroke them, and soon was engulfed as they ecstatically panted and slobbered over and around him, almost knocking him from his knees in their enthusiasm.

'He likes dogs,' Simon said, more by way of apology than explanation, and Adam nodded again, this time in frank astonishment that any man could wish to coddle a working animal. To his way of thinking it was a certain sign of lunacy, the same as petting a cow or a lamb. There was no profit in behaving that way with farm animals.

After Simon's introductions, the farmer grunted his assent to answering the bailiff's questions and led the way to the log-pile. Foreigners were welcome, his actions showed, to pass their time any way they wished, but he still had a living to earn and work to do. Their enquiry was conducted to the steady chop of his hatchet.

Regretfully leaving the dogs, Baldwin squatted on a thick trunk while Simon stood nearby. It was Simon who began.

'Adam, you've lived here all your life. Have things changed much over the years?'

Without looking up, the farmer considered for a moment. 'No. The moors are the moors. They change with the seasons, but that's all.'

'Have the miners made a difference?'

'They've got more greedy. Before, there was only a small number. Now there's lots, and a few own all the mines. Used to be that all tinners were like that Bruther or Smalhobbe, just one or two men with a little place. Now there're lots all covering the same bit for the likes of Thomas Smyth.'

'I suppose at least you're safe up here, anyway. There aren't many come all this way to trouble you.'

The axe paused, then fell again. 'If you've got rights of pasturage, they come close enough. They dig all over the place, and leave their holes in the ground for animals to hurt themselves in. I had a heifer break her leg last year, but I can't get money from the miners, they claim stannary privileges. I lost my cow, but I'll get no help from them even though it was their fault.'

'And it's worse than it used to be?'

'Ah, yes. Time was, they used to come no closer than five miles from here. Now they're only a mile away, and right where I lead the herd.'

'And you think they're being greedy?'

'We have ancient rights here, bailiff, we who live in the common land of the moors. We've been here since time out of mind, my family and a few others, but now our lives are being made hard by some few foreigners. There are robberies done by some – there was one on the night Bruther died. They demand money not to take our land, and if they aren't paid, they dig it and take the water so we can't use it. But we can do nothing. Who's going to protect us who live out here if the miners choose to attack us or steal what's ours?'

'You say there was a robbery? Who was attacked?'

Adam Coyt jerked his head in the direction of Widecombe in the Moor. 'Old Wat Meavy at Henway. He was knocked down and had his purse taken.'

'I wasn't told,' said Simon with a frown.

'When these things happen, we can't run to Lydford every time. Anyway, one minute he was riding into Chagford, and the next he was on his bum in the middle of the road and lighter by some pennies. There are too many miners out here to worry about just another robbery, bailiff. It happens all the time.'

'And it's getting worse, from what you say.'

'Yes.' He suddenly looked up and pulled a wry smile, shrugging. 'But isn't it the same all over the country? The King's warden knows how things are going, doesn't he? From all I hear, it's not just here, it's everywhere.'

'But if people are suffering badly, you should tell the chief warden, or at least me as a bailiff. We might—'

'Suffering badly!' the farmer cried, and let the axe fall from his hand. 'And what do you think has been happening here? Whole vills have emptied with the bitter weather, the last people leaving before the land eats them up, like it has their fathers, their mothers, their wives and children. Do you need us to come and tell you how places like Hound Tor have emptied? The menfolk worked on while their women sickened and their children died, just as we have to, we farmers. We have our farms to look after, but what good are they when our boy-children are gone? Why keep toiling and straining when there is no one to pass your profits to? Up at Hound Tor, there were only three left, out of eleven four years ago: all dead, all gone! Had you not heard, bailiff?'

His wide, staring eyes held a misery and near-desperation which struck like a mace at Simon's heart. The famine had been appalling, he knew, but somehow he had never associated it with the troubles here on the moors. During the worst of the suffering he had still been living at Sandford, far to the north and east, where the farms were not so badly affected.

Seeing the understanding on the bailiff's face, Adam bent slowly and painfully to retrieve his axe. Grunting as he straightened, he peered at it as if he no longer recognised it. When he spoke, his voice was contemplative. 'I had a wife and a son – just the one, the other children all died young; they have to be hardy to survive out here. There's no midwife, no wetnurse to help. There was always only me, and often enough I was out working when my wife gave birth. I think it was the last birth that was so hard on her, she never really recovered afterwards. She looked so pale and weak for the next year and a half. Then when she had been out working one afternoon, she died in a snowstorm on her way home. And then my boy started to fade too.' He blinked suddenly, then swung the axe viciously. 'I'm not alone,' he said resolutely. 'There are many like me round here. Lots of us have lost our own, had to take them to Widecombe or Lydford when the snow cleared to have them buried. We've all suffered enough. So if we forgot to tell you before, sir, at least you know now.'

Baldwin had been silent, but now he cleared his throat and leaned forward. To offer sympathy would have been insulting, he knew, and would have been taken as patronising. 'Adam, could you tell us about the night Peter Bruther died. Where were you that day?'

The axe dropped and a branch leapt away. Picking up the twigs, the farmer tossed them onto the growing pile by the door, then sighed and walked out, crossing the yard to the house, returning with a large earthenware jug which he upended, taking a long draught. Wiping his mouth with the back of his hand, he passed it to the knight, who smiled appreciatively. Tipping it, Baldwin found it was filled with cider so strong he could hardly swallow, and he had to control an urge to cough at the pungent fumes. It was with relief that he passed it on to Simon.

'That afternoon, I was up to the north of here, seeing to some peat up near Longaford Tor, where the ground is flat before the marsh. I often go there, it's good fuel,' Coyt said, glancing at the bough before him. 'And wood is not plentiful here. It's too valuable to burn. Anyway, it took longer than I expected, and my old pony isn't as fast as she used to be when she has a weight to carry, so I was late coming home. I was near the Smalhobbe place just as dusk fell. Young Henry, he was game, I'll say that for him. He tried to get one of the men waiting, but there were two others got him first.'

'Did you try to get help?'

'Help? Up there? Where would you expect me to go? The nearest place was that miner's, Bruther's, about a mile or so north, and how was I to know that one miner would want to help another? It was miners attacking Henry, and what good would bringing another do? And what difference would one more make? Even if I ran all the way there, the three would have been gone by the time I got back.'

'How was his wife?'

'She was making a row – screaming and such. But the men didn't hear her. They just kept beating her man.'

'Was anyone else out there?'

'I saw a couple of riders before, while I was cutting peat.'

'Did you see who they were?' asked Baldwin sharply.

Coyt glanced at him in faint surprise. 'I think it was that miner, Smyth, and his man. They were off north of Smalhobbe's.'

'What, heading up towards Bruther's?' Simon demanded.

'Yes, up that way, I suppose,' Coyt said disinterestedly.

'You're sure it was them?'

'They passed me later on the road, just as it was getting really dark. I recognised their horses. It was them.'

'I see.' Simon and Baldwin exchanged a glance. If the men were coming along the road, they were coming from the direction of Wistman's Wood. Baldwin continued, 'And you kept going south-east?'

'Yes, down to the road, then over and east. There's a path there which brings me to my door. It took some time with my poor old pony.'

'And you saw nobody else on the road? No one else passed you?'

'No. At least . . .' He frowned again.

'It could be important,' Baldwin prompted.

'I don't know, but someone did overtake me, just about when I got to the road to Chagford. It was dark by then, but there was someone north of me, riding quietly. I didn't see who.'

'How long after you saw the pair of riders would that have been, do you think?'

'Not very long. I had to cross the Cherry Brook, and the pony was slow, but not more than a few minutes.'

'He was far off?'

'I didn't look.' The farmer's voice had fallen to a sullen mutter, and his axe rose and fell only sluggishly as he was pressed.

'Why? Surely it was strange to hear a rider at that time of night, especially off the road?'

Face reddening, the farmer struck again at the log and made no answer.

'Coyt? I said, why didn't you look?'

Suddenly the farmer whirled and faced him, not aggressively, hut with belligerent shame. 'Because I thought it could be Old Nick. That's why!'

'Old—'

Simon quickly interjected. 'The Devil, Baldwin. The Devil.' And Adam Coyt turned and walked away from them.

As soon as he was out of earshot, Baldwin threw up his hands in despair. 'The Devil! In God's name! Why do these people still insist on such ridiculous beliefs? If he'd only glanced round, he could have seen who it was. It could have been Robert, John – or neither! But because of a stupid—'

'Not so stupid, Baldwin,' said Simon shortly. 'He had no idea that someone had been killed, had no idea that the rider so near could have been involved. These moorland farms are so remote, far from anyone. Have you not felt the loneliness of the moors? It is easy for a man's mind to turn to things like this out here. And there are many stories about the Devil.'

'Simon, really! That's no excuse. If this man had just taken a quick look, he might have—'

'I might have what?' Adam Coyt had returned unnoticed. '*You* don't know these moors, you haven't been out here. You don't live here all year like I do, and you haven't seen the things the moors can do to a man. You just can't understand like we do. Take that man Bruther. Yes, the horse riding past me might have been carrying his murderer – but so what?'

'What do you mean?' Baldwin's face was screwed into a mask of irritated confusion.

'Bruther brought it on himself. He was far out into the moors, and the moors look after themselves, that's all I'm saying. This area is all different when you live here. You might think I'm foolish to believe in Old Nick or Crockern. It's easy for *you*. You'll leave here and go back to your own village. Me, I've got to stay and live here. And I can't do that if the land won't let me. Bruther didn't believe either, he thought it was all superstition. I heard him once, laughing at the thought that Crockern might decide to have revenge on miners living too far out on his moor. He said he didn't mind Crockern, he said he'd offer a fair price. It doesn't do to make fun of the spirits on their own land.'

'So you think it was this Crockern who killed Bruther? Not the Devil?' Baldwin's tone was derisive.

'I don't know. And I don't care. Whoever killed him was keeping Crockern happy, that's all I know.'

# CHAPTER FOURTEEN

'Myths and superstitions!' Baldwin muttered frustratedly as the four left Coyt's house and began to follow the road into the moors. If the man had only looked, they might now have a fresh witness, or at least the name of someone who could have seen who the two riders were. It was possible that this man could have been Bruther's murderer, too.

'If men behaved normally and ignored the old wives' tales,' he said bitterly, 'not only would they be less scared all the time, they would probably manage to work better and be happier in their lives. Crockern and Old Nick!'

Simon smiled faintly at the knight's disgust. 'There's not much else here for people, though, Baldwin. Anyway, the question is, who *was* on that horse?'

'If we take the word of that farmer, it was the Devil.'

Simon knew how little regard his friend had for the old stories – Baldwin had ridiculed them often enough before. The knight was a well-travelled man, with more experience of the world, and Simon found it hard to argue the case with him. Even so, he found the knight's irascible outbursts against deeply held local beliefs very insulting.

'Simon?' Baldwin gave him a shame-faced grin. 'I am sorry – but I have seen too many people harmed by rumours and stories to want to have any truck with them. You are right, old friend. We need to discover who the single rider was. It could have been one of the Beauscyr sons, of course. Robert can give us little account of where he went that night, and John was away from the inn, although he has not admitted this to us yet.'

The bailiff was mollified by his change in mood. 'So now we must try to find out about three men, not two,' he mused. 'The pair of riders seen by Samuel and Ronald, and the single one heard by Coyt.'

'Yes. It is odd, though.' Baldwin's face was pensive. 'After talking to Sir Robert, I could have sworn he was one of the two riders – he looked so guilty. Perhaps he was the lone rider who later overtook Coyt?'

'But if he was, did he kill Bruther? Or were Smyth and his man responsible? And if it was Smyth who killed Bruther, what *was* Sir Robert doing out there?'

'If it truly was him,' Baldwin murmured. 'Anyway, the killer must belong to one of the two groups, surely? Miners or men of the Beauscyr demesne.'

'I think so, yes. Unless . . .' Baldwin glanced at him. Simon chewed his lip and shrugged. 'There is another group, I suppose, Baldwin. Farmers, like Coyt himself, have been affected as well. Their moors are being dug, the water in their streams diverted, their pastures ruined.'

'Is that reason enough to kill?'

They had arrived at the clapper bridge again, and Simon let his horse pause to drink. 'I don't know. It depends on what people thought of Bruther, doesn't it? What sort of person was he? From Sir Ralph's story he would appear to have been a bold enough fellow, at least when he had other people with him he was. And he was rude to Robert, too, just before we first came here.'

'Yes. Most say he was a rash young man, always making enemies,' Baldwin admitted. 'Though Smyth spoke well enough of him.'

'It's not like olden times when villeins were always subservient. This man seems to have taken wilfulness to an extreme. I mean, how many runaways would dare to insult two men like Sir Robert, his master until recently, and Sir Ralph, a man who is well-versed in battle and clearly prepared to defend his name?'

'He did not, though, did he?'

'No, but only because there were a number of miners there and it would have been foolish.'

'The same goes for when Sir Robert was insulted by Bruther. The fellow must have had a death-wish to have been so forthright.'

Simon stared at his friend. 'Baldwin, how often have you seen people behave that way?'

'A villein, you mean? Never.'

'What about other men?'

Shrugging, Baldwin drew his mouth into a glum crescent. 'For someone to be rude to a knight is mad, and—'

'You miss my point. The only time I've seen people intentionally demean a knight or a man-at-arms is when they *knew* themselves to be the more powerful!'

'Well, yes, but you are surely not suggesting that a mere serf could feel himself more powerful than, say, Sir Robert? One only has to look at them to see how different they are. One is poor and lives in a rude hovel, while the other is wealthy, the heir to a great hall and money, with a rich estate, and born into the King's highest esteem. How on earth could a miserable peasant like Bruther think he was the equal of such a man – let alone superior.'

'But he *did* didn't he?' His horse was watered, and Simon kicked its flanks to cross the stream. 'He did think he was at least equal, to have dared to speak so forwardly. He knew how he was considered by the Manor: as a runaway. And yet he faced them and bested them.'

'Only because of the men with him,' Baldwin protested.

'And why did he feel safe with them?'

'Well, because they were miners like himself, I would imagine. You yourself told me that the miners have their own laws and rules down here. No doubt he knew that with others of his kind he would be safe enough.'

'No, Baldwin. We know that Thomas Smyth is a harsh master, and he's enforcing his will on the miners round here, that's why Smalhobbe was beaten, wasn't it?'

'Well, yes, but perhaps Bruther banded together with other small miners in the area for protection from Smyth?'

'If there was such a group, they failed pretty miserably, didn't they? If you were going to organise men, and then insulted your enemies, would you leave the others and go home alone in the evenings? I doubt it! After making your mark with an enemy you'd all want to stick together for defence.'

'Yes, I suppose you are right,' said Baldwin musingly.

217

'So, if Bruther had so many men with him, why was he apparently alone and defenceless on the night he died? Where had the others gone, and why? Why had they left him there?'

'Perhaps they had a disagreement with him? Maybe they wanted to do something which he disapproved of, and—'

'No, no, no – do you remember how Sir Ralph described his meeting with Bruther? It was like the younger man was in charge, wasn't it? He was the only one who spoke – none of the others did. And it was the same when he insulted Sir Robert. Bruther spoke, the others simply observed and fingered their weapons. No, I think he was in charge, but *why* was he left all alone? If a leader disagrees with his company, some may leave, but others will stay, even if it's only a few.'

'Perhaps they did. There might have been others with him when Bruther was killed, but they escaped before they too could be hurt.'

'I don't think so. Look at it like this: we are working on the assumption that there were three people on the moors nearby that night. If Bruther had even one other man there with him it would have been hard for three to take him on without one of them getting hurt or killed.'

'Well, then. Maybe they did. Maybe they killed the other and threw his body into a bog. And even if they didn't, if it was one of the knights, they might have been happy to have simply got the man they hated and not cared about the others. You are building bricks without straw, old friend. All of this is guesswork, nothing more.'

Simon shook his head. 'I don't think so. Let's visit Smalhobbe. Maybe he can shed some light.'

\*     \*     \*

Following the trail, they were retracing the steps of Adam Coyt on the night of the murder, and Baldwin found himself glancing around with interest. The road ran reasonably straight, keeping to the lower ground. Stunted shrubs lined the roads, with occasional clumps of heather. After a short way, a small copse appeared, with hills rising on either side. When he asked, Simon told him that this area was called Bellever. The main east-west road was only another mile away, and they should be able to quickly cover the ground beyond to where the outlying miners lived.

The Smalhobbes' property looked more cheerful now. Smoke drifted idly from the roof, and the grey stone building set in the broad plain appealed to Baldwin. It was the picture of tranquillity, curiously at odds with the recent savage events.

Before the door was Sarah Smalhobbe, seated on a stool and plucking the feathers from a hen while others pecked madly and scratched at the ground. She gave them a slow smile of welcome and called for her husband. After a minute he joined them.

'Bailiff, Sir Baldwin,' he said, ducking his head to them respectfully.

'Henry, we'd like to speak with you for a little,' Simon said, climbing from his horse and passing the reins to Hugh. Smalhobbe looked very tired, he could see, but well enough apart from that. At least he could walk again. The miner was clad in a heavy leather jacket over a thin woollen shirt and short hose. A long knife was at his thick belt. His left arm was wrapped in cloth from the wrist to the elbow, and there was a bruise on one cheek and a cut over a blackened eye.

Smalhobbe sat on his wife's stool and sighed. 'It still hurts to move more than a few yards, sirs. My back is one mass of lumps and bumps where the whoresons laid into me.'

'They won't be back,' said Simon shortly. 'The men have been found, and they are being held at the miners' camp.'

'What, by more of Thomas Smyth's miners?' His face registered dismay. 'But they were his men! You can't trust him to keep them guarded, he'll want them to get out and carry on.' He stared at them both, then at his wife, who stood a short way off, listening with an air of dejected concern.

'They will not, I think,' said Baldwin reassuringly. 'They will have other things to occupy them. Thomas Smyth will not come out here again for quite some time, if he ever does.'

The miner did not look convinced. His eyes flitted over the horizon as if expecting to see bands of marauders approaching at any moment.

Simon tried to gain his attention. 'Henry, we are finding it difficult to discover who could have killed Bruther. Who do you think might have done it? Do you think it was the same men who attacked you?'

'Harold Magge and the others, you mean?' The miner stared at him. 'No, I doubt it. Beating someone up – they could do that . . . but killing Peter? I don't think so.'

'You had seen no one else that night, until you were set upon?'

'No, nobody. I was at my works all day and it was quiet.'

'You never went near Wistman's?'

'No.'

Baldwin interrupted. 'You were late home. Why?'

'I was smelting,' he said simply. 'It sometimes takes time.'

Simon nodded. 'Do you know who Bruther's friends were?'

'Friends?'

Squatting before him, Baldwin held his gaze. 'We know he had several men with him in the days before his death. Sir Robert Beauscyr saw them with him, so did Sir Ralph of Warton – some seven or eight men who looked as if they were miners too. Do you have any idea who they were?'

The miner looked hopelessly at his wife. 'No, I don't know.'

Baldwin saw her quick glance, the pleading expression in her husband's eyes, and knew the man was lying. 'Very well,' he said quietly. 'Perhaps you can tell us this, then. What sort of a man was Peter Bruther?'

'He was a miner,' Smalhobbe said off-handedly. 'He had not been here for long, and he was learning how to get tin, the same as me.'

'Yes, but what was he like? If we know what sort of man he was, we may be able to guess why someone should want to murder him.'

'He was quick, and self-assured, I suppose. It was hard for him to make friends and trust people, but he seemed happy enough.'

'Was he by nature aggressive?'

'Not that I saw. I mean, he was capable of a fight when he had been drinking, but that's all.'

'Did he often go drinking?'

'Once or twice a week. He used to go to the Fighting Cock over towards Chagford.'

Simon frowned. 'How could he afford that? Paying for ale in an inn should have been impossible for a man like him, a

221

runaway villein now working as a miner. Where did his money come from?'

Shrugging, Smalhobbe did not answer. It was confusing to the knight watching and listening. The miner clearly knew something he was not prepared to talk about. He had been attacked by miners, his neighbour had been murdered . . . and yet all he could do now was shrug sulkily. Sarah Smalhobbe's big brown eyes were still glued on her husband. She too was anxious, Baldwin could see, but he had no idea why.

Meanwhile the bailiff had moved on. 'So, you say he went to the inn a couple of times a week. Who did he mix with?'

'I never went with him, so I cannot say.'

'I see. But you heard of him getting into fights?'

'Yes. He once fought a merchant who he thought had insulted him, and then there was a moorman who he said was simple in the head.'

'Was it Adam Coyt?'

'I don't know.'

His attitude was beginning to annoy Baldwin, who leaned forward now and said harshly, 'There seems to be a lot you don't know today, Smalhobbe. Your nearest neighbour was a closed book to you. You have no idea who his friends were, you cannot recall anything about his money, fights, enemies or anything. Do you want to protect his murderer?'

Henry Smalhobbe stared at him, and now Baldwin saw his mistake. The man was not scared; the defiance in his eyes contained slyness, which spoke of self-interest. Then something occurred to the knight. He studied the chickens, and the miner began to look nervous.

'So, Henry. Who have you been to see this week? Or when did he come to see you?'

To Simon's amazement, the little man's face fell, and he stammered: 'Who, sir? I don't know who you mean, I . . .'

Baldwin rose, standing menacingly over the miner with his hands on his hips. For a moment Sarah thought the knight was going to hit him. 'Enough of this lying, Henry Smalhobbe!' he thundered. 'You have been paid to keep your silence, haven't you? When we first came to see you, you had no chickens. Where have these appeared from? Someone wishing you well, I have no doubt, for it is a goodly-sized little flock. Tell us who it was.'

'No, sir, honestly, they were—'

'Henry, we have to tell them the truth!' His wife dropped to her knees before him, her hands going to her husband's like an oath-giver, and like a man taking the homage due to him, her husband put his hands around hers as he stared into her face. 'Henry, tell them! They are trying to help people like us, who live out here on the moors,' she begged. 'Please, tell them!'

Smalhobbe's eyes rose to meet the bailiff's, and he sighed. 'Very well. I'll tell what I know.'

'Thank you,' said Simon with relief. 'The men with him. Who were they?'

'Miners from the camp. They work for Thomas Smyth. They used to stay out on the plain beyond Bruther's cottage, and help him work his plot.'

Baldwin scowled. 'You are telling me that Thomas Smyth would let his men go and help a man out on the moors?'

'I don't know why, sir. All I can say is what I know. Those men were his, and yet they helped Bruther.'

'Are you sure that they weren't miners from further north?' Simon asked. 'Couldn't Bruther have associated with other small tinners for all of their defence?'

'No. You see, I knew some of the men from when we first came down here to the moors. We met them during our journey to Dartmoor, and they reappeared with Bruther.'

'What were they doing there?' said Simon, puzzled.

'Protecting him. It was known that he was a runaway – oh, there are probably plenty of villeins here in the moors, it's the best place in the world to hide – but Bruther came from a manor close by, so he could have been caught and taken back at any time. He needed men to look after him.'

'Why on earth should Thomas Smyth protect him?' Simon demanded. 'He wanted people like you and Bruther off the moors, I thought.'

'He wanted me off,' admitted Smalhobbe. 'But Bruther? I don't know. His works were some way out, deep into the moors, away from the roads and so on. Maybe Smyth didn't care about the land up there. I know the only reason he wanted my plot was because he thought it should be his, and it was that bit closer to his camp. Maybe Bruther's place was just too far away for it to be worth scaring a man off.'

'But still, why would he send men to protect the man?'

'Smyth would want any miner to be safe from the attacks of a foreigner,' explained Smalhobbe. 'Anyone who came here to take Bruther would be stating to the world that the miners were just ordinary people, without special rights. Smyth is a strong, bold man. He would not want to have others think him weak, or any other miner on the moors, either. How many of his own men are trying to lose their pasts by coming here? How many were draw-latches, robbers-men or outlaws? How many of his miners would Smyth lose if anyone could come to the moors and take their runaways back with them? He would not want that, it could disrupt all his workings. I think he felt he had to look after Bruther, to protect the other men in his camp.'

Simon took a few minutes to consider this. He saw the knight nod slowly in agreement: it made sense. Many barons would behave in the same way, putting men in to protect a neighbouring small fort, not for profit, but just to deter a possible aggressor. 'Very well,' he said eventually, 'but why were these men not with him on the night he died?'

'That I do not know, sir.'

'Do you have any idea why he should have been at Wistman's Wood?'

Shaking his head, the miner said, 'No.'

Baldwin asked, 'You said he used to go to the inn. Could he have been on his way there?'

Turning to him, Smalhobbe shook his head again. 'No, if he had been going there, he would have gone straight east. He knew that way well enough. Wistman's is south and west from his place; there'd be no reason for him to go down there.'

'And when he was drunk he often fought with others?'

Nodding glumly, Smalhobbe sighed. 'Yes. Often. He never knew when to stop. I suppose at Beauscyr he never had an opportunity to drink too much, but here he started going to the Fighting Cock regularly, and would have fought every time if it wasn't for the men he had with him. Others swal-lowed his insults and boasting while his guards were protect-ing him.'

'And Smyth allowed this? Surely he would not want to have the locals upset by one loudmouth whose only saving grace was that he was setting a precedent of safety for others? I cannot believe this!'

'I don't know why it was, all I know is, that's what happened.'

'I see. In that case, there's only one other point: who bribed you to keep your silence about Bruther?'

'Sir, I—'

'His name, Smalhobbe! You have caused enough delay already. *Who was it?*'

'I can't tell you. He'd kill me!'

'So it was Thomas Smyth, then.'

The expression of shock on the miner's face was almost comical. 'But . . . How did you know that?' he gasped.

'You have spent the last few minutes telling us how he is the most powerful man here on the moors, and we know he has had you beaten to enforce that power. It is obvious. There is one thing, though,' Baldwin said, frowning and leaning forward. 'Why did he pay you to keep silent about Bruther?'

This time the shrug was helpless, but Smalhobbe's eyes were lidded with resentment and he refused to answer.

'Very well,' Baldwin continued at last. 'But you can tell us this: is it true you used to be an outlaw?'

Sarah felt her breath catch. Henry's truculence fell away, and she saw the outright panic in his eyes. After so long, she knew that their attempts to begin a new life were finally failing, and with that realisation she could not help the thickening in her throat as the sobbing began. Her belly churned and she had to put both hands to the ground as she stared at the knight. 'Sir, it's not true,' she said, her voice broken with emotion.

Baldwin gave her a comforting smile as she knelt defence-less before him. 'Tell us the truth, then. We care more for a murder than someone's past misdeeds.'

Ignoring her husband's desperate cry of 'Sarah!' she said, 'Sir, I trust you. Do you swear that we will be left alone if we had no part in Peter Bruther's death?'

Throwing a quick glance at Simon for confirmation, Baldwin gave a slow nod. 'Yes, unless your past includes other murders.'

'That's fair. Well, then, sir. My husband used to work for a fair and decent master, a burgess in Bristol,' she began. 'Henry was his bottler, and we lived with him happily until two years ago.'

'The Rebellion?' Baldwin prompted.

'Yes,' she nodded. 'Our master was Robert Martyn. The King imposed huge taxes on Bristol in 1316, and ignored the city's pleas to reduce them. We sent men all the way to London to explain how they were too high, but he wouldn't listen. In the end he sent the Sheriff of Gloucester with the posse of the county, and laid siege. They drained the ditch, broke the castle mill and set up siege engines, hurling rocks at us until they took the city.'

'Robert Martyn was outlawed, wasn't he?' asked Simon.

'Yes, sir. And he has left the realm. But what could we do? We had no home, no money, no master. We were thrown from the city at the height of the famine, and if it was not for some people we met . . .'

Henry spoke at last, his voice dull and heavy. 'They were outlaws, but they took mercy on us and fed us. One man came from the moors here and we decided to see if his stories of tinning were true. He taught me how to hunt and fight, but on my word, I never robbed or stole anything, and I've never killed anyone.'

His eyes held Simon's defiantly, and the bailiff believed him.

# CHAPTER FIFTEEN

On their way to the Fighting Cock they rode past the front of Thomas Smyth's house, and Hugh could not help craning his neck to stare long after they had passed by. The hall looked quiet, with only a few grooms and a cowherd wandering in the yard, shovelling old hay and muck on to the pile in the corner up close to the entrance. From here it would be collected by cart and taken down to the hall's strip-fields behind the village for rotting down to manure.

After hearing all that the miner had said, Hugh was intrigued. He had assumed that the death of the miner was a simple killing, a hanging by someone with a grudge against him. He would have placed money on one of the Beauscyr family being responsible. Now, though, he felt sure that it must be something to do with the master tinner in his great hall. Why else would he have paid the Smalhobbes to keep quiet?

MICHAEL JECKS

It was with a degree of reluctance that he turned to face the road ahead once more, but soon his mood lightened. Hugh was not a man given to long introspection. Before him was an inn, and there he would be given food and good, strong ale. He sighed happily.

Simon found the inn a little less busy than the last time they had visited it. Now there were several tables free, and he strode to a large one under a window away from the hearth, where there was a chance of uninterrupted conversation. Sitting at a bench, he gazed round the room. Two girls were circulating with drinks, but he could see that this was not their best time of day. He caught sight of them yawning extravagantly, and spotted another asleep on a bench at the far wall: their lives were more skewed to the evening than lunch. *(dinner)* evening meal would be supper.

Baldwin and the others joined him, the knight taking his seat opposite his friend, and soon they had ordered. The girl to whom they had spoken before was nowhere to be seen, and Simon decided to wait until they had eaten before they asked for her. Their food was a thick, rich stew, with the meat minced so small that it was impossible to identify. Baldwin prodded at it suspiciously with his wooden spoon before looking up at Simon questioningly. 'What do you think this is?'

The bailiff gave him a bland smile. 'I don't think you should ask that.'

'Why not?'

'Because it could be anything. Out here,' his hand waved airily, encompassing the whole of the moors around, 'there's not much in the way of food, and a man must survive as best he can. There are wolves, of course, but the main animals

230

here are the forest venison: deer, boar and so on. They are all the King's, and nobody here would dare to break the forest laws by hunting them, of course. I suppose this meat must have come from Chagford.'

'Ah!' Baldwin smiled, and dipped bread into the bowl. As he had expected it had a strong gamey flavour, and the wine he had ordered combined with the food to give him a feeling of comfortable well-being. Finished, he sat back and studied the other people in the room while the others ate in silence.

The girls were working hard to keep tankards and pots filled. One caught his eye. Slight, dark-haired, with an almost boyish figure, she moved with a cool assurance between benches and tables, often carrying several pots and jugs at the same time with a calm efficiency. She did not look like other moor women. Most of the girls in this area were pale-skinned with dark hair, but this one appeared quite dark-complexioned. He beckoned her.

Simon was wiping his mouth with the back of his hand as she drew near, her expression pleasant, but reserved. When Baldwin asked if there was a girl here called Molly, she gave a cautious nod. 'I am,' she said.

The men quickly introduced themselves, and when she declared herself nervous of upsetting her master by not carrying on working, Baldwin called the innkeeper over. Hearing who his guests were, he glanced guiltily at their empty bowls, gave a sickly smile and speedily offered Molly for as long as the men wanted to speak to her. The knight thanked him graciously, then persuaded the girl to sit.

In age she could only be a little older than Alicia, Thomas Smyth's daughter, but born to a harsher life with none of the pampering that Alicia expected. Grey eyes stared at him without curiosity. She was not dimwitted, but she had no interest in any of the men at the table.

When Simon began, he could see her boredom. 'We're trying to find out what happened on the night Peter Bruther died,' he said. 'We've been told by John Beauscyr that he came here with a friend that night. Do you remember it?'

She nodded. 'Yes, they were both here about two hours before dark.'

'You were with Sir Ralph for some time?'

'He wanted me. I stayed with him for some hours, until late in the evening. Then he left me and returned to the Manor with John.'

'We know John was not here all the time his friend was with you, but I understand he was back by the time Sir Ralph left?'

Again she nodded. 'He was here when we came back.'

'How did he seem? Did he look the same as when you left him?'

'I don't know what you mean – I suppose he was a bit excited . . . he was flushed. But he had been when they arrived.' Her eyes took on a distant look. 'No, he wasn't quite the same. When they arrived he was angry, swearing under his breath most of the time, and ignoring me and the other girls. He's not usually like that: normally he'd give us all a smile and have a joke. He wasn't himself that night. He just came in with his friend, took a drink and sat at a bench.'

'Did he talk to anyone?'

'Might have,' she said carelessly, and yawned. 'I don't know. Sir Ralph, he was taking up my time. All I know is, John had a black mood on him, and I was keeping away.'

'I see. And he wasn't the same when you came back down?'

She nodded. 'That's right. By the time we came back, he was more cheerful. He bought a drink for me, and joked with Sir Ralph. I thought he must have rested with one of the other girls, but they said no, he'd been out for a while and returned in a better mood.'

'Did he say where he'd been, or why he was feeling better when he got back?' Simon asked, chewing at a fingernail.

'No, at least, not that I heard. All the girls said was, he'd gone out for an hour or so, and when he came back, it was like his troubles were all over.'

'I see.' Wearily he waved his hand. Clearly the girl knew little. At that moment, though, Baldwin leaned forward.

'Molly,' he asked, 'how well did you know Peter Bruther?'

'Well enough,' she said, her eyes sharp with suspicion. 'Why?'

'We want to learn as much about him as we can, that's all.'

'Well, I don't care what they say,' she stated with a quiet passion, glancing at the bar where the innkeeper stood occasionally looking over at them.

'What do they say, Molly?'

'That he was bad, that he was cruel. He wasn't like that!'

Her vehemence surprised him, but not as much as the sudden watering of her eyes and the way that her shoulders gave a slight shudder. 'Molly, I'm sorry, I didn't realise you—'

'No. No one ever thinks about us serving girls having any feelings, do they? We don't matter.' Her voice was hard, not with self-pity, but a kind of regret.

233

'It isn't that, Molly,' Baldwin said gently. 'I just did not realise you knew him. You did, didn't you?'

'He wasn't like the other men, they always promise anything. Like John and the others, they often say they'll take us away from here, set us up in our own cottage and look after us. It happens, but most men just don't care about us. Peter was different. He really did care. When he had the money, he said, he'd come and get me, and we'd live somewhere else, far away. He said he'd take me to a city, to Exeter or somewhere, and he meant it. With the others it was just a way to try to get me to be more friendly, but Peter, he really cared, I know it. And now, well . . .'

'How long had you known him?'

'Peter? A good year. He started coming here as soon as he ran from the Manor.'

'We've heard that he used to get into arguments.'

'Sometimes. He hated me working here, and he didn't like me going with the other men. It made him mad. He's been thrown out several times for arguing in here.'

'And John Beauscyr used to see you too?'

'Yes. But I never liked him, he's cruel. He hurts the girls. Peter was never like that. He knew what it was like to be owned, he said, and how good it was to escape – and that's how he understood what I wanted, to get away and live free. How could John Beauscyr understand that? All he knows is how to take what he wants, use it and throw it away.'

'Was Peter Bruther here the night he died?' Baldwin asked quietly.

'Yes, but he left just before John and Sir Ralph arrived.'

'You are sure?'

'Oh yes,' she said emphatically. 'He'd embarrassed master John's knight. The fool had threatened to tie up Peter and drag him back to Beauscyr, and didn't notice Peter's friends standing behind him. He had to leave with his tail between his legs when he saw the others. And Peter kept his rope, too!'

'His rope?'

'Yes. Peter and his friends brought it here to show me the night he died. He was really proud, you see. It was like a prize, taking the rope from the man who thought he could haul him back to be a serf again.'

'And Peter took it with him when he left?' Simon asked the girl.

'Oh yes, sir. He wouldn't leave it behind.'

'And he was on his way home before John and his friend arrived?'

'Yes, sir.'

'Do you know which way he would have gone home from here?'

'Down the road, then over the moors once he was past the miner's house by the stream. He always took the same route.'

'So, if John and Sir Ralph were coming here from Thomas Smyth's house, they would have passed him on the way, wouldn't they?'

'Yes, sir, they . . . What are you saying? That *John* could have killed Peter?'

'I don't know. How long after you had gone upstairs would John have left, I wonder?'

'Nobody saw him go as far as I know. After I'd gone with Sir Ralph, somebody noticed John's seat was empty, but no one saw him go out. Later on, Alison went to help a farmer to his horse, because he couldn't mount it on his own, and she saw that John's horse had gone too. That was when she realised that John had ridden off.'

'I see,' said Baldwin, and lounged back, glancing at Simon.

The bailiff frowned at the table top as he thought. 'Molly,' he said after a moment, 'you say Peter Bruther told you he would take you away and make you free when he had the money. He had his own mine, so why didn't you go there with him?'

'He always said it would be too dangerous, with the Beauscyrs trying to get him back. He was afraid there would be a fight.'

'You knew he had guards from the miners' camp with him. I don't understand. We've heard that the miners wanted him and the other small tinners who weren't working for Smyth to leave the moors. Why did they agree to help him and not others? Why should his neighbour, Henry Smalhobbe, be beaten and threatened while Bruther was allowed to stay – and not just that, but was given men to protect him?'

'I don't know, but that evening, the day when he was killed, he said there wouldn't be a need for guards any more. He said he could start his new life, free.'

'What did he mean?'

'Something had happened the day before. He had seen Thomas Smyth, but didn't say what they had talked about. All Peter said was, he'd soon be safe and I'd be able to leave this place and live with him. I'd be safe too, he said.' Her eyes brimmed with tears. 'And the next day I heard he was dead.' Suddenly her face was animated, and she hissed, 'Ask that bastard Smyth what he did! Ask him; he must have killed my Peter!'

She sprang up and walked away, keeping her back to the small group of men huddled round the table. When she finally heard her name called, she glanced round just once, quickly, and saw that they had all gone.

'Hello, Molly,' said George Harang. He leaned back in his chair and grinned up at her wolfishly. 'I think I'll have a pint of ale first. Then I'd like to speak to you – alone.'

There was little talking among the four as they made their way to the great house of Thomas Smyth. At the hall they passed their horses to a groom on hearing that the master of the house was indoors, and soon they were sitting inside, while the bottler poured wine for them. In a moment Thomas Smyth arrived, striding through the door, ever the man of affairs with little time to talk, and too much to do.

'Bailiff, Sir Baldwin. Welcome again. How can I serve you?' he said, dropping into a chair.

Baldwin watched him impassively. Simon was angry that so much information had taken so much searching out; he was convinced that Thomas Smyth knew more than he liked to admit. It must be the miner's approach to life, he thought, keeping everything to himself until he was sure it could not be used to bribe or threaten someone else to his own advantage. That was why he had not mentioned the men protecting Bruther, Simon was sure. He had seen no advantage to be gained in it. Simon meditatively sipped at his wine, then set the goblet down. 'When did you first send men to protect Bruther?'

'What does it matter?' Thomas Smyth's face still held a smile, but it was less broad than before.

Baldwin could see that the man was close to exhaustion, and he was less self-assured than at their first meeting. 'It matters because the bailiff asked you the question,' he said firmly, and was rewarded by a cold stare.

'Why did you put men there in the first place?' Simon said.

'Because I did not want a miner to be taken by the Beauscyrs,' he said. 'It would have been embarrassing to have a worker from the stannary taken away.'

'Eight men just for that? And at a time when you were trying to get other men removed from the same area? It was a very generous act. It would have been easier to bring Bruther to your camp – there was no need to send men all the way out there, surely?'

'It didn't occur to me. Anyway, if I had let him go to the camp, he would have lost his mine – I couldn't let the Beauscyrs think they had beaten a miner like that.'

Simon studied him. It made no sense, he thought, frowning. He too could see the lines of strain on Smyth's face, and even as the bailiff spoke, the miner's hand twisted nervously at a loose thread on his shirt. 'But you wanted the men to leave that part of the moors,' he insisted. 'You said so yourself. Why look after one person so extravagantly?'

'In God's name!' The sudden outburst made them all sit up. 'Why shouldn't I look after him? He . . . He needed help, and I could give it, and that's all there is to it! For God's sake forget it and get on with finding the poor soul's murderer, that's what matters now!'

'We intend to, Thomas. But to do that we have to understand what sort of man Bruther was, so that we can find who had a reason to kill him. Take you, for example . . .'

'*Me?*'

'Yes. You wanted men like him and Smalhobbe off the moors. You had your three men to enforce that, as we well know . . .' As he spoke, Simon was aware of movement behind him, and Christine Smyth walked in. Thomas Smyth gazed at his wife as she walked to his side and rested a hand on his shoulder. 'So why did you not have your men beat him up as well?' Simon persisted. 'Why was he free of attack when you proceeded against his neighbours?'

'All I can say is, I had no reason to harm him, and every reason to protect him. I have told you why: because his Manor wanted him back.' He took hold of his wife's hand.

To Simon they looked a tragic pair, she standing beside her man like a loyal servant, he staring at Simon with the lines of pain and tiredness carving tracks in his face. The bailiff sighed. If the man would not talk, he could not be forced. 'Very well. Another point: you were seen riding towards Bruther's place on the evening he died. Why?'

The miner's eyes slitted. 'You accuse me of his murder?'

Christine Smyth tightened her grip on her husband's shoulder. She knew he was depressed for some reason, had been since first hearing of Bruther's death, but he would not tell her why, and she was scared. Under her palm she could feel the tenseness of his muscles, and she longed to caress him like a child as she felt the breath catch in his throat.

'No, I just want to know why you were there.'

'I wished to speak to him.'

MICHAEL JECKS

'You already had, the day before. What did you want to talk to him about?'

'That had nothing to do with his murder.'

'Your refusal to answer seems odd in the circumstances.' Simon waited, but the miner held his gaze steadfastly. 'Very well. Why did he lose his guards, then?'

'This has nothing to do with Peter's death, and I'll not waste time with this nonsense!'

'Well, at least tell us this: what sort of a man was he?'

'He was a strong, vigorous man. What more can I say? He struck me as an independent sort, the kind who would have done well out here, and who would have worked hard.'

'Did you know he was often involved in fighting at the inn?'

'Fighting – Peter? I find it hard to believe.'

'He had a woman there, too. One of the serving girls.' Simon said it carelessly, but he saw the faint sadness in the man's face.

'I'm not surprised. It was how he was made, looking after others.'

Frowning, Simon glanced up at his wife. 'Madam, you were out on the day that this man was killed, weren't you?'

'Yes, I was in Chagford with my daughter. And George Harang.'

'George was with you all the time?'

'Yes. Until we came home.' She could feel the tension tightening her chest like bands of iron round a barrel. 'Then he had to go out with my husband to see to the mining.'

'When was that?'

'Early afternoon – when we returned.'

Simon looked at Thomas again. 'And when you got back from the camp, was Bruther here? Did you see Bruther that evening?'

'No, no. Peter did not come here that day.'

'He was at the inn that afternoon, according to his girl. He came back this way afterwards, to go home. He would have passed your door, and you did not see him?'

'No, I told you.' Thomas Smyth's face was haggard. 'I did not see him that day. He did not come here.'

'He left the inn a little before John Beauscyr got there, apparently. He and Sir Ralph had come here with his father, but Sir William and he parted at your door.'

'No. He was not here.' Now Christine felt the suppressed emotion in her husband's grip. His fist was tightening on her hand, squeezing the blood from her fingers, and she pulled it away gently, walking to a bench nearby and sitting composedly.

The examination continued, but she kept her eyes on her husband, filled with foreboding. She knew that he was hiding the truth, but did not know what it was. He was scared, that much was obvious to her, and she feared that his questioners might notice. As the meeting continued, her husband became more and more agitated.

It was the first time he had kept anything from her. Normally even the smallest details of the mining camp would be discussed with her, the vaguest problems thrashed out, but she had no idea what his connection was with the young man, Bruther. She felt scared. Thomas had always been a strong man, determined and self-assured, but now it was like watching the render flake from a wall, first a chip, then a

241

crack, then more pieces falling until the whole wall was unprotected. That was how she felt, that his reserves of strength and determination were being eroded under the steady impact of something to do with this dead man. But what it was she had no idea.

Last night he had not been able to sleep. She had woken suddenly, and reached out for him, but he was not there; and when she blinked around their solar, she saw he was gone. She found him in the hall, sitting in his chair before the fire, grasping a pint of wine. He had said nothing, but she could see that his eyes were anxious and fretful. Even the dogs had known something was wrong. They sat by his side like guards, peering into his face with devoted concern. But even then he still would not explain what it was that plagued him so.

'It comes to this, then. When Sir William came in, you did not see his son or Sir Ralph and you did not see Bruther – is that right? And while you were out, did you see Sir Robert on the moors?'

And Christine bit her lip and threw her husband an anguished glance as he answered, 'No.'

'I think there's little else we need to ask now, Thomas,' said Simon, rising slowly to his feet and staring at the miner with a degree of distaste. 'But think on this: if you want the law to protect people here, and not just your men but you and your family as well, you've got to tell us everything. I know you're keeping something back.' He stalked from the room, closely followed by the two servants and Baldwin, who gave Christine a smile and nod.

As soon as the curtain had fallen, she rushed to her husband's side. 'Thomas,' she began, but he cut her off.

'Get a messenger to find George. Tell him to get back here right away – I need to speak to him. And fetch me a jar of wine. I'm thirsty as a rabid bear.'

She ran to do his bidding. Her husband's voice carried his old authority again, and she was sure that he had found a way through his troubles. Christine Smyth was right . . . but if she had guessed the course his thoughts had taken, her heart would have sunk into despair.

# CHAPTER SIXTEEN

Climbing on to his horse, Simon took up the reins and wheeled to face the east. Baldwin sprang up, and seeing the bailiff's quick glance, followed his gaze. At the top of the hill, east of them on the road, a rider was approaching. By the time Hugh had managed to clamber on to his mount it was clear that it was Alicia.

'Good afternoon,' Baldwin said pleasantly as she drew near. 'Been far?'

She laughed, happy after her exercise, her face warm and flushed. 'Almost as far as Chagford.' She patted her mare's neck.

The knight moved forward and studied her horse. It was a small chestnut, almost a pony in size, but strong-looking, with firm, solid legs and a heavy neck. 'How old is she?'

'Meg? She's just over three.'

'Tell me if you ever have a foal from her; she looks like a good, sturdy animal. Ideal for this land, I imagine.'

Simon joined them. She gave him a coquettish glance and tilted her head. 'Are you here to interrogate *me*, bailiff?' she teased. 'I don't know if I can be any help to you, but maybe you should force me to tell what I know.'

'I don't think I need question you too hard,' he said, without returning her smile. 'We have already discussed this matter with your father.' For all the good it did us, he added to himself.

Baldwin could guess at the reason for his friend's sourness. 'Tell me, Alicia,' he said smoothly. 'You were in Chagford with your mother on the day Peter Bruther died. You didn't see him at all on that day, did you?'

Her face froze and her hand stopped its patting. 'Me? No, I didn't see him in town. We weren't there for long, though, we were back here in the early afternoon.'

Trying to relax her, Baldwin smiled, and she did as well, but tentatively, unsure of his next move. 'Do you often ride out so far?' he asked.

'To Chagford? Sometimes, not very often.'

'It could be dangerous, surely? There are a lot of men out here who would like to hold the daughter of Thomas Smyth.'

'How do you mean, Sir Baldwin?' she asked innocently, and Simon turned away to hide his broad grin.

The knight's sudden discomfort made his voice harsh. 'I think you know full well, Alicia. In the same way as your friend Sir Robert Beauscyr, I imagine.' It was her turn to blush – not from shame but from a kind of youthful pride – and Baldwin nodded seriously. 'You should be careful. There are many different types of wolf on moors like these.'

He was thinking of what they had heard of Smalhobbe as he said this, but she misunderstood. 'Oh, but that's ridiculous! Robert isn't like that. I don't care what Father has told you, to me he's always kind and gentle. I just don't believe—' She broke off, and her hand twitched, as if wanting to grab back the words before they could reach the knight.

'What don't you believe, Alicia?' he asked softly, but she shook her head firmly.

'Please forget what I have said. It is unimportant.'

'No, I am afraid it is not. You see, if we are to make sure that it was *not* Sir Robert, there are certain things we need to know. For example, at present we don't even know where he was on the day Bruther was murdered. Now, he admits he was on the moors, but will not give us any way of checking it. It is almost as if he thinks he might get somebody into trouble if he says where he was.'

Her eyes would not meet his. She sat perfectly still, gazing at the view, and her voice was small. 'You can't really think he was involved in the murder, can you? He's such a calm, even-tempered man.'

'Whoever murdered Bruther was probably a very calm man,' said Baldwin. 'You have to be calm to take someone by the neck and strangle the life from him, holding him from behind until he stops thrashing and his death-throes are done.'

She winced. 'Is that how he died? I hadn't realised.' After a moment her head lifted and she met his gaze with resolution. 'Very well, I will answer your questions.'

'You saw Sir Robert that day?'

'Yes. He was in Chagford when we got there, and I saw him. Mother didn't, and she didn't see me go to him. He had been drinking, and was very unhappy because of my father demanding money. I told him I would try to speak to Father and get the ransom reduced. He wanted to talk to me, but Mother was calling and I had to go, so I agreed to meet him later, out at Longaford Tor. We ... we have met there before.'

'I see. So you went there in the afternoon and saw him?'

'It was evening by then, getting close to dark, but yes, and he was fine. The drink had worn off. I hadn't managed to speak to Father yet, though. As soon as Mother and I had got back from Chagford, he went out – he'd only been waiting for George to return. There was some sort of trouble at the mine, apparently. I was going to try to talk to him later. I spent the afternoon with Mother. Later, when she went up to rest, I slipped off to the Tor to see Robert, and was with him in the early evening. When I came home, Father was back and talking with Sir William, so I was too late. Sir William had already paid the money.'

Simon interrupted. 'What did your father think of you seeing Sir Robert?'

'I love Sir Robert . . . and I will marry him.' Alicia tossed her head haughtily. 'Just because Father is not happy with his family is not my concern.'

'Marry him?'

'Yes. We agreed yesterday.'

So that was the reason for the youth's evident pleasure the previous evening. Baldwin smiled. 'You have made him very happy. But tell me: on that night, did you see your father arrive?'

'No.'

'Or see Bruther at the hall?'

'Bruther? Why – was he here?'

He studied her face, but could discern no falsehood. 'Where did you go with Sir Robert?'

'West, then south. When it got late we came to the road and back to the hall.'

Simon quickly butted in, 'So you went down to the two bridges?'

'Yes,' she said, turning to him in surprise. 'Yes, we were there.'

'Did you get there just as it became dark? Did you see two men on horses?'

She nodded. 'Yes, but they had left the road before we got to them. They went north, up towards Wistman's Wood.'

Simon and Baldwin exchanged a look: the two riders were undoubtedly Samuel Hankyn and Ronald Taverner. 'That answers one question, anyway,' said Baldwin, recalling his certainty that Sir Robert had been there. This girl was the other rider seen by Samuel, then.

'But it leaves one unanswered,' said Simon, and faced the girl again, who was staring from one to the other inquisitively. 'Alicia, where were you just before that? Had you gone there by road?'

'Yes, like I said, we stuck to the road. There was no point going off it, and anyway, we wouldn't. Not after dark, not in the moors. It's too dangerous – you can't see the bogs and mires. Why?'

'Did you see another rider?'

'No, only the two. Why?'

Riding back from the hall, Simon was silent and preoccupied. They were no nearer discovering who had killed

Bruther; all they could come up with were conflicting testimonies. The mystery of the two riders seen by Samuel was answered . . . but rather than clearing up the mystery it merely served to highlight how poor was their understanding of the matter. Thomas Smyth had been to see Bruther the day before his death but refused to say why; John Beauscyr had been out and refused to say where; Sir Robert could have killed Bruther before he met Alicia.

'Back to Beauscyr, Simon?'

His friend's calm voice broke into his depressed silence, and he grunted agreement. They were almost at the lane to their left which led down past Adam Coyt's farm to the Manor, and now the sun was getting lower and the wind felt bitter and chill. Baldwin pulled his cloak tighter round his shoulders.

'I thought this was summer,' he shivered.

Simon gave a gloomy shrug. 'The weather here on the moors can always surprise you. This wind feels like it could start raining again soon.'

'Let's hurry back, then.'

Setting spurs to their horses they quickened their pace. Above them, huge grey clouds, their edges tinged with white, moved across the sky with alarming speed. The land, which had looked so calm and soft, green and purple under its velvet-like covering, now showed itself in a darker mood. The moors took on a more menacing aspect, the heather now a gloomy dark carpet, the tors great black monsters crouching ready to leap.

Even Baldwin gave a shudder at the sight. Though he instinctively rejected any suggestion that there could be ghouls or ghosts seeking out souls in the way that Adam

Coyt and other people in the area believed, it was easy to understand how such fears could arise. The huge open space of the moors with its almost complete lack of trees made a man realise how small he was when compared with the vastness of nature.

Glancing at Simon, who rode glumly, hunched against the chill, Baldwin said, 'There is a strange feeling about these moors when the weather changes.'

'Yes,' Simon muttered. 'I'm glad you've noticed. Especially after your words about Coyt.'

'Oh, there is no need for superstition. All I meant was, one can sense . . . There is a certain . . . A malevolent . . .' His voice faded on an apologetic, confessional note, and he carefully avoided the bailiff's eye.

'"One can sense"? "Malevolent"? And you try to deny you hold any superstition?'

'Simon, one can feel an atmosphere without blaming imaginary ghosts and ghouls!'

'And yet you can blush when a young girl flirts, and sense malevolence because the weather cools!'

'It is not *just* that the weather has cooled!' the knight declared hotly, avoiding talking about Alicia.

'Oh no?' A cynical eyebrow was raised. 'You thought nothing of the moors until the clouds came over.'

'That has little to do with it. It is the way that—'

'Yes?'

'There are times, Simon, when you can be infuriating.'

'Yes. But my wife makes good ale and you like my store of wine,' the bailiff pointed out smugly.

'Sometimes I wonder whether that is enough to justify our friendship.'

Reaching the lane, they made their way silently down towards the Manor. A light drizzle began, spattering them and creating tiny explosions in the dust at their feet, but at the same time the weather felt warmer, and Baldwin shrugged the folds of his cloak away. The rain was a relief after the heat of the last few days, and he had always enjoyed the feeling of the droplets pattering against his face. Simon, he saw, was not so content. The bailiff rode with his back hunched against the elements wearing a grimace of disgust.

'So, Simon,' he said, 'what do we do now?'

'We're no nearer an answer, are we?' Simon replied despondently.

'At least we are beginning to understand a little about this man Bruther,' Baldwin said.

'Are we? Smyth says he was a paragon, Coyt says he was a devil-may-care sort who would twitch the tail of Crockern if he had the chance. The Beauscyrs and their guest thought he was some kind of madman, a rogue who would stop at nothing, even threatening and making fun of a knight. Smalhobbe seems to have been fearful of him, or at least wary. Molly and Smyth say he was kind, hard-working and honest, while others think he was *dis*honest.'

'Well, yes, but look at it from the other point of view, Simon. The Beauscyrs and Sir Ralph would naturally be disgusted by a man like Bruther. He goes against the natural order of their lives: not only did he dare to run away, but afterwards he showed no remorse or guilt. That marks him out as a danger, someone who is prepared to stand in opposition to all that they hold dear – and the worst of it to them was that they could do absolutely nothing about it. To Coyt he was almost impossible to comprehend: a man who showed no fear of the moors, nor any terror of Crockern. To a farmer who has spent the whole of his life out here, that is surely understandable.'

'But what of the others?' Simon said. 'Smalhobbe appeared to dislike him.'

'Yes, but a measure of that could be his own position. He is scared of being denounced as an outlaw, though he can fight, from what Magge said. Any man who realises he is being ambushed and then circles his attacker must have had some military skill, whether it came from conventional training or . . . or some less wholesome experience. In any case, he clearly resented the fact that he had failed to protect himself and his wife, while Bruther succeeded somehow.'

'And as you say, Molly and Smyth almost revered his memory.'

'Molly's motive at least is understandable, thank God! She clearly felt he was going to rescue her from her life at the inn and make her his wife.'

'But what about Smyth? There's something very odd there.' Simon fell silent, deep in thought.

'What?' Baldwin prompted.

'It may be nothing but . . . everyone we have spoken to so far has referred to him as "Bruther", except two. Molly and Smyth both talked of him as "Peter". I don't know, but both appeared to know him well . . . At least, both seemed to know him better than the others. Did you notice that?'

'No, I didn't,' said Baldwin, and his brows pulled together into a frown. 'But you're right – they did. Why should that be?'

\*     \*     \*

Tossing his reins to the ostler, George Harang jumped from his horse and ran to the hall. Inside he found Thomas Smyth sitting at his chair before the fire, gripping a tankard. He looked up as his servant entered, red-faced and dirty after his ride through the light rain, his face showing his concern.

'Sir? I got your message and came as soon as I could, but what is it? The boy said that the bailiff and his friend were here, that they were asking questions – is something wrong?'

Thomas Smyth gave a weary smile. 'No, old friend. Not the way you think, anyway. But I know at last who killed Peter. On the night Sir William came here to see us, he rode over here with his son, that bastard John. John left him when they reached the hall and rode on to the inn. And at the inn was Peter, the poor lad. He set off home, according to Molly, a little before John arrived.'

George frowned. 'So they must have crossed on the road.'

'Yes. And afterwards Peter disappeared. So who could have killed him? That runt; that bastard – John Beauscyr!'

'What do you want to—'

'Don't be stupid!' Smyth spat the words jeeringly. 'I want his *head*, here, now, on my lap! That pathetic little worm killed my Peter, and probably thinks he can get away with it. The bailiff's incompetent – or is being paid to be so by Sir William. I don't know and I don't care which it is; all I do know is, John murdered Peter, and he must be made to pay.'

'So you want me to tell the bailiff, then?'

'Didn't you hear me? The bailiff is *no use*! *We* have to get him and bring him to justice. Peter was a miner, a tinner, and he came under the stannary laws. We, as miners, can obtain justice. We can't rely on officials, they have their hands in the Beauscyrs' purses, and have no need to see to our compensation. What does this bailiff care for our hardships? He's no use to us, we have to catch this Beauscyr on our own. I want a force of men, all armed, to take John Beauscyr prisoner tomorrow. He's a murderer – and he shall pay.'

George rushed from the room, his brain churning. He hadn't had time to tell his master about his conversation with Molly at the inn, and he hesitated a moment, undecided whether to return to the hall and tell Thomas. But then he shook his head. His master had new proofs. Anything George had heard from the girl was unimportant now. He ran out to his horse.

Alone once more, Thomas Smyth turned back to his solitary vigil by the fire. Strange, he thought abstractedly, that the flames did not warm him any more. Since Peter's killing he had felt no rest or peace of soul, and the tiredness of inaction had eaten into his bones. Shuddering, he grinned wrily to himself. This, then, was old age, this exhaustion which sapped the will and eroded the hunger for money and power. It was not like before, when each day had been a new opportunity, a new chance to expand his mining area and enhance his wealth. Now nothing seemed to hold any interest for him.

His wife Christine opened the solar door. She saw his strained, taut features and hurried over to him, feeling as if her heart would burst. When she put her arms round him and held him, she felt the same as she had when she had rocked her children, offering protection and security; performing this little service to her man made the breath stick in her throat like the stone from a plum, and tears of sympathy sprang into her eyes. Of her children, six all told, only the one had lived. All the others had succumbed to the cold and the illnesses which assailed the young of wealthy and poor alike.

Thomas finally pulled away and looked into her tear-stained face with a sort of wonder, slowly reaching up with a hand to touch the heavy drops at either cheek; then he sighed and pulled her down on his lap in a snug embrace. While she sobbed in her own turn, gulping and moaning, he rocked her, and felt himself gain strength from her weakness. The abstraction and despair left him, and he was filled instead with a rigid determination. Come what may, he would avenge Peter Bruther.

Christine Smyth slowly felt her abject misery subsiding and the grip of her man increase as his strength returned. When she eased herself away from his embrace, in his now black eyes she saw firm purpose, and she sighed as she wiped the tears away with a hand, feeling her inadequacy anew. Taking a deep breath, she managed to say, 'So you will go with the men to find his killer?' before the tears welled up once more.

'You heard us?'

'I did not eavesdrop; you spoke loud enough for the miners at the camp to hear.'

His face was serious. 'We will go tomorrow.' He hated to see her vexation, but there was nothing he could do. She must understand that; he had a duty to Peter Bruther.

She gave him a brittle smile. 'And you will catch John Beauscyr and hang him – lynch him like a common killer?'

'Did he treat Peter any better? Beauscyr throttled him from behind like any outlaw. What do you expect?'

'I expect him at least to be able to defend himself.'

'Why, so he can brief a lawyer for himself? What good would that do? We know he did it; no one else was there.'

255

MICHAEL JECKS

'But Thomas, what if it wasn't him?'

'It was,' he said harshly, and putting her from his lap he stood and strode from the room.

Her eyes sorrowfully followed his figure as he went. Though she dared not speak out loud, her lips framed the words again: *'But what if it wasn't him?'*

# CHAPTER SEVENTEEN

Simon and the others arrived back at Beauscyr just as Sir William was returning from a hunt, tired and frustrated after a long day in the saddle with nothing to show for it. All the animals seemed to have disappeared. Those areas which usually guaranteed food were empty: the rabbits in the warrens had suffered from a predator; the wood pigeons appeared to have moved to another site; the fishpond was free of herons. He had finally decided to get back home and tell the cooks to kill some doves from the cotes for his guests.

Seeing the four men did nothing for his humour. To his eye they were always there whenever something was wrong, as if they brought misfortune with them. Had they helped him earlier on, when Peter Bruther had first run away, he would feel different, but the bailiff's ineffectual response to the crisis – or, as Sir William felt, his complete lack of under-standing and unwillingness to assist – had left him with a sour opinion of the man. As for his friend, he had appeared to derive amusement from the Manor's predicament. So it was with a jutting jaw that the elderly man nodded to Baldwin and Simon. His anger was not dissipated when the bailiff immediately asked for an interview.

'Now?' he snapped. Surely the bailiff could understand that he wanted to get changed, then wash and relax for a moment before any more questions, but the bailiff was insistent and eventually the knight agreed, but with a bad grace. Hugh and Edgar went to see to the horses while the three trooped up to the hall. Here they discovered a number of guards playing dice before the fire; they showed little desire to move to the guardrooms, which were draughtier. In the end it took a furious bellow from their master to persuade them that he was not of a mood to be trifled with, and they moodily took their things and left.

'Right. What is it?'

Simon sat, and, realising after a minute that the meeting could take some time, Sir William also dropped into a chair. Baldwin sat some feet away, watching the knight with interest. His anger was clear, and Baldwin could understand how he felt. As far as Sir William was concerned, the death of Bruther was none of his business. The murderer had saved him considerable trouble, and that was all. Conversely the law, represented by this bailiff to whom he had turned at the outset, had been of little help. He had behaved properly, calling on the King's official when he had seen the problem, but it had given him no comfort. What had appeared to be a simple, straightforward case of a runaway snubbing the estate had become a tangled web of political manoeuvring between him as the landowner, and the miners – and the bailiff had, in his eyes, taken the part of the miners in preference to his own claims. And the bailiff was still trying to find the man who had cleared away his problems like snow swept from a path. For all Sir William cared, Simon could search until kingdom come. Yet he could still be summoned to speak to the bailiff whenever the damned official wanted.

And the worst of it for the old knight was, the bailiff could do so when he wanted, Baldwin knew. Old he might be, but Sir William was no fool. Though he had an alibi, he knew full well that his sons did not, and any reticence on his part could be considered suspicious, especially since Sir Robert thought Peter Bruther's death could benefit his inheritance. Even so, to be called to discuss the affair immediately after a day in the saddle was at best discourteous from a guest.

So now he sat regally, his brows beetling as he tried to hold his temper at bay, and his mood was not improved by the long, measuring stare to which Simon subjected him. 'Sir William,' he said at last, 'we too have spent many hours on horseback today, and have been to see several people . . .'

'Get to the point, bailiff,' Sir William growled.

'Very well. On the day Peter Bruther died, you rode out from here with your son John, your guest Sir Ralph, and two men-at-arms. Is that right?'

'You know it is.'

'Yes. On your way to Thomas Smyth's hall, did you see anybody else on the roads?'

There was an edge to Simon's voice which seemed to indicate that the question was important; Sir William considered for a moment, his face fixed into a scowl of

MICHAEL JECKS

concentration. 'We went up past Coyt's farm,' he said at last. 'There was no one on the road there, that I know.'

'How about the rest of the way? Was there anyone else on the road between there and the hall?'

'No. I'm sure there wasn't.'

'Good. Now, when you got to the hall, what exactly happened?'

'I dismounted and John and Sir Ralph decided to leave me there. They preferred to ride on to the inn rather than wait with me.'

'What of the men-at-arms?'

'I had told them to leave me beforehand, shortly after quitting Coyt's road. I didn't want them to hear what I was to discuss with Smyth, but I had to tell John. It was hardly an impressive position to be in, was it? Why should I let my men hear of such things? Anyway, I told you all this before. Why do you need to hear it all again?'

'It's important, Sir William. Now, did you see anyone on the road ahead when you left your son? Was there someone approaching the hall from the east?'

'No, of course not!'

'From there the moors roll away and you can see for a great distance. Did you see anyone on the moors?'

He glared at Simon, then at Baldwin, irritation sharpening his voice. 'No! Why? What are you suggesting now, bailiff? Who should I have seen?'

Simon remained silent, but Baldwin eyed the knight tentatively. 'We know that Peter Bruther was at the inn that night, and that he left shortly before your son got there. It seems likely that they must have met on the road, but if they did, why does your son not tell us?'

'Who says John saw the man? Bruther must have hidden from view when he saw my son approach.'

'Not out there, Sir William. You know the land as well as we do. There are no places for a man to hide, not near the road. And we already know that Bruther was accustomed to passing on to the moors near the hall. He did not leave the road until he got to Smyth's place. That would seem to indicate that your son could have met him.'

'What if he did? Are you saying he killed the man, dragged the body all the way to Wistman's Wood, then raced back to the inn? I assume he was at the inn that night?'

Simon sighed. 'Well, yes, but . . .'

'And did he arrive with Sir Ralph? Or was he later than his master?'

The bailiff squinted at the fire. 'They arrived together,' he admitted.

'And yet you dare to insult my son's name in front of me, in my own house!' Sir William's eyes were wide in rage. 'You suggest that my son is a murderer, a man who would strangle another and then hang him from a tree, when you have no evidence whatever?'

'Sir William, please!' Speaking slowly and keeping his voice level and calm, Simon said, 'I have no wish to insult you or your son, Sir William. You know that. But it seems clear that John was in the area, just at the time that young Bruther was there, and must very likely have seen him. I do not say that your son alone saw him. Obviously Sir Ralph was there too, and it is possible that Sir Ralph remembered his humiliation at this Bruther's hands. He would not be the first soldier to kill someone who offered him an insult. As far as I can see, there is no real reason for John to have murdered the young man, but Sir Ralph had cause, didn't he? In any case, you have confirmed that you did not see Bruther on the road. The people at the inn were certain that he left only a short time before John and Sir Ralph got there, so I assume that they must have passed him on their way to the inn.'

The old knight stared, aghast. His shock was plain to both men. 'But . . . But . . . Surely he must already have passed, before we got to the hall,' he stammered.

'As I said, Sir William, if he had passed already, you would surely have seen him up on the moors. From the road to Beauscyr, you can see for miles, and it's the same all the way to the inn. If he was on the moors, you must have seen him.'

'We weren't looking for him, though,' he was pleading. 'He could have been up there, but we weren't looking. Maybe he hid behind a rock? There are plenty of them up there, and it would take only a moment to duck behind one. That must be it! He saw us, realised who we were and dropped out of sight – he would know that Sir Ralph would want to exact vengeance for the insult he offered when they last met.'

'No. It will not do, Sir William,' said Baldwin. His manner was precise, leaving no opportunity for misunderstanding. 'We have ridden past there several times over the last couple of days. If Bruther was there, then you must have seen him. You did not, and neither did your men. You had the men-at-arms with you, and they would have been looking for miners or anyone else who could have posed a threat. Likewise, your son and his master would have kept an eye open. They are men-of-war, and unused to peace. Even if you were concentrating on your meeting with

Smyth, I find it hard to believe that your company were so careless as to forget to keep a lookout. Of course, Bruther could already have passed, but if he had, he would surely have been seen by Samuel and Ronald after you dismissed them.'

'Why? They would have gone in the opposite direction to get back here.'

'But they went to the Dart, to the alehouse. That's how they found the body – they left the road because of two men they thought could be miners. So that means Bruther had not yet passed by. And *that* means that your son and Sir Ralph must have met him later.'

The old man gazed from one to the other, his face suddenly waxen. His eyes, large and almost luminous with fear, seemed to betray his own doubts about his son, but then they fixed on Simon with desperation. 'But there's nothing to suggest that John would kill, like you say. It must have been his master, Sir Ralph. Why would John kill the man? They had nothing to do with each other.'

Simon glanced at Baldwin, trying to avoid the pitiful spectacle of the disintegration of the knight. Sighing, he looked at his hands resting in his lap as he said, 'I am sorry, Sir William, but there is more. Both men arrived at the tavern together, but a short while later your son left, and did not return for a long time. He could have dragged the body over the moors to the woods and hung it there before returning.' He forced himself to meet the gaze of the old knight. 'I am truly sorry,' he said simply.

Sir William raised a hand, making a curious, futile little gesture as if slapping at a fly, knocking away the suggestion that his son could have been involved. He opened his mouth to speak, but before he could, the door opened and his wife walked in.

She appeared surprised to see the little congregation, halting as she took in the mood of the room, but then her brows drew together, and she paced slowly and menacingly towards them, her eyes glued accusingly on the bailiff. 'I heard that my husband had returned, bailiff. I had not realised that you had monopolised his company since then. Usually a guest will leave his host to be welcomed by his wife after a day apart.' Her voice was cold as she stood by Sir William.

Simon sighed. Matillida Beauscyr was almost shaking with fury, and he had no desire to suffer the lash of her tongue, but that was his fate, he knew, if he raised even a suspicion about her youngest son. Already the presence of his woman had instilled a new strength into Sir William, and the bailiff could see that she was not of a mood to let the interview continue without her.

He said, 'My apologies, lady. I did not mean to detain your husband any longer than necessary, and did not wish to annoy you, but there are still some points to talk through.'

'Please do not let me stop you,' she said with icy politeness, and sat. 'I will wait here until you are done, and then I can welcome my husband. In peace.'

Her arrival acted like a tonic on her husband, and Sir William sat more upright in his seat. Glancing at him, Baldwin saw that the old man's eyes were steady again; they had lost their wavering anxiety. Baldwin coughed lightly, a mild clearing of his throat which made the Beauscyrs turn to him. 'If you wish to stay, madam, please take a seat. In the meantime, Sir William, would you mind sending a servant to fetch your son?'

She flashed a look of rage at him at having her desire for solitude rebuffed, but before she could speak her husband gave a small sigh and nodded. When he remained seated and silent, Simon bellowed suddenly for the bottler. The grey-haired man bustled in nervously hopping from foot to foot like a frightened rabbit, and soon John was with them, a sardonic smile fixed to his face. Sir Ralph followed. The knight, Baldwin noticed, looked pensive, as if expecting to be accused of something himself.

John grinned at the assembled group, then sauntered to a bench and straddled it easily, folding his arms and staring at Simon with an eyebrow raised in enquiry. 'And what can I do for you today, bailiff?'

'On the day that Peter Bruther died, when you left your father at Thomas Smyth's hall, you rode straight to the inn, didn't you?'

'Yes. As you know.'

'Did you meet anyone on the way there?' Simon asked, and Baldwin saw that he did not meet the young squire's eyes as he asked the question; it seemed as if he was listening intently to the phrasing of the answer and did not want to be diverted by the youth's expression or gestures.

John reacted well, Baldwin thought. He was startled, that much was obvious from the way he took a sharp breath and shot a glance at his father, but he swiftly recovered and eyed Simon thoughtfully. 'I might have done,' he said unconcern-edly. 'I can't really recall.'

'You can't recall,' said Simon heavily, then spun round and stared at him. 'You're wasting my time and that of my friend, *Beauscyr*! You saw Peter Bruther walking back from the inn, didn't you? We've heard about your arrival at the inn already, and about Bruther's departure. What happened when you saw him?'

The contempt in Simon's voice sliced through the boy's arrogance like a hot axe through lard and John recoiled from his anger, a hand rising as if to ward off a blow. 'No! I didn't kill him, and you can't say I did.'

'*What happened on the road that day?*' Simon was half up from his chair now, glaring at him, and Sir William made ready to protect his son. It was this which made the boy regain his calm. He saw his father lean forward to lever himself up, and sighed. His face showed his nervousness, but he met Simon's eyes with resignation. 'We did meet Bruther,' he admitted.

The room was suddenly still. Everyone there was listening to John Beauscyr. Baldwin thought Simon looked as intent as a hunter studying his prey. Sir Ralph had a kind of sick fear on his face which added to his pallor; Sir William seemed to have shrunk, staring at his son with the anxious concern of a thief watching the jury deliberate over his guilt; Lady Matillida seemed stunned.

'He was walking back from the inn, cocksure as a young rooster, and just as arrogant.' He sneered at the memory. 'We rode along without noticing him at first, but as we came close, he gave a sort of laugh, and that made me look up and I saw who it was.'

'He was alone?' said Simon, and the boy shook his head.

'Oh no, bailiff. He had some of his miner friends with him, otherwise we might have killed him ourselves. It would have been easy if he had been alone. But sorry to say, he wasn't.'

'Did you see the men who were with him? Can you give me names?'

'No. I don't normally associate with such vagabonds.'

'Sir Ralph? Can you confirm this?'

Baldwin glanced at the knight as Simon asked the question. Sir Ralph nodded. 'Yes. It was embarrassing to have to submit again to his mocking, but we had little choice. We could have attacked, for we were on horseback and they were on foot, but we were not on fighting horses. My little mare would have been no good – at the first blow she would have shied and they could have pulled me from her while I tried to control her. If I had been on my warhorse I would not have hesitated.'

'Why? What did they say?'

'They made various comments about us, calling us foreigners and trespassers, telling us we should leave the moors before the tinners threw us off them. And more in a similar vein.'

'And he showed you your rope?' Simon guessed.

The knight nodded. 'He did not miss the opportunity to remind me of my humiliation,' he said tightly.

Simon turned back to John. 'And then you made your way to the inn?'

'Yes, for the love of God! What do you expect – that we followed them all the way to their camp? We weren't that foolish,' John jeered, confident he held the upper hand.

'And you stayed there?'

The smile was a little too fixed, Baldwin felt. John was clearly unsettled by that question as well. 'Well, of course. Why should we want to leave? It is a pleasant place to while away a few hours.'

267

'I don't know why you wanted to leave, John, that's why I asked. Where did you go when you left the inn? You returned there a long time later – so where had you been?'

All at once the colour came back to his face, two red spots of anger flaring high on his cheeks. 'So you have been enquiring about me? Asking the roughs in an inn about me as if I were an outlaw? How dare you—'

'Enough! I want to know where you went, and why. And who you saw. Who can confirm where you went and what you did, how long you were there for, and when you went back to meet your master?'

'I will not answer!' He stood, glaring at the bailiff, then made for the door.

'A moment, John!' Simon's call made the boy halt, but he did not acknowledge the bailiff by word or movement, did not even turn to face him, simply stood as stiff as an oak while Simon spoke forcefully. 'You may leave this hall now, John, but you cannot leave this Manor, I tell you that now. If you do, I shall declare you an outlaw and will demand a posse to capture you. I do not know what happened that night, but I do know that you are being obstructive, and that makes me suspicious. You are the only man who does not seem to be able to account for his actions that night, and therefore you are the man most to be suspected. There will be a coroner appointed to hear and record the events surrounding this miner's death, and he will be a stannary coroner. You know what that means? A jury not only of Devon men, but one with tinners in it will be asked to judge whether they think you could have killed the boy. Think on that! Think on it long and hard, because if you don't start to answer some of my questions, I'll have you in irons at

Lydford Castle. Now go! I will talk to you again in the morning.'

Without responding, the boy strode from the room, and as he left, Simon looked over at his mother and father. They sat rigid, like statues on a tomb, their faces set into masks of shock and horror. 'Sir William, Lady Matillida, I am sorry that it has come to this. Please forgive me, but I can't betray my duty. If you can, speak to your son and persuade him to tell me the truth.' He stood. Not wishing to be left alone with the parents, Baldwin swiftly rose too and followed his friend.

Matillida stared after them. She could not comprehend the enormity of the straits in which the family found itself. Her head moved from side to side in silent denial of her son's guilt. It was impossible, incredible, that he could be an object of suspicion. John, her son, always so bright, so honourable . . . Her thoughts moved on swiftly to the implication of that. John had known of Bruther's act, running from the Manor and bringing shame and embarrassment on the family, and had plainly heard of the insult offered to his master. If he had then been angered by another humiliation to Sir Ralph, it was possible he could have determined to avenge it and by so doing exorcise the spirit of evil that Bruther had imposed on Beauscyr. He was wild and headstrong, always had been, and surely he was capable of murder.

Only one man could shed some light on all this. She looked at Sir Ralph, who was gazing at the door with a perplexed frown. 'What did the miners say to you both that night?'

Startled from his reverie, Sir Ralph scratched his head. 'They were obscene, lady. Insulting us both, and our parentage. They made some comments about you, and it was that which angered your son most of all.' He stared at her bleakly.

'Did he kill Bruther?' she asked, her voice even, as if enquiring about the weather with no quaver to show her inner turmoil. Though he did not answer, his haunted eyes told her what he thought. She had to swallow hard before standing unsteadily and walking out to the solar.

# CHAPTER EIGHTEEN

Hugh and Edgar had been waiting at their favourite place down by the kitchen, where they had set the bottler to filling jugs with his best strong ale. When Simon and Baldwin rejoined them, the bottler scurried for more drink. They took their seats at the bench, Simon resting his head in his hands and massaging his temples. When he looked up, he found a pot beside him on the ground, and he took a long draught.

'That's a bit better,' he sighed and wiped his mouth with his hand. Burping, he glanced at his friend. 'So what do you think?'

'Me? If the boy won't answer, it will go badly for him,' said Baldwin quietly. Instantly their servants set themselves to finding out whom the two were discussing, and Baldwin explained what had happened in the hall. 'John is keeping something back,' he concluded.

'From his behaviour, it seems clear enough that he has at the very least had a hand in the murder,' Simon told them.

'Why else would he go so quiet? But why did he not even invent a story, that's what puzzles me.'

'What, no alibi?' Edgar set his pot down. 'Didn't he have any kind of explanation to offer?' he asked, surprised.

'No. Nothing at all. He refused to discuss where he had gone.' Simon shook his head, troubled. 'It's not as if he's a fool. He must know what we're bound to think. If he makes no effort to show his innocence, there can only be the one assumption.'

'That *is* strange,' mused Baldwin, so softly that the other three almost missed his words. When they turned to him with mystified faces, he went on: 'I mean, it seems odd that John and Sir Ralph should go to the inn for Molly – the same girl whom Bruther apparently wanted. I wonder . . .' He frowned into the distance.

'What?' asked Simon after a minute, irritated by the pause.

'Hmm? Oh, I was just thinking: if John really wanted to annoy Bruther, surely the best way would have been to say that he was going to bed the miner's woman. There would be nothing he could do about it, after all. Except maybe . . . offer a challenge!'

Simon stared at him open-mouthed. 'He could have, couldn't he?'

'It would explain the facts: Sir Ralph and John see the miner, words are exchanged, the squire threatens to go and see Molly, the miner promises a fight if he does, the knight and his man go to the inn, meet the girl, the miner returns in their wake, sees her going with the knight and waits outside. A little later the squire goes out, they agree to fight, meet out on the moors, fight to the death, and—'

'And the boy dies. John takes the body to Wistman's Wood and hangs it, then . . .'

'Yes, that's the trouble, isn't it?' said Baldwin as Simon faltered.

Hugh stared from one to the other. 'Surely that explains it, doesn't it?'

'No, Hugh,' sighed Baldwin. 'It doesn't. Firstly, John would not be afraid to admit it. The challenge issued in front of the miners would give him witnesses and make it self-defence, clearing him from a charge of murder. Secondly, the whole inn would have been aware that there was going to be a fight. And thirdly . . .'

Simon leapt in, 'And thirdly, since when did men fight to the death with only thin cords to strangle each other?'

Glaring at the ground truculently, Hugh said, 'Maybe they fought with knives or swords and you didn't see his wounds?'

Baldwin glanced at him coldly. 'No, Hugh. There was no stab – I would have seen it. Bruther died from the cord round his neck. It bruised, and bruises only appear on a live body. The mark was thin, and the cord which killed cannot have been any thicker. If someone lives, their bruises smudge and diminish with time. The more clear the outline, the more recent the wound; but if someone dies shortly after a blow or, in this case, strangling, then the changes in the marks don't happen. It is as if they are frozen. I was told it was God's way of helping us to find how a man died.'

The servant looked amazed. 'How can that be?' he frowned. 'Are you sure?'

'I have seen many dead men, Hugh,' said Baldwin, and his voice was sober. 'Too many, maybe. But I have lived through wars and seen their effects on the victims. That is how I know.'

They were all silent for a moment. Simon could see that his friend was sunk into a gloomy reverie, but could not think of a way of pulling him back. To his relief, Edgar did it for him. The servant contemplated his master quickly, then, with a motion as if of disinterest, said, 'So, where did these miners go to?'

Simon suppressed a grin as Baldwin turned distractedly to look at his servant. 'Eh?'

'I was just thinking – there were miners with Bruther on his way back from the inn that night, but they can't have been with him when he died. Where did they go?'

Baldwin mused, 'We only have the word of John and Sir Ralph that there were any men there at all.'

'If you're right,' Hugh broke in suddenly, his face still holding his doubtful scowl, 'couldn't John have offered a fight anyway?'

'What?' sighed Simon, throwing his servant a look of long-suffering exasperation.

'Well, if John agreed to meet Bruther alone and fight, maybe he went out early, before Bruther expected him, and got him by the neck. That would explain it, wouldn't it?'

Simon stared, then turned to Baldwin. The knight nodded. 'If, as you say, John had agreed to fight him, had left for the inn and then sneaked off to ambush Bruther, it would make sense. It could also explain why Sir Ralph would keep his silence, for the knight could feel that blame could attach to him, after the way that Bruther had insulted him before. And he might feel guilt for the behaviour of his squire, because it would be bound to reflect poorly on him. But,' he sighed, 'I find it hard to believe that Bruther or John would have trusted the other enough to agree to meet alone.'

Edgar poured more ale, then topped up the other pots. Setting the jug down, he said, 'One moment. Surely there are no other witnesses to say that there were any miners there, only Sir Ralph and John? What if the whole roadside meeting was an invention? Could it not be that the two came across Bruther, throttled him and hid his body, and then went on to the inn for an alibi? Afterwards John slipped out, took the body again and rode over to Wistman's, where he hanged it?'

'His guards *were* there – or so Molly said,' Baldwin insisted.

'And yet they must have gone before Bruther was killed.'

'Yes,' said Simon. 'Where did *they* go? And why?'

'And when?' muttered Baldwin.

Hearing a door slam, Simon glanced up to see John and his father standing at the top of the stairs. Sir William half-raised a hand as if to beckon him, but then grimaced and let his hand fall.

'Baldwin,' the bailiff said softly, 'unless I am much mistaken, our young friend has been persuaded to give us more information.' He stood, finished his ale and set his pot down, and Baldwin rose to join him. They strode together over the yard to the steps and stood at the bottom, gazing up expectantly.

John's eyes were downcast, but the flaming colour of his face showed more humiliation than anger. It was his father, Baldwin noticed, who wore the cloak of absolute rage, his eyes unblinking in the white face. When he spoke, it was with a strangled voice, as if the very act of speaking was intensely difficult.

'Come with us, please, bailiff. And you too, Sir Baldwin. My son has much to tell you. Much! Come on, you cretin!' This was to John, and as he spoke the old man knocked his son on the back. John looked up and met Simon's steady gaze. There was no fear there, the bailiff saw, just defiance. Walking jerkily, like a prisoner going to the gallows, John descended the stairs, went past the stables and made for the flight of steps that gave on to the wall. These he climbed with every appearance of infinite tiredness.

Simon was astonished at the sight. He trailed after the boy in a state of confusion, glancing every now and again at the lad's father, who seemed consumed by his temper. If it was full night, the bailiff thought, Sir William would be incandescent.

Up at the wall, Sir William motioned curtly to the guard, and ordered him to leave them alone. Then he led the way to the barbican. 'This is the most private place in the Manor. Anywhere in the hall we could be overheard, and this wastrel has done enough already to bring shame on our house.' He cast a bitter eye over his son. 'Tell them.'

John had his hands on the wall, staring out over the land before him with a kind of wonder, as though he had not seen the view before. 'We did see Bruther,' he said. 'And he was with his friends, like I said. They jeered and catcalled, insulting us both and holding up Sir Ralph's rope, but we could do nothing against so many, not while we were on our riding horses. We had to swallow our pride and carry on.'

'Tell them the rest! Tell them what sort of son I've raised – tell them how you have dishonoured my name! *Go on!*' As Sir William shouted, the spittle flew from his mouth, and the boy flinched at the white face so close to his own.

'I have been a soldier for years now, up in the north. We never suffered such humiliation there; if a man gave us offence, he died. That was the rule – and why not?' His eyes met Baldwin's, and challenged him. 'That's the way of a soldier, after all. When we fought for Sir Gilbert, we would think nothing of killing, for that was our duty – until Sir Ralph forgot his honour when he heard about robbing the cardinals. He decided we must leave Sir Gilbert's service, just when Sir Gilbert needed our help. We had to scurry down here like rats running from a burning house, to our shame. Well, it seemed to me that being insulted by Bruther was as bad. The villeins here have forgotten their duty of service and respect to their betters, that is clear. I was ashamed when we got to the inn that night. Sir Gilbert would not have allowed such rabble to escape unpunished. But Sir Ralph said we should forget it, said we should leave them, leave Bruther, and carry on with our plan to run from the country. I said to him, "But they will think they can insult a knight and escape justice!" but he just gave that dry little smirk of his and said we would be alive, though. Honour means nothing to him!'

'So what did you do?' prompted Simon quietly.

'I had a pot or two of wine, but the air smelled foul to me in there. Everyone was trying to enjoy themselves, but no one took any notice of me. Sir Ralph went off with a girl, and I was alone. I decided to go out and clear my head. It was a still evening, and I wanted to avoid any trouble, like Sir Ralph had told me, so I headed away from the moors and the mines and went off towards Chagford. I don't know exactly which way I went, but after some time I found myself near a wagon. There was a man on it, and when I ordered him to tell me where I was, he made some comment about fools who should know better than to ride out with no idea where they were. So, I . . . I hit him. And then I saw his purse. It seemed stupid not to take it, and he had been so insulting, I thought it would teach him—'

'So it was *you* robbed Wat Meavy!' Simon gasped.

'Is that who it was? I didn't know. Anyway, yes, it was me. And then I rode back to the inn. I was a little confused in my mind, but I didn't want anyone to hear about my encounter.'

His father turned from him in disgust. John raised a hand as if to touch his shoulder, but hesitated, then let it drop, his head hanging dejectedly. Baldwin thought he looked as miserable as a whipped hound. 'You did not see Bruther again after the meeting on the road?' he asked. John did not look up, merely shook his head.

After a moment, Simon sighed heavily. 'Very well. You may go for now.'

'But I—' He looked at his father, who suddenly spun round.

'You heard the bailiff. Go!' he shouted tersely, and with a cowed air, John slowly turned from them and walked to the steps.

'So you see, bailiff,' said Sir William, once his son was out of earshot, 'he had nothing to do with the murder. He's only a *thief*!' He spat the word contemptuously.

Baldwin contemplated him for a moment. Then, speaking calmly, he said, 'There are many men who do foolish things when young, Sir William.' The old knight's head shot round to stare at him. 'I do not say this to offer you unfounded hope. Many learn the pleasure of power while young but grow into honour later. Your son has started badly, but if he joins an honourable company of mercenaries in Italy, he can still redeem himself. Do not be too hard on him.'

The old knight nodded thoughtfully with a strangely suspicious expression that also showed a stirring hope. He turned to Simon. 'That depends on you, bailiff. Will my son be held as a robber? Or will you let him carry on to go to Italy?'

Simon did not answer immediately. He was mulling over the boy's story. It certainly fitted the facts as they knew them . . . but it left him with the same problem as before: who was the rider heard by Coyt on the moor?

'If you will make good Wat Meavy's losses, I see no reason why I should trouble myself over the matter. He has not yet reported the affair to me, so if you reach him quickly and refund his stolen money, I may never hear more of it. And if I don't, there's little point in my getting involved, is there?' Sir William nodded, relieved. 'But I would ask that you don't tell John yet. Let him suffer his feelings of guilt for a while, because it may make him realise just how serious his behaviour has been. Let him stew, and we will talk again about him later.'

Sir William nodded again. Uttering a deep sigh, he walked off in the same direction as his son. Baldwin crossed to his friend's side, staring after the bent figure of the old knight.

'It is hard to believe that he was once a great and feared man, isn't it?' he mused.

Simon was faintly surprised at the sympathy in his voice. 'Yes,' he agreed. 'It's easy to forget that someone like him was once young and full of fire.'

'Oh, I do not know about that! He was full enough of fire earlier on, when he had just learned what sort of man his son was.'

'Yes – but look at him now.' Their eyes followed the knight as he went to the stairs to his hall. At one point, he stumbled and nearly fell. In the shadows near the stables stood a man-at-arms, and he stepped forward quickly to help the old knight. As he moved into the light, Simon saw it was Samuel Hankyn. Sir William stood suddenly still as if shocked at his own lack of coordination, a man forced to recognise his own old age. Simon felt his heart lurch in sympathy at the sight. Sir William Beauscyr was old and worn down by too many crises – a man who had lived over-long and seen his son turn to dishonour, a man waiting for death. The bailiff turned away from the miserable sight as Hankyn escorted his noble employer to the comfort of his chamber.

'Poor old man.' Simon felt Baldwin's keen eyes on him even as he spoke.

'Perhaps. I wonder if Bruther would feel the same compassion for his old master, though.'

# CHAPTER NINETEEN

The clamorous tolling of the chapel bell brought Simon to instant wakefulness, and he lurched to his feet. In the hall it was still half-dark, with the early sun failing to reach high enough to enter through the windows. Standing, he felt a surge of angry resentment. He hated fast wakings. At home, if he was shocked from his slumber he was as fractious as a child for the rest of the day. Now it was worse, for he could see no reason for the interruption of his rest. Hugh sat up on his bench, rubbing bleary eyes, Baldwin stood frowning, and two of the Beauscyr servants scratched and yawned nearby. Only then did they hear the row from outside.

Grasping his sword and belt, Simon fumbled with the buckle as he stumbled to the door. Baldwin joined him in the screens, not bothering with his scabbard. He had simply snatched the blade from its sheath and now stood beside the bailiff with the cold white steel flashing and glinting, Edgar by his side, his face inscrutable. A moment later Hugh was with them, his long dagger gripped so tightly that his knuckles showed white. Simon tugged the door open.

At first the bailiff was convinced the fort was under attack. It was mayhem, with men rushing pell-mell from one end of the courtyard to the other, some holding helmets in their hands, others struggling with belts and shields, all woken by the alarm call. Then he smelled the acrid stench of burning, and when he glanced to his left, he saw that smoke was billowing from the stables. From the look of the column of smoke it was a miracle that the building had not been engulfed, but then, as he knew, grass and straw made a lot more smoke than they warranted.

He was blinking furiously from the stinging fumes. There appeared to be no order or sense to the panicking men. Guards stood at the walls, bellowing and waving, some shouted back from the courtyard, and all was madness: men mindlessly rushing to and fro, and others roaring commands.

Suddenly, Sir William appeared in the courtyard beneath the stairs. He quickly took in the situation and began barking orders. Under his control the men stopped their mad racing and a semblance of calm took over. Horses were pulled from the stables while a chain of men formed from the spring, passing buckets to and fro and hurling water on to the flames. At the knight's bellow, servants ran to the sheds by the kitchen and grabbed the long poles and ladders stored there. Thatch smouldered above the stables, and these men clambered up to the roof and used the poles to drag it down to the ground, where others stamped on it. Soon all was done, and the men stood or shuffled in the thin light of early morning, laughing in their relief and chattering like children at a fair.

As soon as he saw that the fire was well under control.' Sir William pointed to a guard, and Simon saw it was the captain who had fetched Samuel on their first day in the fort. 'You! What the devil happened?'

'Sir, I don't know.' The man shrugged in bafflement. 'The guard just found the hay on fire, and when we came out, it was all as you saw it.'

Simon glanced at the kitchen, quiet and deserted this early in the morning. Kitchen fires often released sparks which caught on the thatch of other buildings, and all too often the kitchens themselves would blaze up. That was why they were commonly separated from the hall and other buildings, but it did not stop the odd glowing mote from travelling to other roofs, and that was what must have happened here. There was no mystery in it. He shrugged, gave Baldwin a tired grin, and was about to return to the hall and wait for breakfast, followed by a nap if he could manage it, when another man ran to the foot of the steps.

Ignoring the guard captain, he stared imploringly at Sir William. 'Sir William, you must come quickly!'

'What is it now?' the old man snarled.

'Sir, it's Samuel Hankyn and Ronald Taverner – they're dead!'

Simon felt his mouth gape, while beside him, the knight froze in horrified shock. Baldwin recovered first and leapt down the stairs, agile as a deer, while Simon rushed after him. Both ran to the little room where they had spoken to the two men.

In the gloomy interior it would have been easy to think that Ronald Taverner was merely sleeping. He lay on his palliasse, his eyes closed and his head resting on his bundle of clothes as if he was shortly to wake, and Simon was tempted to call to him. But the blanket had been pulled aside, and his pale chest could be seen, the evil puckered stab wound showing clearly like a small purse-lipped mouth. Simon groaned and turned away while Baldwin, his face screwed into a frown of intense concentration, slipped forward and surveyed the body. There was a man kneeling beside the bed, and Baldwin was speaking to him as Sir William came in, his son Robert beside him.

'So what is this? Is Taverner dead?'

'Yes, Sir Robert. He's dead. Another murder,' said Baldwin shortly.

'A murder? And in the fort itself this time? Are you sure?' demanded Robert.

Baldwin did not attempt to answer. If the young man could not see the wound, that was his affair, and the knight had more important work to do.

Sir Robert noticed Simon standing by the doorway. 'So, bailiff, it appears you are as incapable of preventing murders as you are at solving them.'

Simon gave him a slow and contemptuous glance, then moved to Baldwin's side. Something dug into his foot and he bent to pick it up. It was a die, and he handed it to Baldwin, who took it and tossed it up and down as he considered the body. 'Well?' Simon asked. He felt miserable at another needless death, and could not take his eyes from the still form before him.

The knight gave a helpless shrug. 'He was stabbed, you can see that for yourself. It must have been very recent. His body is quite hot, not at all cold. You can see there's almost no blood. I've only seen that once or twice before; it's rare.

Normally I would expect to find more . . .' His voice trailed off.

'Sir? Do you want to see Samuel now?'

The knight looked up with sharp interest. 'Where is he?'

'Just out here.' The man led the way through a low door in the far corner. Beyond was a tiny room used as a storehouse. Just inside it was a number of fallen barrels, and here, slumped among them, was Samuel. He lay face down. One arm was twisted up behind his back as if to slap at a mosquito or horse fly, the other resting beneath his head. His body was contorted. He had suffered agony in dying, that much was clear.

Simon could not stare at the crumpled figure before him. It was one death too many, and it radiated a tangible sadness and pain in this little room which had become a mausoleum. He found himself putting a hand to his head, partially covering his eyes, as if to hide from the sight.

Striding out, Baldwin snatched a lantern from a gawping boy, then jerked his head at Edgar. 'Get these people out. Hugh will help you.' He jabbed a finger at the man who appeared to have discovered the two bodies. 'He can stay.'

Nodding, Edgar began to shepherd the crowd from the little room. It was some moments before they had peace; the men in the courtyard were trying to squeeze through the little doorway as Hugh and Edgar forced them back. At last, when he had the door barred, Edgar noticed that Sir William and his son had remained where they stood. The manservant was considering asking them to leave as well when he heard Baldwin's call, and forgetting them he hurried to the door. Baldwin gave him the lantern to hold so that he could study the figure.

At first he surveyed the position of the body, standing stock still while his eyes roved over the limbs, fixing their position in his mind, memorising where the toppled barrels lay and then glancing round at the other stacks of goods. He could see that the man must have fallen forwards. Apart from the collapsed pile of barrels on to which he had fallen, there was no other sign of a struggle. He crouched and examined the nearest barrel. Right beside it on the ground was a circle, and he nodded to himself. 'Look, Simon, this one tipped over from where it had stood.' He rocked the barrel tentatively. 'Not very heavy, either. The others must have been stacked on top of it.'

Letting his eyes take in the scene again, he moved up to the body. A few inches above Samuel's hand was a sharp tear in the wool of his coat. Touching it lightly, Baldwin could feel the stickiness, and his lip curled in distaste. 'Yes, he was stabbed too. In the back.'

'What can have happened?'

'I'm not sure.' Baldwin's eyes went to the other body on the bed. Taking the light from Edgar, he strode to the palliasse. 'Ah!'

'What?' Simon followed him. 'What have you found?'

'Look.' Baldwin turned, and in his hand was a short-bladed knife, its steel dulled with dried blood. 'This must be what killed them.'

Sir William's voice came from the store-room. 'Sir Baldwin, there's a knife out here too.'

'What?' The knight's face registered astonishment for a moment, then he darted through to where the old knight stood frowning at a thin-bladed knife, turning it over and over in his hand.

Baldwin took it from him and studied it. 'So what has happened here, then?' he muttered.

'I can guess,' said Sir Robert. 'There were regular gambling games down here. The guards get bored too often, and then they resort to playing at dice. These two were obviously playing at some game, began arguing and soon came to blows. They stabbed each other.'

'That is a truly magnificent hypothesis,' murmured Baldwin, and the young knight gave a slight smile, pleased with the older man's approbation. Simon could hear the dry sarcasm in his friend's tone and for a moment his mood lightened.

'It would explain it, wouldn't it?' the young knight said, glancing smugly at Simon.

'Oh, yes!' Baldwin's voice registered emphatic agreement.

Smiling, Robert walked from the store-room, stared briefly at the body on the bed, then went out. Hugh closed the door after him. Sir William had watched his son depart, but now his gaze returned to Baldwin, who was again studying Samuel's figure. 'So you aren't convinced, Sir Baldwin?' he asked, his voice calm and steady.

'No. Not at all.'

'Why?'

'It is too simple on the one hand, and too difficult on the other. Oh, I am sure that the poor lad in there on his mattress died almost instantly from his wound. There was no blood, and I think that means he was dead in an instant. No blood always does seem to indicate a quick death. But this one, Samuel – he managed to stagger all the way out here, over from the bed, before dying.'

'So?'

'Sir William, this man bled a lot. Feel the back of his coat if you don't believe me. There's a good pool of blood here where he lies. Yet there's no blood on the floor by Ronald's palliasse, or from the bed to here. He was not stabbed there, he died here, where he fell.'

'But . . . but surely he could still have been killed by the other. Ronald must have stabbed him here, and then made his way back to his bed where he himself died.'

'I fear not. As I said, Ronald died almost instantaneously. What is stored in these boxes and things?'

The question caught Sir William unawares. 'Out here? Food and some drink, I think. And spare cloth. Nothing much. Why?'

'I just wondered why this man would have wanted to come out here.' Baldwin's gaze was travelling around the room as he spoke. There was no window, just a small door which gave onto the courtyard. When Baldwin walked to it and tried it, it was barred.

Simon gave him an enquiring look, and the knight shrugged. 'It means nothing,' he said. 'It is barred now, but the murderer might have got in last night and barred it afterwards, once he had killed Samuel.'

'What are you saying – that someone in the garrison killed these two?' demanded Sir William, his face reddening.

'Hmm? Oh, yes, without a doubt as far as I'm concerned. Somebody came in here, probably through the locked door, and called out or kicked over a stack of barrels to attract Samuel's attention. Why else should he come here? When the poor man entered he was grabbed and stabbed in the back. It would not have taken long for him to die, not with a wound that high on his back. Then the same man went through to Ronald's room and stabbed him through the heart, possibly while he was asleep, but that's a guess. Whether the dice were already on the floor or not is unimportant, but it is possible the killer scattered them as an afterthought to suggest the idea that there had been a gambling fight. Then it was simply a matter of dropping knives about, after dipping them in blood, to leave us with the clear inference that they must have slaughtered each other. I have no doubt we were expected to think that these two had fallen out over money, but I find it hard – no, impossible – to believe that, after seeing the two of them together. They were too friendly.'

Sir William appeared to shrivel as Baldwin spoke. Simon half-expected the old man to fall to the floor as the knight finished talking, he looked so frail and weak. His face took on an introspective look. 'And is there anything else? Anything to indicate who it could have been?' he asked, but Baldwin did not respond. He carried on searching the rooms in his quest for clues while the others watched. They were still there when the servant began pounding on the door and shouting once more for Sir William.

Sir Robert watched his brother with a dry, humourless smile. He had heard of the row of the night before, and was amused to see how it had affected his brother. John stood apart, not wanting to talk to the men-at-arms who helped Robert to his horse, or to the men who climbed on to their own horses to join in the hunt. He waited like a sulking child at the periphery of all the noise as the men prepared.

There was still an all-encompassing smell of burned wood and straw from the stable, and it was partly this which had persuaded Robert to go and search for food. He had no desire to wait in the fort and supervise the men clearing up. After the night before he knew that John would prefer to be leaving the Manor for the morning too, and that gave him cause for a certain sadistic pleasure, knowing he could not go. On a whim he walked his horse over to where his brother stood.

'Come, brother. Why don't you join us?' John looked up, and Robert saw the despair in his eyes. It made him regret his sarcastic, bantering query, to see his brother so smothered by fears. When he spoke again his voice was softer. 'John? Are you all right? Would you like me to stay with you? The men can go alone, if you want to talk.'

'To you?' For a moment all Robert could see was the surprise, and he gave a twisted smile. It did sound odd. For the last few weeks they had quarrelled incessantly, neither wanting to approach too close to the other. Their ideas were too different, their motives, their interests, their very souls, were worlds apart. Each time they came together they sparked, like flint and steel. But it left Robert with a hole he could feel in his heart. He wanted a brother he could call his friend, a man to whom he could talk, with whom he could discuss his anxieties and his hopes, a man he could speak to of his love for Alicia, and who would understand and give encouragement. It was more than that: he needed somebody he could trust wholeheartedly, a man he could rely on, especially now he was to become master of Beauscyr. And especially since the death of Bruther. He leaned forward in his saddle, so that his head was close to his brother's, and no one else could hear his words.

'Look, John, if you want me to, I'll stay here to speak to you. You'll be going soon, I know, and I don't want you to leave with any bad feelings.' An air of uncertainty crept into his brother's face and John peered up at him, biting his lip. It emboldened Robert. 'When Father is dead and I am master here, you'll always be welcome to visit, and—'

The spell was broken. With those few words, John lost his indecision. A sneer twisted his features into a grimace of disgust and he took a half-step backwards. 'So you can feel generous to me, you mean? So you can allow me the scrapings from your table, like an old man begging alms at your door?' Robert wanted to cry out, to stop the flow of spite and jealousy, but the words stuck in his throat. 'How kind, brother. How very kind! So you will let me come back here every now and then to see how well you are: how profitable your estate is; how plentiful your children are. I fear, brother, that I might not be able to. I fear that I might prefer to stay in Italy. A gaol there would please me more than to see you living here happily, and as far as I am concerned, once our father is dead, I will have no wish to see you or the estate ever again. So thank you, brother. I hope you enjoy your hunt.' *And break your damned neck!* he added inwardly.

Robert stared, all colour drained from his face, As though carved from marble, he sat rigid and unmoving on his horse, and only then did John see that there was no pride in his attitude, only hurt rejection. Then John ached to take his words back, to try to explain . . . but it was too late. The damage was done.

His spine stiff and straight, Robert kicked his horse into a canter and swept through the first, then the second gate, out to the open moors beyond. It would not do to let the rest of the hunting party guess at his torment. Up in front was the rising land, a broad expanse topped by a small clump of trees, towards which he headed, the hooves of his followers' horses pounding behind him. There was a thick lump of despair in his chest. He could hardly think coherently, for every thought led him back to John and the terrible contempt in his younger brother's eyes.

That was why the ambush was such a dramatic success.

# CHAPTER TWENTY

George Harang watched the men approaching with a feeling akin to panic. If only there hadn't been that fire, he thought. The Manor would not have been awake so early, they would all still have been at their breakfasts, not up and active – and it was far too early to send out a party to hunt. He slapped a fist into his cupped hand. The preparations were not even half-completed.

And yet the men were coming on, as if they had not seen his group of miners lying in wait. It was a strong force of men-at-arms, one man out in front ignoring the others, riding as stiff as a board of wood, apparently uncaring whether his guards could keep up with him or not.

Harold quickly assessed the chances of success, and then signalled urgently to the man next to him and gave his instructions.

If only John had not been so quick to take offence, Robert lamented as he lashed his horse up the slope. Why should he be so swift to anger just because the older of the two was to inherit the estate? It was the natural way of things, not some curious new injustice.

He clenched his jaw resolutely. There had been no need for John to spurn his attempt at reconciliation, it had been offered in all sincerity. And yet the jeering withdrawal of his brother had made it clear that there could be no friendship between them. But despite his own anger, Robert could still feel the prickle behind his eyes.

Then he saw the figure of a man standing up on the skyline before him, waving his arms urgently. Robert set spurs to his horse and increased his speed. At least someone wants my help, he thought, a bitter grin twisting his lips.

As he came closer, he saw that the man was familiar. The body stocky and trim, the legs short, the trunk thick like an oak tree. It was George Harang.

'*Now!*' bellowed George.

Suddenly the ground was full of miners. A group appeared in front of him, and as he whirled, Robert saw that he was surrounded. More were behind, some facing him with smiles of disdain at his stupidity while others turned back towards his men, fitting arrows to bows. Robert stared, stunned. The blood pounded in his veins, thundering at his temples like the steady beat of a warhorse at full gallop, and he felt a chill creep over him.

George walked down towards him, laughing loudly, issuing orders and keeping a wary eye on the members of the hunting party. 'Tie him up!'

\*    \*    \*

'Sir William, Sir William!' The pounding on the door sounded as though it was going to shatter the timbers to dust, and the old knight lifted his eyes to it with resignation. Was there never any peace, he wondered. Irritably he walked to the door and tugged it wide.

'What the devil is—'

'Sir William, it's the miners. They've come and they've captured your son – we saw them from the walls, sir. They—'

Baldwin and Simon raced up and listened at either side of the old knight as the messenger stuttered and stammered, his pale, round face wrinkled and anxious, reminding Baldwin of his old mastiff, who was no doubt lying comfortably in front of his fire at Furnshill. Shaking the idea from his head, he caught the end of the message: 'And they took him, knocked him from his horse, and—'

Baldwin grasped him by the shoulder. The man had greying hair and black, misshapen teeth in a revolting, slack mouth. Blue eyes stared back, the terror in them plain to see. Gradually he calmed under the serious stare of the knight's dark brown eyes. 'Good, now, start again. You say that your master's son has been taken. Which one?'

'Sir Robert, sir,' the man gulped.

'And he was taken by miners?'

'Yes, sir. The men at the gate saw it. There was George Harang and others, and they caught Sir Robert just at the top of the hill, when he went out to hunt. There were lots of them, and they tied his hands and took him away.'

'Where to? Which way did they go?'

'Towards the miners' camp, I suppose. One of the men has followed. We're getting the rest of the horses saddled now, sir.'

'Good.' Baldwin stared at Sir William. 'We must hurry; this cannot be permitted. It is one thing to take moormen hostage, quite another to take a knight captive.'

'Do you know of any reason why they should have taken your son, Sir William?' asked Simon.

'No, I've no idea why they should do this,' declared the knight with frank astonishment. 'We've always lived side by side with the miners on the moors, and there's never been anything like this before. We've paid when they wanted money, we've not intimidated them, I've recognised their power, and it would have been stupid to try to curb them – that would only have led to more troubles. No, I've no idea why they should have done this.'

Simon slowly nodded. 'Very well. Let's get ready, then.'

Hugh and Edgar trailed after them. Baldwin's man wore a happy smile, and he clapped Hugh on the back as they went. 'Don't worry,' he said cheerfully. 'It'll be fun,' and began whistling.

'Fun!' muttered Hugh contemptuously and sniffed. He had the unpleasant suspicion that there would be blood shed, and he had no wish to see the colour of his own.

In the courtyard they found a mass of confused and anxious men. Some wore helmets, some mail, but most simply had their leather or quilted jackets. All gripped weapons, rough agricultural tools or long-handled pikes; only a few wore swords. One stood with shy embarrassment clutching a worn billhook. Pale faces or flushed, all held the same quiet concern. It was one thing, Baldwin knew, to accept a master's food and lodging, but when it came to protecting him, the nature of an oath of allegiance took on a wholly different and more fearsome meaning. All these people were aware of how little Sir William must value each of their lives against that of his oldest surviving son, and in their eyes he read the age-old calculation: would their leader be able to win without throwing away his men's lives needlessly? It was there in the narrow watchfulness, in the slow, unhurried movements, in the careful stroking of a hand over the haft of a lance. All these men felt the same tension as they looked at Sir William.

Baldwin was about to turn and mention this to the knight when the older man pushed past him, going to the stairs and climbing halfway up them. But this was not the same Sir William. A few moments before, he had been an elderly man bent with his cares, his vitality sapped by recent events. No longer. Now he was a warlord.

There was no shout from the crowd to welcome him. At a hanging, even the victim would get cheery applause, but not Sir William. The men stared up at him, and he stared back, and a strange stillness slowly settled on them all, curiously out of place for such a sizeable group. It was no surprise, Baldwin reflected. After all, these men had seen the steady decline of the head of the Beauscyr family. They all knew that he had few enough years left. His walk had gradually slowed, he tired more easily, and the strength which had marked him out as a great warrior had begun to fail him.

For several minutes there was no sound but for the whip and crackle of clothes drying in the gusting breeze on the lines by the kitchen. The sun peered between some clouds and added a tinge of warmth, but still Sir William stared. Some men began to shuffle, their feet restlessly slapping in the little puddles of sloshed water from the buckets.

'You all know what's happened to my son.' His tone was pensive, almost sad, but carried clearly. 'He's been captured by miners and taken away. I don't know why. It could be that the tinners want to hold him to ransom. They've done it to others before, though they've never dared do it to *me* in the past. It's probably because I agreed to pay them not to damage the Manor's lands. Now they feel so powerful, they think they can threaten even me. It's my fault, if they think that. I should have realised. But I could do nothing, because they threatened other things if I tried to use force to keep them from here. I had to pay. I am sorry, because it means that you all must now fight to help me free my son.'

Now he stood upright, and there was no sign of his age as he glowered down. 'But understand this, all of you. This is not just for me and my family. It is to save *you*! If the miners get away with this, they'll know they've beaten the strongest in the moors. They can't be permitted to take hostages freely whenever they wish. If they do that, no man will be free any more, not just knights, but farmers and merchants, villeins, even the men in the tenements – all will have to submit to the miners. Do you want that? They will feel able to go anywhere, into your fields, ruining your families' crops. That is what will happen if we allow them to win now. They will know they have the power to order.'

His voice grew, swelling until it filled the square yard, and the men stopped shuffling and listened closely, many with frowns of understanding darkening their faces. One or two glanced at friends, nodding with a new conviction. Sir William carried on. 'I don't ask any of you to follow me to free my son. Few if any of you feel the need to defend him, beyond your duty to the Manor and to the land's heir. But you have to come with me today. Not for me or for him, but for yourselves and for the other people of the moors, to protect yourselves and to keep the land free for all. We have to break the arrogance of these miners and make them understand that they cannot continue to threaten and extort, steal and harry. They have to learn that we will stand our ground and defend ourselves. And the way to do this is to free my son. I do not want to fight, I'm old and my time for war has passed, but I will not let robbers and outlaws take my land without holding a sword to them and saying, "No more!" No, I do not want to fight – but I will if I must, and now, today, I may have to. So may you. Not for me, not for my son, *but for yourselves.*'

Suddenly he grasped his sword and whipped it from its scabbard, holding it over his head. 'Is any man among you not prepared to fight for your land?'

The yard erupted in a great bellow of denial, the shouts echoing round the buildings and making the horses stamp and snort. A hound barked, deep and mournful.

'Then mount your horses and follow me!'

Baldwin cast an eye over the men, now cheering and waving their arms. It was a good effort, he admitted to himself. Men who a few minutes before had been muttering blackly about standing up for the son of a knight who should have seen his peril, or who had nervously fingered weapons while thinking about the miners' own, men who had wondered how much the tinners would ask for Sir Robert's life and whether it would be too much, who flinched at the thought of injury – for in the heat of summer a wound could fester, and that spelled a slow and tortured death . . . all now raised swords, daggers and polearms over their heads and applauded. The first lesson that a warrior captain has to learn, he thought drily, is how to persuade the men fighting for him that they are fighting for themselves. Sir William had been a soldier for many years, and that lesson was one he had not forgotten. One man, he saw, had his arm slashed by a carelessly handled knife; he stared dumbly at the dripping blood for a moment before waving and cheering again. The sight made Baldwin sigh. It was strange how men could decide to throw in their lot with someone just because of a pretty speech.

'Impressive.' Sir Ralph had walked up unseen by the others, and Baldwin glanced at him with a question in his dark eyes. He had not seen the knight all day, not during the panicked rush to put out the fire, nor when the bodies were found. Now he stood surveying the men in the square with a kind of sad recognition. 'I used to be like them,' he said musingly. 'Full of fire and honour. Keen to defend my rights and privileges, come what may and the Devil take my enemies. Now it's just for money I fight, and money doesn't last as long as a cause. Nor does it flame the belly as well.'

'At least it keeps your belly filled for a while,' said Simon lightly from behind.

Sir Ralph did not meet the bailiff's gaze, staring instead at Baldwin. 'Only for a while. Only for a while. And when the money's gone, there's nothing else. No cause, no honour, no great freedoms. Just a search for more money.' He glanced at the crowd. 'At least they have their cause today, even if it won't last.'

Baldwin mulled over his words as they fetched their horses and prepared to ride out. The man's face had held an infinite sadness, as if he sorely missed times past when he had honourable battles to fight, one loyal and chivalrous man in a company of similarly motivated warriors. Baldwin could understand his feelings of loss and the sense of missing purpose: it was the same lack of direction he had known when his Order had been destroyed, which had consumed him until he had undertaken his search for the man he felt must be responsible. Yes, Baldwin could easily comprehend his feelings.

Simon was on his horse and waiting long before Baldwin. In the mêlée which was the yard, simply keeping the horses calm enough to be saddled was taxing Hugh and Edgar, and thus it was that Simon was the first to see the younger Beauscyr brother. From his vantage point, looking over the heads of the crowd, he could see the boy clearly at the foot of the steps, his thumbs in his belt as he cast a sullen glance over the milling people. Sir William spoke to him, then looked around for Simon. A moment later he strode over to the bailiff's side.

'Bailiff, I want John to join us today.'

'I don't think we'll need him,' Simon said, gesturing at the men-at-arms all round. 'I think we have a strong enough force.'

'That's not the point and you know it,' said the old knight firmly. 'Robert is his brother. John has a right to aid us in freeing him.'

'Perhaps. Wouldn't it be better to leave him here, though? He can see to the Manor's defences.'

'My wife is more than capable of doing that. No, his place is with us.'

Simon paused for a moment. Both were aware that there was no need for Sir William to ask – if he wished, he could have the bailiff bound and kept under guard while he took his men. 'If you tell me why, I will agree.'

Sir William gave a terse nod. 'Very well. The two of them argued this morning. John thinks that it was because of their quarrel that Robert rode into the ambush in such a head-strong manner. If they had not fallen out Robert would have been more careful, and at the very least would not have ridden so far in front of the hunting-party and thus have been captured so easily. John feels very bad about it, bailiff. He wants to help free Robert.'

Simon shrugged, then nodded. 'That is just cause. Bring him.'

All the men were ready now. Baldwin was up on his heavy rounsey, and their servants were mounted too, Edgar still wearing his excited air. The courtyard went quiet as Sir William and his son climbed on to their horses, and then the mounted men rode out through the gates and off up the slope before the fort. Others would follow on foot.

At the trees on top of the hill they were met by a messenger, red-faced and panting after his mad dash over the moors.

'Thank God I caught you, Sir William! The miners who hold your son are at the tin workers' camp out on the moors.'

'Good. Get a fresh horse and follow.'

Sir William kicked his horse and rode on, vaguely aware of Simon and Baldwin behind. At his side was his son and Sir Ralph, but the old knight kept his eyes fixed ahead, in case his face betrayed his doubts and fears. He simply could not understand what Thomas Smyth hoped to achieve by taking Robert.

It was not as if they had constantly argued and fought. The Manor had long accepted the unpalatable fact that the miners had rights on the moors, and had not molested them like many other landowners. Some men took a tax on all tin mined on their estates, but Sir William had early come to the opinion that it would be better to leave them to their work. There were other ways to make money that would not involve upsetting the King's officials and bringing ruin on the family. By and large the miners and he had managed to coexist. That was what made this hostage-taking so incomprehensible. If there had been a long-established grievance, he would have been able to understand, but as far as he knew there was no reason.

He cast a surreptitious glance at his other son. John rode hunched up, as if nursing a private grief. Sir William would not be surprised if his younger son were responsible somehow for this débâcle. He clenched his jaw angrily as he enumerated the problems caused by the squire: his constant bickering with Robert, his arrogance and rudeness, his stupidity in robbing that man over towards Chagford, all now seemed to have led to this latest disaster. Somehow, the old knight felt, it *was* all John's fault.

That led him to wonder what the bailiff thought of his son. Simon had made it more than clear that he doubted John's word, and considered him at best unreliable. Sir William would not have been surprised if the bailiff thought that the lad had killed Bruther – and probably stabbed the two men-at-arms as well. There was no clear motive for him to have committed the three murders but John simply appeared to have a lust for mischief and crime – he himself had confirmed that when he confessed to the robbery. And again, that was an offence with no good reason. If John had needed money, he could have asked his father for it. There was no need to take to the road. His only saving grace, Sir William knew, was in his youth. Many men, he acknowledged ruefully, took to the robber bands, to the marauding companies which roamed widely wherever the rule of law had fallen down. John's crimes, whatever they might have been while he was a shavaldore in the north, were surely not so heinous compared with some others.

There was only one thing that mattered right now, though, and that was gaining Robert's release. He must free his older son, no matter what.

Baldwin was still thinking about the two dead men. So much had happened already this morning that he felt as exhausted as if he had been up all night. The fire, then the deaths, the ambush and taking of Sir Robert . . . all merged and blurred together in his mind, and he was trying to set them into a logical sequence. It was offensive, he knew, to drop the murder investigation like this, but while Robert was alive it was the duty of anyone who could help to try to get him freed. And if it was possible, the bailiff must attempt to stop any fighting, though after Sir William's speech that would be harder. Now all the men from the Manor were anticipating a battle. The blood of a western man was always slow to be warmed, God knew, but once stirred, he would fight to the death for what he thought was right.

Baldwin thought again about the two dead men, his mind casting around for a logical explanation. Who could have wanted them dead? It was a mystery, for both seemed pleasant-enough men. True, fights often broke out among garrison troops who were bored when posted far from the nearest town, that was why modern castles were built with separate quarters for loyal men compared with hirelings: so that arguments among the troops could be contained, and the lord and his loyal men could bar their doors and keep out any fighting. In such cases, the fighting was commonly due to gambling arguments. Perhaps that was what had caused the murders here, too. Somebody could have been in the room with Samuel playing at dice, and an argument might have developed. Whoever it was might have walked from the room into the stores, knocked over the barrels to make a disturbance, and when Samuel followed to find out what was the matter, stabbed him in the back. Ronald could have heard the scuffle and woken, so he too was killed . . .

Baldwin frowned. No, that did not feel right. There were too many little details which niggled at him. Such as, when the barrels were knocked over, why had Baldwin himself not heard it? Any soldier would know to put a hand over his victim's mouth when stabbing him in the back – that would be common sense to prevent any hue and cry – but the row of the barrels falling must surely have been loud. Why was it not heard in the hall above? Baldwin and Edgar were both light sleepers after so many years of living as travellers and soldiers, and any such sudden noise during the night must have awakened them.

No, such a row could not have happened while they were asleep; it must have occurred while they were *outside the hall*. What is more, both bodies were still warm, which meant that the men had died later in the morning, probably while he and Simon were awake and in the yard . . . With all the noise of the bell and the fire-fighting, nobody would have noticed the dull thud of barrels falling. Nor could it have been connected with a gambling argument. Soldiers would play dice at any time of day, but so early in the morning?

'There it is!'

The call from the rider in front woke him from his reverie. Time enough later to go through the details again. Right now, there was a boy to rescue and, if possible, a fight to avoid. Sighing, he felt for his sword and loosened it in the scabbard, praying that there might be no more deaths this day.

Before them, the camp had an air of calm sleepiness. The little cottages lay dotted with smoke rising from their hearths like a peaceful village, and the lack of a stockade gave it an aura of confidence and stolidity, as if it had no need to fear nature or other men – and indeed, few would attempt to rob a miners' camp. Anyone so foolhardy as to try would discover how attached a tinner was to his profit. There had been an occasion Baldwin had heard about down in Cornwall, when an abbot had decided to levy his own tax on the metal mined in his lands and had sent a force to demand payment. The abbot had soon learned that under provocation, men can swarm like bees and sting – and he was forced to reduce his demands.

A few paces away, Sir Ralph was half-expecting Sir William to ride in like a warrior of old, razing the place to the ground in a wild orgy of destruction, horses thundering down the plain, the men reaching out with their swords and lances, slashing and stabbing at all in their path. That was the old way, the *chevauchée*, the riding out of chivalry.

But Sir William had learned his warfare among men like these miners and he disdained a mad rush. From what he had heard, his adversaries understood how to site archers, the same as the Welsh, against whom he had struggled with the old King Edward. Back in those days, he and others had been impressed by the skills of their enemies, especially their ability to use the land to funnel horsemen into small areas where the horses could be slowed and their riders pulled down. He had no wish to be tricked like this, nor to lose any lives unnecessarily, especially that of his son.

Sir William carefully scrutinised the lie of the land. It dropped from here down to the stream, with the little buildings dotted around like pebbles scattered on a board. There was no apparent defence, no barricades or walls behind which archers could hide, just the close-positioned huts. It was these which would offer protection. The alleys and lanes between would allow ropes to be strung to knock riders from the saddle. Men could be lying in wait behind the cottages, ready to spring out and club or stab. There could be little doubt that the miners already knew that he and his force were here. They must have had a lookout watching from on high. He glanced to either side. To the left was a small cluster of rocks – the ideal site for a guard, commanding a good view all over the land to the east. It would have taken no time to leap down, climb on to a pony and gallop for the camp.

Sir Ralph and Baldwin joined him. The mercenary jerked his head down towards the vill. 'Where do you think they'll have put him?'

'I have no idea. He could be in any of those huts.' Sir William suddenly felt exhausted. Slumping in his saddle he turned a tired face to Baldwin. 'What do you think. Sir Baldwin?'

Studying the area, Baldwin did not answer for a moment, then pointed. 'There, in the blowing-house. It's the safest, most secure place. That's why the three miners were kept hidden there. The store-room has only the one door and no window. However, the other buildings all around make it hard to get to,'

'I think you're right,' the old knight nodded.

'Let's go and find out,' said Sir Ralph, his gaze going from one to the other in some confusion. 'Why are you waiting?'

'Because I know this tin-mining bastard,' said Sir William heavily. 'He was a soldier with me many years ago in Wales. He's no knight, maybe, but he was a good warrior nonetheless, and crafty.'

Simon moved up to their side. 'If it's a trap, he's baited it well. It's a tempting morsel he's put down. May I suggest we draw its teeth before we stand on it?'

'Speak plainly, man! What do you mean?' asked Sir William tetchily.

'I'll go down and try to speak to him. There's no sense in running in there at full tilt. Like you say, if he's had any experience of warfare, he'll have placed his men where we won't be able to get to them but where they can pour arrows into us. It makes no sense for us to run into that. He's unlikely to harm me, anyway. I've got nothing to do with this and he's not going to want to upset the warden and the King by hurting me.'

'I will join you, Simon,' said Baldwin. 'I should be safe too.'

'If you're both quite certain,' said Sir William, staring at them with apparent surprise. 'Are you sure you'll be safe?'

'As I say, he won't be in a hurry to upset the King – this *is* the King's land. He may be proud enough to offend you, but if the King heard that his bailiff was hurt, he would be down here in force and the miners would find their lives more difficult. No, we should be safe.'

Seeing Sir William's shrug of acceptance, they set off slowly down the long slope, loping cautiously with their servants.

'I thought it was a good idea back there,' said Baldwin musingly.

'And now?'

'It is very quiet, isn't it?'

He was right. Simon could hear the rhythmic gurgle and splash of the water round the wheel as he approached. The cottages all looked empty, but he had the uncomfortable sensation of being watched. It was like riding into one of the old farmsteads long since deserted, only here it was more alarming, for the smell of smoke lay all over. There should have been the bustle of people, with men cooking and hammering, chatting and shouting as they worked, and the silence was oppressive.

'Damn this! Let's ride in like men and stop this slow torture,' he muttered and was about to kick his horse, when Baldwin pointed with his chin at the ground.

'Not if you love your mount, old friend.'

Frowning, Simon followed his gaze and saw the little squares in the grass. There were holes dug all over the smooth, level area leading to the blowing-house, the turves relaid above to hide them. He gave a shame-faced grin and reluctantly nodded. Each turf hid a hole a foot deep, dug to break a horse's leg and stop any charge.

In among the cottages Baldwin glimpsed men waiting. In most ways they looked the same as those commanded by Sir William – a rough, scruffy crew used to working with the heavy picks and mauls they gripped, staring anxiously at the four men riding slowly in to speak to their master. The knight sighed. No matter what the dispute, he knew, it was always the way with war: the wealthy bickered and the poor fought and died for their cause.

At the blowing-house they stopped and waited, remaining seated on their horses. Looking at Baldwin, Simon saw that he was quite calm and at ease, and the bailiff gave a grimace. His own stomach was bubbling, and he could taste bitter acid. At a sudden noise his horse skittered nervously, and he cursed it, gripping hard with his knees. When he looked up again he found himself meeting the enquiring gaze of Thomas Smyth. The miner stood grasping a heavy falchion, an old sword which had chips from its single edge to show its past had not been peaceful; he appeared surprised to encounter the bailiff and his friend.

Simon felt his fear dissipate. It was hard to be scared of a man who looked so sane and normal, and even if his meetings with the miner had not always been pleasant, Smyth was at least businesslike. 'Thomas,' he said, feeling suddenly tired and flat. 'Just what in damnation do you think you're doing?'

# CHAPTER TWENTY-ONE

They sat on the bench outside a cottage and sipped rough ale while Thomas Smyth watched them, his brows lowered. To Baldwin he had the air of a man pushed beyond patience. His black eyes were red-rimmed and sunken, making them appear bruised, and the lines in his face had deepened. Like Sir William, he had aged in the last few days.

'It was the final straw – when I heard about that whelp John Beauscyr, I mean, and how he'd been to the inn that evening. He must have passed Peter on the way there, after he had left his father at my hall.'

'So what?' asked Simon.

'John Beauscyr must have followed Peter afterwards and killed him.'

'But the miner had men with him – you knew that already.'

'Yes. I knew that. But I also know that the miners left him a little later and came back here. He told them he would not need them that night.'

'So when he went on to his cottage, he was alone?' Baldwin asked.

'Yes. All that way over the moors, he was on his own. It would have been an easy job to kill him.'

'You know how he died?' Simon said gently, and the tinner nodded sombrely.

'Throttled. Then hanged. It'd be easy enough for John Beauscyr to do that.'

'Perhaps. But why would he want to, that's what I don't understand.'

'He's a Beauscyr, isn't he? Peter had run away from their lands and made them look like fools. John wanted to get rid of the man who had shamed his family.'

'That's not how the boy thinks, Thomas. No, I find it difficult to believe that would have led him to murder. In the main he seems to enjoy seeing his brother at a disadvantage. I think he liked the runaway getting off the Manor's lands. At least, until he was shamed by Bruther himself.'

'How was he shamed?'

'The night he died, Bruther insulted John and Sir Ralph on the road, and that caused them to lose face.'

'Yes? Well, I'm sure Peter was provoked.'

'Provoked? When he had a force of men with him?' Baldwin's eyebrows rose. 'You suggest that when two men are confronted by eight the two will try to provoke the others? I do not find that entirely credible, Thomas.'

'Maybe it was unintentional. Knights can be arrogant fools.'

'So can villeins,' the knight observed caustically, and Thomas fell silent, throwing him a nervous glance.

'Any man can,' said Simon pacifically. 'It still doesn't tell us what this is all about,' and he gestured at the armed men nearby.

The miner stared at him. 'What this is all about? I'd have thought it was obvious! If the boy killed Peter, I want him to pay for it. My men couldn't get him, but his brother rode out, so they caught him instead.'

'And what now? What do you intend to do, now that you have captured Sir William's son? Kill him – or just hold him for your pleasure? Either way, there is a good-sized force led by the knight himself waiting just outside your camp, and he wants his boy back. Are you prepared to see more miners die just because you want to avenge Bruther?'

'Yes! I shall exchange Robert for John, and the whelp will get miner's justice for what he did.'

The emphatic confirmation made the bailiff and his friend exchange worried looks. Both men wanted to avert what promised to be a bruising and vicious battle. The miners numbered more than the force of forty mounted men-at-arms that Sir William could field, but other guards from the fort were on their way by foot, and if the old knight thought he had the advantage he could attack.

Baldwin leaned forward and met the unflinching, determined eyes of the miner. 'This makes no sense. You have lost a man, but that's hardly a good enough reason to risk the lives of all these others, Thomas. And we do not know that it *was* John who killed Bruther. Yes, he might have had an opportunity, but we think he was not in the area when Bruther was killed. He was over towards Chagford.'

There was a quick doubt in the miner's face at that. Baldwin continued softly, 'And Robert himself was nowhere near the place. We know that on the words of three people who saw him.' He saw no reason to say that one of the three was Smyth's own daughter. 'He was not involved.'

'So who did kill Peter?'

'We wondered about *you*,' admitted Simon frankly. 'Adam Coyt saw you near Bruther's place that day. What were you doing up there?'

To his surprise, the miner gave him a twisted grin. '*Me?*' He turned and beckoned to Harang, who stood sharpening a long dagger some feet off, staring up the plain to the group of horsemen. 'George, come here a minute. Right, tell these two what you and I were doing on the night that Peter died.'

The thickset man stared at Baldwin and Simon suspiciously. Seeing Thomas Smyth nod, he shrugged. 'We were here at the camp for most of the afternoon, checking on the blowing-house and seeing how it was working. When it got late, we left to go and see Peter up at his house. The day before, my master had offered him a job overseeing the smelting. It would make sense having someone here we knew and trusted to look after the ingots. We went to hear his answer, but the place was empty so we rode over to see Sir William at the hall.'

'You must have trusted Bruther to offer him that,' said Simon, pouring more drink. The jug was misshapen, the earthenware cracked and the spout broken, but it was not this that made him spill the fluid. It was the miner's next words.

'He was my *son*, bailiff.'

The two men sat back and gaped. Baldwin found himself thinking: So that is why he always called the young man by his Christian name – why did I not realise!

Simon stammered, 'But why . . . Surely you . . . Why the hell didn't you tell us!'

'Why the hell should I? Would it have changed the way you investigated his death? What would *you* have done, bailiff, if he had been your son? The same as me, I would think. I wanted to find out who had done it so that I could meet the killer and treat him the way he served my son. My only son.' He groaned in despair.

'I do not understand, Thomas,' said Baldwin gently. 'You say he was your son, but . . .?'

He looked at the knight and smiled weakly. 'My wife is a decent woman. Sir Baldwin. She has been good to me, and she gave birth to many children for me. But only Alicia survived; all the others died at birth or within a few years. Then poor Christine could not have another, and I learned to be content, because I had Peter.' His eyes took on a faraway look. 'His mother was Martha Bruther. She was lovely, widowed young, and I got to know her before I married. I had not even met Christine when I wooed Martha. I wanted her, I wanted her so much I was prepared to marry her, but she wouldn't have me. She'd tried marriage, she said, and preferred life on her own. Her husband used to beat her and it put her off taking another – she had no need of a man. But she was proud of Peter, our son.' He stopped, staring past Baldwin's shoulder as the memories came back.

'You could have saved us hours if we had known this before,' Simon said peevishly. 'We could have concentrated on the other suspects.' And then he cursed his insensitivity.

'I couldn't tell you before,' Smyth explained, 'not with my wife there. It would have hurt her too much. So I kept it back and tried to help you as far as I could. I didn't think it mattered.'

'And no more does it now,' said Baldwin compassionately. 'But we come back to the main issue: what will you do with Robert Beauscyr? He is innocent, I am sure, and you do not want to hurt the man who could become your son-in-law, do you?'

The miner's mouth dropped open, but before he could respond, there was a shout, and a man ran up to them, pointing to the plain. 'They're coming! They're coming!'

Smyth stood and gave Baldwin a brittle smile. 'I think Sir William has decided for us. We defend ourselves.'

It was the arrival of the foot-soldiers from Beauscyr that made Sir William decide to attack. His seneschal had rounded up all the men in the demesne as well as the spare guards from the hall, and made them hurry to join their master, all grasping whatever was at hand when the call came. Mattocks, peat shovels, axes and hammers were their meagre weapons, and all wore the same fixed and anxious stares, too scared to run off, but fearful of the outcome of the day. If it was a battle to protect their children and wives, they would have fought to the death with stoic determination as their sires had against the French, the Danes and the Normans, but this was not their fight. This was an argument between miners and their master, and they had no wish to leave their families fatherless in another man's feud.

As they came to the plain, a lookout saw them and rode straight to the knight, who told him to get back and order the men to rest. Sir William would soon lead them into battle.

For some time he sat watching the vill, frowning. The bailiff and his friend had been gone for too long: it was not his imagination, the sun cast strong shadows in this light, and he had watched his own move over a heather bush and on. John sat moodily on his horse beside him, while Sir Ralph gazed down at the camp with a kind of tranquil boredom, as if in this wasteland there was nothing else to hold his attention. When he heard a horse snort loudly, Sir William glanced over his shoulder at the man behind, and saw there too that he had the same quiet stillness. Few looked at him; their eyes were all fixed on the camp.

He had never expected to ride out again at his time of life. Seeing his men, all the guards from the fort and the servants who could ride, he felt a curious sensation that this was all wrong. It should not be him here, it should be one of his sons leading the men. He was too old. His time had passed, even as the old King's had, with the fierce and brutal clashes in Wales over thirty years ago. Then he had been young and eager, a forceful leader of men, a man of honour with other renowned names at his side.

They were good days. The risks had been high, the plunder great, and for all the men who survived there was a feeling of achievement and pride. Even after the débâcle of the expedition from Anglesey the tall man from Beauscyr had taken a good portion of the spoils for himself.

A quick frown darkened his brow as he thought again of the short, dark man with the flinty eyes who had been in his company, who had stood apart from the others and fought alone, as if he was no part of the rest of the group but an outsider who had joined merely to offer assistance when needed. Now this same man Thomas Smyth had caught his son, thirty years on, and for no reason.

Whirling his horse round, he motioned to a man nearby. 'Take a message to the others,' he said, issuing instructions quickly and sending him on his way. His eyes stayed fixed on the rider as he galloped up the hill and disappeared over the other side, then he glanced at his son. 'Come, John. Let's free your brother.'

Simon and Baldwin watched grimly as men poured over the brow of the hill and walked, a straggling mass, towards the vill. From his place behind his master, Edgar could see some of the defences prepared for them. True, there was no high rampart or wall like that at Beauscyr, but all over the camp large rocks had been scattered, making it harder for horses to travel fast, and these, along with the holes dug out on the plain, should stop any charge. The miners stood in small groups, with outlying men at each side who carried bows, while in the middle was the greater force of men with arms, holding swords, picks and iron bars in fists gone suddenly clammy.

Thomas Smyth strode around, offering brief words of support and encouragement, laughing at the words of one, slapping another on the back, and experimentally touching a rusty weapon here and there with a show of amused disgust. To Baldwin he was like any number of men who led others, smiling, instilling confidence by his own display, and always remembering the names of his men. Like all good commanders, he knew, the knight could see, that if a man would fight and die for his master, that master must show respect for his man. And like all good commanders, he knew how to position his troops for best advantage.

Chewing at his moustache, Baldwin tried twice to go to the miner, but now George Harang had his sword out and was guarding the two men and their servants with five others. His eyes never left the bailiff and his friend, not even when the shout went up from the Beauscyr force, not when the stumbling feet began to stamp and pound as they ran towards the camp, their steps sounding like a rushing river of noise. For all that, it was strangely peaceful. A lark sang above the camp, the murmur of the leat called softly behind the blowing-house, and Baldwin had a sense of unreality. It felt impossible that he was truly here, and would shortly witness the climax of years of arguing between the tinners and the landlord, that he would again be involved in a battle in which he had no part. He had no interest in either side's claims or demands, he was only here to help his friend try to find justice for a man who had been captured.

The running men had lost any semblance of formation now, and he could not help his lip curling in disgust, quickly replaced by sympathy. These men were just like the troops he had seen at Acre. Poor, untrained levies hurled at the enemy to try to batter a way through while the cavalry searched for the best point to smash a breach in the lines. Like at Acre, they would be destroyed. Here, there was no line to be broken, no defence where cavalry could focus. When he heard the whistle and snap of the bows, he winced, and had to turn away, but not before he had seen men stumble and fall, two with the feathered darts jutting obscenely from their chests, one with a shaft embedded in his throat. Another wave of arrows rose into the air, sounding like a flock of geese in their hollow swishing, and the solid thump as they hit flesh was terrible.

But he had not realised how well Sir William had been trained. As the torrent of men reached the camp, almost simultaneously, or so it seemed, there was a great shout behind. A strong party of horsemen had ridden round and were now attacking from across the river, behind the defenders. The call acted like spurs to the Beauscyr men in front, and their weapons rose and fell, swords meeting axes, pikes meeting hammers, daggers meeting daggers, in a cacophony of discordant clanging like an army of ironsmiths beating their anvils together.

And now there was a fresh rumbling and pounding as the knight led his men at the gallop. Baldwin could see the two men leading, Sir William Beauscyr and Sir Ralph, their swords high, the sun sparkling on their mail and plate, glinting from their swords as they whirled overhead, flashing from the sharp edges of the lances, while the land shimmered under the thunder of the hooves. When they came upon the pot-holed ground, many fell, but most reached the edge of the little town.

Simon was fretting. He did not know what to do for the best. It was impossible to stop the brawl, but he could not stand by and see so many men killed or wounded for no reason without lifting a finger. George Harang and his men anxiously fingered their weapons and cast wary glances over the two men. Thomas Smyth had not asked Simon or Baldwin for their swords or daggers, but neither felt it would be safe to draw them. The miners had no reason to feel that they were enemies as yet, and both men would prefer matters to stay that way.

Between the cottages Simon caught occasional glimpses of the struggling men. He winced as he saw an axe fall and take a man's arm off at the shoulder. There was a short wail, swiftly cut off, and he spun round to see a man sinking to his knees with a bloody mess where his throat should have been. Suddenly he felt waves of nausea breaking over him, and he gasped, his eyes still on the man who slowly toppled to one side, eyes wide and staring as if in surprise.

That was when his anger flashed into full flame. Shoving one guard away, he snarled at George Harang: 'Take me to Smyth!'

The miner gazed at him uncertainly. 'I was told to keep you here.'

'I don't care! How many more must die while those two fools fight with other men's lives? Take me to him now! This isn't just madness, it's futile!'

George hovered, undecided. Thomas had told him to stay here with the two men, but he, too, was shocked by the brutality of the battle. This was not what he had expected. It was no way to avenge Peter – it was merely a slogging match in which men with the least reason to fight were pitted against each other. Yet slowly, unwillingly, he shook his head. He had never yet failed his master.

Baldwin walked forward casually. Simon was standing a short distance from George, his face reddening in fury, and the knight moved alongside, aware of the heightened tension in their other guards. 'George,' he said. 'Simon is right. We have to stop this. Look at it.'

The miner risked a glance and saw men grappling with each other, men holding each other by the throat, one who sat numbly, his head bleeding profusely from a wound in his scalp, and bodies . . . everywhere he looked there were figures lying on the ground. Then he saw a young man fall after a blow from a club. Gritting his teeth, he addressed Simon. 'Come with me,' he said quietly.

He led the way past the guards, who stared dumbly as if unsure whether to join the fight or stay where they were, between the cottages on the left, and to a place where the ground rose. From here they could see Thomas. He was wielding his heavy sword as if it was as light as an arrow, and against him stood John. Glancing round the field, Simon made out Sir William on his feet a little behind, and Sir Ralph was with him, also off his horse. A man stumbled by carrying a lance, a bloody gash in his arm, and Simon swore viciously. The man could only have been twenty, no more, and he was crying, unseeing, just walking to avoid any further fighting, and the sight inflamed the bailiff. Before Baldwin could stop him, he had shoved past two struggling groups and drawn his sword, knocking John and Thomas apart and standing between them.

Baldwin stared in astonishment, but then, seeing that two miners were rushing to Simon thinking he was going to attack their master, he leapt forward with a muttered prayer, and stood facing them, his back to the bailiff and his sword outstretched while his brown eyes held theirs unblinkingly. They hesitated, exchanging a glance, before slowly circling round him to get closer to Thomas Smyth, but he moved to bar their way. At the sound of the bailiff's voice they halted.

'Stop this madness!'

Risking a quick glance behind him, the knight saw that his friend was bellowing right into the miner's face. Thomas stood white with rage, his sword gripped in both hands, and Baldwin thought for one terrible moment that he was going to attack Simon. But then the fire died from his eyes and he seemed to shrivel. While the deafening clamour of the battle ranged all round them, the miner was locked in his own private world of pain and grief.

This was not what he had wanted. He had tried to get hold of John, the man he believed had killed his son, but when George Harang had come back with Robert, he had intended somehow to use him as a bargaining chip to capture the real culprit. He had not wanted this. All he had wanted to do was avenge his son, not cause more hurt. The bailiff was staring at him with open disgust, and it shook Smyth, making him look all round.

Theirs was a distinct island of calm in the middle of the battle, fringed by men hacking and stabbing at each other. Their allegiance was a mystery, for in the height of battle all were reduced to a bland uniformity, faces set, wielding their weapons with the fixed and fearful determination to kill before they could be harmed. Thomas found it difficult to distinguish between his own men and those of the Beauscyrs. The men were all involved in their own private battles, small groups of three or four with various weapons, some clinched together in a mortal fight for control of a single dagger, some slipping and sliding at the bank of the stream, faces and clothes streaked with mud and soil, others standing and making slashing arcs in the air with steel and iron. Here and there men stood warily glaring at each other, panting, already too exhausted already to continue, snatching rest in the midst of the killing. And all over the ground were the bodies. Some writhing, some rolling, some screaming, and more just still, features fixed, with stabs or great marks in their skulls where a mace or pick had dashed out their brains.

Simon saw the miner's face change. A look of understanding came into his eyes, and with it an infinity of sadness. He nodded, his sword dropping, and stood up from his crouch, and Simon knew that the fight must soon end.

'STOP THIS NOW!' he roared, and Simon was surprised at the power in his voice. 'ALL OF YOU, STOP!'

Some of those nearest paused and turned to stare. Baldwin saw one man try to look to Thomas, and as he did, his opponent sprang forward, ready to stab, but before he could strike Baldwin had knocked his falchion aside. Immediately the other faced back and tried to swing his axe at the Beauscyr man, and Baldwin had to knock that away too. 'Stop this now!' he snarled. 'If one of you tries again I will take your arm off!'

Simon strode through the mass to Sir William. He was standing white-faced while a man tied a dirty cloth round his head. A flap of skin on his cheek hung loose where a slash from a dagger had caught him. Now he stared dumbly as the bailiff approached. 'Tell your men to stop. Now!' Simon rapped out. 'The miners will stop if your men do. Order them to lay down their arms, Sir William.'

'What of Robert?'

'If you tell your men to stop, we can ask, can't we?' bellowed Simon nastily. 'Is having all the Beauscyr men killed going to help? Tell your men to CEASE FIGHTING.' To his immense relief he saw the old knight sigh and nod.

# CHAPTER TWENTY-TWO

The fighting had spread to cover almost a square mile, and it took several minutes of bellowing to halt the battle. Gradually, uncertainly, and in all cases with their eyes fixed cautiously on their enemies, men pulled apart, fingering weapons newly notched or snapped. They backed together, forming small sullen circles, gasping for breath, here three miners, there four Beauscyr men. Several peasants stood and tried to calm a youth who sobbed and clutched his smashed wrist. All were taut, expecting a sudden renewal of the fight; all were scared of being surprised, and no one trusted their opponents.

Baldwin saw this, and took Thomas by the arm, pulling him to where Sir William and Simon stood. 'Thomas, you must order your men to pull back a little. Sir William, you too. Your men must stand back and leave you two here, so they can all see that there is no deception. Tell them to form a ring around us.'

With a slow shuffling the two companies separated when the leaders gave the order. One scuffle broke out when a man saw a friend lying dead, but his companions pulled him away. Simon could not even see what side he was on. There was a slowly increasing space as the two sides paced backwards, all scowling at their enemies. Now and again they stumbled over a body. Fortunately, few had died. Those who were hurt were collected and taken away to have their wounds seen to, and soon there were clumps of men ferrying those who could not walk over to the bank of the stream where they had their limbs washed and bound. Fires were lighted to heat the irons that would cauterise the worst of the injuries.

Simon forced himself to look away, ignoring the angry mutters that came from all sides, and faced Beauscyr and the miner. John was there as well, standing beside his father and peering round with haughty amusement. Edgar and Hugh were with Baldwin, and although Hugh had blood spattered on his tunic, he seemed well enough.

'Right, Sir William, and Thomas. This nonsense has to stop,' Simon said as he marched towards them, then stood with his hands in his belt. 'First, Thomas, I want you to order that Robert Beauscyr is released. There is no profit in keeping him here.'

'Why should I? I think this miserable cur killed Peter, and I want to keep his brother until I see what will happen to him.'

Simon spoke loudly, so that all could hear. 'John Beauscyr has told me what he was doing on the night that your son was killed, and I am content for now with his word. He was *not* the man who murdered your son.'

As his words sank in there was a complete silence. The old knight was the first to speak, his voice low and shocked. 'Your son?'

'Peter Bruther was my son. I knew his mother before I married, and it was for my wife's sake that I never admitted to him, but he knew he was my flesh and blood. That was why he came to the moors. I told him to, so that he could learn the ways of farming tin and make himself wealthy. It was why I made sure he always had a guard to protect him from you and your men.'

John, too, was gaping. 'Peter was your son?' he said, shaking his head from side to side in disbelief. 'But none of us knew that!'

'Is that why you killed him? Because you thought he was unprotected?' roared the miner, taking a quick step toward him. Baldwin moved to stand between them.

'Wait, Thomas.' The deep brown of his eyes held and quieted the glinting black flint of the miner's. 'Look around you! There has been enough harm done already. Let us listen for a time and talk before you decide to cause more deaths.'

'I didn't cause the deaths here, it was the Beauscyrs who attacked the camp.' But his voice was toneless, and he looked away. After a moment, he nodded.

Simon addressed the old knight. 'Sir William, I want to prevent further bloodshed. I am sure that you and your men don't want any more killing either. We are not a court here, we have no coroner to conduct an enquiry or clerk to record it, but we can investigate here and now, while there are all these men to witness it. I can report later to the chief warden at Lydford. Will you be content to continue?'

MICHAEL JECKS

The old man nodded, still staring at the miner, and Simon felt that he was wondering how he would feel if he had been Thomas Smyth, if he had lost his son, a young man he could not recognise publicly, and whom he had tried to help by bringing him out from villeinage to a new life where he could be protected, only to find that he had been murdered. Sir William's face displayed his horror and compassion. The sight gave Simon some relief. The knight would be compliant.

'Thomas?' the bailiff prompted, glancing at the miner. Thomas Smyth nodded slowly. 'Good. In that case, we should have chairs brought. There's no need for us to stand when we can sit.'

The bailiff sat in the middle, flanked by Baldwin and Hugh. Edgar stood nearby, while Sir William and his son sat to Simon's left, Thomas to his right. The miners and the Manor's men crouched or sat all around, reminding Simon of the stannary courts he had attended. It was strange to be in control of a meeting like this; usually it would be the chief warden or a judge who would sit at the throne to listen to evidence in an inquest or court session, but the bailiff had no time to feel anxious about his lack of experience. This matter was too serious to be left alone, as the battle had shown. He was determined to resolve the argument between the miners and the Beauscyrs.

'All of us are here to try to find out what really happened on the day that Peter Bruther died,' he began. 'You all know me. I am the bailiff of Lydford, and my duty is to find the murderer. I call on all here to witness the words of the men who come before us today. You must listen and see that we

328

are fair to all.' He glanced round. 'First, I want to see the three men who were sent to Henry Smalhobbe and beat him.'

It took a little time for the three to be fetched. Harold Magge stood resolutely defiant, the others looked cowed and nervous before all the men. Simon saw that their bruises had reduced, and nodded to himself while Thomas instructed them to tell the truth. Then he stirred. 'You went to Henry Smalhobbe and attacked him on the day that Bruther died, didn't you?'

Magge nodded. Quickly Simon took him through the evidence he had given before, how he had sat in wait for Smalhobbe, how the man had nearly taken him by surprise but had been bested, and how they had returned to the miners' camp. Simon glanced at Thomas as he asked, 'Who beat you afterwards? Who caused your bruises?'

'Thomas Smyth did it. He thought we must have killed Bruther, and he had told us not to attack him. When news arrived about Bruther being found at Wistman's Wood, he came straight to the camp and ordered us to be brought to him. He had us beaten to get us to admit to killing Bruther.'

'Had you killed Bruther?'

'No!'

'Had you seen Bruther that night?'

'No.'

'Who did you see that night?'

Magge hesitated, glancing at Thomas, and Baldwin saw the old tinner give a small nod. 'George Harang and Thomas. We saw them riding back from the direction of Bruther's place, after we had left Smalhobbe. They were heading southwards to the road.'

'Thomas?'

'Yes, it's true.' He looked up bleakly. 'We went to see him but he wasn't there. I waited some time, but when it began to grow dark it seemed better to get home again, to meet Sir William. There was no sign of Peter.'

'I see. Now, Harold Magge. Where did Henry Smalhobbe come from when you ambushed him?'

'From the south.'

'Could he have come from Wistman's Wood?'

'Smalhobbe?' There was a sneer to his voice. 'He's only a smallholder. He'd hardly kill another miner.'

'He was nearly able to surprise you, wasn't he? If his wife had not called out, you yourself told me that he might have overcome you, and if he had, he might have beaten off the others, mightn't he? Now, please answer the question: could he have come from Wistman's Wood?'

'He was coming from the south. Wistman's is south and west from there, but he might have walked keeping to the lowlands rather than over the hills. And he was late that night, later than he usually was. I suppose he could have been to Wistman's Wood.'

'You never told me this before,' said Thomas Smyth. His voice was tired, his visage pale, and he was staring at his man with a kind of hopeless sadness.

'You didn't ask us about where Smalhobbe had been, sir,' Magge said shortly. 'You asked us what *we'd* been doing – not about him. I didn't know Bruther was your son. I just thought we'd done something to displease you . . .' He trailed off as the bailiff held up a hand.

'Harold, would you say it was possible?' He instinctively trusted this man's opinion. Somehow the miner gave off an aura of wholesome stolidity, and Simon recalled how the

330

first time he had seen Magge he had thought instantly of a farmer from the moors. Now, like a farmer, Magge paused and considered the question for some time in silence.

'I reckon it'd be possible but I don't think it was him. Smalhobbe's not a killer, no matter what others say.'

'In that case, I'd like to speak to Robert Beauscyr next,' said Simon. The young knight was soon standing before them. He did not appear to have been mistreated, which was a relief. Baldwin had wondered what might happen if he had turned up wounded. The Beauscyr men could easily be tempted to hurl themselves into a fresh attack if the boy had been harmed. After all, he was the reason why they had been commanded to fight.

Simon asked him to tell everyone what he had done on the night of the murder. Nervously, Robert told of his flight from the hall and how he had ridden to Chagford, where he had met Alicia, and of his subsequent agreement to meet her. This brought a wry smile to Thomas' face. He had not realised how involved his daughter was with the boy. Looking at him now, he wondered about Robert Beauscyr as a son-in-law. To his faint surprise he found the idea less distasteful than he expected.

'But you saw two men on the road, didn't you? Over towards Wiseman's Wood,' Simon prompted.

'Yes.'

'And nobody else?'

'No, bailiff.'

Simon glanced at the miner. 'The two riders were men-at-arms from the Manor. It was they who found Bruther's body shortly after.'

'Are they here?' Thomas asked, surveying the men ranged opposite.

'They are dead,' said Baldwin shortly, and a dangerous new wave of tension gripped the watching men.

'How? How did they die?'

It was Sir William who answered, sounding as tired as the miner. 'They appear to have got into a fight over a game of dice. Both were stabbed.'

'When was this?' the miner demanded.

Simon told him. 'Early this morning. When we found them, their bodies were still warm.'

Thomas Smyth turned to peer at John. 'It was *you*, wasn't it?' His voice shook with emotion. 'The men could identify you somehow, and you killed them to conceal your guilt.'

'Be silent, Thomas!' Simon said, but John had gone white with fury.

Leaping out of his chair, he faced the miner, grabbing his sword's hilt. But before he could draw it, Edgar slapped his hand away. There was an angry rumble from the Beauscyr men, met by a sudden movement from the miners at the other end of the space where the tinners sat and listened. Simon quickly stood, hands held high. '*Be still!*' he bellowed, and then looked from Thomas to Sir William. Both also stood, slowly and unwillingly, and calmed their men. Meanwhile, John stood glowering furiously at Edgar, who smiled back calmly, his eyes never moving from the boy.

Simon glared at the youngest Beauscyr. 'Keep your hand from your sword, squire. I'll have no more blood on the moors today.'

'You expect me, *me*, the son of an honourable knight to accept being accused of common murder? By a miner? By God, you have no right to—'

'Silence! I have every right, and every duty, to investigate a murder. Stand before us, and keep your hand from your sword. Do I have to remind you that this is a lawful investigation into murder? If you don't obey I'll have you arrested and kept at Lydford prison.'

For a moment, Baldwin thought John was going to argue. He glared fiercely at the bailiff, while he considered his position. Simon was red-faced with fury, his anger simmering, ready to boil up and scald the lad. At last, giving a scornful shrug, the boy strode off to stand beside his brother.

'John Beauscyr, you were out on the moors that day. Did you see anyone else? Someone who could have been involved in the murder of Peter Bruther?' His rage ebbing, Simon realised he must leave out the boy's admission of robbery. In the present climate it would be too much to expect the miners to control their ire if they were to discover that John had been involved, on his own admission, in banditry. John spoke shortly about that evening, about the ride to Thomas Smyth's house and the subsequent journey to the inn. When he talked of the meeting with Bruther on the road, a hush fell, and everyone seemed to be listening intently.

Baldwin thought he made a good witness, strong, upright, and speaking with a controlled certainty. His very stance implied conviction, his legs a short distance apart, his arms crossed over his chest. He was the image of all knightly virtues.

Simon carefully took him through the meeting with Bruther, how he and his men had left the young Beauscyr and his knight, jeering at them as they rode on to the inn. 'And you saw no one else on the road after you left Bruther?'

'No, nobody.' Again his flat statement carried no room for any doubt.

'So, then, it comes to this,' said Simon, speaking loudly now for the benefit of the miners and Beauscyr men ranged all round. 'Bruther went home from the inn. At his father's house his men left him and he carried on alone over the moors. Some time later, Adam Coyt came along the road on his way home, and he heard a rider to the north of him on the moors. He didn't look to see who it was.' There was a slight lightening of tension in the crowds, even a nervous ripple of laughter as he added drily, 'He thought it might be the Devil or Crockern at that time of night. Now, listen to me, all of you!' He stood and surveyed the watching crowd. 'It's certain that Thomas didn't order his own son to be murdered. John Beauscyr was with his friend at the inn. His brother was with Alicia Smyth. None of these caused the killing. I don't yet know who was responsible for Peter Bruther's killing. But I will find out, and when I do, the man will be arrested and held for trial.'

There was a shout from the crowd behind him, a voice sneering, 'You're playing at this. Why should you care about a miner? You don't care about Bruther. All you want is to help your friends the Beauscyrs.'

'Do you think I'm paid by the Beauscyrs?' Simon roared, his face flushing a dark red. 'Do you think I'm held by Sir William's purse? You might just as well suggest I'm paid by the miners. It was I stopped Sir William from riding out to bring Bruther back, it was I told his sons to leave the miners in peace, it was I who tried to stop this madness. I'll not have it said I'm a hireling who'll dishonour my position for bribes.' His furious gaze swept round the men in the crowd, and Baldwin saw with a small grin, quickly covered, that those who caught his eye immediately looked away. No one was keen to risk the bailiff's wrath.

Simon calmed himself with an obvious effort. 'This affair is sad and unpleasant, but fighting between the miners and the Beauscyr men must stop. There is no point in further loss of life. I don't want to hear of any more killings. I'll find the killer of Bruther, just as I'll find the murderer of Samuel Hankyn and Ronald Taverner. Three men have died, and God only knows how many have been killed – and how many more will die – because of the fight here today. It must stop.' He looked at Sir William and Smyth. 'Both of you must settle your differences. I can't stop you trying to kill each other if that's what you're determined to do, but, by God, if I hear that there's another battle here I'll get the King to send troops and impose his peace on the moors! Now I'm going, and Sir William, I want you to take your men back to the Manor. I'll see you there later. Thomas, I expect you to release Sir Robert immediately.'

Baldwin watched, still seated, as the miner and landlord agreed, and their men began to gather up their weapons. Gradually, the Beauscyr men set off away from the meeting place and up the hill, some collecting horses from those holding them, and mounting. The miners were sullen, staring and muttering among themselves as their enemies slowly departed, a few tending to the wounds of bleeding friends.

He sighed. There were so many murders nowadays that all too often the killer would escape. A merchant could be stabbed on the roads and the local people might never have seen his attacker, or even if they had, they might not know his name. Sometimes if a man was known and he was caught red-handed, he could avoid justice by running away. After all, if he was never captured he could not be made to pay. It would be down to the local people to pay taxes to the Crown for the breaking of the King's peace.

The area was clearing quickly now, men on all sides gathering into small clumps and moving apart, the tinners starting to walk to their huts, the soldiers riding or slouching off. Baldwin watched Simon talking to Robert. The young man was pale and drawn, but Baldwin put that down to fear of his potential father-in-law. That he did not seem to have suffered at the hands of the miners was a relief.

John mounted his horse, snapped his reins and cantered away, and Baldwin's eyes followed him until he was a small figure on the horizon. The boy was irritating, certainly, but that did not mean he was a murderer. Even so, he had been out that night, and though there was a witness of sorts in the person of the robbed man towards Chagford, it was possible that John could have killed Bruther earlier, then hurried east to create an alibi. Baldwin did not share Simon's conviction of John's innocence.

That brought Baldwin to thinking about the other men who had been abroad on the moors when Bruther was so brutally murdered. Adam Coyt, for instance. He could have invented the story about a man riding past near the road as night fell. The knight was inclined to believe him, but only from a liking for his type: strong and individualistic, working in a harsh environment to scrape some sort of a living. There was no other reason why he should trust his word.

Of the Beauscyrs, Sir William had been at the miner's hall and Robert with Alicia Smyth on the afternoon Bruther died – but there was a period, though Simon had not mentioned it to the crowd, when, according to Alicia, she was away from Robert, between the time she returned home to meeting him again on the road again, later. What was he doing during those lost hours? And then Baldwin's mind came back to John: always there was John ... malevolently spreading rumours and lies for his own amusement, trying to undermine his brother from jealousy over the inheritance.

Deep in thought, Baldwin strolled back towards the main camp, where his horse was tethered. There were the others, too: Samuel Hankyn and Ronald Taverner. Their deaths were a mystery. The two appeared harmless enough, especially poor young Ronald. It was ridiculous to suggest that they could have been involved in some kind of fatal brawl over a game of dice. The way that Samuel had tried to look after his friend showed how nonsensical that idea was. If there had been a fight there must have been another man there, someone who murdered Samuel first presumably, since he was fit and healthy, and then stabbed poor Ronald while he lay on his bed.

He glanced at Simon. The bailiff was talking to Hugh now, giving instructions in a clipped monotone which showed how his anger was still bubbling. Hugh knew it too, from the way that he hung his head and listened, not daring to interrupt or argue. It was so unlike his usual truculent manner that Baldwin could not help a quick grin as he turned away.

So who *could* have been with the two men in the room, he wondered. Perhaps he could get an answer by questioning the guards, those who were out in the early morning, but somehow he doubted it. Something was wrong. There was something he had missed.

Looking out at the departing force, he saw where the small squares of turf had been trampled; their danger was visible to all now. It was a simple enough trick, he knew, to make horse warfare difficult. Yes, the miner was capable of defending his land. He had displayed the tactical skills of a warrior, and Baldwin recalled Sir William's words that Thomas Smyth had been a soldier long ago in Wales. Surprise had been essential to Sir William's success in not losing more of his men. All he had needed to do was divert attention from the miners' front, making them fearful of heavily mounted troops with lances and spears behind, to allow the knight to charge safely. It was the same as the fire which had diverted attention from the two dead men.

Suddenly Baldwin's frown intensified. So *that* was why the murders had not been heard, he realised – because of the sudden alarm about the fire. The tolling of the fire-bell had drowned all other noises.

Simon finished giving instructions to Hugh and looked round the camp. The miners were returning to their work and the Beauscyr men had almost disappeared over the brow of the hill, transporting their dead and wounded with them. Nearby was a small pile of bodies, five tinners who had died, and Simon eyed them sourly. For a bailiff to fail in preventing a single murder was bad enough, he knew . . . but a full-scale battle on the King's forest was a major event. He would be called to account for this! Sighing, he suddenly felt exhausted. The events of the morning had taken their toll, from fighting the fire to stopping a battle, and all he wanted now was a chance to sit meditatively and drink a long refreshing draught of ale. Seeing Baldwin, he stretched, and grimaced as a bone clicked. Then he strolled over to him.

'So, Baldwin. At least that's over for now,' he murmured, and Baldwin's head snapped round. 'Baldwin? What is it?'

The knight explained about his new insight about the two dead men and the attention-distracting fire. Simon listened, but could not help glancing at the small and pathetic bundles of the dead. 'I know,' said Baldwin, following his gaze, 'but that's the way of warfare. I feel the fate of Samuel and Ronald is worse, somehow. Their deaths were premeditated, and they were killed before they could defend themselves – just like Peter Bruther. He was grabbed from behind and garotted, while Samuel was stabbed in the back and Ronald was slaughtered while he lay helpless in his bed.'

'If what you say is right,' Simon mused, 'the killer must have begun the fire, then slipped into the room to murder Hankyn and Taverner.'

'Yes, but I still cannot understand why he should have enticed Samuel into the store-room. At that time of day, surely he would have found both asleep – in which case, all he needed to do was stab Samuel first where he lay.'

'Oh, that's easy. Whoever this killer was, I think he started the fire, then entered the store-room from the courtyard itself. He waited there until the alarm was raised, and when it was, he kicked over the barrels to make a noise. It woke the good Samuel, who walked in to see what the row was, and he was grabbed round the mouth to stop him screaming as he was stabbed. After that, all the murderer needed to do was walk back into the room beyond and finish off poor Ronald where he lay.'

'Yes, but *why*, Simon? That's what I don't understand. Why kill them?'

'That's something we can only find out by asking the killer, but I expect whoever did it thought the two men had seen him on the moors when Bruther died. It would explain the matter rather well, wouldn't it? He thought they had seen him, so he made sure they could not tell anyone.'

'If that is correct,' Baldwin said, his voice low, 'then it must have been somebody in the fort. The fire began *before* the gates were opened. Adam Coyt, Thomas Smyth and his men . . . everyone who was outside the fort must be innocent. Whoever killed Bruther and then the other two must have been inside last night.'

'Oh yes, Baldwin. I've got no doubt about that,' said Simon grimly, and he led the way to where Hugh and Edgar held their horses.

Quickly swinging himself up, the bailiff glanced round the camp. Almost all the signs of the fighting were gone now. The bodies, the evidence of the battle, had been covered and would soon, no doubt, be taken to the little church at Widecombe. Two men were shovelling earth into the traps and stamping on top to level the ground, while others were walking over the terrain collecting arrows. These would be put back in the armoury in case of another attack. Apart from that, the camp had regained a little of its calm atmosphere, slumbering in the warm summer sunlight.

Kicking his horse up the slope, Simon said, 'It's as if nothing has happened here, it's so quiet.'

The knight nodded in agreement. 'Indeed. You could hardly imagine what carnage was here only a few hours ago. The grass is flatter, but that is all. The moors are good at hiding their secrets.'

'Yes. Whether it's a single man like Bruther, or a group like the ones here, all soon disappear.'

They were at the furthest fringe of buildings now, and Hugh looked back pensively. 'I wonder where Bruther *did* die.'

'What do you mean?' asked Baldwin, staring at Simon's servant.

'Well, we don't know *where* he died, do we? He might've been killed where he was found, only it seems a bit odd for him to be up at Wistman's Wood, so far out of his way. All we know is, he died somewhere between Thomas Smyth's hall and his own place.'

'Well done, Hugh. So all we have to do is hunt over all the moors between those two places and we'll find where he was killed. That should be easy enough.' Simon's tone was witheringly sarcastic.

But Baldwin was thoughtful as he stared at the servant. 'It shouldn't be too hard, really. After all, we know that Bruther was careful and wary. If he was walking over the moors and heard someone behind him, he'd turn to see who it was. And if somebody was lying in wait, Bruther must surely spot him. These moors are so flat, even a beetle is visible a mile away.'

They were almost at the top of the hill above the plain now, and Baldwin turned to survey the landscape. 'If a man was going to ambush someone, he would want to do it far out in the moors, surely? Even if he had men with him, he would prefer a quiet place with no chance of a witness overhearing, wouldn't he? Now where could a man do that on the moors?'

'At a tor, I suppose. Or a group of other rocks.'

'That is right! There are rocks behind which a man could hide, but would John have been able to get to them to ambush Bruther, unseen by his victim?'

Simon considered a moment. 'It would depend on which route he took from the tinner's house. The killer must have been in place when Bruther passed, then gone on to

Wistman's Wood with the body, had time to hang it, and then escaped. I wonder how long that would have taken him?'

'A good while,' Baldwin judged. 'And that is what I do not understand. Everyone seems to be able to explain where they were, apart from Sir Robert and his brother. Of course, John might not have had time if he rode immediately to Chagford to rob this farmer.'

'Which means it was Sir Robert.'

'Yes.' But Baldwin's expression was doubtful.

Simon sighed. 'We still don't know where or exactly when Bruther was killed. It must have been some time before dark.' He stopped. When he spoke again he was deep in thought. 'I never thought of that before. He was dead some time before the two Beauscyr men passed by, so he would surely have been killed in daylight.'

'Let us assume he was killed in daylight, then,' Baldwin said. 'His body must have been carried over to the woods, because if he was going straight home, his route went nowhere near Wistman's Wood. The wood is over a mile distant from any point on the path, so he must have been taken there on horseback. He would have been too bulky to carry.'

'Yes,' Simon nodded, thinking hard.

'If John had too little time, could it have been his brother?' Baldwin mused.

'Didn't Alicia say she met Sir Robert when it was getting dark? He would have had time to kill Bruther between leaving Alicia and seeing her again later.'

'True, but I find it hard to believe it was he .'

Hearing this, Edgar whirled in his saddle to stare at his master. 'Could it not have been Adam Coyt, then? He had a packhorse there.'

For once Baldwin was sharp with his servant. 'Don't be ridiculous! Coyt *admitted* being there, otherwise we would not have known. Why should he confess to being there if he was the killer and had no need to admit to being even remotely close? And another thing: Coyt dislikes miners generally, it is true, but he had no real dislike of Bruther except insofar as Bruther damaged the moors, to his mind, and for that he expected . . . um . . . Crockern to protect the land. Anyway, Coyt was not in the Manor last night. He could not have killed the other two.'

Simon shrugged. 'The murders *could* be unrelated. It's not something we should ignore, anyway.'

'It is too unlikely, Simon. Think about it: a man is killed; two men find the body and may have seen something; shortly afterwards, these two are also murdered. It would be too much of a coincidence for them to have died for different reasons. No, they must have been linked in some way.'

'So you think it was definitely one of the Beauscyrs, then?'

'Yes.'

Hugh screwed up his face and glanced at Simon. 'What about Sir Ralph? We don't know when Bruther was killed, like you say, so Sir Ralph could have done it.'

'No, Hugh. He was with Sir William and John on the way to the tinner's house. They all said they were together then, and I believe them.'

'Then it must have been the other one,' announced Hugh. 'I never trusted that Sir Robert. He always looked too arrogant.'

'Robert? I suppose it's possible,' said Simon, with a faint smile at his servant's relish. 'I feel he's not a killer, though. I'd have thought his brother was more likely.'

343

'John could have hared after the man who had insulted him,' Baldwin agreed. 'It's quite possible that he could have overtaken Bruther, waited for him to pass, then jumped out and strangled him.'

'If it *was* John,' Simon said, 'I still wonder if he had enough time to murder and hang Bruther?'

'He had as long as it took to get over to the road to Chagford,' said Baldwin shortly. 'Anyway, what were you telling Hugh to do before we left? You were speaking to him for some time.'

Simon gave a short laugh. 'Telling him to find out whether there were many robberies here that didn't go reported. That attack on Wat Meavy interests me. I wanted to see if Coyt was telling the truth, and that there were more than I realised.'

'And?'

'You tell him, Hugh.'

'They said that there hadn't been many until a few weeks ago. Since then they've been getting worse.'

Baldwin shot the bailiff a quick look. 'You think John has been robbing since he came home?'

'It wouldn't be the first time a squire turned to pillage. He's been trained in it up north, I'd guess, and he's carrying on as he always has.'

The knight shrugged. 'Possibly, but I do not quite see how that can help us.'

'Look at it this way: how long would it have taken John to get to Chagford to attack Meavy?' Simon asked. 'When was this Wat Meavy attacked? Did he see who attacked him? Was it really John who did it? We don't know yet, do we? Fine, so we think that John could have been involved in a series of raids, stealing from the people here – but that doesn't make him a murderer, though if he was found guilty of it, he would still be punished for breaking the King's peace. No, but he might have had time to leave the inn, go and kill Bruther, hang the body, and then ride east until he came upon someone to rob. By chance he meets Wat Meavy and robs him – it could have been anyone, so long as whoever he found was scared of the name of Beauscyr and would not accuse him of theft. All he wanted, if I'm right, was to have someone he could call upon to say he was not anywhere near Bruther in case somebody at the inn told us he was not there all night. That was why I also asked Hugh to find out where this Wat Meavy lived. And he did.'

'Is it far?'

Simon gazed to the north and east, then shrugged and smiled.

Sighing, Baldwin stretched, then nodded. 'Ah, I see. Well, then. Let us go there now and find out what *did* happen.'

# CHAPTER TWENTY-THREE

Henway, the small vill where Wat Meavy lived, lay some four miles from the camp. The four men followed the road, turning north over the moors when Hugh pointed, down into a steep valley where the air was cool and fresh. Small clumps of bushes and trees lay at the bottom on the banks of the little stream, all covered in thick moss, and the sound of rippling water mixed with the green light of the sun filtering through the trees gave a feeling of peace and calm.

Trailing along the line of the water, they soon came upon Wat Meavy's house. It was a sturdy stone building, with a cluster of outbuildings forming a stockade, a low wattle fence keeping his animals in and wild creatures out. Smoke rose from the house and drifted towards them, carrying with it the delicious aroma of fresh bread.

They clattered up the small rise into the yard and dismounted slowly, easing sore muscles. From here the farm looked wealthy, with fresh white limewash on the walls, well-maintained byres and a barn. While they stood, a woman came out of the house, wiping her hands on her apron.

From a distance, she looked as though she was in her twenties, but as she approached they could see that she was older, probably nearer her late thirties. Baldwin could see some of her children peering inquisitively round the doorway at the guests. He winked, then turned to the woman, listening with half an ear as the bailiff introduced them. The woman was of medium height, strongly built, with no hunching at the shoulders so common in peasant women. Her face was wrinkled with age, and tanned from a life spent outside helping her husband, but the brown eyes were clear and sharp as she glanced at the small group. When Simon had finished she asked them to go with her, and she led the way to the house.

Here she sent children scurrying to fetch bowls and platters and benches, and insisted that they join the family in their meal when her husband arrived, which he did a short while later, clumping in from the yard with his heavy boots. Nodding at the men as if he had expected them, he walked to a bench a short distance from his fire and sat. Ale was brought and drunk, then bread, still warm from the hearth, and cheese. Watching carefully, the farmer waited until his visitors were served before beginning to eat, while his wife helped the children keep pots replenished. Baldwin had to keep smilingly shaking his head as the children tried to refill his pot, but one was insistent and each time he averted his gaze he found there was more to drink. Eventually he had recourse to the simple method of leaving the pot full, but felt guilty when he saw the reproachful glance of a young tow-haired girl, surely not more than nine years old, who stood steadfastly staring at him, jug ready, until he grinned in defeat and sipped a little. Her sudden smile was radiant, and he felt more warmed by it than by the food.

He darted little glances round the room while he ate. The house was smaller than he would have expected, and he assumed it had once been a long house. All too often these immense buildings suffered catastrophic collapse and fell in on themselves. This one appeared to have fallen at one end, while the rest of the place had been rescued. Before, the cattle and other farm animals would have been kept in one end of the house while the men and their families used the other, but since the loss of half the house it looked – and smelled – as if the animals did not come in any more. He guessed that the area behind the new stone wall at his back gave on to a new building constructed with stones from the old one – a byre or shed where animals could be kept. The room had a wholesome smell of smoke and rushes, its atmosphere that of a great hall. Hams hung drying from rafters in the smoke from the fire, adding their own pungent odour. In the knight's experience, most farmhouses reeked of cattle and dung, sweat and urine, but not this one.

When his gaze finally rested on Wat Meavy the knight was disconcerted to find that the man had been subjecting him to a detailed scrutiny. Faded blue eyes met his unflinchingly from a round face the colour of old leather. His russet tunic was scratched and torn, but the farmer wore it with as much pride as a great lord would wear his armour. A thin stubble of greying hair lined his jaw and top lip, and lank grey hair stuck out from his head in unruly disorder above a grubby band. It looked as if it covered a wound. The farmer used his food like he used his tools, Baldwin thought. Massive hands grabbed hunks of bread and cheese and crammed them into his mouth while his eyes moved from Simon to Baldwin and back.

Hugh was fully at home. He had been raised on a small sheep farm over to the north-east, near Drewsteignton, and this was the company he felt most at ease with, farmers and their children. This room was much as he remembered the main room at his parents' home, though it was many years since he had been there. The people were friendly, the food good, and the ale – he took a long draught and sighed gratefully as the strong-flavoured liquid washed down his throat – the ale was fine.

As the men all finished their food and settled, Hugh belched and grasped his pot, a warm glow encompassing his spirit as he sat back and took notice of the others again. Baldwin, he could see, was thoughtful as he stared at the farmer, while Wat Meavy appeared caught between nervousness and suspicion, his broad square brow lined. Seeing his guests had finished, the farmer sent his wife and children out, and when they were gone, Simon leaned forward and smiled reassuringly.

'We're here because we want to ask you about the day you were attacked, Wat Meavy.' Briefly he explained who he and Baldwin were, before resting his chin in his hand. 'I know you weren't going to report it, but we need to hear all about it. It may prove important in another affair, a murder.'

'Peter Bruther's, you mean?'

Simon nodded. The farmer considered the bailiff for some time without speaking, but then gave a slow nod. 'What do you want to know?'

'You were going up to Chagford?' Simon prompted.

'No. I'd been there all day and was coming back. I had had a sow and some piglets to sell.'

'I see. What time of day did you leave to come home?'

Wat Meavy gave him a slow smile. 'Late, bailiff. I'd been in Chagford all day, and it was thirsty work standing there in the sun. There was no need to hurry, my wife wasn't expecting me yet, so I went to the tavern there in the town. I suppose I must have been there for some hours before I left.'

'Was it dark yet?'

'No. Not quite.' He gave a sudden frown of concentration. 'But it was getting that way, I think.'

'I understand you were attacked just outside the town, is that right?'

'Yes. I'd just got past Coombe, and was beginning to head southwards. There's a place there where an oak used to stand in the wall, only it fell some years ago and old Stephen Thorn, he's never got round to mending the wall. Its stones are still all over the ground. Just beyond, the lane curves sharp to the left, and narrows too, and then there's another lane comes up from behind you. Well, that's where this man came from, I reckon. At the time I thought he rode up from nowhere, that's how it seemed. He just appeared, and he had a great sword in his hand, and shouted at me to stop. I thought it was the Devil! Well, my horse, he just stopped dead anyway, he's not used to having men turn up like that. Before I knew what was happening, I'd taken a knock on the side of my head and the bugger'd cut the purse from my belt . . .' His eyes took on a faraway look. 'My sow and two piglets. Thieving bastard! They were worth good money, too. I'd sold them for five shillings, and most of the money was in that purse. Five shillings!'

Baldwin cleared his throat. 'So, er, what happened then? This man hit you, and you came straight home, is that right?'

'Yes, sir.'

'Did you recognise him?'

'Oh yes, sir.' He eyed the knight with sudden wariness, as if wondering whether to continue.

Simon broke the sudden silence. 'Do not have any fears. Just name him for us and nothing can harm you. We think we already know this man's identity, but we must have you confirm it.'

'What if him and his family come here? They could burn our place to the ground, yes, and kill my wife and the children. What then?'

'They won't come here, Wat. I'll make sure of that.'

'I don't know . . .'

'Wat, the culprit's father has promised me already that he'll make good your loss. Does that help? He had no idea his son was here. But I must hear who it was – you must tell me.'

'It was John Beauscyr.'

The flat answer made Simon sink back exhausted. He had thought that this man might tell him something he did not know, but here was the proof. There was only one other point which mattered. His voice was low and serious as he spoke. 'Wat, do you have any idea when this attack happened? Was it dark yet, or was it still light?'

'I don't know,' said the farmer, baffled at the question. He pushed out his lower lip and frowned with the effort of recollection. 'Let's see. I'd left Chagford in daylight, and I'd only got past Coombe. That would have taken bugger-all time, I suppose . . .'

'How did you recognise him?' asked Baldwin, shooting a glance at Simon and leaning forward.

'His face, of course.'

'Did you have a lantern?'

'No.'

'Then it was light enough to see, surely?'

Suddenly a great smile broke over the farmer's face. 'Yes, of course! I was to the west of Meldon Common, and as I passed by, the sun was sinking before me, and I remember thinking it was late – yes, it was just as dusk was coming on.'

'I see,' said the knight. 'And it was late when John left the inn, was it not, Simon? I think John could not have murdered Bruther and got here in time to attack Wat.'

Simon nodded dejectedly. 'No. It looks like he's innocent,' he agreed. 'But that being so, who was it?'

Baldwin gave him a sympathetic smile. 'I have no more idea than you,' he said. 'Wat, I am grateful to you for your help.'

'That's my pleasure, sir,' said the farmer, following the men to his door. Once he was outside, Simon turned slowly, struck by a thought.

'Wat, you said he just sprang from nowhere. How did he look? Did he seem anxious or worried? Could he have been tired from a fast ride?'

'Tired? No, not at all. No, if anything he was rested.'

'How do you mean?'

'He was . . . how can I describe it? He was all eager, like a hound smelling a scent. It was like he was determined to prove something. He kept muttering things.'

'What sort of things?' Simon was frowning now as Baldwin wandered back to listen.

'Something about someone . . .'

Baldwin smiled, then touched Simon's arm. 'Come on. I think we've taken enough of this farmer's time already. He hated Bruther, I expect he was saying he'd like to get even for the insult the lad gave him on the road.'

'No, sir,' said Meavy, his face wrinkled into a scowl. 'No, it wasn't that so much. He was saying he was no worse after all, and his father was no better than him. That he might as well copy his father, and the sooner he was away the better. I don't know, it was hard, my head was aching, but I think that's what he was saying.'

'That he might as well copy his father?' Simon's face was a picture of confusion.

'Yes, sir. That he might as well copy his father.'

The sun was slowly edging westwards by the time they jogged out of the small farm and took the road back to Beauscyr. Simon led them, gazing unseeingly at the ground in front of his horse as he ran through the farmer's evidence. Wat Meavy had impressed him with the clarity of his account. Though he was probably quite drunk when he was attacked after an evening spent at the inn, the farmer could nonetheless recall his journey home. He knew what the daylight was like, he knew where he was attacked, and all that after being clubbed round the head. His word must be believed.

'Simon?'

Turning, the bailiff saw his friend riding alongside, with a puzzled frown drawing his eyebrows so close together they made one thin black line on his brow. Simon grunted. 'What?'

'Suppose, for a moment, that the farmer was right. Suppose John Beauscyr *was* muttering imprecations about his father. What would that mean?'

'That his father had given him a talking to about robbery, I suppose.'

'But this was before we heard about him being a robber. It was because we thought he was involved in killing Bruther, that he admitted robbing Meavy – to show us and his father that he could not have been near Bruther when he died.'

'Yes. So what?'

'Are you being intentionally dense?' Baldwin sighed. 'Look, he was muttering about copying his father. Why would he want to do that – rob Wat Meavy, I mean. It seems to me he must have heard something about his father that day which made him decide to rob.'

'Something he had heard made him choose to rob Meavy?' Simon repeated blankly.

'It is possible. And yet, why would he say that he was "no worse, after all"?' Baldwin stared hard at his horse's neck. 'Simon, I just wonder . . .'

'What?'

'If he had already been told by Sir William not to steal and rob any more, and then had heard that his father had used to rob as well, maybe that would have been enough to drive him to attack someone.'

Simon was dumbfounded. 'That's a very big guess,' he managed at last.

'If Sir William had already told his son to stop stealing, he would certainly be enraged to hear about Wat Meavy.'

'Yes, I suppose so. But to suggest that Sir William himself . . .'

'We know Sir William fought for the King during various wars; it would hardly be surprising if during that time he had a chance of spoils which were not strictly legitimate.'

'But how could John have heard something about his father?'

'Bruther.' Baldwin avoided Simon's eye.

'*Bruther!*' Simon exploded. 'How in the name of God do you come to think that? There is nothing to suggest that Bruther knew anything about Sir William, and now you say blithely that Bruther caused John to go beserk like this – what's got into you?'

'I think,' said Baldwin slowly and precisely, 'that it is possible that Bruther heard from his father about something that Sir William had done in the past. Perhaps a long time in the past, I do not know. We do know that Sir William was a soldier, like I said, but Thomas Smyth was too. The battle today proved that. He was highly efficient in the way he set out his troops, and if Sir William had not responded so effectively, it is likely that Smyth would have slaughtered the Beauscyr men. It is possible that Thomas knows something about Sir William. It would explain a lot, after all. Think how easily Sir William gave in to the miner. He said it was because Smyth was legally entitled to be there on the moors, and that may be so, but I find it difficult to believe.'

They had come to the main track across the moors now, and turned south-west on to the packed earth of the road.

'If I am right, Sir William was fearful of the miner because of what Thomas Smyth knew of his past. And perhaps . . .' He suddenly broke off and stared ahead blankly. 'Simon – I have been a cretin! Of course, there's only the one explanation!'

'What?' asked Simon sarcastically. 'That Thomas Smyth threatened the knight with exposure if he didn't let the tinners farm tin on his land? Or do you think that the knight knew something about the tinner that made him keep from his land anyway? Baldwin, I think you've—'

'Simon, listen! Please, just for a minute.' Baldwin was smiling broadly. 'Think on this: Bruther normally had men to protect him, all the time he was on the moors. Yet on the very night that Sir William met Thomas Smyth, Bruther suddenly did not need those men again. Strange, don't you think? Then again, think about this: John met Bruther that night and they certainly exchanged words – and we hear that he rushed off shortly afterwards to Chagford and attacked the first man he met. Hardly the behaviour of a rational squire, I would have thought.'

'I think you must have drunk too much of good Farmer Meavy's ale – you're babbling,' said Simon, but he kept a suspicious eye on his friend. After a few minutes, he lost his patience. 'All right, then, Baldwin. So what do you mean? What do you guess from these two hints?'

'Ah, Simon, later, later, old friend. I see we're heading for both Beauscyr Manor and Smyth's house. Why don't we go to see Thomas Smyth first? It is not far out of our way.'

And he refused to discuss the matter further.

# CHAPTER TWENTY-FOUR

By the time they trotted into Smyth's yard, Hugh was becoming desperate. He did not dare stop while the others carried on, for he knew how his slowness annoyed the knight, and was sure that if he stopped to water the roadside Baldwin would refuse to halt, and the three would leave him. Hugh was still too nervous of the idea of Crockern to want to be left far behind while his master and the others disappeared into the distance. So he lurched on painfully, his lips pressed firmly together in mounting anguish as the liquid sloshed painfully in his bladder.

The yard was busy, with servants leading horses out for exercise or cleaning the stable of manure and soiled straw, while others were unloading a wagon of provisions for the kitchen. In the midst of this bustle, Hugh dropped from his horse and tossed the reins to Edgar, who received his mute plea with supercilious amusement, and rushed to the stable wall. After only a few seconds of agony, the relief was intense, and he smiled foolishly at the stones of the wall before him. Looking for his master, he saw the three walking behind George Harang towards the hall. He knew he should go after them but he could not hurry. There was no point, he thought. Simon and the knight were only going inside to ask more questions, and they had not needed his help so far.

Inside the hall, Simon and Baldwin stood in a huddle with Thomas Smyth and stared round sadly.

The room held almost twenty men injured in the morning's fighting, and Smyth's servants rushed hither and thither, carrying bowls of water and torn cloth for bandages. His wife was there too, holding a man's hand and offering words of comfort. She glanced up as Simon entered, wiping at her forehead, but he could see her mind was on the wounded man. A surgeon knelt by another figure, obviously hard-pressed to see to all the slashes and stabs.

While Simon watched in fascinated horror, the surgeon finished inspecting a head wound. The bailiff could not drag his eyes away as the doctor gently pushed a finger into the thickly clotted wound on the scalp. Quickly now, he took the proffered razor and shaved the man's head. While the assistant held the white-faced tinner by the shoulders, the surgeon crouched by his head with a pair of large forceps. At a signal, the forceps were inserted into the wound and quickly hauled back, now with a fragment of white bone gleaming amid the gore. After a shriek, the wounded man stilled and calmed, panting, with his eyes wide in fear and pain, but now when the surgeon investigated the wound again, he wore a smile. Washing the blood away and cleaning it with egg white, he appeared well pleased, and sutured the skin together carefully, taking a pellet of thick pitch-smelling medicine and smothering it over the wound. Then he rose with a sigh and moved to the next man, a youth of only one or two and twenty, who had the broken shaft of an arrow jutting from his shoulder. He wept openly as the surgeon approached, thick tears of terror falling from his thin and dirty cheeks.

Thomas Smyth watched sadly, but looking up, he caught his wife's eye. She stiffened, upright, holding his gaze, then flashed him a quick smile before turning her attention back to the figure before her. That brief recognition made his chest tighten in pride. After the drama out at the camp he had known he must explain about Martha Bruther and his dead son before Christine could hear of them from others. Even as the men were being carried indoors he had pulled her to one side.

She had said nothing as he spoke, and he felt his panic rise at the thought of the hurt he was causing her. But then she ducked her head. 'It was a long time ago, Thomas. Before I even knew you. And you kept your sadness over his death to yourself to save my feelings?' He could say nothing, mutely staring at her, and after a moment she touched his arm gently. 'Come, husband. We must make sure that no more die like your poor son.'

And now the bailiff and his friend were back to question him again. Smyth rubbed his eye. He was tired after the horrors of the morning, and suddenly sickened.

'Let's get away from this spectacle,' he muttered, and led them to the door. Simon was pleased to see he stopped often on the way, patting a shoulder or the back of a wounded man, and always having a word or two with his men. He cared for them, Simon saw, and they knew it. As he approached, some even tried to sit upright, as if to show their respect.

Simon was relieved to be out of the room and back in the open air again. The aura of pain and death in the hall was depressing, and he inhaled deeply, strolling behind the tinner, who meandered over to the stream, his head down and hands in his belt. There was a bench overlooking the water, and Thomas Smyth sat here, glowering ahead. Simon and Baldwin stood before him, Edgar waiting a little behind.

It was Simon who broke the silence. Casting a suspicious eye at his friend, which told Baldwin more precisely than any words that the bailiff still had no idea of the direction his thoughts were taking him in, Simon said, 'Thomas, we have been to visit Wat Meavy at his farm since we left you at the camp. He has confirmed that he saw John Beauscyr on the night that your son was killed.'

'He saw Beauscyr that night?' The miner's puzzled glance rose to meet Simon's firm stare. 'I don't . . . You mean Beauscyr was there when Peter was murdered? It wasn't him who killed Peter?'

'No. From what we've heard, it wasn't John.'

The tinner was overwhelmed. He looked away, over the moors to the east. 'My God! And I've caused the death of my men for . . . But how can this man Meavy be so sure? Are you saying that—'

Baldwin intervened smoothly. 'Thomas, this morning I was very impressed by your method of setting out your defence – the way that you sited the archers compared to the footsoldiers, and forced any frontal attack to concentrate just where you wanted it. Yes, it was masterly.' The tinner stared at the knight in silence. Imperturbably, Baldwin carried on. 'If it was not for the second attack over the river, you would surely have carried the day with ease, wouldn't you? There would have been a great massacre there. Where did you learn to fight like that?'

Thomas shrugged. 'It was just luck, that's all. It seemed the best way to put the men.'

'So it was not from your experience as a soldier in the wars with Sir William?'

'He told you?' The astonishment could not have been faked.

Baldwin smiled, his moustache lifting wolfishly. 'Why shouldn't he?'

'Because it only serves to discredit the man,' he said shortly. 'Why should he tell you about it? It's true, I fought in the Welsh wars, and I knew Sir William there. That was part of the reason I came here, because I had heard from his men about tinning, and thought I might as well try it myself.'

Simon was looking from one to the other with confusion, and the knight noticed. Gesturing mildly towards his friend, he said, 'Perhaps you should explain. The bailiff was too young to have been involved in the wars.'

'Very well,' said Thomas, throwing a faintly disgusted glance in Simon's direction as if at the bailiff's lack of knowledge of recent history. 'It was back in the '80s. King Edward, father to our Edward and much the greater man, called on his lords to help him put down the Welsh once and for all, even offering to pay the troops himself. The Welsh had always been a thorn in his side, and back then, before his son proved so incompetent at Bannockburn, he had the Scots under control and could spend time in bringing the Welsh to his will. My lord joined the army, and I went with him to join with the men under Luke de Tany. I was only twenty then, back in '82, but strong, and prepared to win some honour from a battle, and I soon became the leader of a small company.'

'Sir William was there too?'

'Oh yes, and like his son Robert he was as arrogant as a young knight can be. I think it was his first war, though he's been on many a raid since. But he was a knight, and wouldn't speak to me. I was just there to obey orders and nothing else. We were there under de Tany for ages. I remember we marched in Maytime, early in the month, and had to go to Neston, in the Dee estuary. I was a crossbowman, and I was one of the group put on the fleet of over sixty ships called from the Cinque ports. Many of us bowmen were there on the ships to serve as marines when we arrived in Anglesey. We took the island and built a bridge over the Menai Strait so that we could attack through to Bangor, but then that was it. By the end of September we were ready, but we had to wait until we had an instruction from the King to carry on, for we were to throw the enemy into confusion by diverting his armies just when the King's own men started a new attack.

'It went well. The King and the Earl of Lincoln moved up the Clwyd Valley, Earl Warenne advanced along the middle Dee, and Reginald de Grey went on from Hope. The Welsh had no chance against such forces, and the whole affair should have been finished quickly, but Archbishop Pecham decided to try to stop the killing. He mediated for some time and held up the attack – a stupid waste of time. It was obvious that the Welsh were merely taking the opportunity to regroup their men for more fighting.

'Meanwhile, we in Anglesey were stuck with nothing to do. It was miserable, with no decent camp and too many men in a small area. Men fell ill, and we were all fretful and bored. We just wanted to get on with it and push the Welsh back. Well,' he glanced up at his attentive audience, 'that was why Sir William did it, I think. Boredom!'

A faraway look came to his face as he continued, every now and then his hand rising to his cheek to scratch at an insect bite. 'You have to understand, first, that until then the soldiers had been well enough behaved. We had attacked the island and won it, we had set up camp as ordered, and we had built the bridge as we had been told. But the tedium of just sitting out there with nothing to do was dreadful! We knew that at any time we could be thrown over the bridge to meet the Welsh, and that was worrying. Those madmen with their long knives are vicious warriors. In the heat, and with more and more men falling ill from fevers and then dying, fights began to break out – little disputes flaring like charcoal when the bellows blow. Normally they would have been forgotten, but there they became reason to kill. And for a young knight seeking glory and wealth, it was maddening.

'It was November when we began to move. We had waited there for months, and I think de Tany was as keen as the rest of us to get moving, so we crossed over the bridge and into Snowdonia. Our leader thought he could make a decisive attack which would throw the Welsh into disorder and end the war. It's been said de Tany wanted to ruin the peace negotiations – I don't know, he might have – but all I can say is that we all wanted to go by then.

'At first, things went well. We rode out into the country, but the main host got entangled in a fight with Welshmen. When this happened, I was out on the flank with Sir William, and he ordered me to join him. We thought it was to attack the rear of the Welsh, but no, he took us round behind and then on into the country.'

Now his eyes rose to meet Baldwin's. 'He had heard of a nunnery some miles away – I still don't know the name of it – where the nuns had gold and jewels. That was his aim, not to fight in some vainglorious battle, but to make a profit from a war he thought foolish. He took us there and we attacked it. They had no chance. There were some hundred and fifty of us, and the nuns only had twenty-odd men to protect them. They were all killed, including the women, but not of course before they were raped.' His voice was cold and bitter as his face hardened. 'And Sir William was the first, taking two women before he let his soldiers in.'

There was silence for a moment, then Baldwin stirred. 'And you?' he asked softly.

'Me? I was there, but I didn't rape or kill or steal. How could any man be so barbaric towards women who have dedicated themselves to God? These weren't tavern sluts, they were holy. I couldn't touch them if I'd wanted to. No, I turned my horse for Anglesey, and a good thing too. If I hadn't, I might have said something to Sir William, and that would have earned me a slow death and no honour.

'No, I returned, but by then the battle was lost and de Tany dead, drowned in the Menai Strait. The men had been routed, and I had a hard time of it winning my way back to the camp. There seemed little point in telling of Sir William and his exploits. The situation was bad enough, and most men were talking about getting back on to the ships and sailing for Rhuddlan or Neston, but the ships refused to take anyone. I think they were scared of what the King might say and do to them. So we were stuck there, until we were lucky enough to have Otto de Grandison arrive to take over. And that was when I had my shock, for suddenly, here was Sir William again, but now apparently covered in glory and wealthy to boot.

'He had taken all he could carry, him and his men, and run away, riding as fast as they could to avoid the Welsh, for I suppose by now they had heard of the defeat of the army. So it was Sir William who brought news of the battle to the King, and it was Sir William who was rewarded by the King for acting so bravely as a messenger!'

Falling silent, he frowned darkly at the water in the stream. 'Of course, I was only a poor trooper, a mounted crossbow-man. I could not accuse a great man like Sir William of outlawry. If I had, I would likely have been killed for my presumption. So I tried to forget it. I was with the soldiers when Otto de Grandison led us over the Strait again, this time successfully, and was with his army when it closed in on Snowdonia and took Caernarvon and Harlech. There was no great booty, but at least I came out of it alive, though bitter to see how easily a knight could win renown, wealth, and the King's favour. Afterwards, I travelled around the country. The war had left me feeling unsettled, and it was some time before I recalled what other men in Sir William's retinue had said of tin mining and how a man could live on the moors free of anyone, making his own money from his work. The idea sounded good to me, so I came here.'

Simon puffed out his cheeks as he sighed. The tinner's story was all too common, he knew. He had met other soldiers and seen their bitterness at how they had been betrayed, their disgust with the rewards given to some who least deserved honour, while others who should have been

fêted were forgotten. It was the way of war. 'And it was definitely Sir William who led the attack on the nunnery?' he
asked.

Thomas Smyth grunted assent without looking up.

'Tell me, Thomas,' said Baldwin, 'when did you mention
this to Sir William?'

Now the tinner looked up with a smile playing at his lips.
'How did you guess that?' he asked. 'No matter! I told him
on the day Peter was killed – when I saw Sir William.'

'What, when you saw him that morning at Beauscyr?'
asked Baldwin, suddenly intense.

'No, that evening, when he came here.'

'What did you say to him?'

'I had asked him to come to my hall to discuss what I
should do about the tin on his land,' said Thomas, and gave
a quick grin. 'I think you know what I mean. He brought
money with him, and he thought that was all . . . but then as
he was about to leave, I told him that I remembered the
convent, and he was quiet, like a dog is quiet when it sees a
peril and crouches ready to spring. I told him all that I have
just told you, all about the campaign, how he took men away
from the battle to further his own fortune, and how he gained
favour with the King. I think he was shocked.'

'Why did you tell him all this now? You have kept it
hidden for years, so why bring it up now, so long
afterwards?'

'I wanted my son to take on more responsibility for the
mines. I didn't tell Sir William he was my son, of course. I
just let him know that I wanted young Bruther to be able to
live free of attack. And I told him that if there *was* an attack
on Peter, I would revenge him by telling my story. After all,

the situation was different now. Before, I had been a worth-less crossbowman, whose word could be doubted. Now, I was a powerful man in the area, with money and men to back up my words. He knew he could not deny it, and he went white with anger.'

Baldwin's face was serious. 'I see. And that was why you thought Peter did not need his guards any more?'

'It was nothing to do with me. If I'd been here, I'd have made sure he kept the men with him. But he felt safe, I assume,' said Thomas Smyth, sighing sadly and staring down. 'I'd told him the whole story the day before – and that I was going to confront Sir William. I thought then it could be useful for him to know what sort of a man Sir William was, but I'd no idea he'd leave his guard behind that night.'

'I presume he felt he would be safe since you had told Sir William what you knew about him,' said Simon.

'Perhaps,' said the tinner sadly. 'It's all the same now, anyway. My Peter is dead.'

'There is one thing I still do not understand,' said Baldwin gently. 'You say that Peter came past here and his guards left him here before he made his way back over the moors, but why should he come past here in the first place? It surely is not on his way back to his hut – that would take him over the moors from the inn. Was it only to leave the men that he came over here?'

'He usually came this way on his journeys back from the inn. The path from here is safer, with fewer bogs.'

'But you did not see him?'

'No. I was out with George that afternoon, over at the encampment, then up at Peter's hut.'

'And Sir William was here when you returned?'

MICHAEL JECKS

'Yes.'

'I see. Very well!' Baldwin slapped his hands together decisively. 'In that case, I think we can leave you alone now. I am sorry to have had to ask you about these matters which are, I am sure, painful to remember, but you have cleared some points.'

'Good,' said the tinner with frank astonishment. 'But I don't see how.'

'It is nothing much, just some things I was unsure of. For now, good day to you.'

As he shook himself and tugged his hose back into place, Hugh noticed the old bottler glaring at him a short way off and emptying a bucket into the drain. Hugh gave him an apologetic grimace as the old man said, casting an offended eye over the damp patch on the wall: 'It's not a privy, you know.'

Hugh felt his embarrassment mount. 'I'm sorry, I thought—'

'I suppose it's too far for a bailiff's servant to walk another six yards to the drain?'

'Look – I didn't think it'd matter . . .'

'Matter!' The bottler's tired old eyes stared at Hugh with distaste, then back at the stain. Shaking his head, he turned away. Hugh scampered to walk with him, feeling guilt at causing his disgust. In the face of his mumbled apologies the servant unbent a little, and by the time they reached the hall door, he was almost sorry for his words. 'Forget it. We're all on edge here, since Bruther got killed. Our master has not been himself since then, and now there are all these wounded men too.'

Hugh nodded. From the doorway, they could clearly hear the cries and calls from within the hall, and Hugh hesitated before entering. 'They're all in there?'

'Yes,' the old bottler sighed. 'First poor Bruther, and now this.'

'This was because of Bruther, you know. Your master wanted to catch his killer.'

'Bruther's dead. It's unfair to blame *him* for all this, even if it was done in his name,' the bottler said with asperity. He could see the trepidation on Hugh's face and took sympathy. 'Come here into the buttery and have some ale,' he said more kindly.

Recognising the olive branch, Hugh traipsed after him. In the room with the casks and boxes he sat on a wine barrel while the older man rested carefully on an old stool, settling slowly with a grunt before filling two pewter pots with ale. He paused at a high shriek from the hall, and Hugh stiffened, but then took the proffered drink gratefully and drank deeply.

Nodding towards the door, the bottler said, 'There's a surgeon and his assistants in there. They don't need you or me to get in their way.'

'You knew Bruther?' Hugh asked, trying to change the subject.

'Yes. He was a good young man to me, very polite, and always had time to share a quart of ale.'

'It's very good,' Hugh nodded, and the bottler refreshed his pot.

'Bruther always said so. Mind, he liked his drink anyway. It never mattered much what sort it was, but he did say mine was the best ale in Dartmoor.' There was no need for Hugh to speak. The old man wanted company, not talk, and they sat quietly for some minutes. Stirring, the bottler continued, 'He was brave, too. Did you hear about him and that knight? He didn't just send the fool on his way, he took the rope too.'

Frowning, Hugh glanced up at him. 'Where did you hear that?'

'He told me, when he came here the day he died. Not for long, he was hoping to see my master, but Thomas was at the camp. Still, he shared a cup or two of ale with me, while his old master bellowed for more wine in the hall.'

'Sir William was here too?'

'Yes. The old bastard was stomping round the hall in a high old mood at being kept waiting for my master. When he wasn't howling for wine he was cursing and muttering enough to raise the dead. Bruther thought it was funny.'

'Did they speak to each other?'

'No, of course not. Bruther stayed out here with me until he left.'

'So he never went into the hall?'

'Not that I saw. Mind, I wasn't here all the time.'

'Eh?'

'I had to go out. There was a problem with the fire in the kitchen and I went to help the cook.'

'You left Bruther here?'

'Only long enough to finish his ale. He came and gave me his farewell in the kitchen. Poor devil. He seemed happy again.'

'He was happier when he left than when he arrived?' Hugh asked carefully.

'Yes. He was in a miserable state when he got here, something about a girl, I think. But he always had said that my ale cooled his brain and settled his temper. After a few pints he was happy enough. I watched him go. He turned and waved, down there by the fields near the stream, really cheerful, he was, the rope coiled over his shoulder.'

'But Sir William was still here?'

'Oh yes. I saw him when I got back from the kitchen. He was cooler than before. Not as wrathful, thank God! He just asked where I'd been, didn't even shout at me. Then requested more wine.'

Hugh scratched at a bite on his scalp. 'You were away for some time, then?' he hazarded.

'As long as I could be,' the bottler shrugged. 'I didn't want to be there with him shouting at me. I stayed with the cook for a good time, until I heard my master's horses.'

'Oh,' said Hugh, deflated. 'So you would have heard Sir William ride off if he had gone somewhere, if you could hear your master in the yard.'

'Eh?' Shrewd old eyes glanced up quickly. 'Why? What are you . . .? No, I couldn't. The kitchen's out back. I heard my master on the road.'

'Would you have heard a man mounting his horse in the yard and riding off if he went over the moors?' Hugh asked slowly and carefully, suddenly feeling a hollowness of expectation in his belly. He did not need to hear the answer.

# CHAPTER TWENTY-FIVE

Back at Beauscyr, Simon and Baldwin sat on chairs close to the unlit fire. Sir William was not there yet. John, anxiously tossing a dagger in the air and catching it, stood near them and looked disapprovingly at Edgar as he lazily leaned against a pillar. Sir Ralph was there too, standing with his back to a wall, arms crossed negligently. For all his appearance of indolence, Baldwin could see the watchfulness flickering in his eyes. Both looked surprised to see Thomas Smyth enter after the others.

Some moments later, Sir Robert Beauscyr and his mother entered. As always, Lady Matillida swept in regally, ignoring her guests as she walked lightly to the table on the dais and seated herself at her chair. After a moment's thought, her elder son followed, sitting at her side and staring at Simon. At last the door was thrown open and in walked Sir William.

To Simon he seemed to have regained his youth. He marched in with one hand resting on his sword hilt as he moved to his wife's side. There he touched her shoulder briefly, then sat down, leaning forward on his elbows. Acknowledging Thomas Smyth, who stood tensely behind Simon, the old knight confronted Baldwin and Simon.

'Well, what do you have to report? I want an enquiry into the affairs of the miners. That is crucial now, after their taking of my son.'

'Sir William, I don't think that would be a good idea,' said Simon gently.

'Why not?' cried Robert, leaping to his feet and staring at the bailiff. Simon sighed, but stiffened as the boy continued, 'I suppose they offered you too much money to refuse, did they? Do you have any idea what it is like, to be taken like a common felon? To be dragged away like that, and—'

'Yes,' mused Baldwin. 'It must be difficult for someone to be carried off like that. I mean, a merchant might be able to forget it in time, but a noble knight? Someone who wants to impose his will on his demesne? That must be very hard.' And he smiled winningly at the youth.

Robert opened his mouth to speak, but then caught sight of the dangerous glint in Baldwin's eye, and suddenly snapped it shut. There was something about the knight which had changed over the last few hours, he saw. All diffidence and softness had fled, leaving in their place a strange harshness. It was as if he had made a decision and intended to carry it through, no matter what.

'Yes,' Baldwin said again, standing and strolling towards Sir Ralph. 'It would be difficult for a knight to take such an embarrassment, wouldn't it?' The northern knight's eyes met his for a moment, then he looked away. Not from nervousness, Baldwin could see, but from a kind of ennui.

MICHAEL JECKS

'What is all this about, Sir Baldwin? You may feel that this is a good time to insult your hosts, but I do not find your attitude at all impressive, let alone amusing.' Lady Beauscyr was white-faced, but whether from anger or fear he could not tell.

'Very well, lady. My apologies for upsetting you, but I am afraid there is nothing else for it.' He remained beside Sir Ralph, but now his gaze was fixed on Thomas, as if he was explaining the whole matter to the tinner, and the others in the room were merely an audience to the drama.

'These murders have been confusing. At first, when it was only Bruther, there seemed no end of people who wanted to kill him and who could have done it. Another miner – we wondered about you yourself – perhaps even a moorman. And many could have benefited from his death.

'But when the two men-at-arms died, it became clear that the killer must be someone from inside the Manor. The gate is closed and barred at night, and it is too much to think that an assassin could enter. No, the killer was inside.

'At first we thought it had to be Sir Ralph. He came down from the north, where killing is commonplace and the coroners have a hard time keeping track of the dead. Would it be so surprising if he was involved? But he was with a woman that night, at the inn. Unless she and the others there were lying, he was never away for long enough.'

The tinner nodded, watching as Baldwin ambled to John, who stood with his eyes downcast, flicking his dagger up and down. 'And John?' Baldwin said, contemplating the boy with his arms crossed. 'He was a problem, too. He was with Sir Ralph all the way to the inn, but once there, he left. Of course there was his brother, too, we thought. Robert,

374

who ran from the hall that day and spent it riding over the moors. But we find that he was with his lover almost all the time, and certainly when Bruther was killed. It was not him.'

Simon observed John, who had slowed his knife-throwing and had now stopped. The boy's jaw jutted aggressively, and his voice was dangerously low as he said, 'Are you accusing *me* of the murder, Sir Baldwin?'

The knight surveyed him silently for a minute. Simon answered for him. 'No. And for several reasons. For one, we can't believe you could have ridden from Wistman's Wood to Chagford in time. Bruther was at the inn just before you, and you saw him on the road. He had men with him, so you could not have killed him then – there were too many witnesses. After your slanging contest, you carried on to the inn and stayed there for a while before riding off. To have gone to Wistman's and killed Bruther, then hanged him, and made your way to Chagford would have been impossible. Oh, and there's another thing in your favour: you thought Bruther had a load of men with him. You weren't to know he left them at his father's hall. No, you didn't do it.'

Robert rose, stuttering in his astonishment. 'Are . . . are you suggesting it was me?'

Sir Ralph glanced anxiously at Baldwin as he said, 'No. You did not kill Bruther. You were with Alicia, like you said. And from what she has told us, you could not have had time. You left her late, she says, and I believe her.

'No, whoever did commit the murder had to have had a great hatred for Bruther, and reason to think he would profit by the young miner's death – or perhaps that his family would profit, I do not know which. In any case, as far as I can tell, this is what happened:

'Bruther was drinking at the inn that night. He went there as often as possible to meet the girl he loved. It was sad that she was the one he chose, for she could not keep herself for one man. Even when she heard of Bruther's death, she was only sad for herself, saying that he was one of the few who seemed to want her seriously. All others only wanted their brief pleasures of her. Anyway, he left to return home, and on the way he met you, John, and taunted you. I expect he insulted you and your master. Did he dangle the rope in front of you? And then, I daresay, he started talking about your father, how Sir William had been a hell-raiser in his youth, and your father was no better than any common outlaw. He told you about a certain convent in Wales where your father had besmirched the family name, or so I would guess. And you replied in kind, saying you were going to have your fun with his woman.'

Thomas Smyth groaned in understanding. The events fitted together as neatly as a bolt on a crossbow as Simon took up the story. 'You carried on, but you were furious with him, weren't you? Angry to hear about your father's past, and mad to think the bugger could get away with humiliating you,' he said, looking at John. 'You knew Bruther was probably right, your father *had* been involved in the sack of the nunnery in his youth, and you decided you might as well use his example to help you get money, especially after Sir William had declared that you were low in his esteem after news of your doings in the north. That was why you were so angry when you attacked Meavy, and why you muttered about your father as you stole the poor man's purse. You knew Sir William had done worse when he'd been young. Much, much worse.'

Baldwin nodded appreciatively and smiled. 'And Bruther carried on *his* way. He arrived at the hall where his father lived, as he always did, but that day was different. That day he knew about Sir William's past, and he thought Sir William had been told to leave him alone and make sure that his men did too. He was free of any fears about the Beauscyr family and friends. Before it had been because of the security of the guards round him, but not now: now he left the guards at the hall's doors. Why should he have done that if he did not think he was safe?'

Simon leaned back and sighed, folding his arms. He took up the tale. 'Because, of course, he thought Sir William had already, that morning, been given the threat. He thought he was free of serfdom, because his father had said that after this day he need not be worried about the Beauscyr family. The good knight's horse was outside the hall, and so Bruther went in. He insulted you in there, didn't he, Sir William? Feeling safe from you, I imagine he taunted you too, passing comments about you and your son. And then he walked back towards his works, confident he was in no danger.'

'He was not to know that his father had not yet spoken to Sir William, was he?' said Baldwin. 'Thomas Smyth did not return until it was almost dark. It took him some time to get to Bruther's hut and back, and he arrived a little after you, didn't he, Sir William?'

'Yes,' said the older knight. His face was pale, and it was almost as if, Baldwin thought, he would be able to see the stones of the wall through the older man's parchment-like skin.

Simon leaned forward, frowning, but Baldwin held up a hand for silence. 'Yes, he was there a little after you, but it was a little after your *second* arrival, wasn't it? Bruther came into the hall while you were there and . . . well, let us say you were unhappy about his attitude. When he realised his father was not there, he walked out again, and you were left there brooding on his words. He knew your past and you did not want that to come out, so you went after him, and lay in ambush. There was no need to let him go too far, you had plenty of time. When he appeared, you jumped on him, strangling him with the first thing that came to hand – what was it?'

'A thong from my saddle. It had been loose for days. I pulled it free when I left my horse up in the rocks and settled to wait for him.'

'I see. And then you thought it would be a good idea to leave a permanent message to any other villeins who thought escape to the moors might be a good thing – so you carried his body on your horse to Wistman's, and left him hanging there.'

'It's true,' Sir William said quietly, his face terrible in its pallor. 'I hauled him to that cursèd wood and hanged him, then made my way back. I swear I never knew he was Thomas Smyth's son. I thought he was interested in Bruther because it would embarrass me.'

'Will.' Matillida put a hand to his forearm but he shook it off.

'I did kill him. But the law is on my side. He was my villein, damn him, and he had no right to run away and then taunt me and mine. He was my villein, and I owned him. I tried to persuade him to come back, but he rejected my offers, and then, when he began to insult me . . . *me!* . . . in Smyth's hall, and threatened me, telling me to keep my son away from his whore or he would tell of my past, I saw red. I had to do something. I chased after him and ambushed him out on the moor, and then I thought that his body would be the ideal symbol to keep others from trying the same thing. Once I had done that, I rode back as quickly as I could to the miner's hall and waited for Thomas Smyth to arrive.'

'The bottler did not even know you had gone out, you were so quick,' said Baldwin.

'How did you know, then?'

'You were the only person who was alone and without an alibi. We had thought you were with Thomas, but he only got back around dark. Samuel and Ronald finished drinking about dusk and were leaving the alehouse, so you must have been at the hall for ages. They had time to ride to their inn, drink, and then leave again and yet we had been told you arrived at Thomas' hall a little before him. It was only today, when we heard the bottler had left you alone for a long time that we realised. If it was not for that, we might never have guessed.'

Robert was staring at his father. 'But why did you kill him, Father? There was no need to murder him!'

'Brother, I think there is a lot you need to know about being a strong knight,' sneered John. 'A strong knight does as he wishes, and ignores the weak.'

'Are you that much of a fool?' Sir Ralph strode to his side, quivering in suppressed rage. 'Do you really think that's all there is to being a knight? Have you understood nothing about chivalry? It doesn't mean stealing and murder. How can you expect your name to live on in honour if all you're known for is killing and raping? That's not what a knight is; a knight is the leader of the flock, the enforcer of God's will.'

'He may be to you, Sir Ralph,' the boy returned. 'You who were always so honest and pure! But not here, not when there are weak serfs to control. You call me a fool, but you deserted your master when he needed you, and—'

The swinging fist caught the boy on the point of his chin, and his head snapped back under the force of the blow, hitting the wall behind him with a loud smack. He was quickly up again, eyes glittering with animal fury and his knife was in his hand. It scythed upwards in a silvery arc, flashing wickedly. Simon watched in startled horror, incapable of moving, as it rose straight towards Sir Ralph's chest.

Not so Edgar. As soon as he'd seen Sir Ralph's hand forming a fist, he'd grasped his sword, ready to intervene. Now, as the dagger rose, he brought his sword down on the boy's wrist, using the flat of the blade. He was trying to be gentle, but all in the room heard the bone snap as the two met, and John was left staring blankly at his loosely dangling hand while his blade tinkled on the stone floor.

'No more!' Baldwin bellowed, whirling to face the dais. 'No more deaths in this accursèd Manor! Why did you decide to kill Taverner and Hankyn, Sir William? Was it because they saw you on their way back from the wood that night, and that made you anxious in case they might speak of it?'

Sir William gave another tired nod, his eyes firmly fixed on his youngest son. 'Yes,' he admitted heavily. 'Samuel saw me, and put two and two together. He told me yesterday. I knew it was only a matter of time before his story got out. They wouldn't've been a problem if it wasn't for that.'

'So you began a fire to make a diversion,' said Simon incredulously, 'then slipped back and stabbed Samuel when he walked into the store-room, before going over to Taverner's bed and slaying the sick man while he slept?'

The tired old eyes turned to him, but now there was a degree of contempt in Sir William's voice. 'And what would you have done, master bailiff? Left them to black-mail you? You can be sure that's what the weasel-faced little devil was planning to do to me. Oh, yes. And, I suppose,' his voice dripped with sarcasm now, 'I suppose you would not have raised a finger to protect your name and that of your family?'

To Simon's surprise, it was Robert who answered. He stared, open-mouthed in his shock. 'Of course, Father! Why did they have to die? All you were protecting was yourself, your misdeeds of years ago. There was no need to kill two men who had served you loyally for years. Your honour was false, unreal – so why was it worth three men's lives? All you managed to do was heap injustice upon dishonour!'

'Shut up, idiot!' Matillida snapped. When she looked at Baldwin, her face was a mask of cold indifference. 'Well, Sir Baldwin, this has been very interesting, but not very rele-vant. It is nearly dark outside, and the gates will be closed already. Tell me, why do you feel we should listen to any more of this?'

'Because, my lady, Sir William here has committed three murders, and we have to produce evidence of this at the next court at Lydford. I am sorry, but there is nothing we can do about it.'

'But surely,' she said softly, 'you do not want to ruin us? Will it profit the men who are dead? There is little proof that my husband has done anything wrong, after all.'

'Lady, he admits it!' said Simon hotly, but she held up her hand.

'No one has yet tried to accuse my husband of anything. We could easily forget this unpleasant affair. We are not so very wealthy, but we can offer land and money to our friends.'

Baldwin stared at her with his brows drawn. 'You are suggesting an accommodation?' he said at last, and she nodded. 'I see.' He turned to the miner and motioned him forward.

'In that case I should make my opinion plain,' said Thomas heavily. He pointed a shaking finger. 'Sir William, I accuse you of the murder of Peter Bruther, of the murder of Samuel Hankyn, and of the murder of Ronald Taverner.'

'I think that says it all,' said Simon calmly. 'Sir William, you are under attachment to come with us to Lydford. Lady, I hope that makes our view plain.'

She glared at him with soaring rage, and then opened her mouth to scream for the guards, but before she could speak, Robert put a hand to her shoulder. When she attempted to slap it away, he held her hand. While she stared at him in horror, he said, 'Mother, be silent. The knight is right – Father is guilty by his own mouth. I'll not have more honest men killed to protect the guilty. Sir Baldwin, you have my support.'

His father had a wild fear in his eyes. 'Robert? What do you mean? You don't expect me to go to the castle at Lydford, do you, because I'll kill anyone who tries to take me there, and I don't care who it is! The guards in this Manor are—'

'Mine, and when they hear that you are a murderer, who has confessed to killing two of their friends, condemned from your own mouth, they will obey my orders. Do you want me to have you bound to prove it?'

# CHAPTER TWENTY-SIX

Sitting once more in the sun outside Simon's house at Lydford, watching the villeins working the fields behind the village, Baldwin was relaxed and drowsy. It was a more or less satisfactory end to the enquiry, he felt. Sir William had been held by the court, an event which caused some initial disquiet to the burgesses of the village who would never have expected to keep a knight in the chilly and damp cell under the ground. But they had quickly become used to the idea, and now some relished the depths to which the knight had sunk – metaphorically and physically. Fighting between Beauscyr men and the miners had all but stopped. Now the only recorded fighting was the normal fisticuffs outside the inns and an occasional dispute on the moors about who had bounded a particular parcel of land for mining.

Hearing a shrill scream and the thunder of small feet in the screens behind him, Baldwin smiled and groaned, slowly rising to his feet. In a few moments Simon was with him, his daughter clinging to one arm. 'Fetch your poor father some wine, Edith,' he said, carefully depositing her on the grass, and giggling, the eight year old ran back into the house. His eyes followed her slight form until she disappeared, then he slumped into his seat with a contented sigh, casting a baleful eye at his friend. 'I trust there *is* a little wine left?'

Baldwin grinned and up-ended his pot to show that it was empty. 'I don't know, but I hope so,' he said, his eyes slitted against the brightness. 'How is our friend Sir William this fine morning?'

'Oh, much the same as usual. Insists on being freed, insists on his innocence, insists the food isn't good enough for a dog, insists I'll be in there instead of him soon enough when the King gets to hear of this indignity . . . You know the sort of thing.'

'How can he say he's innocent? He confessed in front of us, for God's sake!'

'Yes, but he doesn't appear to remember that. Now he says that he was nowhere near the area, and he's almost rabid in his denial of throttling Bruther, let alone stabbing the other two.'

Baldwin nodded, but his eyes strayed to the view again. Simon's next words dragged his attention back just as Edith returned, closely followed by the slim, fair figure of Margaret, Simon's wife. A wetnurse deposited Edith's sleeping brother nearby, and the bailiff's voice was quieter as he watched his son, feeling again that sense of mystified wonder that he could have helped create the tiny figure. 'John Beauscyr and Sir Ralph are going soon. Ah, thank you, Edith. Yes, it tastes wonderful.'

Eyes snapping wide open, the knight waited eagerly to hear more while Simon ruffled his daughter's hair, an assault upon her dignity which she loudly deprecated, and spoke to his wife. After a few minutes, Baldwin could not bear to wait any longer, and burst out, 'Your pardon, Margaret, but your husband is surely the most frustrating man in Christendom! What do you mean, John and Sir Ralph are going away together? What has happened to them to make them friends again?'

Throwing him an amused glance, Simon smiled easily. 'Sorry, Baldwin. I forgot you weren't there at the castle yesterday.' He was referring to a meeting he had arranged between the miners, represented by Thomas Smyth, and John Beauscyr. They had asked the bailiff to sit in and witness their agreements so that there should be no argument in the future. Baldwin had been out with Edgar, riding to the north at the time, and Simon had not been able to talk to him since. 'The two of them came in cheerfully enough, and I think Thomas has realised he has a new son in Robert who may not always bow to his will as he would like, but who is nonetheless a fine friend, and honest – the one good result of much reading, as his brother wrily admits. Anyway, they agreed what they needed to, as to where the tinners would go, where the Beauscyr Manor would prefer them not to, and how much the miners will pay the Manor for using the demesne lands. After that they were pleased to announce that Alicia will be married to Robert, and they invited us to the ceremony. That means you too, Baldwin. At the end of the meeting, Sir Ralph and John came in. It would seem that Sir Ralph was horrified to hear how John spoke about honour and loyalty on the day you accused his father, and had no idea that he had been robbing people all around. It seems he's determined to give the lad a better idea about knighthood, and he's taken him under his wing once more to make sure that he learns what it involves, especially regarding the chivalric virtues. The boy has agreed – rather, I think, to Sir Ralph's surprise! Seeing his father humbled has been a profound shock to young John, and I think he has been forced to look again at his own actions.'

Margaret leaned forward, wielding the heavy pewter jug to fill Baldwin's pot. As she bent, Simon took one slim wrist and held it for a moment, and she smiled at him, feeling the warmth of her love for her man. Glancing at Baldwin, she said, 'Surely that's not surprising? After all, the lad is only young still, and all his life, from what you have said, has been spent in power. First here, where he grew up with his father having authority over wide lands, then when he went to the north, where he was constantly fighting. Is it so odd he took it for granted that he could take whatever he wanted from anyone, whenever he wanted?'

'No,' said Simon, 'but will it really change him?'

'Give him the chance, Simon,' Baldwin laughed and sipped wine as he leaned back in his seat. 'I think I said this to you some days ago. He's still young and has much to learn: how to command respect and loyalty, how to earn renown and honour, and, not least, how to understand himself. Think about that robbery of poor old Wat Meavy – that was not the vicious action of an outlaw or shavaldore, that was the confused and bitter attack of a lad who does not yet know what he wants, who thought that it would prove to his father that he was a man like him, that he was strong and resolute. Maybe he felt it would endear him to Sir William.

MICHAEL JECKS

Give him a chance and you may be surprised how high he can rise.'

'He'll have the opportunity where he's going. Apparently they are setting sail for Italy.'

Baldwin nodded sleepily. The sun was warm on his face and there was a soft breeze from the deep gorge nearby which lulled and soothed. It was hard to keep his mind on the knight and his squire. 'They will have opportunities there to win the glory for which John yearns.'

'Sir Ralph said – damn, what was it? Ah yes – he quoted from a book, and said he was going to teach John how to be a real knight.'

'What book?' asked the knight.

'Something by a man called Lull, I think.'

'Ah! Ramon Lull. I have seen his book on chivalry. It is not bad, though not as good as others – but it is the type which Sir Ralph would like, I suppose. Lull claims that the most faithful, strong and courageous men are chosen to be knights. He suggests the principle that after the Fall from Grace, when Adam and Eve were thrown from Eden, chivalry was created to defend and restrain the people. Not the worst book for John to learn from, I suppose. So long as he takes on board the ideals of *service* to the people and not just the elements concerning power.'

'Baldwin,' Margaret smiled, 'you are rambling.'

'That, my dear,' he replied without opening his eyes, 'is because I am a rambling soul and at present almost asleep. Now why don't you tell your husband to relax and sit back quietly to enjoy this weather? From all I have seen, it is rare enough that you have a chance to feel the warmth of the sun in this benighted Manor. Why not just enjoy it?'

388

Simon grinned, and turned to his wife, but it was not long before they gave their son to the nurse once more and left, walking to the fields with Edith. After all, it was unreasonable to expect her to be quiet when the rasping breath of the sleeping knight threatened to waken the dead in St Petroc's churchyard almost half a mile away.

# Michael Jecks
# Templar's Acre

## The Holy Land, 1291.

A war has been raging across these lands for decades. The forces of the Crusaders have been pushed back again and again by the Muslims and now just one city remains in Crusader control. That one city stands between the past and the future. One city which must be defended at all costs. That city is Acre.

Into this battle where men will fight to the death to defend their city comes a young boy. Green and scared, he has never seen battle before. But he is on the run from a dark past and he has no choice but to stay. And to stay means to fight. That boy is Baldwin de Furnshill.

This is the story of the siege of Acre, and of the moment Baldwin first charged into battle.

This is just the beginning. The rest is history.

**Hardback ISBN 978-0-85720-517-9**
**Ebook ISBN 978-0-85720-520-9**

# Michael Jecks
# City of Fiends

It's 1327 and England is in turmoil. King Edward II has been removed from the throne and his son installed in his place. The old man's rule had proved a disaster for the realm and many hope that his removal may mean the return of peace to England's cities.

Keeper of the King's Peace Sir Baldwin de Furnshill and his friend Bailiff Simon Puttock had been tasked with guarding Edward II, but they have failed in their task and now ride fast to Exeter to inform the sheriff of the old king's escape.
In Exeter, the sheriff has problems of his own. Overnight the body of a young maid has been discovered, lying bloodied and abandoned in a dirty alleyway. The city's gates had been shut against the lawlessness outside, so the perpetrator must still lie within the sanctuary of the town.

When Baldwin de Furnshill arrives, along with Sir Richard de Welles, a companion of old, he is tasked with uncovering the truth behind this gruesome murder. But, in a city where every man hides a secret, his task will be far from easy…

**Paperback ISBN: 978-0-85720-523-0**
**Ebook ISBN: 978-0-85720-524-7**

# Michael Jecks
# The Oath

**Amid the turmoil of war, nobody's life is safe…**

In a land riven with conflict, knight and peasant alike find their lives turned upside down by the warring factions of Edward II.

Even in such times the brutal slaughter of an entire family, right down to a babe in arms, still has the power to shock. Three further murders follow, and Bailiff Simon Puttock is drawn into a web of intrigue, vengeance, power and greed as Roger Mortimer charges him to investigate the killings.

Michael Jecks brilliantly evokes the turmoil of fourteenth-century England, as his well-loved characters Simon Puttock and Sir Baldwin de Furnshill strive to maintain the principles of loyalty and truth.

**Paperback ISBN 978-1-84983-082-9**
**Ebook ISBN 978-1-84737-901-6**